MW01517966

THE STARCHARTER SERIES

BOOK 1: PROTOSTAR

BOOK 2: RED GIANT (COMING 2022)

STARCHARTER
PROTOSTAR

For Jackie
&
Martin

EVAN CHAIKA

STARCHARTER: PROTOSTAR

Cover art by Miblart
Editing by Bonnie Ryan-Fisher

Published by Evan Chaika, Edmonton, Canada

ISBN Paperback 0-978-1-77354-172-3
ISBN Ebook: 978-1-77354-211-9

Publication assistance and digital printing in Canada by

PUBLISHING
PageMaster.ca

For Miss Minsky, the best schoolteacher
that a kid could ask for.

CONTENTS

DERRON

I 1
II 61
III 169
IV 258
V 340
VI 408

JOSHYA

I 16
II 100
III 146
IV 227
V 322
VI 370

JAIR

I 32
II 124
III 219
IV 297
V 402

GRELHYM

I 46
II 155
III 238
IV 316
V 421

ALGEN

I 74
II....................137
III 213
IV................ 270
V 350
VI...................381

ALMOND

I 87
II................. 180
III 252
IV................328
V 390

ORLO

I 108
II.................201
III 282

RYMUS

I 116
II................. 191
III 243
IV................289
V 358
VI.................413
Epilogue 426

CHAPTER 01

DERRON 1

*M*illions *of miles from home, and the sunrise still never ceases to disappoint.* Derron stood and let his mind wander as the sun's warmth cascaded over him, melting the snow crusted on the tips of his boots. Crackling red leaves hung loosely off ancient trees and shone around him like a crimson fire, autumn's last breath of life before the coming chill. At forty-nine years Derron had weathered many long and bitter winters, surviving weather harsher than most would ever know. But even now, he could tell deep in his bones that this one would be the worst of them all. He looked up to the sun again and rested against his walking stick, enjoying the moment's respite. He knew that in a few moments time, the thick grey clouds would pass overhead again and swallow his warmth.

A foreigner on a foreign world, Derron thought to himself. To his knowledge, no one else had ever ventured to this planet. No matter where he ventured across the surface, he could find no signs of settlement. That was good; it meant that no one else had yet discovered its secret. Derron closed his eyes and reached to the string around his throat, grasping the wooden bear paw that his daughter, Carissa, had carved for him. He felt the rough grooves in the wood and smiled a sad smile. His daughter was lightyears away, at a home he might never see again. When he thought of her, Derron couldn't help but think of his other children. Some were grown themselves, scattered throughout the Starscape, unconscionable distances from their home just as he was. One day Derron hoped to bring them all back together, to be a family once again.

The Starscape was massive: an expansive realm of countless stars, planets, and moons. And although travel from one world to another was impossible by normal means, rips in space known as "rifts" connected one world to the next, as easy as stepping through an archway. That was how Derron was able to get to where he was now. No one knew where the rifts came from, or even when they came into being. Truth be told, few even gave it much thought. To most of the inhabitants of the Starscape, rifts were as normal as rivers, flowing from one place to the next. Countless rifts were well documented and well travelled, but that did not mean that all were. New rifts were being discovered nearly every year. The particular one connecting Derron's homeworld to this one had been al-

DERRON

most impossibly hidden. Derron had only discovered it by following a map he'd come upon nestled in an ancient book that was tucked far away in a dusty, old castle library. Whoever had once maintained the castle's records must have either died or given up on the job long ago, and it was clear that no one had taken up the position since. That did not matter to Derron, as ever since he had been a young boy, he'd practically lived within the confines of the densely packed library shelves. Finding the map was easy; finding a group to go with him had proved much more difficult.

When Derron had finally assembled his small scouting party, no one had truly expected to find anything of note at the location the old map denoted. But when at long last they had found the rift, tucked away on a small wooded island well out to sea, murmurs of astonishment and excitement had risen around cheers of success. Derron hadn't doubted himself for a minute. While the others debated what their next move should be, he was already stepping through the doorway into realms unknown. Though now, after six and a half months of overcast skies, dense forests and unforgiving rain and sleet, he was beginning to falter in his convictions.

Sighing, Derron watched as the last rays of sunlight were smeared out in the sky, and the world once again returned to the visage of stale grey that he had long since come to know. He raised the carving to his lips and gave it a light kiss. Derron hoped that soon he would see his family again, but his stomach rumbled and suddenly he instead hoped that soon he might

DERRON

happen upon a stream with fish or den with game. His small party had scarcely eaten in the past few days and he grimaced at the thought of letting them go another hungry night under the two foreign moons that rose above them with the stars each night.

Derron scratched at the coarse whiskers sprouting from his chin. His once dark brown beard had started to show the first signs of greying, a prospect he was none too happy about. A crack from the underbrush behind him made him pivot, walking stick cocked in hand, ready to take a swing at any animal that may have ventured too close. The animal put up its hands in a show of surrender.

"It's just me, Captain."

"Mollens," said Derron, lowering his weapon, "I thought you were gathering fruit in the southern grove."

"I was, but all the fruit has gone dry there; I thought I may have more luck in this area of the woods."

Derron shook his head. "I wish it were so, but the winter here seems to come earlier than our own. I can't seem to find any food either, and by the looks of this weather it will only get harder from here on out."

"Ah."

Mollens slouched down on a stump and lowered his eyes. Derron felt for him. Mollens was a loyal boy, no older than twenty. He was a man grown in reality, but a good five years younger than anyone else in Derron's company. Bright eyed and curious, he had been happy to come along despite multiple

DERRON

warnings of the dangers they would inevitably face. The first month off-world had been kind to him, but the same couldn't be said for the rest. His clean-cut hair and peach fuzz had grown to thick tangles and a short scraggly beard that helped mask his young age.

"Head back to camp," Derron told him. "I'll catch us something and bring it back."

"I'll help you!" Mollens stood, but Derron shook his head again. Taking his walking stick, he pointed it at Mollens' malnourished stomach.

"The way you're looking, something's bound to catch you."

He tried to give Mollens the warmest smile he could muster, but he knew that the boy was beyond consoling. Back at home Derron had five children, three sons and two daughters, all of whom he missed deeply. Out here in the wilderness, Mollens had become a sort of foster-child to him in place of his own. Similarly, Derron had become kind of a foster-father to Mollens. However, unlike Derron, Mollens would not have a family to go back to when they got home. The boy looked disappointed, but understood and nodded. Brushing the hair from his eyes, he returned to the underbrush.

When Mollens was no longer in earshot, Derron begun moving down the path once again. Not long after, he spotted a game trail, but it quickly led nowhere. About one hundred yards ahead and another dead trail. Then another. Derron was about to head back empty handed when he spotted a small bird resting in a tree. *Not enough meat to feed everyone, but enough to feed a few.* His thoughts returned to Mollens and his fatherly instinct kicked in. Hunting birds would be hard for some, but Derron had learned how to make a sling as a child, and that information had been retained though his many years. He pulled out the one he'd made a few nights ago and placed a small, smooth river stone in the pouch. Whirling it twice about his head he let it fly on the third and struck the bird on its right wing. A few moments later he found it on the ground, flapping its one unbroken wing frantically. A small twist soothed its suffering. It made Derron sad to end such a life, but his stomach was speaking to him louder than his heart.

It was close to nightfall by the time he returned to camp. The fire blazing at its centre had guided him back after the light was too dim to see the path. Since there was no one else around besides themselves, they needn't worry about their camp being discovered, thus the fire burned large and bright at all hours. It also had the added bonus of attracting the curiosity of the local wildlife. Any animal brought close was quickly killed, skinned, and eaten as an easy meal. Sadly, they had found no such luck in days, so Derron was more than a little surprised when he discovered a small pig roasting on a spit as he entered the clearing.

"Welcome home, Captain!" called up a blonde man with scruffy whiskers and tight curls for hair. One of the man's legs was elevated on a stump and bound by long grass and twigs, the closest thing they could make to a proper cast out here after he had fallen from a tree scouting the area a few weeks prior.

 DERRON

"And hello to you, Will!" Derron called back, tossing him the bird. "Pluck this for me, would you? Unless of course you've got somewhere to be?"

Will smiled up at him. "Only if you're up for carrying me."

"That'd be something I'd like to see!" said a short, dark haired man named Anthon. He sat on a stump nursing a cup of hot pine tea.

"You mock an old man. I don't want to hurt my back."

Anthon laughed. "I've seen you wrestle a bear before, so don't give me that old man horsecrap."

Will looked up, puzzled. "Did that really happen?"

Derron allowed himself a slight smile. "It was a small bear."

That night the group feasted upon pork and beets. It seemed root vegetables were the only produce they could find anymore. Collectively, they decided to save Derron's bird to break their fast on the morrow. Only eighteen of the twenty-one in the company were present that night. Fortho and Mallard were out exploring a cave the group had found weeks back while bushwhacking, and Melwick was off on a mission to map the local area.

"Melwick should have been back by now," Derron announced to the group. "I need two volunteers to go searching for him tomorrow."

"I'll go." A burly balding man named Roman spoke up; his mouth was dripping with grease. Manners were the least of anyone's concerns out here.

"So will I," said Skoma, the next youngest to Mollens.

DERRON

"I volunteer," said a voice from the brush outside camp.

"Melwick!" exclaimed Anthon. "You could have chimed in earlier."

"I could have, but I like it when you all talk about me." He smiled and looked over at Derron. "I finished your map, Your Grace."

Your Grace. Melwick was the only one who still called him that. Sometimes Derron would forget the status himself. Out here in the wilderness, what did it matter? Back home, Derron was King Derron of Ursa Major. He was the ruler of entire star systems. Out here he was the King of Brush and Bramble. In all honesty, Derron preferred that. He never enjoyed the power of rule or the luxuries that came with it. He had always been more concerned with books and nature than laws and land disputes.

"Thank you, Melwick. Bring it over."

Melwick handed him a large folded parchment with charcoal lines crossing the page. A few had smeared but it was legible for the most part. The camp was marked with an "X" surrounded by the clearing. Most of the map denoted dense forest, apart from a large lake to the northeast, a cave to the northwest, and a grove due south of them. Melwick had also circled four points on the map in red sap. Derron looked them over stoically and nodded. He folded the map and placed it in his bag.

"Thank you Melwick. This will be very useful."

Melwick smiled and took a seat close by the fire. Someone tossed him a hunk of steaming pork rump and he caught it in both hands. Taking a bite, he smiled.

"Haven't eaten this good in weeks. Has this been the norm around here?"

"Har!" burst out Roman. "I wish!" Grease sputtered from his mouth as he spoke.

"That's a no then." Melwick took another large bite from his roast.

"We found those walnuts two days back," chimed in a man in the back.

"And you ate them all!" shouted another, to which everyone laughed.

By the time the moon was highest in the sky, everyone was asleep, save two camp guards and Derron himself. He lay inside his makeshift shelter made of oak logs and mud. By this point, the group had been at this camp so long that the shelters had started to feel like true homes. He listened to the sound of raindrops beating against the logs above him and contemplated the situation he found himself in. Tomorrow the group would move on, which meant it would be the last night they would spend with this camp as a shelter. The coming days would most certainly be colder and wetter than they already were, and without a roof over their heads, however makeshift, sleeping would be near impossible. On top of it all, there would assuredly be a day when snow came to stay. Exactly when was anyone's guess, since it was impossible to know without knowl-

DERRON

edge the ecosystem of the unknown planet they were on. He figured it was better to move now while they still had time. Derron could have mentioned the coming hike at the fire, but he had instead decided to give his boys one last solid night's sleep without stressing about the journey ahead. Leaning over, he picked up his dagger and carved a notch into the exposed wood of his shelter wall. "198" He counted out loud. "198 days since I've seen my family." He hoped that the number wouldn't rise much higher, but he knew deep in his heart that it would.

The morning came with a thin mist hanging in the air, accompanied by a light frost covering every visible surface. Derron stretched and scratched at his beard, feeling the briskness of the early morning in his bones. He said a brief hello to the man tending the fire and walked off into the brush to relieve himself. Coming back to camp, he saw the others beginning to stir. Melwick was putting a pot of water over the fire to boil, and Will was preparing the bird Derron had caught yesterday for roasting. Anthon stood awkwardly trying to scratch the small of his back to no avail. Derron could see Mollens prepping to head out in search of berries. He put a hand on his shoulder and shook his head. Then, turning to the group he announced:

"Pack your things and get ready to move; we're heading out when the light gets over the trees." He turned to Roman's lean-to where the big man hadn't yet woken. "Roman!" he shouted.

DERRON

The burly man jolted awake and *shwacked* his head against the roof of his lean-to, knocking a snow-sodden log loose.

"Bugger me, Captain!" he cried.

"Get yourself up. You'll be carrying Will."

"Then I better get his portion of the partridge," Roman retorted, rubbing his scalp.

Will hobbled over beside Derron. "My leg may be broken but my stomach isn't."

The lot of them sat around the fire, everyone trying to edge as close as they could to the flames. It was becoming more than a little apparent that the day would be a cold one. Half the men owned rough blankets fashioned from the furs of animals they had caught and eaten, though none really knew the intricacies of tanning so the garments were itchy and smelled. But regardless, they were warm and that was all that really mattered. Sitting, Derron pulled out the map again to study it. He looked up to see Melwick standing over him.

"Tea, Your Grace?"

"Thank you."

He placed the map on a dry spot beside him, graciously took the cup from Melwick and took a sip. The liquid was brownish-green and piping hot. It tasted faintly of herbs and pinecones, and it reminded Derron of the forest that surrounded him. He smiled to himself and took a long swig. Soon after, another man, Gar, brought him a small portion of the bird he'd caught yesterday. Derron pouted at it, annoyed that he had gotten a larger portion than the others. *Don't make a fuss*, he thought

to himself. *After all, you are still their king.* They found the
bird tasted somewhat like bluebird from back home and everyone seemed to enjoy it. Will gave a part of his ration to Roman,
who graciously accepted.

"That's so you don't drop me," Will told him.

Roman stuffed his face with the meat. "I still may drop
you, but at least now I'll feel bad about it."

When the bird had been eaten down to the bone, Derron
began to instruct them on how the day would go. Derron himself would lead the group north towards the lake Melwick had
discovered. The plan was for them to follow directly alongside
a stream close-by to their camp that eventually emptied into
the lake. By Melwick's estimate, the journey would take approximately five days, although that was assuming the weather
held up.

"Melwick tells me that there is a small underground cave
approximately a day's walk north," Derron finished. "We'll rest
there for the night."

Skoma looked concerned. He sat fiddling with the hilt of
his sword as he often did. "And what of Fortho and Mallard?
They will come back to find us gone."

"I have written them a note as to where we are going."
Derron pulled a small folded parchment from his bag and
placed it next to him on the ground. "They will find us."

Skoma nodded. Like most of his group, Skoma could not
read or write. Within his group only four men could: Melwick,
Fortho, an older man named Alymer, and Derron himself.

 DERRON

Derron had also begun to teach Mollens the basics, but the boy had been less than interested in learning. He lifted himself up off the ground and retrieved his walking stick from where it rested against a nearby tree. Without having to say anything, the rest of his group fell in line behind him as they began the journey out.

The first day of the trek north was a grueling one. Twice the company happened upon brush too thick to muscle through and had to double back. A few squirrels and jays were caught along the way, but nothing major was found. When the clouds darkened and night grew near, they were still a good hour away from their cave destination. In the dark, Derron risked one of his men tripping and breaking a leg or worse. When the light finally dipped over the tips of the canopy and the grey sky turned black, Derron motioned for the company to stop.

"We camp here tonight."

Roman placed Will not so gently to the ground and took a seat on a wet pile of leaves. Will looked as if he were about to complain but held his tongue when he saw that Roman had already fallen fast asleep. Two men started making a fire and Anthon went downhill to the stream to wash himself. Derron rubbed his face and let out a grunt of annoyance. They'd have to weather the night in the open. *I shouldn't have been so over-zealous. We should have stopped to camp much earlier.*

"Melwick!" he called out.

"Your Grace?" The smaller man was suddenly beside him.

"Have you been cataloguing this trip as I asked?"

DERRON

"Yes, Your Grace."

"Good, give me the document."

Melwick fumbled in his sack and produced a large stack of parchment. Derron took it and sat himself down on the ground. Roman snored loudly to his right. He flipped to the most recent date. *Day 189* it read across the top. Derron frowned and wondered which of them had made a mistake. He skimmed the half-page Melwick had jotted for the day. The only note Derron saw that interested him was the mention of the location of some wild strawberry bushes. Derron frowned, annoyed that his friend had never mentioned them. He loved strawberries, even if they were overripe and wrinkled. Melwick looked at him, confused.

"Your Grace, is there a reason you wished to see my notes?"

Derron handed him the stack. "I notice that you've never made any notes of the weather."

Melwick bristled. "Would you like me to?"

"Yes, starting tomorrow make sure to take note of everything that has to do with the climate here: weather patterns, temperature, plant health, all of it."

Melwick took his notes and nodded. "As you command."

The next three days of walking went by much more smoothly. The forest seemed to thin as the group got closer to the lakeshore. The lake itself was much larger than Derron was expecting. Its north shore stretched past the horizon and made the lake look as if it went on forever. A thin layer of ice covered

 DERRON

the surface and reflected the early day light. The sun itself was still hidden behind thick grey clouds. He turned to Melwick.

"Did you circle this entire lake when you were last here?"

Melwick beamed. "Why did you think it took me so long to get back?"

Derron took a quick look at the map and glanced at the red circle on the edge of the lake.

"How far away?"

"About half a day along the coast."

Derron looked off into the distance. "Tell the others to set up camp, and that I'll be back soon."

CHAPTER 02

JOSHYA 1

Down in the Scorpio Tunnels, day and night melded into one. Oil torches lined bedrock walls and lit its thousands of winding pathways with a foreboding orange light that cast flickering shadows whenever someone walked past. The torches had to be constantly replaced by runners as soon as each burned low, as letting one go out meant a section of tunnel returned to a state of pure blackness. Joshya had lived his entire life within the confines of the dirt and stone maze he called home. Never in his life had he seen the sun, or felt the rain on his face, or heard the chirping of birds fill his ears. Not a single person living in the tunnels had, as the entire population had been completely shut off from the surface for close to eighty-three years now.

As Joshya moved through the tunnels, he felt the smoothness of the stone floor against his bare feet. His soles had become so callused that he wondered if the stone was truly smooth, or if he simply could no longer feel the rock's coarseness against his skin. He wished he could know what the feeling of grass between his toes was like, as his grandfather had, but he knew dim light and hard floors were a small price to pay for safety. Joshya's father constantly made it a point in conversation to remind him of the dangers lurking aboveground, remind him of embroiled enemies and longstanding feuds.

Years ago, an invading army had forced the Scorpio people from their homes and down under the surface. The Scorpio's King at the time, sensing defeat, ordered every tunnel entrance be sealed using massive boulders, making it impossible for the enemy to get in. But in doing so, the King sadly also made it impossible for the Scorpios to get back out again. The general assumption was that even after all these years, the enemy still lurked above them, waiting for the Scorpios to crawl out in surrender, for an opportunity to be rid of them once and for all. A chance to finish what their forefathers had started. Of course, no one knew for sure. No one had seen or been to the surface since the war, and no further attack had ever come. Even if there were an army above them, Joshya knew the Scorpios were hardly going to come out grovelling. They had built a life in the dreary tunnels that they now called home, and for many, the surface was just a fantasy.

Before the war had even started, the tunnels had acted as a major part of the Scorpio's lives. They had served as the site of mines and barracks for the greater Scorpio land lying above.

But as large as they were in importance, they were even bigger in size. The tunnels stretched out and covered miles in every direction, and even further lengths down into the ground. All tunnels eventually converged on their most central structure: a great granite castle carved directly out of the surrounding rock. It would be a sight to behold if anyone ever could look from the outside in, like a hidden tower inside of an ant hill. From top to bottom, the castle was over two-hundred feet tall, and still the very top sat far below the surface, so much so that a passing traveler walking atop the land above the massive structure would not notice so much as a hill. It made for the perfect defense. A group of invaders could stand directly atop the castle, and never even know it, which was lucky with the constant looming danger of the enemy perched somewhere upon the surface.

Joshya himself had never even travelled all of the tunnel corridors, and that wasn't because he wasn't allowed; far from it in fact. Joshya was son to King Artemis, Lord of the Scorpio Tunnels and all its inhabitants. In all honesty, the King himself probably hadn't seen them all either. The sheer vastness of the tunnel system made it exceedingly easy to get lost. Single pathways forked into three, four or even five offshoots. Some tunnels crossed, others doubled back, and others abruptly ended. Some even seemed to go on forever, with no end to be found. Eventually, even the torches stopped lighting the walls. That was when you knew you'd gone too far. The leading theory among the more enlightened living among them was that giant wurms had created the original tunnels thousands of years ago before going extinct. While no one could prove it, there hadn't been any better explanations, and so the theory stood. A few times Joshya had attempted to carve a map for himself on a stone tablet, but he had soon given up. Living underground meant there was no access to trees, which in turn meant no access to wood, which in turn meant no access to paper. People were condemned to using stone and clay. Writing had become such a labour-intensive activity that most citizens had given it up entirely. Roughly seventy percent of the five thousand odd people in the tunnels were illiterate, and the number was likely to increase as fewer and fewer could pass the knowledge down to future generations.

Living in constant darkness and dampness had its other effects on the population as well. An increasing number of people were relying less on their eyesight and more on sounds and vibrations to navigate the cramped world they lived in. Joshya himself could never get used to the idea of straining his ears and fingertips, and elected to continue using his eyes in the dim light; for the most part his eyes had adjusted. Today in particular, he passed by an older woman walking with her eyes closed and feeling the texture of the tunnel wall as he ran by. Joshya prided himself on knowing the tunnels better than anyone else, but some days it felt as if the tunnels were constantly shifting. He had been set to meet with Vylarr, his father's captain of the guard, hours ago. Despite eight decades without conflict, the King had insisted his son be trained in the way of

sword, bow, and lance. Joshya had protested at first, but his father was firm in his beliefs and would not bend. So every week
Joshya made his way to the lower levels of the central palace
for weapons training. Normally, he had no problem finding the
chamber, but today he must have taken a wrong turn somewhere in the agriculture tunnels and now had to backtrack
from chamber to chamber.

"You're late," a voice said from behind him as he entered a
familiar room.

Joshya turned his head to see his arms trainer leaning
against the wall beside the doorway. The torch beside him
flickered, sending waves of light up and down his crimson armour. Vylarr always made sure to dress as befit his rank, even
when it wasn't even close to being necessary. Joshya had never
been a fan of his grizzled trainer. Broad shouldered and balding, Captain Vylarr made an intimidating sight. Put a horned
helm on him and one may have mistaken Vylarr for a bull, although a bull would probably have had a better personality.

"No, I'm not." Joshya tried to bluff, but he knew deep down
it would get him nowhere.

Down below the surface, there was no accurate way to tell
time. The colony in the castle used general increments to try
and keep a semblance of flow to their day. Terms like Hour of
the Rat, Hour of the Wurm, or the Bat, Beetle, and a number of
other creatures were commonly used. But the hard truth was
that no one could really keep track, and one man's Hour of the
Beetle was another's Hour of the Rat. Joshya had once heard

 JOSHYA

stories of surface peoples who used the sun to tell their time, but that was hardly an option in their position. Vylarr was having none of his excuses, glaring at Joshya with his condescending eyes.

"I'm sorry, Vylarr," Joshya said, more annoyed than actually sorry. "I'll be on time tomorrow."

Vylarr pushed himself from the wall. "You are the King's son. You should know these tunnels like you would know your own veins." He frowned. "And when we are training, you'll refer to me as Captain."

Vylarr picked up a blunted training sword from the rack on the wall and tossed it underhand to Joshya, who caught it easily.

"I still don't understand," Joshya said, feeling the weight of the blade in his hand. "We've never been attacked. Why do we need to train in combat?" Vylarr was testing the weight of his own sword, seemingly only paying half attention to his pupil. He looked up.

"Never?" Vylarr asked rhetorically, stepping forward in the typical sparring stance, blade extended. Joshya met his stance, and tapped the tip of his blade to his teacher's.

"Yes," he stated again. "The Scorpio Castle is hidden in these tunnels. No one on the surface knows where it is or we would have been attacked by now. And we've never been besieged."

Vylarr made a slow swing to Joshya's head and he blocked it easily, deflecting it downward. "We've been over this half a

JOSHYA

hundred times. Our people have been under siege for the past eighty years. You need to pay more attention when that scribe of yours teaches you history. I assume you've heard of the War of the Crow King?"

Joshya made his own swing at Vylarr, who knocked his blade upwards and elbowed him in the chest, sending him stumbling back. "Of course I have." Joshya spit a gob of phlegm on the ground. "But that was back when we still ventured to the surface. My grandfather put an end to that." He lunged at Vylarr, but was easily blocked and went tumbling into the wall, nearly knocking a torch from its sconce

"Yes," said Vylarr, "your grandfather did do that, but only after your great-grandfather was slain in combat by a lowly boy. And you know why that happened?" He raised his sword, pointing the tip towards the prince lying on the ground. "He died because he was never properly trained how to fight!"

Vylarr rushed headlong at Joshya, landing blow after blow. Joshya was able to get to his feet in time to block the first five, but made a misstep on the sixth and felt the consequence of a hard chop to his side. Then, before he could even process the pain, a chop came down over his shoulder, sending a stinging jolt up his collarbone and forcing him down to one knee. Vylarr looked down at him in disgust and pointed the tip of his sword at Joshya's face.

"Your baby sister could fight better than you do," he spat out. That annoyed Joshya.

"And who taught you how to fight?"

 JOSHYA

"My father, who learned from his father, who, unlike your ancestor, actually survived the war." He turned. "Get up." Vylarr returned to the sparring stance, awaiting the tap of Joshya's sword. When Joshya didn't move, he repeated himself. "I said get up."

"And why would you want to train me then?"

Vylarr sneered. "Oh, I don't want to train you. Your father told me to train you, and he's the king, so I do what he tells me."

That made Joshya mad. He hated being treated like an object belonging to his father. He sprang to his feet and lunged towards Vylarr, who used his momentum against him and sent him sprawling right back down to the ground. Joshya never looked, but he knew that his teacher was smirking at him.

Hours passed before Vylarr allowed him to leave. By that time Joshya had a dozen new bruises to nurse and sweat beading into his eyes.

"Where are you off to now?" asked Vylarr, dabbing his balding hairline with a yellowed towel older than he was.

"I have a lesson with the scribe in the Hour of the Beetle."

Vylarr rolled his eyes. "A trip to the hot springs first would be more courteous. Aldar is an old man; the smell of you may be enough to tip him over the edge of his grave."

Joshya liked Aldar about as much as he liked Vylarr. The scribe was older than four times Joshya's age and sour as a spoiled beet. Regardless, he was well respected by his father and, as such, demanded respect from Joshya. When he arrived at the door to Aldar's chamber-room, he knocked and awaited the old scribe to open it. Minutes passed before it did.

"You're late," came a voice though the door.

"I'm sorry. I was held up with Vylarr in the training room."

"You should pay more attention in those classes you know," scolded Aldar. "You never know when you'll need them."

"Funny, Vylarr said the same thing about your classes."

The fact Vylarr and Aldar liked each other so much made Joshya even more annoyed. Nonetheless, he took a seat in a chair across the table from Aldar. Down in the tunnels there were no trees to make furniture from, so the craftsmen had to make their chairs, tables, beds, and other furnishings from the one resource that the Scorpio's had in abundance: clay. The chair was hard and rough, but cool to sit on and felt nice on Joshya's warm sweat-soaked skin. He'd spent half a moment's respite resting his sore muscles before a pile of books were thumped on the table in front of him, making him jump and ending his moment of bliss.

The books were old, written in a time when the Scorpios still ventured aboveground and could access the trees on the surface. Joshya wondered what a tree actually looked like. No pictures existed in the books. He found it ironic that none of the illustrators had thought to draw the very thing they were using to draw on. Aldar rubbed the wrinkled skin of his pale, stubbly chin and flipped the first book open to a detailed map of the Starscape. Joshya had seen it a thousand times before. Using a long thin piece of iron, the old scribe pointed down at the page, tapping the end on the inked system northmost on the page. Joshya knew the answer without having to be asked the question.

"That's Ursa Major," Joshya answered. "Symbol: A great bear. Ruled by King Derron."

"Good," said Aldar, moving the point of his stick to another system.

Joshya knew it well. "Gemini. Symbol: the twins. Ruled by King Fayvius."

The stick moved again.

"Cygnus. Symbol: The swan. Ruled by King Nymor."

The stick flicked the table with a long SMACK. "Wrong, Nymor was killed in his sleep a fortnight ago. His eldest daughter, Princess Myrella, is the new Queen.

Joshya looked up quizzically at Aldar. "How was I supposed to know that?"

"You will one day rule when good King Artemis passes. You need to know these things."

"But how do we even know these things? We're cut off from the surface!"

"Your father has his ways."

"He's never shared them with me."

"He will. Be patient."

Aldar flipped his book to a new page, covered in the faded ink of some old hand. Dust filled the air and covered the interior of Joshya's nose, as he held back the urge to sneeze.

"The War of the Crow King." Aldar covered a spot on the page with his pointer. "When and why did it begin?"

"It began in the year 754... no, 756."

"Good." And what caused it?"

Joshya thought for a moment. "King Olathe of Corvus broke the terms of the peace treaty between himself and my great-grandfather. Olathe had agreed not to settle the sand mountains north of our tunnels, but he killed all the men we had posted there and built The Olathefort. My great-grandfather assembled his troops and tried to take it by force. When Olathe refused to surrender, my great-grandfather burned it to the ground.

Aldar nodded. "And what happened to your great-grandfather?"

Joshya reflected for a moment about what Vylarr had said to him. "He died."

The lesson went on for what seemed like days, but was in reality only a few hours. By the time Aldar let him go, Joshya's mind was brimming with knowledge about high families, history, agriculture, law, masonry, and all sorts of other subjects. He had no doubt that he'd forget half of it by the time he next met with his mentor.

That night, Joshya made his way down to the drinking chamber. It was the one room in the entire underground castle he seemed to have no trouble finding. When he reached the entrance, he paused, and brushed his hair down over his eyes. Joshya never liked to be recognized when he went on one of his drinking excursions. A king's son was not meant to be seen drunk amongst the commons. He often smeared dirt and dust on his face to obscure his features. Next to the other tunnel diggers and brick makers it made him look like a common worker. Although, Joshya was never sure whether it really worked, or if everyone else was just too drunk to care. Satisfied with his look, he entered. Inside, he saw all sorts of rugged folk: tunnel diggers, masons, kiln-workers, gardeners, all had come for relaxing, drinking, and all-round having a good time. There were no peak hours for business, since everyone had completely different schedules. One person would always be starting work just as another finished; such was the way of living in tunnels where there was no measure of a day. In recent months, the drinking chamber had been expanded to three times its original size and was growing still, yet it never seemed large enough to contain the people within. There was never a moment wherein a drink was not being ordered, drunk, or smashed drunkenly against a wall. Joshya walked through the crowds to the clay counter and ordered his favourite drink. The server handed him a ceramic cup filled to the top with a murky grey liquid. The concoction was made from ground-river water, sugarcane, and a special fungus that grew on the outskirts of the tunnels. The liquid made him dizzy, but in a good way, and it caused him to see in interesting shapes and colours. Joshya took a long drink and then looked over the seating area for someplace quiet to sit and think and let the drink take its course. He decided on an empty chair in a dimly

JOSHYA

lit corner, but as he made his way over someone grabbed him by the arm. Joshya spun around, expecting to find one of his father's guards, but was instead met face to face with a red-faced teen about his age.

"Esho!" he said, happily giving his friend a hug. "I thought you were off tending to the root gardens?"

Esho laughed. "I suppose I should be doing that, shouldn't I?" He raised his own glass of fungus ale to his lips and slurped.

Joshya took a sip of his own. "I should report you to my father."

Esho tapped Joshya's glass with a muddy knuckle. "And if you do that, I'll tell him where you've been hidin'."

They shared a mutual grin and Esho led Joshya back to a table where two other boys were arguing fervently over something. Five near-empty glasses of various drinks littered the table.

"No, no," said one of the boys, voice thick with a drunken slur. "A Virgo warrior-maid could never outmatch a Cancer mutant."

The boy was around Joshya's age and had a pudgy belly and curly, dusty black hair that puffed out past his ears. The other boy had jet black hair that protruded from his forehead, almost as pointed as his nose. On his tunic was a patch in the shape of a Crow, symbolizing the Corvus faction of his ancestors.

"It depends on the mutation!" the Corvusi boy argued. "Are we talking a barnacle mutant, or a lobster mutant? If you're trying to tell me a barnacle mutant can take on the wrath of a warrior-maid, you're sorely mistaken!"

The Corvusi boy downed the last half of his cup and placed it next to the pile of empties. "I need more ale if you're going to keep talking wurmshit," he said, standing. When he turned, his eyes met Joshya's and he smiled a drunken smile.

"Joshya!" he called loudly, despite Joshya being right in front of him.

"Joshya?" The curly haired boy looked up, and gave Joshya an equally drunk smile. "My Prince," he said with a mocking bow.

Joshya knew these two boys as well. The curly haired boy was named Mathas, and was studying to become a scribe, perhaps to replace Aldar in the event of the old man's passing. The other boy with the crow patch on his chest was Himrel. Back in the War that sent the Scorpio's underground, a small number of Corvusi soldiers had turned traitor on their own and given aid to the defenders. Afterwards, when the surviving Scorpios were forced underground, the allied Corvusi went into exile along with them. Himrel was the great-grandson of one such warrior. Unlike most of the descendants who had soon assimilated into the Scorpios, Himrel was proud of his heritage and boldly displayed his Corvusi badge on his chest, the same tattered and faded one his great-grandfather had worn in the war itself. Wearing it in the present day, however, only brought Himrel looks of disdain from others, a constant reminder of the bad blood that sent them into hiding. Joshya and his friends, though, couldn't care less. Perhaps that's why Himrel spent so much time around them.

"Which do you think would win," Himrel pointed a finger into Joshya's chest, "warrior-maid or mutant?"

"What does it matter?" asked Joshya plainly. "Neither will ever find the likes of us."

Himrel gave Joshya a look like that a baby would give his mother for taking away his toy. Then he belched loudly and sat back down. "Guess that means no one wins the bet."

Mathas looked disappointed and Joshya frowned, feeling like the death of the party, but three cups later he'd brought it back into full swing.

Hours afterwards, Joshya stumbled back out into the tunnels. His face was flush and his pants had ripped somewhere along the cuff. He wavered, and fell against the hard wall. It felt cool to the touch and for a moment he thought about staying there. He shook his head to himself, knowing he had to get back to his bedchamber before his parents thought to worry about him. Well, his mother at least. His father was probably still in court doing kingly things. As he pushed his way back up, he accidentally bumped his shoulder into the chest of a tall man he'd never met before, sending both sprawling to the ground. The dirt on his face was all but smeared off so Joshya looked away in a feeble attempt to mask his identity.

"Sorry sir." he muttered, trying to sound as sober as he could.

 JOSHYA

The man said nothing, only taking a second to lift himself up off the ground and to slip something back into his pocket. He then disappeared into the darkness of the tunnels. Joshya scratched at his shaggy hair and brushed off the dust from his shoulders. *Where's he off to in such a hurry at... at...* Joshya couldn't remember what hour it was. But it didn't matter; soon he was passed out asleep in his own little corner of the universe.

CHAPTER 03

JAIR 1

From outside, the faint sound of the rabble penetrated his ears. Jair sat cross-legged on the hard cobblestone floor, sharpening the end of his ceremonial long-axe with a whetstone. The metal head shone bright, as befit its status. When polished to an incredible sheen, the light reflected off its razor edge and danced across the walls. For a moment, Jair pondered why an executioner's axe need be so pristine if moments later it was to be plunged into some vagrant's bloody throat. The thought quickly exited his mind. It wasn't his place to question his duties. As royal executioner, Jair's job was to carry out the sentence, not to question the whys and wherefores.

Many of the other palace guards envied Jair for his position. Behind his back he knew they mocked him, gossiping amongst themselves about how cushy his job must be. And yet each time he descended the steps to the chopping block, Jair prayed he would be lucky enough to trip and take his own head before the execution. He frowned to himself. It would obviously be easier to be punished for some petty crime. Maybe steal from the royal treasury, or denounce the King in the public square. Both crimes carried death sentences in his city. Jair had been the one to carry out the sentence many times himself. He'd do it, but he didn't think he could stomach the moments leading up to an execution, with all the waiting and the knowing. And so, he carried on with his job of ending other people's lives when he only truly wanted to end his own.

The whetstone made long scratching noises as he ran it across the length of the axe head. The sound calmed him. It brought him back to his days in the palace guard, before he had been up-jumped to his current status. Back then he was a man in a thousand. Nobody but another face in the crowd. He had kept his service sword, hanging it above his bed on a pair of stakes. Every now and again he'd take it down and wax it to keep it from rusting; for whatever reason, he could never let it go. His quarters were humble and the only other adornment was a white cloak, neatly draped from a hook on the wall. It was a gift from the King himself, made from lamb's wool and embroidered with the golden altar of Ara. In truth, he should be wearing it, but he could never seem to do so. *The fabric itches my neck*, he would tell himself.

Jair's mind wandered back years ago, to the day he had been promoted. Back then he had been stationed at the city's southern gate, but due to an abundance of new recruits he had been reassigned to the dungeons. Jair had protested, explaining to his commanding officer that he was not fit for the job, that he was too inexperienced. His commander had simply laughed and told him that the royal dungeons were the most boring place for any soldier to be positioned. That had been just two weeks before the riot.

While he had been on duty, a small group of captured Lacerta insurgents had broken out and began overpowering the stationed guards. In their struggle to reach the exit, they had killed five guardsmen, as well as the previous royal executioner. Jair himself had been making his rounds, checking on prisoners all the way on the other side of the dungeon. He'd heard the telltale sounds of a struggle and went running. When Jair had seen the rioters begin to break, he'd picked up the executioner's gold encrusted long-axe and began halting each rioter one by one until none of them remained alive. In the end, he was the only guard to survive. The King had been so impressed by Jair's feat of bravery and strength that he had personally appointed Jair to the newly vacant position. A great honour to be sure, but an unwanted one.

Jair lifted himself from the floor and stretched his arms. He was only thirty-one years old, but the long years of swinging his oversized weapon had jarred his shoulders and elbows. As he bent his body, his joints popped so loudly Jair was sure the people far below could hear it. Cracking his knuckles, he moved towards the dark wooden cabinet propped next to the window. From it, Jair removed his ceremonial armour: a chest piece of gold and jewel which shimmered as he held it in the light. He pulled it over his head and adjusted the metal until it rested comfortably on his back muscles. As a palace guard, the armour he had worn was solid steel, sturdy and unbreakable. This armour though was made of the much lighter material of aluminum, and was covered in gold plating. Jair was half convinced the piece would shatter if he were to drop it. Reaching back into the cabinet, Jair retrieved a matching gold-plated aluminum mask that covered his features. He ran a finger over the metal. Smooth, meticulously crafted. There was no hole for his mouth, only two small ones for his eyes, and another two even smaller for his nostrils. He donned the mask before gazing out the window.

Jair's quarters were high up in the main tower of the palace. Ninety feet above the courtyard, it was only below the city's judicator, high scribe, and royal treasurer. The King himself had the largest quarters, but those were on the ground-level, next to the central fountains. Peering over the landscape below, he watched as farmers rolled bales of hay amongst their disinterested livestock. Most of the surrounding lands to the castle were made of such farmland, all except to the southeast which housed the King's Forest. The dark green swath stretched for miles, all the way from Teardrop Lake in the west to the Rumblefall Mountains of the east. As Jair stood and watched, the autumn wind rustled the tips on the pines and the whole wood seemed to sway like some large green entity.

When he finally saw the King's procession approaching the gate, he knew it was time. Sighing, he reached down, picked up his axe, and straightened his back, donning the unfeeling persona of his position. Jair had to descend a hundred and fifty steps just to reach the ground level. From there, he passed noble and not alike to reach the portcullis. Outside, the light of the morning sun was blinding, reflecting off his mask and into his eyes. He was met with a wave of shouts and cheers by the mob of onlookers in the square. In front of the castle, surrounded by jeering people, an elevated wooden stage had been erected with a block at its center. If he wasn't wearing a mask, they would have seen the look of disgust on his face. *Death should be quick,* he thought to himself, *not cheered on as if it were some sport.*

There were castle guards posted periodically all the way from the portcullis to the platform, cordoning off a pathway through the crowded masses. Jair began the uncomfortable walk from castle to stage. The last royal executioner, he remembered, had reveled in this walk, waving to the crowd and pumping his axe in the air. Jair preferred to take a much more somber approach: facing forward, unwavering, with his long-axe resting upon his shoulder. Taking his place to the left of the golden executioner's block, he surveyed the crowd in front of him. Old and young, women and men, all had come to see the day's scheduled murder. His attention then turned, as it usually did, to the executioner's block itself. "The most ornate butcher's block in the universe," the city folk called it. The gold

 JAIR

was shined and waxed to a sparkle; no one would have known by looking that it had been covered in a traitor's blood not three days past. The stage for the execution was raised at least eight feet from the ground, so all could see clearly. Jair looked down at the jeering masses before him and cursed at them under his breath. There were significantly more here today than normally. I must be taking the head of someone interesting. The thought brought him no pleasure.

Guards were also posted all around the stage to make sure no rowdy fool had the bright idea to try and rush the stage to save whoever it was losing their head on that particular day. Jair was curious if he knew any of the guards from his time in their ranks, but all were facing the crowd and it was less than likely one of them would be stupid enough to turn around.

A trumpet sounded from somewhere behind the stage and Jair turned to see the King and his retainers descend from the palace and make their way down the path to the block. The King himself looked as though he'd seen better days. He had been away on diplomatic missions across his kingdom when an urgent matter had cut his trip short. At once he'd begun the long journey back to the castle. He had asked the execution be delayed until he returned, so that's what had happened. If Jair cared, he may have asked the Judicator why the King was so interested in this man. But alas, he did not. A head chopped off today is the same as a head chopped off tomorrow.

Jair supposed it had been at least two years since he'd last laid eyes on his King. He wondered if His Grace had always looked so old. His snow-white hair came down in wisps across his shoulders, held together by a golden crown upon his head. The guards assigned to the stage's stairs parted and the King's company made their way onto the platform. The King himself took a seat in an ornately carved chair to the back left of the stage. To his right stood his personal guard, Sir Harkin, hand ever on his sword hilt. Harkin had once mocked Jair for his lack of knighthood. It was widely known that the only men Harkin truly respected were other knights, despite himself not gaining the status until well into his thirties. To Jair's left there were two other guards that had come with the King. One he vaguely remembered from his own service time, but the other was a complete stranger, and looked no older than twenty. *They're filling the guard with untrained boys and play-knights*, he thought with a sigh.

The last retainer to take the stage was the King's personal scribe, whose name Jair did not know, and who was currently fumbling with a scroll. The man was small and bald as an egg, looking more than a little anxious to begin. The rest of the procession dispersed amongst the crowd.

"Silence!" called the scribe in a meek, squeaky voice. "There will be silence!"

The crowd hushed for a moment, but before long seemed to become even louder.

"Si..." The scribe tried again, but was cut off by a woman shouting up obscenities at him.

 JAIR

Jair could see this would get them nowhere. He took two big steps forwards to the front of the stage and paused. Then, with all eyes on him, he lifted his heavy axe into the air and thumped the butt of it down thrice onto the planks of wood below him. An ominous sound echoed across the square and the crowd soon came to a hush.

"Thank you." The scribe looked relieved. He opened his scroll and read aloud. "Today we gather to witness the final moments of an enemy to our people, a murderer and a villain." He lowered the scroll. "Bring out Captain Vikron of Taurus!"

The crowd collectively looked to the right as a triad of guards marched out of a small tent next to the platform. In their center walked a man a good head taller than any of the guards that held him. His beard looked as if a small furry animal had attached itself to his face. He wore tattered clothes, ripped and stinking, but even still they had allowed him to wear his captain's helm: a steel war helm adorned with two large bull's horns. Jair took note that the ends had been significantly blunted. The crowd's murmurs started to rise again at the sight of him, but no one dared shout too loudly. Captain Vikron made his way to the stage and stood behind the golden block, a guard on each side and one behind. Jair didn't recognize any of them.

"Captain Vikron," the scribe began, not turning to him, but instead speaking into the crowd. "You have been charged with the crime of murdering forty-six members of the Ara ruled town of Ganton, including women and children. How do you plead?"

"Guilty!" Vikron growled without hesitation. "But it be forty-seven people I killed, not forty-six. If you're going to name my crimes, at least get them bloody right!"

The scribe reddened. "The punishment for these crimes is death, Captain Vikron. Do you have any last words?"

"Aye, I do." Vikron stared out into the crowd. "I'd like everyone here to know that I'm 'membering each and every one of your faces right now. And one day I will personally watch the life drain from every one o' you, and I got the memory of an ox, so don't be thinking I'll be forgetting any o' you."

The guard standing behind Vikron shoved him down onto his knees.

"Especially you, 'cutioner. Don't think you can hide behind that mask o' yours."

He smiled up at Jair; his teeth were yellow and rotting. Then he closed his eyes and rested his chin softly on the block. Vikron's bushy beard splayed out like a nest. The speech seemed to amuse the scribe, who had finally turned around and was now staring gleefully at Vikron.

"And how will you do that, when you have just seconds left to live?"

Vikron smiled without opening his eyes. "This ain't the end, bookworm. It's only the beginning."

The scribe chortled. "Then I'll see you in the afterlife, scUUUGH!"

 JAIR

The scribe's eyes widened, and he tumbled to the floor. Jair could see a small crossbow bolt protruding from his lower back. The crowd began to stir. Sir Harkin already had borne cold steel in his hand, scanning the crowd for the source. The King himself was staring incredulously at his fallen friend, before standing and shouting something at Jair, but he too was cut off when a second bolt came soaring from the crowd and pierced him square in the chest. The King's eyes rolled back in his head and he crumpled back down into his chair, crown falling from his brow.

A woman in the crowd screamed, and Jair could see a man up front was weeping. One of the guards on the platform was at the king's side, feebly trying to help quell the bleeding. Sir Harkin had leapt down into the crowd and Jair lost sight of him. The guards posted around the stage were now moving into the scatter of people, searching for the mystery assailant. Jair watched them panning through the city folk, ripping off cloaks, hoods, and anything else that could conceal a weapon. Before long, the guards had dispersed themselves too far and Jair watched as one guard went down with a knife in his back. Another seemed to disappear into the sea of onlookers without reason.

Jair heard a snicker from behind him and turned to see Vikron laughing to himself, head still resting on the block. Jair raised his pole-axe and made a quick stride to end his merriment, but the captive captain was quicker than he looked. Standing, the burly man caught the two guards beside him

off guard as he pushed them open palmed in the chest. Both
went tumbling off the side of the stage into the crowd below.
He didn't make an attempt on the third guard behind him.
When Jair made a wide swing for Vikron's torso, the spared
guard came forward and raised his own blade, deflecting the
blow. *He's in on this too*, Jair realized suddenly. Turning on the
ball of his foot, in one swift motion Jair pushed the man off
balance, spun around, and drove the pointed tip of his axe up
through the man's throat. Warm blood washed over Jair. The
lifeless body of the turncoat guard fell to the ground, revealing suddenly that Vikron had somehow gained possession of
two hand-axes, and was charging forward. Unprepared for
the much bigger man, Jair made a poor attempt to raise his
long axe in defense as Vikron rushed him. He was sent flying
backwards, dropping his weapon as he went. The force of the
impact sent Jair over the edge of the stage, and he landed on
his back with the jewels on his armour popping out and spinning off into the crowd. The wind was knocked from his lungs
and his teeth clamped around his tongue hard enough to draw
blood as he laid writhing and gasping for air.

Jair ripped off his mask in a feeble attempt to free his air-
ways. He turned and spit a glob of blood onto the grass. To his
right, he could see Sir Harkin in a mad rage, hacking down city
folk in a paranoid attempt to find his king's killer. Jair watched
one man pleading to the knight of his innocence, but the king's
guard was having none of it. Harkin raised his sword above his
head, but before he could bring it down, another one of the city

folk drove a sowing needle up between the rings of the knight's chainmail right between the ribs. Sir Harkin fell to his knees. The pleading man took no time in fleeing, disappearing into the crazed crowd. The small woman who'd attacked Harkin began undoing his armour, even as the dying knight still clung to his last few breaths of life.

When his own breath returned to him, Jair stood and took a few sweet seconds before jumping and pulling himself back up onto the stage. The guard helping the king lay dead with a gash on the back of his head. Jair crawled over him and checked the king for a pulse. It was there, but faint and fading. His golden crown lay beside him in a pool of blood. Jair frowned, thinking how he should be feeling something for his king. Sympathy perhaps, or anger. A voice from behind broke his thoughts.

"I told ya, bookworm."

Jair turned to see Vikron holding the bleeding body of the scribe.

"Please. P-please." The scribe stuttered, his voice heavily slurred with pain.

Vikron smiled. "Was never talking about the afterlife." He smirked, and then twisted the scribe's neck until in snapped.

Jair could only stand in stunned silence. The city square was littered with bodies. About two dozen or so people were left, either cleaning knives or collecting arrows. The rest had died or fled. Taurus loyalists, Jair thought bleakly to himself. The only two who remained alive on the platform were himself and Vikron, who was now looking at him with smiling eyes.

"Well, 'cutioner, I can see your face now. It's a prettier face than most of the women on my homeworld have, I'll give you that." He then bent over and picked up Jair's long axe. "So 'cutioner, you ready to be 'cuted?"

Jair fell to his knees and nodded. *Yes,* he thought. *Finally.*

Vikron frowned. "That's no fun. I was expecting a fight out of you."

When Jair didn't move or speak Vikron unsheathed one of his hand axes and threw it onto the stage next to Jair.

"Fight, dammit!"

Jair looked over at it, uninterested.

"Bugger you," said Vikron, as he turned back to his people. "I thank you all for coming!" he announced. "I owe my life to each and every one of you." He smiled. "But none o' you will ever get it!"

A laugh rose up from the square. *So close,* thought Jair. *I was so close.* Vikron continued his speech.

"This city is small; it won't be long 'til we're run over with guards. Pick the bodies of what you fancy then follow me. Nathanyel, with me!" When no one in the crowd moved, he spoke again. "Nathanyel!"

The small woman who'd killed Sir Harkin cleared her throat. She was holding Harkin's chainmail in her arms. "Nathanyel is dead, Captain." The square went silent.

"Bugger me."

For the first time in the day, Jair thought Vikron looked worried. Then, as if he'd had a brilliant idea, Vikron smiled. He moved towards Jair and lifted him off the ground by the collar of his tunic under his broken armor. The action choked Jair and made him cough in Vikron's face.

"Well, 'cutioner, looks like I'll be needing you after all. I assume you know the castle as well as any common palace guard?"

Jair wasn't sure what Vikron was getting at, but he nodded anyway. He glanced back to where his King lay, and for a moment he thought he saw movement, but he wasn't sure.

"Good." Vikron grinned and dropped Jair to his feet, before giving him a shove forward. "Take me to the King's quarters."

JAIR

CHAPTER 04

GRELHYM 1

"Spill a drop and the next thing you'll be fetching is your own coffin." The words rang in his head as he ran down the corridor.

If only the chef hadn't taken so long, Grelhym thought. *I wouldn't have to worry.* Grelhym was no older than fourteen, but had already spent a third of his life in his Lord's service. He hoped that within the year he'd be allowed a chance at knighthood, but it was a far-off dream. Knighthoods were only given to squires who supported their charges in the field of battle. Grelhym wasn't even sure if his slobbish Lord had ever even held a sword, let alone fought in as much a skirmish. And besides, Grelhym himself was more oft seen reading than training in the castle yard.

Grelhym had known Lord Rygar for as long as he could remember. He'd been orphaned as a child, and soon after been taken into the castle's service as a dust boy, crawling into the various fire pits around the castle and scrubbing soot. At the age of eight, he had been chosen alongside several other boys to serve the Lord as his personal attendants. Back then there were six of them, and Grelhym hadn't had to worry about being the central focus for his lordship. He could lay back and coast his way through his duties, knowing no one would look to him if anything went amiss. But as his time went on, the other attendants who worked alongside him began to pass. The first one got the flux, another succumbed to a chill, two boys were slain in a botched attempt by a thief to make off with half the Lord's treasure, and one died in an unfortunate accident involving a donkey and a castle whore. With each one's passing, the number left to do the work diminished, meaning Grelhym's duties had mounted. He could no longer slack and instead found himself doing his Lord's bidding all hours of the day and half the night. So, when Lord Rygar's former squire had drowned in a swamp, the pool of candidates His Lord had to choose from had become quite small.

Ever since, Grelhym had found himself running back and forth, fetching food and water and ale and pillows and whatever else His Lordship found himself fancying. *But at very least I'm one step closer to my knighthood.* That's what he would always tell himself. A fortnight ago, when Grelhym found out that his Lord had been chosen to attend a parley off-world, he rejoiced in the knowledge he'd get a well-earned break. He imagined the host would have servants to do his duties for

GRELHYM

him, but on arrival he had found no such luck. Being taken along meant he had to act as the Lord's retainer, as well as his squire. The only thread of hope Grelhym could hold onto was the knowledge that someday he would be knighted. He often daydreamed while doing his duties about what the common folk would call him as he rode past gallantly on his stallion. Sir Grelhym the Great was a favourite of his, though he found it to be too simple. Sir Grelhym the Gallant was another. But Sir Grelhym the Glum was more likely. Ever since arriving at the parley, Grelhym had been miserable, having to run back and forth nonstop and being yelled at all the way.

The day was hot and muggy, and Lord Rygar had a craving for dried grapes and red wine. He'd already retrieved the dried grapes, but they had been hard and not very flavourful, which only served to annoy his master. Sending him back for the wine, he'd grabbed Grelhym's arm, bushy moustache quivering.

"Spill a drop and the next thing you'll be fetching is your own coffin," he had said, before giving his squire a hard shove in the back.

It only made matters worse that the cook couldn't find a single cask of red in the entire storeroom. Grelhym had stood quietly, shifting his weight back and forth from one foot to the other and making a nervous note of the time. When the cook finally returned bearing a cup of what Grelhym hoped was red wine, though it looked more purple than anything, he grabbed it and started the long walk back to the great hall. He made

 GRELHYM

it back without spilling a drop, saving his position and most likely his life. Rygar took a swig and wiped his mouth with the back of his hand.

"Sit boy, we're about to begin."

Grelhym took a seat among the other squires and various other men and women in waiting. An elderly man stepped gingerly up to the high seat at the head of the Roundhall. Grelhym knew who the man was, as did everyone. The old man currently fluffing a red velvet seat cushion was Meikal, the personal scribe to the King of Sculptor. A man of eighty-eight years, Meikal had traveled most, if not all, of the Starscape. Along his journeys he had met countless thousands of people, and was well liked and well respected by all he encountered. It made him the perfect judicator for the upcoming debates. As an honoured scribe of over sixty years, his skills would also come into play, although his hands were too frail to write on his own, so he had brought a flock of young pages to attend to that. Grelhym looked around the room to the faces of the honored guests settling in for what may be several long and tedious days. Many of the faces he did not know, but a few he recognized.

Closest to him, he noted the great warrior, Sir Velaron of Lacerta, known as the Knight of the Sandstorm, who sat worrying the clasp on his cuff. Brown skinned, dark haired and handsome, Velaron was the secret love of all girls lowborn and highborn alike. He had earned the name "Knight of the Sandstorm" after crossing the Raza desert in the dead of night during a great sandstorm to warn the people of Lacerta of an oncoming attack. He then led the defense, and staved off an army thrice the size of his own. Recently, there had been a rumour spreading around the squire's quarters that Velaron had six toes on his left foot. No one had, as of yet, actually seen if it were true, not even his own squire.

A few seats down from Velaron was King Emerton of the Crater Faction, stroking the snow-white ermine that he brought with him everywhere. Most figured he must love that ferret more than his own sons and daughters. The ermine gnawed happily on a carrot while the King smiled.

A burly man sat down next to him. Grelhym knew him as Damien, the eldest son of Derron, the wayward king of Ursa Major. With his father off on some secretive mission, Damien had been left to tend his father's people for the past half a year. He could not have been older than thirty, but the grey hairs starting to sprout amongst his dark brown beard showed that the role had begun taking its toll.

And though Grelhym didn't know his name, he immediately knew the delegate from the Cancer Faction. The Cancers were known for being sick and twisted fish-like mutants, though the reason as to *why* was a closely guarded faction secret. The man sitting at the roundtable had an elongated head like that of a hammerhead shark, with fins on the backs of each of his wrists. His skin was grey and rough. The sight made Grelhym queasy. Across from the abomination, as distantly placed as they could be, he saw the delegate from Aquarius glaring. Pale

 GRELHYM

skinned and radiantly blond, the Aquarii were the antithesis of the monstrosities that were the Cancers. Both shared a home-world and loathed one another's people. It was amazing that the two were not at one another's throats.

Grelhym looked back to his own Lord, who was now whis-pering to an older gentleman wearing a leather jerkin with the symbol of a ship painted on the shoulder. The two seemed deep in discussion when Meikal stood and tapped the end of a long pointer on the table in front of him. He only needed three slow taps before he had the room's attention. Grelhym marvelled at how lucky he was to be able to see such a living legend with his own eyes.

"Greetings," Meikal began.

His voice carried, but was clearly laboured with age. A few delegates around the table mumbled their greetings in return. Grelhym saw one overzealous delegate salute the scribe, which made him chuckle. Meikal continued.

"I'd like to begin by thanking King Terreon of Sagittarius for organizing this parley." He motioned towards the man im-mediately to his right, who stood and took a small bow. Meikal cleared his throat.

"Today we gather to address a serious issue. As I am sure you are all aware, the various worlds we dwell upon have each experienced the same serious problem." His beard reached halfway down his chest and rustled with each word. "For the past fifteen years or so, our homes themselves have begun to die." He paused and looked up at a man close-by where Grelhym sat. "Reuso." The man at the end of the table sat up straight. Meikal rested his pointer on the table in the man's direction. "Your people make the majority of their livings on trade by the lumber harvested from your Great Forest, correct?"

He nodded. "Yes, your honour."

"And how is the Great Forest these days, Your Grace?" Meikal looked as though he already knew the answer.

"It's dead, your honour." Reuso frowned and sat.

Meikal coughed, nodding his acknowledgement. "Sir Telling."

The man with the ship painted jerkin stood next.

"The vast majority of your homeworld is covered by ocean-water, is that correct?"

Sir Telling looked melancholy. "Not anymore, your honour. Our ocean 'been drying up. Most of it has turned salt flats and sand at the moment."

A few mumbles of astonishment rumbled around the room. Grelhym had never visited either planet they spoke of, but he did know his own. The world he lived on had once been covered in thick swamp and dense pine. The swamps had always been dangerous, but recently the fumes had become so noxious that the roads through had become impassable. Mass swaths of pine forests had become black and brittle, and even the wildlife had fled the area. Hunting had become near impossible close to their castle, and many nearby villages had been abandoned.

"My birds have all died!" yelled a voice from across the room.

A young woman stood suddenly and slammed a fist on the table. "My people are starving!" she yelled. "Our grain is all but gone!"

"Ours too!" came an older voice. "We need it more than all of you!" The old man who cried out began coughing as soon as the words left his lips.

Meikal began tapping his pointer on the table once more, and the room began to quiet down. He then leaned over to one of his pages and whispered something. At the same time Grelhym noticed that the shouting old man's squire had got up to go run him a vial, presumably something to ease his throat. Meikal rested back in his chair, already looking exhausted.

"We have all suffered from recent events. We are not here to argue about who has been most affected, or who deserves the most pity. We are here to discuss the possibility of a solution."

A soft voice came from the back of the room. "But only one of you will gain use of the artifact." A hush fell over the room. King Terreon stood and laced his arms behind his back. Grelhym could get a good look at him now. The man had smoky brown hair and a beard meticulously trimmed to an inch in length and uniform throughout. His tunic was cadmium red and was emblazoned with the light brown arrow of Sagittarius on his left breastplate.

"The artifact is a last resort." His voice carried with the weight of a true king. "We are here to discuss what we can do for each other. And if anyone's specific problem cannot be helped, they will gain access to the artifact."

He moved his gaze along the edge of the room and made eye contact with each delegate before sitting back down.

"Thank you Terreon." Meikal produced a small bowl from under the table full of small folded pieces of parchment. "This bowl contains the names of every faction across the Starscape. When I draw your faction's name, the representing delegate may make his or her case for why they require use of the artifact. Each…"

At that point Grelhym stopped listening and sunk into his chair. *This will take forever. I'll be older than Meikal when I'm finally relieved of duty.*

As name after name was drawn and called, delegates stood to make their cases. Some took the route of logic and came with long documents of stats and charts as to why they should have access to the artifact. Others made pleas for mercy and tried to guilt the other delegates into choosing them. One delegate from Taurus made the argument of might, and all but threatened war on the rest of the delegates if he was not chosen. Meikal listened intently to each one, but the same could not be said for Grelhym. His mind wandered thinking of everything from food to girls to the bugs landing on his legs. He scratched at a bite on his ankle that had turned to a hive. Beside him, one of the other squires had fallen asleep. Unfortunately, the boy was soon after called upon by his master, resulting in a very painful slap awake. By that time, the sky outside the Roundhall had

GRELHYM

gone dark and the cool dusk air wafted in. Less than half the delegates had spoken their peace, and a few had already left for their quarters. As the King of Octans finished his speech about the lack of any clouds on his world in ten years, Meikal yawned and raised a hand.

"We break for the night and reconvene in the morning."

The room quickly emptied of all important occupants. The squires and other lesser helpers stayed behind to tidy the room for the next day. Grelhym noticed that Meikal and King Terreon had also stayed behind. The old scribe looked as if he would fall asleep in his chair, and Terreon sat studying notes he had taken through the day. Grelhym wondered if he'd even noticed everyone else had left. One woman attempted to take the empty glass from in front of the Sagittarius King, but he waved her away. Grelhym himself took up a broom and began sweeping the large cobblestone floor.

At sunrise the next morning, the hall was packed again. Meikal began by announcing that Hentro of Monoceros, the older coughing gentleman from yesterday, would not be joining them as he was feeling ill, and that his squire had been sent back to his homeworld with a request for a replacement delegate. Grelhym groaned and wished that were him. It had only been a day and already he'd give anything to go back home. The squire sitting next to him leaned over to Grelhym.

"I heard that the parley is rigged," he said. "Meikal is hiding the parchments for those he wants to speak first in his sleeve."

Grelhym turned to him. "Why would he do that? If every-one gets to speak eventually, what does the order matter?"

The other squire shrugged, then turned to speak to the squire on his other side. Grelhym yawned. As a common man in waiting, he didn't have to be up until well past sunrise. He missed those days. But as a squire, it was up at dawn no matter what. *I bet a knight doesn't have to wake up this early.*

"Grelhym!" He heard his Lord yell.

Grelhym staggered to his feet and swiftly ran to him. "Your Lordship?"

"I desire dried grapes. Get them now."

"As you wish." Grelhym hurried off back to the kitchens. When he entered, he met his favourite kitchen girl and she gave him a warm smile. "Lord Rygar requests dried grapes." He elected to use the word "requested" over the far more accurate "demanded". It meant he'd get the food much more quickly, and of much better quality. *And less likely to be spit on.* He knew the kitchen staff despised the arrogance of the various high-types they were having to serve and you always had to check for spit in your Lord's food before giving it to them. The girl reappeared and handed him a hardy bowl of the dried fruit. He thanked her and hurried back to the hall, where a noble look-ing man in a blue silk robe adorned with golden swans was al-ready starting to make his case. Lord Rygar snatched the bowl from his hands as Grelhym walked up to him. "Give me that," he growled. "I have a splitting headache and the likes of you aren't making it better."

 GRELHYM

Taking his seat, Grelhym soon found himself drifting off. The talk went much like it had the previous day. At one point it looked as though two delegates were going to come to blows, but Meikal was able to calm them, much to Grelhym's disappointment. Soon after that, he was fast asleep, dreaming of sweet peaches and freshly caught cod. He was in the middle of floating down a river of cider when he was rudely slapped awake with enough force to knock him to the floor. Lord Rygar stood over him, red as a beet, his moustache twitching. When Grelhym looked around, he saw that the entire delegation was looking at them. He felt his cheek and winced at the tenderness. His eyes met his lord's.

"Fool!" Rygar shouted. "Sleeping on duty? Do you mean to mock me in front of my peers?"

Grelhym wasn't sure what he should say, so he said nothing. Rygar reached down and yanked him by the arm from the floor. He snapped his fingers and one of his personal guards moved in from the seating and stood beside them.

"Sir Thyon," Rygar motioned to Grelhym. "Take this loyal squire to his quarters, and make sure he isn't hit too many times on the way there."

"Yes, Your Lordship."

Sir Thyon shoved Grelhym in the back and forced him from the room, then grabbed him by his collar and dragged him all the way back to his chambers, where he was thrown on the bed. Thyon then unsheathed his sword and backhanded the hilt against Grelhym's side. Grelhym felt the impact against his ribs and doubled over coughing. Sir Thyon resheathed his sword and left without a word.

"Bastard," Grelhym wheezed.

He lay on his back for a moment before getting up to his water basin. The water was lukewarm and salty, but he splashed it on his face anyway. The salt stung his cheek, and when the water settled, Grelhym was able to see his reflection. Lord Rygar hadn't broken the skin, but he had left a sizable welt, and when Grelhym touched it, he grimaced and grit his teeth. When he looked outside, Grelhym was surprised to see that the sun was already going down. He remembered that he was supposed to feed and clean his Lord's horse tonight and thought for a moment about skipping out. But before long he had come to the conclusion that regardless of what his Lord felt tonight, he would only be angrier tomorrow if he had again shirked his duties. And so Grelhym put a dab of witch hazel on his cheek and started out. The air outside the hall was cool with the twilight. Very few people were around, and those who were seemed too lowborn to bother Grelhym for anything. He was still in his squire's garb denoting him as an off-worlder.

Looking out in the distance, he saw the miles upon miles of hard rock plateau stretching off into the distance, culminating on the horizon at Swordpoint, the thin mountain made entirely of a kind of flint. He stopped for a moment and marvelled at the sight of it. As was the case with many planets, Armonth was also facing the grim possibility of becoming completely inhospitable. A decade ago, looking over the ridge you'd have seen

miles of trees and meadows. Now, it was all gone. Grelhym wondered for a moment if the rock stretched all the way to the edge of the world. *And maybe even further.*

The stables were only makeshift. The original had burned down in a riot months ago. What was left had been built up again into a very simple wooden structure, just enough to keep the rain and wind off the horses. Lord Rygar's horse was nearer to the back. Grelhym found him munching on stale oats from a trough laid out for him. Grelhym was puzzled. *I was supposed to feed you, wasn't I?* He hopped into the pen and brushed the horse lightly on his roan red neck. The horse looked back at him and gave him a whinny. Grelhym furrowed his brow and perked up his ears.

"Shhh, boy."

He looked around, and then heard the noise again. Is someone talking? From the corner of his eye he noticed two men entering the stables. One was Lord Rygar. Before his mind had a chance to process what was happening, his legs buckled and he ducked down under the pony wall. Rygar and the other man walked past the pen and to the very back of the stables. Grelhym pressed his ear up against the wooden slats and tried to stay as still as possible as the two men began to speak.

"I take it you understand what you are to do?" said Lord Rygar.

"Bloody hells, of course I do! Just who do you take me for?" said the man he did not know.

"Alright, alright," Rygar was sounding impatient.

Through the slats, Grelhym watched him remove a small glass vial filled with pink liquid and pass it over to the man.

"Two drops, no more, no less."

"I can count. Now leave and let me do my work."

Lord Rygar threw his hands up and left the stable while the other man stood staring at the vial. Grelhym's heart raced. What is that? Before he could get a better look at it, the man stashed the vial away in his tunic, and casually left the stables as well. As the stranger passed the stall he was in, Grelhym thought he felt his heart skip a beat. Soon though, he was in the clear, and decided to leave. He didn't want to be caught if Lord Rygar happened to come back. But before he could get ten feet out, something grabbed his arm. He turned and came face to face with the strange man, and even though he didn't know his name, Grelhym knew the intentions written all over his face.

CHAPTER 05

DERRON II

The lake's edge was rimmed with frost. Dead reed stalks wavered in the breeze, dry and cracking in the cold. Derron took another glance at the map. Any moment now he should find it. The wind picked up and he pulled the collar of his down-filled jacket higher around his neck. Far off in the distance he could see smoke rising from the camp his men had made. No doubt they were enjoying a well-earned fire and rest. He imagined the possibility of fish swimming in the lake and his mouth watered. The thought of another night on nothing but pine nuts made Derron queasy. Above him, a squirrel chirped. *At least I'm not alone out here*, he thought. Derron's mind wandered as he walked. He thought of his home, of the mission, of his future. He thought of his son, Damien, and how he might be handling the responsibilities of being King. Derron wasn't worried. Damien was a man well grown by now, broad-shouldered and fit, as well as being kind and just. Twenty-six years of age, and wiser than men twice that. Derron smiled at the thought. A father's pride.

The ground beneath his feet was muddy, but the cold had hardened it into the strange consistency of icy sludge. Even with his walking stick, Derron was finding it hard to keep his footing. Luckily, the lakeside was covered in a small brush, and he need only reach over and grab a branch to prop himself up. Something rustled to his right, in the treeline some twenty yards from the lakefront. Derron stopped in his tracks, thinking of possible prey, but nothing reared its head and so he kept walking. He still found himself fascinated by the world he was on. Despite the two moons that rose each night, nothing seemed all that different to his own planet, same trees, same animals, same rocks, and even the same climate to a certain extent. *How does that happen?* He considered for a moment that maybe he wasn't on another planet at all, but rather a more northern continent on his own. Yet he quickly dismissed the idea. If the two moons weren't proof enough, no rift had ever connected two points on the same world. Across the Starscape there were thousands of documented rifts and not a single one connected to its own world. Derron pondered the dilemma for the next couple hours as he walked, but came no closer to an answer than when he started.

The freezing rain started pouring down just as the other side of the lake came into view. Looking back, Derron could no longer see the side he had started on, only the faint column of

DERRON

black smoke broke the skyline. The water of the lake sparkled as drops sent the surface to splashing, almost in a dance. It would have been beautiful if the weather wasn't so miserable. Derron decided to take a break and sat on a large boulder under the cover of a huge pine. Finally, dry, he eased his muscles. Without the constant dripping on his head, Derron's mind became clear enough to assess the landscape around him. This part of the lakeside was covered in large boulders, some bigger than Derron himself, and it was sandier than the side he'd started on. The largest rock jutted from the reeds twenty yards away... and was notched. It was hard to see with his old eyes, but there was definitely some manner of a cut on the rockface. His heart raced. *This could be it.*

Derron got back on his feet and hurried as fast as he could without slipping. The closer he got, the clearer it became. As he walked around it, he discovered that there were four notches in actuality, all stretching up and over the top of the boulder. To see the whole thing, Derron would have to climb. In the rain, that proved difficult. The rock was smooth already, and the wetness didn't help matters. On top of it all, the cold made his hands and feet ache with every inch. But eventually, he made it up. The rock was only fifteen feet high, but scaling it made Derron feel as though he'd just summited a mountain. As he knelt, the fruits of his labour were staring him in the face. The symbol was one he'd seen at least thirty times before. A circle, divided into four quadrants with a cross that passed the circumference on all sides. He felt the notches with his hand and smiled. *I'm on the right track.* He looked out over the lake and wondered what the significance was. His contemplation was stopped short, however, by a growling coming from beneath him.

He looked off over the side of the rock to see a coyote, four feet from snout to tail and thin with starvation. One of its ears was half gone and its light beige fur was matted to its body. Head raised, the animal bared its broken teeth in a menacing snarl. Derron jumped when it barked at him, but regained composure fast. He grabbed his walking stick which rested against the rock and started jabbing down at the wild dog. The coyote hopped back and forth, always just out of his reach. Derron leaned forward to get a better angle, but slipped, hitting his arm on the way down and landing hard on his back. The coyote was on him immediately, biting and clawing. Derron put up his stick to defend himself, but the dog was too quick. A claw raked at his jacket and tore out long shreds, bleeding the down from its inner lining. Its jaw latched onto his right forearm and gripped like a vice. Derron cried out and punched at the dog with his one free hand, but to no avail. The coyote twisted his head and the wayward king screamed.

Reaching to his belt, Derron fumbled for his knife, but couldn't reach it. Instead, his hand found the bag with his fishing twine, bait, and most importantly: hooks. Reaching in, he pulled one out and drove the small metal spike into the coyote's snout. It wailed in pain and let go of its grip on his arm for just a moment, but it was enough. Derron brought round his stick

 DERRON

and hit the coyote square in the nose, making it back away in pain. He then scrambled to his feet, his right arm numb and bleeding, and went in for another hit, but the coyote had had enough. With its tail between its legs, it wandered back into the brush.

Derron cursed at the sky and gripped his injured arm. He gingerly slipped off his satchel and pulled out a roll of rough gauze. Rolling up his sleeve, he walked down the waterfront and dipped his arm in the lake, grimacing at the sting and the cold. Then he put a generous wrap around his arm and slipped his sleeve down to hold on the cloth. Feeling the cold wind penetrate to his chest, Derron assessed the damage to his clothing. The outer lining of his jacket had been sheared open by the coyote's claws, and most of the down inside was falling haphazardly around him. Underneath, his leather tunic was scratched, but not ripped. He breathed a sigh of relief for that. The cold air blew again and Derron shuddered. His jacket was next to useless now, but he couldn't bear to take it off. Perhaps they would find another duck and he'd be able to refill it and sow it shut again.

He got his bearings and took a step back toward the camp. It would be a hard trek back. But before he got more than ten feet out, he heard a whimper. Turning, he saw the coyote, tail and ears down, slowly trotting up to him. It pawed at the hook in its snout. Dried blood caked the lower half of its face down from its nostrils. Derron could see now that the snout was broken. For a moment, he felt sorry for the animal, but his past experiences kicked in. *It will just attack you once you've helped it.* He turned back and started walking again, but the patter of paws on mud and a whimper made him pause. He sighed and knelt. The coyote loped over to him and whimpered again. Before he did anything else, Derron held up his right arm, where the blood was already soaking through the wool.

"See this?" he pointed. "You did this to me; don't think I've forgotten that," he said to the dog, not really knowing why. Maybe he was finally going mad.

Very carefully, Derron removed the hook through the coyote's nostril. If he'd tried to pull it back out the way it went it, the metal would snag and tear, so he moved it carefully until the end came all the way through and the bloody hook fell to the ground, staining the snow beneath. Almost instantly, the wound began to bleed fresh, but regardless, the coyote looked relieved, and licked at the blood crusting on its face. Derron couldn't do anything about the broken snout. He'd reset broken arms before, but he had no idea where to begin with a snout.

"You're welcome," he said, again wondering why he was talking to a wild dog.

The trip back to camp was much harder going than the trip out in more ways than one. The rain had turned to hail and the ground was almost un-traversable as it had been covered in a thin layer of ice. About halfway back, Derron almost slipped but caught himself by slamming his walking stick into the ice. He avoided falling, but the sudden movement had sent a jolt of pain through his arm, and that was almost worse. He paused and looked longingly out over the lake. Energy failing, he wondered if he had made a mistake trekking alone. The light was already fading over the horizon and it would still be an hour before he got back to camp. His rumination was cut short, however, when he heard the familiar patter of paws on ice again and turned to see a coyote with a broken snout sauntering up to him, a dead squirrel dangling between its jaws. It stopped a few feet in front of Derron and lay the squirrel down, nudging it towards him. Derron stared in disbelief, but picked up the game and, confused as to what to do next, patted the coyote on the head. When he began walking again, the coyote seemed to follow, and despite himself, Derron smiled.

When he finally reached camp, Derron was an awful mixture of cold, numb, hungry, exhausted, in pain, and dazed. The cloud cover was dark again, and two of his men stood on a hill searching the landscape. When one of the men pointed at Derron, they came rushing towards him, and both reached out an arm to steady their leader. Skoma and Anthon then helped Derron back to the fire, but not before Skoma stopped and drew his sword at the sight of the coyote.

"No," managed Derron, before he passed out.

☆ ☆ ☆

Derron had no idea how many days had passed; all he knew was that his head hurt and his arm throbbed. But at least he was dry and comfortable. When he opened his eyes, there was a lattice of twigs and brambles five feet above him, supported by four trees. Derron was lying on his back, a matt of dry grass cushioning the hard ground. He glanced at his arm and remembered the fight with the coyote. The dressing had been changed and clipped, but his arm still hurt. Slowly, he rotated his wrist, testing his mobility. The skin felt tight, and a jolt of pain made him stop. Only then did he notice he wasn't alone.

"If I may, Your Grace." Melwick was standing over Derron's makeshift bed. "It was not smart to go off on your own. Next time, allow at least some of us to go with you."

"You know I can't do that."

Derron reached for his walking stick where it rested against one of the trunks. He felt his fingers wrap around the shaft, but his grip wouldn't hold. After a few tries he gave up. Derron held up his arm and frowned at it. Melwick looked solemn.

"The arm will heal in time, but it will never be the same. I suggest flexing the muscle a little each day to help stave off any atrophy."

Derron squeezed his hand into a fist and grimaced as a shot of pain rushed up his forearm.

"I suppose my sword-wielding days are behind me, not that it matters out here."

He gingerly rose to his feet, careful not to thump his head on the wood ceiling above him. He reached again for his stick, but this time with his left hand. The movement felt foreign to him. Melwick brushed aside the fur covering the entrance and Derron walked out into a rush of cold air. As his eyes adjusted to the light, he saw his men were hard at work collecting firewood, preparing fish, and constructing lean-tos. He heard clicking from beside him and was surprised to see the coyote gnawing on a chicken bone off to the side of camp. Anton walked over carrying a bundle of dead twigs and smiled.

"That little guy scared the shite out of us when he came up with you, but put a little meat in him and he's as friendly as a housedog." His eyes shifted to Derron's bandaged arm. "Well... to a point I suppose."

Derron looked over to the dog warily. As much as he had warmed to the animal, he knew the danger it still posed. "Keep an eye on it. Remember that it is still a wild animal."

One by one, each of his men checked in to see how Derron was doing. He graciously thanked each one for their concern, but really, he felt nothing but embarrassment for stupidly going off alone and getting himself hurt. When Will entered the lean-to around mid-day, he made a lighthearted comment about no longer being the only gimp in the group. That made Derron genuinely chuckle. He slept the rest of the day until evening, when Anthon woke him and brought him out to a roaring fire and plates of smoked trout. A few of his men were already eating. Sitting, Derron felt the blessed warmth of the fire and held out his hands to warm them. That's when Derron realized that all eyes were on him. Alymer cleared his throat.

"I think it's time you told us the real reason why we're here."

Derron winced. He had been able to avoid that question thus far through one means or another, but he knew deep down that he wasn't going to be able to divert this time. His

DERRON

men were strong, and, more importantly, they were loyal. It broke his heart to lead them out into the dangers of the wilderness without fully telling them why. He couldn't blame them for finally needing to know. Anthon spoke up before Derron could decide what to say.

"You left to go on a hike, alone, and came back with a coyote in tow and a what could have been a lethal wound. You are our King, Derron. We need to be able to protect you; we swore an oath."

The rest of the men nodded their agreement. Derron shifted uncomfortably as his hand absentmindedly rose to stroke at his beard. He allowed himself a quick glance at Melwick, but it was clear he'd get no help there. Sighing, he reached into his bag and produced the map. Lifting himself to his feet he handed it to Alymer.

Alymer took it warily, and glanced over Melwick's scratchings. Derron watched the old man's eyes move from one marking to the next, then back around to the first. The wrinkles on his face stretched with a puzzled expression. "What... What do these circles mean?"

Derron tried to be as vague as he could. "Possible locations - it's the reason why we're out here."

"Possible locations for what, exactly?"

There's no way to beat around the bush this time, he thought. Everyone was looking at him intently.

Derron chose his next words carefully. "Something that could change the entire way we live, the entire dynamic of the

DERRON

Starscape as we know it." He paused. "That is truly all that I know."

Will frowned. "That isn't much to go on."

Anthon gingerly took the map from Alymer and looked at it, puzzled. "And did you find it... the location, I mean?" He pointed to the red circle on the lakeshore. "That must have been why you hiked halfway around the lake."

Derron shook his head. "No." He looked over to the coyote. "Found him, though."

The coyote looked back at him, still content to gnaw at his bone. His tail wagged like a house-dog. For a moment, one could be forgiven to forget that it was a wild animal. In truth, Derron knew more than he was letting on. The book he had found had told him much and more about what he was searching for, but he was adamant to hold his tongue until the right time. Derron just hoped no one would be bold enough to call his bluff.

"Who else knew?" asked Roman.

"No one," he lied.

Skoma ripped off a hunk of a freshly roasted trout and pushed it into his mouth. "So, where's the next location?"

Anthon studied the map. "It says there's something just west of here, and another a league north."

The map was passed around so that the whole group could get an idea as to where they needed to go. Even Melwick feigned intrigue at the circles as if he hadn't been the one to put them there. Derron knew that eventually the group would put two and two together and realize Melwick's extended trips meant he must know something about all this, but he'd cross that bridge when he got to it. Out of everyone, Mollens was the only one to look truly hurt. Will was last to see the map, as Skoma passed it to him where he lay with his leg raised on a rock by the fire. He frowned as his eyes darted around the page.

"If we go west, we'll have to double back for the north location. With the weather the way it is, that could mean getting stranded." He passed the map back up to Derron. "What if we were to split up?"

Derron considered it for a moment. Splitting up meant Derron may not be around when the location was found, and that could be dangerous; although, if Melwick was there, he'd be able to stop the men from looking any deeper than they should. He nodded.

"That is what we will do." He passed the map to Melwick. "Make a copy of this."

Melwick took it and pulled another piece of parchment from his bag, placed it over the original, and began to gently trace his original map. Derron turned to where Alymer sat cleaning his teeth with a fishbone.

"Alymer, I am trusting you to lead a group to the western location, while I lead the rest of us north. Skoma, Melwick, you're with Alymer. The rest of you are going with me."

Alymer nodded, getting up gingerly with his old knees and grinned.

"I won't let you down, Captain."

 DERRON

"I know you won't."

But it wasn't Alymer that Derron was worried about.

CHAPTER 06

ALGEN I

If it were possible for it to rain under the sea, today would have been one of those days. The open water was cloudy with soot, causing the underwater glass dome to become almost pitch black as the light from above was clouded out. Algen wondered if anyone living on the surface had to deal with anything like this, especially on a day like today. It was Algen's sixteenth birthday, the day that when he finally became a man. As everyone did at this time of their lives, he would soon have an audience before the King, and more importantly: he would finally have his transformation.

The thought excited him more than anything had before. The Cancers were unlike any other faction in the Starscape. Each inhabitant was uniquely and intentionally deformed, as was customary. Inside the King's Dome, where Algen had lived his whole life, there was a special chamber built around a site of ancient power. Those who entered the chamber were immediately changed on a biological level, and the person who stepped out from the chamber was no longer human.

Hundreds of years ago, the King of the Cancers had decreed that children under the age of sixteen were too young to cope with such a transformation, and that all would have to wait until adulthood. As such, it was easy to recognize anyone under that age. Algen was often bullied by the other boys in the dome who had recently undergone transformations of their own, but today was Algen's time in the limelight, his time to at long last claim his true form. He stared out into the vastness of the surrounding ocean and let his mind wonder about what he would become by day's end.

Fittingly, all the transformations that happened in the chamber made a person mutate into a kind of half-human, half-sea creature hybrid. The kinds of mutations you could find under the domes were endless, ranging from fish to anemones, seals to rays. Not all mutations were successful, however. Algen had heard the story of his uncle, who upon stepping into the chamber had lost the use of his spine. It had disintegrated in his back and left him paralyzed from head to foot. He hadn't lived much longer after that. Algen's mother had similarly had one leg morph into the rough shape of a tentacle. The appendage was weak and had left her immobile ever since. As well, her skin had become coarse and red, and rough to the touch. Such was the way of the chamber. There was always that chance, but it was a rite of passage that no child wished to forgo, or at least, did not have the option to forgo. His father, Alperen, was another story entirely. He had been blessed with becoming a shark-morph, and a very powerful one at that. Upon exiting the chamber, his father had found himself with a jaw that could rival that of a great white's; with three rows of sharp teeth and a new slick grey tinge to his skin.

The ruling King at the time, had been so pleased with the new morph that he had immediately placed him within his inner circle amongst the King's top guards. Over the years, his father had become one the most renowned warriors of the Cancers, and Algen knew his father wanted no less for his only son. He hoped not to disappoint him.

As he walked through the alleys of the city, mind wandering, he bumped into Naylis, a nineteen-year-old skate-morph. The two said their hello's, before Naylis ran off muttering about something he had to do. Algen watched him as he disappeared around a corner. Naylis was Algen's oldest friend, and had taught him about everything to expect and what to do when he went inside the morphing chamber. Despite having full confidence in his ability to make the transition smoothly, Algen found it impossible not to worry. "Stay as still as you can," Naylis' words rang in his head. "Arms out straight. Like a 't'." That was the most worrying aspect. Sometimes, during transformations done hundreds of years ago, a person's appendages would be placed too close together and would fuse. Even to this day, conjoined toes and fingers were not uncommon.

He wondered what creature he would take on. Most took the form of a fish or crustacean. Skates, like Naylis, were rare, but not as rare as jellyfish. Every now and again, someone would take the form of a squid, or octopus, or sea snake or water bug, or even a coral or conch. A mixture of two or more creatures was rarest of all. Naylis would sometimes boast of all the beautiful ladies that would gawk at his manta ray appearance. Many boasts included Naylis pointing to a deep bite mark on his right arm-fin, smiling a sly grin, and telling Algen that a gorgeous shark-morphed girl had given it to him after she had caught him sleeping with her jelly-morphed sister. More like than not, he had gotten it while drunkenly swimming too close to a real shark outside the dome.

Once at the gate to the King's Palace, Algen stopped and waited. The King's palace was located dead centre in the King's Dome, it's walls carved from a pale white stone and built so high they stretched almost to the apex of the dome's curve. Pearl inlaid bands adorned each of its five towers, which on clear days caught the light and refracted crystal beams down onto the city below. The gate itself was wrought in gold, traded from the peoples of the surface. Algen needn't wait there long. Within a few minutes, one of the palace guards arrived and opened the gate. As Algen entered the stone courtyard, he saw his father, smiling and walking towards him. Dressed from head to toe in his golden scale armor, his father embraced him, his three rows of teeth twisted in a toothy grin that spanned his face.

"My boy," he said. "Today shall be your day."

Algen smiled back, more as a facade than from actual joy. His heart beat so fast Algen thought it would leap from his breast. His father let him go and took him by the arm, up the great stone steps and into the corridors leading to the great hall.

"Alperen!" called an elderly soldier as they came before the door to the hall. He held a spear in his left hand and a shield in the other that bore the red, star-eyed crab of the Cancers. His neck pulsed as gills reflexively opened and shut. "Your boy's grown fast."

"He has indeed!" Alperen gave his son a slap on the back and another big grin, then he opened the door to the palace and ushered his son inside.

Algen saw that seven boys and four girls were already waiting, whispering to one another. The floor of the great hall was lined in polished stones of turquoise and navy and green, and Algen's feet echoed as they slapped against the smooth stone. He grimaced as the others turned to look at him, but soon they were back talking with one-another. Algen overheard one girl who was hoping for a squid-morph. Another hoped to become a fish on her bottom half. As for the boys, they all wanted morphs that would allow them to become great warriors in the King's court, someone like the legendary Rynald the Ripper, A man who morphed almost completely into a giant barracuda and waged war on the Aquarii people of the surface. Algen paid them little mind, as his attention was captured by the throne just feet away from him. The room was mostly dark, but a well-placed skylight above the throne bathed it in a golden light, even on such a gloomy day. The seat itself was carved from whalebone, brittle and cracking from age, but still awe-inspiring. Behind the throne were two archways, and the room fell to a hush as the King entered the hall.

King Caraq was an imposing figure to say the least. Rippled with muscle and close to seven feet tall, he fit the look of a legendary king. His chest was covered loosely in a mail shirt made of silver links overlaid by navy blue scales that rustled as he walked. But the most imposing aspect of the man was his right arm. The entire appendage was made of a greyish-green chitin and ended in a massive crab claw. The pincer twitched as he took his seat on the throne.

"Children," he began, voice booming. "Today you take the first steps in your journey towards adulthood, and join the ranks of the true Cancers!"

A murmur of excitement emanated from the other initiates.

The King continued. "You need not fear the transformation chamber, for whatever you are as you walk in is shed, and you are reborn anew, stronger, and greater. He paused, then pointed his massive pincer at a young boy in front. "You are Umer, are you not, child?"

The boy nodded. "I am, Your Grace."

"Umer, step into the chamber and be reborn!"

The king made a sweeping motion to an ornately carved red wooden door at the far end of the hall. Umer almost ran to it, but collected himself and settled for a more respectful fast walk. One of the King's warriors opened the door for him, and shut it behind Umer as he entered. Algen and the others waited with bated breath. He felt his father's hand squeeze his shoulder. Close to five minutes later, the door opened again. A dark brown hand emerged first, followed closely after by a long leathery body, much flattened. Umer's eyes scanned the room in a dazed frenzy. His jaw drooped and looked loose to Algen, until he realized that it had grown three times its original size. Umer's skin was mottled brown from head to foot and his arms had the pattern of fins on them. The warrior who had opened the door held the new morph under the arm and brought him forward to the king. Umer brought his moist, fishy eyes up and attempted to look as dignified as he could, but the disappointment was all over his face. The King gazed down upon him with annoyance, pincer opening and closing.

Algen knew that this was the point when the King would choose a role for Umer, as he did for every morph. It was the role you served in until you either died, or pleaded hard enough for the King to take pity on you. The latter happened less often than seeing an underwater bird.

"Send him to the seaweed fields," the King decreed, waving him off with his human arm. "He'll work as a cropper until one of you decides you want him for a squire."

Unlikely, thought Algen as the warrior led Umer out the door to the hall, passing by the other initiates on the way. The merry banter of a few minutes ago had been replaced with collective nervous silence. No sooner was Umer gone from sight, than the King was scanning them again. He pointed his pincer at the girl standing beside Algen, the one who had wished for a fish tail in place of legs.

"Child, what is your name?"

"Alanna, Your Grace."

"Alanna, step into the chamber and be reborn."

The girl took a few nervous steps toward the chamber, took a deep breath and entered. When she exited again a few minutes later, her legs were still very much human. Her face, however, was not. Her eyes had grown large, at least by a scale of three, and her skin had yellowed. Under her chin, two long thin fins had sprouted and a longer fin had formed on the back of her neck. Her eyes darted in all directions, looking around at the others. It was clear that she too was unhappy. She drooped her head, which made her dorsal fin fan out in a brilliant shade of orange. Algen thought she looked quite beautiful.

"No," came a hushed voice from behind him.

Algen turned to see that one of the other boys was pale in the face and breathing fast.

"No, I won't go," he said a little louder.

That time King Caraq seemed to hear as well.

"Are you afraid, boy?" The King's voice demanded the attention of the hall. Everyone was listening now, which only made the boy hyperventilate harder.

"I won't do it! You... you can't make me!"

The boy pivoted and ran towards the door. Calm as ever, the King did not move. One of the guards at the door extended his spear across the boy's path. Too late for the boy to stop, the spear's shaft hooked under his chin and swept him off his feet, sending him flailing to the floor. Within a few seconds the guard, as well as Algen's father, had the boy by his arms, kicking and fighting in their grasp. Together they moved toward the chamber and tossed him in. Before the boy could get to his feet, the heavy door had shut behind him, and he was trapped. Algen could hear banging on the door for a few seconds before it stopped and became quiet. After five minutes, King Caraq spoke.

"Let the coward out."

The door opened, but no one appeared. Then suddenly, the boy bolted from the chamber, and knocked one of the guards to the floor. His nose had grown into a long snout, and underneath were rows of thin, needle like teeth, which he plunged into the man's fleshy neck. The guard screamed and writhed but was defenseless against the onslaught. Alperen moved in to save the man, but the king commanded him to stop with a gesture of his claw, a grin apparent on his face. Only as the guard's body went limp did the boy finally get up, still snarling, with blood and sinew dripping from his mouth. He wiped it off with the back of his hand, which had become grey and clawed in his transformation. The King was now smiling outright.

"Boy, what is your name?"

"Ragga." He spit out a hunk of flesh. "But I want a new name with my new body." The speech has heavily slurred with his new mouth.

"And you shall have it! From this day forward you shall be known as Gnash. I think that suits you quite well."

Gnash nodded, and King Caraq turned his attention to the guard standing beside his throne.

"I want this man brought to the training grounds immediately."

The guard nodded sheepishly, and stepped over his dead friend to reach Gnash, being cautious not to get too close. Gnash bared his bloodstained teeth, but made no move to fight, and went with the guard deeper into the palace. The King was visibly in a good mood now, and his attention quickly turned to Algen's father.

"Alperen, I'm to understand your son is with us today."

His father nodded. *I'm next. It's my time.* The guppies swam in his stomach. His father put a hand on his shoulder and nudged him up to the front of the group.

"What is your name, child?"

"Algen, son of Alperen," Algen replied, hoping the second part would make him sound important.

"Well Algen, son of Alperen, step into the chamber, follow in your father's footsteps and be reborn."

Algen strode forward, his father beside him. As they moved closer, Algen could feel a wave of heat emanating from inside the chamber. His feet squished in the blood drying on

the floor. Before he entered, Algen turned back, and gave his
father a smile, one as if to as to say *I won't let you down*. Then
he stepped forward into the chamber. His father was the one to
do the honours of sealing the door behind him. Somehow that
comforted his nerves, but only a little bit. Behind him, the door
closed with a *THUD*.

The chamber Algen found himself in was much larger than
he'd expected. In his fantasies he had always imagined the
room would be so small that he would hardly be able to move,
but in reality, it stretched ten feet from end to end. The roof
was curved like a dome and at its peak was a hole from which
shone an eerie red glow that bathed the room in a dim crimson
light. The walls of the chamber were made of large mirrored
scales that reflected the light in queer patterns along the floor.
And the chamber was hot, almost unbearably so. Algen felt his
exposed skin burn and itch. Suddenly, he remembered Naylis'
advice and stood absolutely still. He spread his fingers and his
toes as far as they could go and splayed his arms and legs. The
itching grew worse and it was hard not to scratch. His temperature rose and Algen did everything he could to not flinch at the
heat. He looked down and noticed his skin wasn't as pale as it
had been, instead it was looking more purple. His heart raced
inside his chest. *It's happening*. His fingers suddenly cramped
and he watched as webbing grew in the spaces between his outstretched digits. His toes soon did the same. He trembled at
the sight of his own hand. Before he could process what was
happening, more changes began. He felt a bubbling on the left

 ALGEN

half of his neck. Gritting his teeth, he resisted the urge to grab at his skin. He twitched as the bubbles on his skin popped and barnacles grew to the size of fish cakes on his neck, cheek, and shoulder. Suddenly, a feeling like he was going to vomit burned in his throat and brought him to his knees. *Gills*, he thought. *I must be growing my gills.* Algen breathed deeply and wondered what the next thing to change would be when all the sensations stopped. The itching went away, his skin cooled, and his throat eased. *No*, he thought. *No, no, that can't be the end*! But the door opened anyway and a rush of cool air swept into the chamber.

It *was* over. His father was just outside the door, peering in, and the look on his face was the worst thing Algen had ever experienced. Rising from his knees, he felt his skin jiggle. He poked at his arm. The flesh was squishy like gelatin, so much so that he could almost pinch the bone. It made it difficult for him to walk, and it took Algen a second to get used to it, but soon he was able to move forward and exit the chamber. His feet jiggled beneath him as he returned to the hall. All eyes were on him. He looked at his hands in the natural light and saw that his skin had become a vibrant, almost shiny, dark sapphire colour. He felt the webbing between his index and middle finger and was surprised how thick and elastic it was. The King's grin had changed to a look of disappointment.

"Well, Algen, son of Alperen, it looks as though you were not blessed with a transformation like your father's."

Algen felt like a failure. "No, Your Grace," he said, or at least, that's what he was going to say. The words caught in his throat and only a hushed whimper came out. He frowned and tried a second time, but again the words were just air escaping his lungs. He tried a third time, louder, and then again. Nothing.

King Caraq looked confused. "Speak to me, boy." He demanded. His pincer hand clacked open and shut.

His father looked concerned and nudged him. "Answer your king."

Algen looked to his father with sad eyes. *I can't,* he thought. *By the Gods, I can't speak*!

CHAPTER 07

ALMOND I

The feast was well underway by the time the last rays of sunshine flickered over the canopy of the autumn trees. Torches around the field were lit to the cheers of the towns-folk, but none were grander than the great fire at the base of the deity statue. As the fire came to life, the townsfolk threw roses into its breadth. The petals burned away from the stems and caught the updraft of the hot air, sending them up into the sky until eventually they turned to ash. Almond stood unmoving, mesmerized by the sight of it. Her attention turned then to the deity statue depicting Auma, the god of summer, sun, and celebration. He stood eight feet tall, carved from solid granite, poised with one hand on his hip and the other outstretched and holding up a rabbit.

The rabbit was the symbol of Almond's people, just as every faction had. She'd heard stories from her grandmother of the days when Auma would descend from the heavens and defend the Lepus Faction from much greater and more powerful factions like the Virgos or the Leos. Wisps of firelight flickering across the stone giant's face made it look as though the man was come alive again, ready to rid the world of anyone who'd dare do her people wrong. Almond imagined what it would be like to travel the stars.

"Look there," her father had told her when she was younger, pointing at a shooting star. "That's Auma's spirit, gone to defend us."

"Where is he going?" she had asked, eyes sparkling with youthful amazement.

"We'll never know that. But we do know that wherever he is, he's keeping us safe."

"I want to go with him!" she had told her father, which had only made him laugh. He leaned over and kissed her on the forehead.

"One day, sweet daughter, but for now stay here with me."

The memory made her smile. She looked up overhead to see another shooting star. Almond wondered how many more she would watch before she'd be the one travelling through space. Her pale orange dress waved in the light breeze and the simple sound of humming surrounded her as the people around her began to sing. She quietly made her way from the statue to find a solitary place to sit. Almond had always preferred praying in silent contemplation to group chorus.

 ALMOND

Somewhere along the way, the smell of roasting meat caught her nose and she trailed in pursuit. From behind her, a tall boy carrying a keg of wine bumped into Almond in his hurry to get somewhere, turning to apologize without stopping. She watched him as he disappeared into the crowd. Everyone in the village of Rimby was here, from bakers to builders, masons to musicians, even Almond's grandmother had made it out for the occasion despite being the oldest person in the village. More often than not in recent times, her grandmother seemed perpetually confused, and she slept straight through the majority of most days. Almond was happy to see her grandmother out and about for the festival, but her uncle Jonah needed to wheel her around in a small cart stuffed full with blankets and pillows. At very least, young children were always close by to give her summer flowers of every colour, but Almond knew that the orange were always her favourite. Almond had always felt as though she had a special connection with her grandmother; they shared the same nut-brown eyes that had given Almond her nickname, being the only two in the family to possess them. Smiling, she plucked a deep orange pansy from where it grew under a nearby tree. Weaving around the other children, she came to the side of her grandmother's cart and kissed her on the forehead, placing the pansy gently on the old woman's chest. Almond had assumed she was dozing, but her grandmother smiled, and a wrinkled, spotted hand cupped the petals gently. And although her grandmother's eyes never opened, somehow Almond could tell that her grandmother knew it was her.

She eventually came upon her father, standing next to a large cook fire serving helpings of beef to festivalgoers. He smiled at her when he saw her approach.

"Almond," he said, sounding as warm and pleased to see her as he always did.

Her father was skinnier than most men in the village, and his hairline had receded to almost the point of baldness, but his smile was welcoming and his fierce blue eyes made him more handsome than most would admit.

"Come." he told her. "It's not every day we get to feast on a roast like this."

She graciously accepted the helping he gave her and began to eat. The meat tasted heavily of sea salt and butter. The piece she had was so tender it fell apart in her fingers and she had to lick the grease off. The man standing next to her father smiled at her.

"You've grown, Almond. How old are you now?" Her mouth was full of meat so she pushed it to one side of her mouth to answer.

"Fifteen," she said, swallowing.

The man nodded. "It feels like you were born just yesterday."

She smiled back at him. "Time goes by quickly."

 ALMOND

From over the hill she could see a dance beginning and she excused herself to go see. Her father offered her more meat as she left, but she declined.

As she got closer, she could hear the music roaring almost as loud as the laughter of the dancers. She watched Patsy the baker's wife dancing with Arnold the blacksmith, and Gent the fisherman's apprentice twirling a giggling, young butter churner. In all, close to fifty villagers were dancing away the night in the field, and over twice that number was onlooking, clapping, jeering, and whooping. Out of the corner of her eye she saw a tent curtain flap in the breeze revealing for just a second a young boy and girl quietly kissing. Almond blushed and hurried in closer to the dance. Her bare feet felt soft against the grass and tingled. Reaching the crowd, she pushed her way through to the front, where she cupped her hands around her mouth and called out to the dancers. Everyone split apart and changed partners. One boy, a little older than Almond, reached out a hand and she took it, being whisked into the circle. Only then did she realize her hands were still covered in grease, and she blushed seeing the stains on the boy's clothes. She giggled and waved goodbye as she turned and disappeared back into the crowd.

Wandering, she discovered another tent and slipped inside. Two large bearded men were sitting opposite and staring intently at one another with glazed eyes. A group of a dozen others beat them on the backs and shouted words of encouragement.

"I bet you a thousand rabbit pelts I can drink mor'n you!" she heard one of the men say. Suddenly, the smell of hard ale filled her nostrils.

"Har! I'd take that bet, and then I raise you my daughter's hand in marriage!" He laughed again, before downing a huge mug of golden ale in three gulps. "You don't *have* a daughter!" she heard the first voice say, followed by a roomful of laughter. The big man spit his drink all over the table, which only caused more laughter.

"No, I suppose I don't," the second man began. "But I bet if I put my son in a dress you'd *still* marry 'im!" That brought even more laughs.

Almond took a look around and saw a tray of chestnut honey cakes left sitting on the edge of a table. With everyone focused on the drinking, she slipped by and nabbed a handful, then slipped back out without a word. Outside she looked around before sneaking away to her special hiding place she'd had since she was a little girl: a small opening underneath the roots of a massive oak tree covered completely by tall grass and weeds. Almond had to crawl to fit, but she could sit relatively comfortably. As a child she had come here whenever she'd wanted to avoid doing her chores. The oakwood roots were crumbling and rotted, but the structure still held, and no one else seemed to know it was here. She enjoyed the feeling of the cool dirt on her back, and tracing her fingers along the texture of the wood. She positioned herself and adjusted until she was comfortable, then began to gnaw on a cake. By the taste, she assumed they had been made by Merrick. The boy was only seventeen, but had already surpassed his mentor at baking sweets. The nuts were soft inside the cake, and the honey was sweet and fresh. She smiled and closed her eyes. A bug crawled up onto her leg and she watched it for a while before flicking it into the soil. The cool dirt and soft sound of the celebration outside soothed her, and before she knew it her head nodded and she drifted off to sleep.

☆ ☆ ☆

When she awoke, the sounds of merriment still rang through the meadow. She noticed no one was around and her heart skipped a beat thinking she had missed the start of the feast. Hurrying out, she almost tripped over her own feet as she ran towards the main tent. She opened the flaps and ran face first into a fisherman named Hagon, who smiled at her.

"There you are, Almond; your father has been looking everywhere for you." He frowned. "You're all dirty."

Almond looked down at her orange dress, which was streaked in mud and grass stains. She blushed. Hagon clapped her on the shoulder.

"Don't worry, no one will blame you for being a bit dirty. Now run along to the front table - your parents are there."

She thanked Hagon and hurried off, brushing loose dirt from her hair. When she finally found her seat, the food was just beginning to be served. Her father smiled and offered her a glass of the liquid she had never drunk before.

"I think you're old enough now to try some of this."

Almond's stomach turned at the sight of it and she politely refused. The festival continued outside, where a dance had started in the center of the meadow.

Above the sounds of laughter, Almond thought she heard something else. She tugged at her father's arm, but he was in deep conversation with a farming couple from a few acres away. He gave her a look that said *not now*, and went back to it. She tugged at her dress in habit and paced back and forth. Looking around she noticed a few others seemed to be scanning the field. *Do they hear it at well?* The sound kept getting louder until Almond could hear a distinct *click-clack, click-clack* over the hill. Looking up, she watched as fifty horses summited the ridge, and descended upon the festival. Screams went out as the meadow was encircled.

"Almond!"

She heard her father cry out, but she was already yards away, running as fast as her legs could take her. Falling to her knees and diving forward, she scrambled into her hole, covering the entrance with just enough tall grass to hide her, while still allowing her to peek through. Her heart raced, wondering if anyone had seen her, but everyone was too focused on the intruders. A few of the villagers picked up sticks and pots to defend themselves, but the Lepus were a peaceful people and few carried true weapons.

Only then did she recognize who had shown up. They were a group of free riders from the Canis Venatici Faction known as the "Hunting Dogs." They roamed their section of the Starscape preying on weaker peoples and taking slaves for the fighting pits of some far-off world. Each member had teeth filed into razor sharp points and wore a heavy leather jerkin dyed coal black. Their captain rode up to her father, who stood firm where everyone else had run closer to the center of the circle. Almond was just close to enough to hear them speak.

"Perro, this is such a nice spread you've laid out," said the Captain of the Dogs. His voice dripped with slime. "I'm offended that you didn't think to invite us."

The captain then dismounted his black steed and came face to face with her father. On his right hand he wore a gauntlet that at its knuckles jutted out into two long daggers. Nonchalantly, he put the gauntlet to his mouth and began picking something from his teeth with one of the daggers. Her father wasn't fazed.

"We've talked about this Jackan. We gave you double last month so that this month we pay nothing and can have our festival."

Jackan bobbed his head back and forth. "*Weeeell*, I suppose that *was* the deal, but we may or may not have already gone through the supply."

Her father stared back incredulously. "You went through two months of food in three weeks?"

Jackan kicked at the ground like an ashamed child. "We got a bit carried away, I'll admit it. No matter though," he smiled. "I'm sure you've got some more kicking around."

Her father pointed a finger accusingly at Jackan's face. "We do not. Now leave."

Jackan clicked his teeth together. "Wasn't asking. Either you give us our supply for this month, or we round up all the little rabbits here and pick a few for the pits. How does that sound?"

Her father stood firm. "No."

"Fine, have it your way."

Jackan grabbed her father on the shoulder with his left hand, and cocked his mailed right hand. Before another word was uttered from her father's mouth, Jackan punched him in the gut. The daggers on the end of his gauntlet burst out her father's back as red as rose. Jackan then whispered something into her father's ear before tossing him like a sack of flour onto the ground. Her father writhed in pain, but managed not to scream.

"Alright boys." He circled a finger in the air. "Round them up!" He then turned to her father. "And someone please get that man a bandage. I don't want him dying." He smiled. "Not today at least."

The Hunting Dogs brought every man or woman of fighting age together in the center of the meadow. Jackan looked them over one by one, and chose eleven, including her Uncle Jonah, that would go to the pits. Then, the Hunting Dogs raided their food stores and took three wagons full. When that wasn't enough, Jackan commanded Almond's grandmother be lifted from her own wagon, which was then filled with more stolen food and roped to the back of a horse. Her grandmother was left to fall unceremoniously to the ground, causing Almond to nearly burst forward, but she knew she could not reveal herself. Finally, the dogs hoisted her injured father unceremoniously onto one of the food carts. Jackan laughed and gave a final warning to the remaining villagers not to follow them, before mounting and leading them away.

Almond felt tears trailing down her cheeks and welling on her chin. She punched at the dirt around her until her knuckles bloodied and then lay still, unsure what to do. Around her, the remaining villagers were busy fumbling around attempting to pick up the pieces. She watched as a woman fell to the ground in tears and lay wailing for her husband. An older man with a bushy beard was trying to rally some of the men to go after the attackers. He waved his cane above his head like a sword, pointing it over the ridge. No one but him seemed to want to go. A few people filled a wheelbarrow with blankets and cushions, then, lifted her grandmother into it. Luckily, she looked no worse for wear. That at least, Almond could be thankful for. Gingerly, she crawled out from her hole and began searching for her mother. She found her at the feast table, head in her hands. When Almond drew near, her mother looked up with sad eyes and held Almond's head against her breast. Almond felt the heaving of her chest as choked sobs filled her ears.

After everyone had collected themselves, no one felt like continuing the festivities. One by one, they all returned to their homes. Almond's mother and one of her cousins wheeled her grandmother home while Almond walked a few paces behind, tugging at her dress. The farmhouse felt empty without her father. Once inside, her mother went to her bedroom and didn't come out, leaving Almond alone with her sleeping grandmother.

"What do we do now, Grandma?" she asked, knowing there would be no answer.

"Everything happens for a reason, love."

Almond stared wide eyed at her grandmother, who turned her head toward her and gave the warmest smile.

"My son is a strong boy. He'll find a way to make this right. Don't worry, child."

"But Grandma... He... That man... He *stabbed* him."

"I've seen men recover from much worse injuries than that." She beckoned with her hand. "Come here, child."

Almond rose to her feet and crossed the room. Her grandmother took hold of her hand and gave it a squeeze. Reaching around her neck, she unclasped a necklace Almond never knew was there. On the end was a key. She reached over and pressed the item into Almond's hand and closed her fingers.

"You are still very young, child, but it is time for this to be yours. There is a box buried beneath Auma's statue. Tonight, dig it up." Her grandmother closed her eyes and fell asleep, leaving Almond confused and scared.

That night, when the moon was at its highest, she returned to Auma's statue. The brazier had gone out long ago, and the coals were cold. Before her, the stone man seemed to stare back at Almond in the moonlight. She fell to her hands and knees, said a small prayer, and began to dig. It didn't take long before she uncovered a long, thin box. Bushing off the dirt, she removed the necklace from around her neck and slotted it into the lock. With a *click* it opened, revealing inside a thin sword only slightly longer than her arm. She could barely lift it above her waist, it was so heavy. Underneath, she also discovered a belt with a scabbard. The leather looked older than her grandmother, cracked and sun-bleached. She wrapped it around her waist and buckled the clasp shut. It was so large that it hardly fit, and she had to keep one hand on it to keep the belt from falling. She then sheathed the sword. It hung so low that the tip scraped along the ground. Even though she would never have the strength to use it, she somehow felt safer with it on. The box also contained one more item: A small pendant that was tucked away in the corner. Almond cupped it gently and held up what looked like a brilliantly orange stone incased in a lattice of gold. She held it by the chain, and twisted her wrist, making the pendant spin in front of her. She was mesmerised by it. Taking her hand off the sword belt, she slipped the chain around her neck and smiled despite her sadness.

CHAPTER 08

JOSHYA II

As he entered the market tunnel, Joshya's head pounded from the antics of the night before. He watched through squinted eyes as busy market-goers hurried from stall to stall, buying all sorts of wares: cricket flour, bat meat, roast centipedes, mushrooms, lichens, moss blankets, river fish, and anything else you could conceivably buy and sell whilst living exclusively underground.

As he watched the people around him, Joshya played with the money in his pocket, fumbling a gold coin between his fingertips. The ore mines had been connected to these tunnels when the Scorpios were sealed in, and although production had stopped during the war, the stockrooms were piled high. Because of this, gold and other precious metals were still the primary means of currency inside the tunnels. And being son to the King, Joshya had a lot of it.

He had come to the market to buy something for his dinner. The Royal Palace did have its own kitchens, but Joshya
had never taken a liking to the fancy food. He much preferred
eating as the commons did, which meant buying from the same
vendors. He paused when a glint of light coming off a vendor's
stall caught his eye. Walking over, he said hello to the smallest
old lady he had ever seen. The lady smiled back at him, trying
to use her lips to cover what remained of her teeth. Across her
clay table lay raw stones of all different shapes, sizes, and colours. They all looked beautiful to him, and Joshya gave a small
silver coin to her in exchange for a sparkling green stone fleck-
ed with silver. The old lady smiled at him and rubbed the metal
between her fingers. Joshya held the stone up to the torchlight
and watched as the whorls in the stone seemed to move in
the flickering light. Placing the stone gently in his pocket, he
smiled and continued on.

If the Scorpios had the ability to trade with other factions,
Joshya had no doubt in his mind that they would be the largest precious ore provider. The tunnels stretched deep into the
bedrock, into caves of pure quartz, gold, emerald, and opal.
His father had promised him that one day he'd take him to
see the caves first-hand, but as of yet that hadn't happened.
The abundance of such precious metals meant that they were
far less valuable than items you could only get on the surface.
Anything made of wood or wool would most likely run you a
price higher than a pound of silver or gold.

Joshya's stomach growled and he returned to his mission. Passing down the stalls, he eventually came to one adorned with clay barrels of edible green mushrooms. Joshya felt around for a few big ones, and ended up with enough for the evening's dinner. When he went to pay, the vendor's eyes widened and he grabbed hold of Joshya's outstretched hand and shook it vigorously.

"No, no, no, I cannot accept your money, my prince."

Joshya frowned. He hated when people did that. Regardless, he felt it to be rude for him to demand to pay, and so he graciously thanked the man for his generosity and began making his way home.

The Scorpio's palace consisted of at least one hundred private chambers for the use of the high family. Most were fitted with fired red bricks that helped the chambers hold their shape and gave them a more regal look than the average tunnel. There were rumours that somewhere in the palace was a passage that led all the way to the surface, but despite Joshya trying hundreds of times, he could never find it. He arrived in the frontmost chamber to find his little sister, Noni, chasing after a bug. When it skittered near Joshya's foot he stomped and squished it under his boot.

"Hey!" his sister cried. "That was my friend!"

Joshya rolled his eyes. "There any plenty of bugs around here, so get a new one." She frowned at him and stormed off.

Before doing anything else, Joshya visited his grandfather's room, where his mother sat beside his bed, dabbing her father's brow. Down in the tunnels there was a common fungus called "The Wart." If ingested, the fungus caused the victim to break out in hives and lose their vision. The symptoms were also usually accompanied by chills and muscle weakness. It wasn't uncommon for ignorant children to fall ill after accidentally eating the brightly coloured fungus, but cases in adults were much rarer. A treatment was discovered long ago, but it hadn't seemed to work on his grandfather, perhaps due to his age. The old man lay shaking under three layers of blankets with at least nine thick hives dotting his face, neck, and ears. One had closed off his right eye completely, but that hardly mattered as he had already gone blind months prior. Joshya placed his hand on his grandfather's shoulder. The weak man stirred and looked with his one blank eye at Joshya, smiling.

"Is that you Joshya?" He coughed. "It's been so long."

Joshya and his mother exchanged a nervous glance.

"I was here yesterday, Grandad." Joshya reached down under the covers and squeezed his grandfather's hand.

"Were you? He frowned. "I can't remember." And then promptly fell asleep.

His mother looked up at him. "He doesn't have long left."

Joshya nodded. "I know."

With his father spending the majority of his time attending to royal matters and his mother indisposed with his sick grandfather, Joshya had de-facto become the primary caregiver for himself and his younger sister. Moving to the kitchen and unloading the big green mushrooms he'd purchased into a bowl, he unlatched the nearest torch from the wall and used it to light a fire beneath the hearth. He then filled a large bucket of water from the basin and heaved it over the fire. When the water was boiling he added the mushrooms and a few other ingredients. The smell of the stew brought his sister into the room, carrying with her a large beetle. Joshya glanced over at her.

"I told you you'd find another one."

Noni looked hurt. "It's not as big."

Joshya wasn't in the mood to argue. "Sit," he said. "Supper will be ready soon."

Joshya spent that evening training again with Vylarr. The Captain wanted him to train extra this week for some reason. Joshya thought to protest, but decided against it. He even thought he was doing well, until the captain had put him in his place once again. Afterwards, Vylarr had brought out a large dummy made of hard clay, solid throughout, and shaped roughly like a person.

"Again."

Joshya struck the dummy across the chest with the edge of his sword as hard as he could. Small chips of clay sprayed off the solid block and onto the floor, where a small pile was forming. No matter how hard Joshya tried, he couldn't seem to break it in half.

"Again!"

So he swung again. WHACK! More chips flew. His arm was on fire from his wrist to his elbow. Joshya wanted to quit, but Vylarr wouldn't let him. The piercing expression his trainer had pinned to his face made Joshya uneasy. Vylarr leaned over and got his nose up to Joshya's.

"That's an enemy soldier coming at you! That's a warhorse charging you down! That's a man trying to take your life and snuff it out!" He closed his hand in a snuffing motion and paused. "Are you going to let that happen?!"

Joshya met his gaze. "No."

"Glad to hear it." Vylarr's face calmed as he backed away, pointing the tip of his training sword at the cracked dummy staring blankly into the distance. "I want you to stay here until that dummy has been broken in half."

Joshya was ready to argue, but decided against it. Once Vylarr left the training chamber Joshya resumed his practice.

WHACK!

WHACK!

Whack.

Joshya's arm tired and his swings became mere taps. Suddenly, he was overcome with a wave of frustration and lurched forward to tackle the dummy. As it hit the floor it cracked and all at once Joshya lay on a bed of broken ceramic. He rolled onto his back and didn't move, irritated at the world, until he heard a muffled noise. Sitting up, he looked around. *What?* he thought. *No, there was definitely a sound.* Joshya pulled a fresh training sword off the wall and moved around the corner. He was so on edge he jumped at the sight of a beetle. He kicked himself for being so anxious. But then Joshya realized that the beetle wasn't moving. He knelt down and picked up something he'd never felt before. It was thin and sharp in the middle, with wisps of what felt like hair coming from the stem. He liked the feel of it and moved it in his hands. Suddenly he heard the clash of steel on steel.

Joshya pocketed the strange object and went running in the direction of the sound. He rounded a corner and came upon a burly brickmaker lying on the ground, blood trickling from his head. Sitting astride him was a slender man, with a capelet made of what looked like black hair, the same hair on the mysterious object he'd found. The caped man held a long dirk and was pressing down on the brickmaker, who was struggling with a metal mallet locked in the hilt of the dirk as the only thing between his chest and the blade. Neither noticed Joshya as he watched. Taking advantage of the situation, Joshya barreled into the assailant, sending the man sprawling to the ground. Joshya's practice sword slid off the man's leather armour, but couldn't cut though. At that point he noticed the man wore a black bandana over the lower half of his face and had long straight black hair covering most of the top half. He seemed almost familiar. The garb he wore was nothing like what Scorpio's wore, but even more shocking was the crest adorning his leather breast piece: a crow, identical to Himrel's. The sight made Joshya pause. The assailant picked himself up off the ground and grabbed a torch off the wall. From behind Joshya, the burly brickmaker stood up and walked next to him, rubbing the side of his head where he had been struck.

 JOSHYA

"Who in hell is that?" he asked no one in particular.

Before Joshya could respond, the man threw the torch at their feet. The oils from within the torch spread and set Joshya's boot on fire, sending him leaping backwards. By the time he'd stamped it out, the man was gone. It was only then that the brickmaker noticed who he was.

"Prince Joshya?" He stared wide-eyed.

Joshya rolled his eyes. "Forget me, what about him?! We need to go after him!"

"No," The brickmaker shook his head." I'm not risking the King's son, and I'm in no shape to do anything myself." He moved his hand away from his head and looked at it. Blood caked between his fingers. "Bugger snuck up on me with my own mallet."

CHAPTER 09

ORLO 1

Orlo picked at the scabs forming under the fetters clasped around his ankles. Blood coated the rough iron and peppered the dirt floor around him with red splotches. There were no windows in his cell, and the only light came from the crack under the door. Every now and again a mouse would crawl in from under the door and visit Orlo. He welcomed the company, but more often than not he'd shoo the mouse away before it got too close. He'd been in this place for less than two days, but it felt like years. And he knew the longer he stayed, the less his chance for survival would be. He also knew all too well where he was, and what awaited him when that door finally opened. This was the Meat Locker, the holding cell for all new fighters destined for death or glory in the Leo's Lion Pit.

The Lion Pit was a massive arena, built for the sole purpose of entertainment through violence and gore. Slaving mercenaries from around the Starscape would bring captives here to act as competitors in tournaments made up of hundreds of indentured warriors. Most of the Meat Locker's residents wouldn't see it past the first round. The Lord of the Pit was cousin to the current King of Leo, and had a dozen or so elite warriors that fought for pay in every tourney. Where the slaves were beaten, starved, under-armed, and under-armoured, the Lord's men were treated like royals: with every whim catered to, donning the finest armour, and brandishing the most lethal of weapons.

Orlo had been captured with ten others while on a hunting trip on their homeworld. He had made a bet with one of his companions on which one of them would last longer in the pits. Orlo had bet a gold coin he'd make it to round three or higher at the time, but now, as hunger sapped the energy from his bones, he imagined he'd be lucky to last five minutes on the field.

Orlo groaned and rested his head against the wall of his cell, thinking back to happier times; times when he was on the top of the food chain, hunting and trapping animals for his shop. Now, he was on the other end of the line, an animal in all but name, waiting for its death. The mouse had returned, and was nibbling on one of his big toes. Orlo didn't feel he had enough strength to move, and so he let it happen. The fetters on his ankles were so tight that he could hardly feel his toes anyway. Suddenly, the door swung open and banged loudly into the stone wall of his cell. The mouse shrieked and scampered off into a corner. Orlo shielded his eyes from the light as a big man with long black hair and bronzed skin walked in.

He wore nothing but a small loincloth that barely covered his manhood and a set of iron keys around his wrist.

"Up," he commanded.

Orlo tried, but his legs were about as weak as the dirt around him. He shook his head. The big man sighed and moved closer. Bending down, he unlocked Orlo's chains from the wall and then the locks around his feet. Orlo breathed a sigh of relief as the pain in his ankles was lessened for the first time in two days. The big man then grabbed Orlo around the waist, and despite his weight of close to one hundred and eighty pounds, lifted him up off the ground like a baby. Orlo decided not to resist, and instead he slumped down, allowing himself to be carried. The trip didn't last long, and Orlo was dumped like a sack of flour back onto the ground, this time in a much larger room.

"Up," commanded the man again.

Again, he tried. This time Orlo got to his knees before stopping. The big man came closer, looking angry. Orlo held out a hand to stop him.

"I can do it. Just give me a second."

Slowly but surely, Orlo was able to rise to his feet. The second he did, the big man tossed a hunk of bread his way. Orlo fumbled it in his hands and it fell to the ground. He bent down and shoved the stale chunk into his mouth, barely chewing. It was the best thing he'd ever tasted. The big man motioned to the door.

"Walk."

ORLO

Inside was an armory, filled with rusty and unmaintained weapons. Lining the walls were chipped swords and broken axes. He looked back at his jailer.

"You're kidding, right?"

The jailer pointed to the wall. "Pick."

Orlo sighed and started leafing through the selection.

"Faster."

If your life depended on it, you'd take your time too, he thought. His eye caught a blue-tinted sword with a black leather hilt. He pulled it off the wall and spun it in his hand. The blade had a slight curve to it and ended in a double point, the front one bigger than the back. He checked the edge, which was rough but still felt sharp. Orlo, being a meat shop owner, was more familiar with a cleaver than a sword, but in his younger years he'd been no stranger to a fight, and had to defend his land on more than a few occasions. He turned back to the big man, and the urge to cut him down and run was foremost in him. As if reading his mind, the jailer shook his head and pulled a large spiked mace off the wall.

"Walk."

Orlo was marched to another room, where he was given a half-helm and a chest piece as thin as paper. The helm fit clumsily over Orlo's round head and shifted from ear to ear as he walked. The jailer stopped before a bamboo door. Orlo could hear cheers from the other side. Then, as the cheers grew loudest, he heard the sound of steel through flesh and the sound of liquid spilling out onto sand. He grimaced.

"You're next."

He looked to the jailer. "I figured that out already, thank you."

The big man smiled and pushed Orlo through the open door. He was immediately amazed by the sheer size of the pit. An oval at least one hundred feet across was before him, with walls twenty feet high before stretching into stands. Wooden seats ringed the fighting area, almost every one filled with a blood-crazed onlooker. At the forefront was the Lord of the Pit himself, sat comfortably in a small wooden throne with a skull for each hand rest. Beside him sat his lady, who drank wine from an ox horn. She wore no shirt and her breasts were borne for all to see. It wasn't uncommon on the Leo homeworld for women to dress as such, the climate was brutally hot, and Orlo already felt himself beginning to sweat.

The ring was littered with dead bodies. He had to step over a few to reach the centre of the arena, where he unceremoniously bowed before the Lord and promptly spat. He was still deathly tired, but being able to move around in the fresh air and sunshine had invigorated him.

From the other end of the pit, a door opened and out walked an equally disheveled man. As he walked towards the center, Orlo could see him more clearly. The man had piercing ruby red eyes, a dead giveaway that his opponent was from the Hydrus area of the Starscape. The man wore metal armour with a sea snake painted over the chest and carried a long pole with a green-tinted glass orb on the end. Orlo cursed under his

ORLO

breath as his opponent took his own bow before the Pit Lord. They then walked back to their own sides of the arena. The weapon his opponent carried was typical for Hydrus infantrymen. It was called a venomer, a staff topped with a sealed vial of corrosive acid. If you were hit by that end, not only would glass shards shred wherever they made contact, but you'd likely lose all the skin and muscle that the acid touched. Even a drop could pierce the skin like a needle. They must have let him keep his weapon. The thought annoyed him but didn't surprise him. The point of the pit was entertainment, and for a group of gore happy onlookers, what's more entertaining than watching a man dissolved alive?

Orlo took a few steps forward, trying to gage how anxious his opponent was to attack. The Hydrus man made no real movement. All he needed to do was wait until Orlo got into range, and one swing of his staff would end the fight. That was what made a venomer so lethal; it was near unblockable. If any part of your own weapon accidentally hit the glass bulb up top, then get ready for an acid shower. Use a shield? The acid would eat through that as well, and then into your arm. Armor? Again, the acid would spray in all direction and seep somewhere in a chink. The best chance you had was to use long ranged weapons. Sadly, Orlo didn't have that option. He knew that eventually he'd have to get in close. The sun glinted off his sword and shone blue. He looked at it and felt the weight. *Light. Really light.*

"Fight already!" the Leo Lord called from above.

That made the Hydrus man move forward. Orlo did the same. As they got closer, Orlo sped up the pace, and the Hydrus man matched him. Ten feet from each other his opponent reeled back and prepared a swing. At the last moment, Orlo ducked and rolled under the attack. The acid tip swung inches above his head. A roar came up from the crowd. Orlo found his feet and stood, just as another swing came. This time he had to bend backwards to avoid it. Orlo then took ten long strides back and stood, sword ready in hand. The crowd booed at him for his cowardice. The Hydrus man was even smirking. His black shaggy hair fell over one of his crimson eyes. He raised his arms out to his sides in a show of power. The crowd cheered. He was clearly gaining popularity already. That's when Orlo took his chance. He cocked his arm and let go. The blue sword flashed end over end through the air, and stuck into the wood of the staff, ripping it from its possessor's hands. The weapon fell to the dirt with the sword still in it. Incredibly, the vial did not break. The Hydrus man stared in awe and the crowd hushed, but before he could move, Orlo slammed into him. The force sent the two of them to the ground. Orlo soon found himself with a black eye, a bruised cheek, and bloody knuckle as blows were exchanged.

Eventually the tussle brought the two of them close to their weapons. Straddling his prone opponent, Orlo made an attempt to grab the hilt of his sword, but his combatant pushed his arm away. He made a second lunge and this time was successful, but instead of bringing the sword up, he cut right through the

ORLO

handle of the spear into the ground. The Hydrus man panted beneath Orlo, and flipped him off in a last-ditch effort, then got to one knee and grabbed his staff, not realizing that the lethal part had been removed. Orlo capitalized on the situation and nabbed the tip from the ground where it still lay. Lunging forward, he knocked the Hydrus man back to the ground, then raised both hands gripping the small handle still on the vial, and brought it down onto his opponent's face.

An inhuman screech erupted from the man's lips as the acid spread across his nose and cheeks, and down into his eyes and mouth. The yellowish-green sludge sizzled and steam rose off his skin. Soon, the screaming stopped and Orlo was left facing a skull with bits of meat loosely hanging off. The cheers of the crowd barely entered Orlo's attention. He was horrified at the sight before him. Grimacing, he looked to his arms and legs, where a few small drops had touched him. The skin was burnt black and the wounds went deep. Getting up, he retrieved his sword and looked to the stands. The Leo Lord was standing and clapping, and sent for one of his men to bring Orlo in and tend to him. As he was escorted out of the arena, he looked back to see two new warriors entering the pit. *And it continues,* he thought. For the first time he noticed a gash in his leg trailing blood from every step. *When did that happen?* Orlo thought. Then he blacked out.

CHAPTER 10

RYMUS 1

"**S**oak it in, little brother. A fish needs the rain as much as the plants do."

Rymus turned in his saddle towards Elkus. His brother sat astride his chestnut coloured destrier, its bridle stained a brilliant blue.

"Today is a good day for a battle," Elkus continued.

"And a battle we shall have!" called Lydus, trotting his own horse up beside his brothers.

The rain was coming down heavy and hard, as it always did before the Pisces began a charge. Somewhere at the back of their ranks, Rymus knew the Shaman was deep into a trace, using smelling salts and muttering unintelligibly to himself. His words were gibberish to the soldiers, but to the skies they were a song - one that brought fog and cloud and torrential rain. The Pisces believed the rain brought power to their armies.

Superstition, to be sure, Rymus thought, and yet the Shaman's powers were undeniable.

The weather had put the enemy off guard. The small encampment below was stirring with soldiers escaping from the rain, running from gate to gate attempting to keep their fires alight. Rymus was close enough that he could see the faces of the soldiers below him on the hill. Yet as close as the they were, the fog hid the hordes of armed Pisces men from view. *They have no idea what's coming.*

Rymus' horse bristled and shook, its mane dripping with water. He closed his eyes and said a silent prayer for him and his brothers, as he did before every skirmish. Each brother would be taking a separate battalion into the enemy encampment. Lydus, being the eldest brother, would be taking a small force directly downhill into the camp to break-up their defenses. It was the most dangerous position to take, but there was no doubt that the tall and muscular brother could handle it. Elkus, the middle sibling, would be taking a larger force around the west side of the camp. At the same time, Rymus himself would be taking an equal force around the eastern side. They would all come together in the centre, three forces against one.

He removed his spear from its holster on the saddle of his horse. Rymus weighed it in his hand, felt it, made it an extension of his arm. By day's end the weapon would be broken in half and he would have to have a new one made. He ran his finger along the edge of the point. The water was beading on the steel and rolling off. *Pristine.*

"Eldrich is a fine smith," Elkus said to him, the rain matting his short hair to his scalp.

Rymus gave the spear a twirl around his hand and held it up. "As long as my arm works as well." He turned his horse and grinned to Elkus, "Fair day to you, brother."

"And you, brother," Elkus grinned back as Rymus rode to his battalion.

The ground was already becoming almost too soggy to ride. They would have to charge soon or risk having their horses slip in the mud. Rymus' second in command, Keldo, rode up to him.

"All soldiers ready, Captain."

"Good, have them wait on my mark."

Keldo nodded and rode back to the columns. Overzealous as always, he thought. Keldo was a stout man. Short, with a fat belly from too much brown ale. His armor was a light blue the colour of the sky, waxed to a shine brighter than crystal. The water of the rain beat off the armor without so much as sticking for a second. Rymus always figured that Keldo was jealous of the high family of Pisces and did his best to look as regal as he could. The showmanship bothered his brothers, which was why Keldo had ended up with him. Rymus would be lying if he'd said that Keldo's obsession didn't annoy him from time to time, but the man was also a great warrior and a cunning strategist. Rymus figured he'd rather have a jeweled war-axe than a rugged hatchet, and so far, Keldo had never let him down.

 RYMUS

The sound of a horn filled the air and Rymus turned in time to see Lydus begin his charge out of the fog and down the hill towards the encampment. Soldiers who were lazing around the camp quickly stood to attention and found their helms and arms. Guardsmen posted at the closest side of the camp drew bows of strongwood and began to fire. Lydus was at the very front and couldn't be fazed or slowed, not even when an arrow glanced off the armor covering his cheek. Some of his men began to falter as arrows pierced their horses. One soldier near the back took a solid hit between the eyes and his horse veered off from the rest, rider slouched backwards. Some of the soldiers who were supposed to be defending the gates were running, and some who were supposed to be running were forming defensive lines. The enemy was utterly unprepared, and that was good.

Lydus was the first over the small stone fence surrounding the camp. His horse had no trouble leaping the structure. He quickly rode down a bowman on his left and cut down another to his right. By that time the rest of the charge had caught up and the camp was swimming with Pisces soldiers. The man his brother had cut down caught Rymus' attention. Writhing on the ground, a large gash had been taken out of him from chest to chin and the blood was pouring profusely. Lydus' sword was a dastardly weapon, a bastard sword sharp as any, but serrated like a scaling knife. Lydus had gotten the idea while catching fish with his brothers years ago, and Eldrich the smith had made it a reality. Lydus had practiced using it each day to get comfortable with the unconventional weapon, and the training had paid off, as now it was being used to remove large chunks of leather armour, skin, muscle, and even bone from any unfortunate soldier to get in its way.

The horn blew again, and Elkus made his descent around the west slope of the hill. That was the cue. Rymus nodded to Keldo, signaling the shiny man to bring his equally shiny trumpet to his lips. The horn blew and Rymus began the decent down the hill. The ground was wet, but luckily not too much so, and within a minute Rymus too was upon the enemy, fighting alongside his brothers. Stabbing left and right with his spear, he reared his horse this way and that, not letting any man get too close. In the distance, he saw Elkus fighting in the mud, his horse lying slain beside him. Rymus rode toward his older brother and ran down a foot soldier coming up behind him. Elkus looked at him, annoyed.

"I knew he was there!"

Rymus bobbed his head and Elkus spun on his foot bringing the ball of his flail into the skull of another foot soldier attempting to get Elkus from behind.

"And him!"

It was short work to sweep through the encampment from there on out. By the end of the battle, the rain had already begun to clear, and the Shaman was out cold and jerking in his sleep. Lydus sat on a rock cleaning his sword. Elkus was off interrogating, and most likely executing prisoners. Rymus himself had found a cask of deep golden wine the likes of which

RYMUS

he'd never tasted, and was currently getting drunker than he'd previously thought imaginable. Keldo walked up to him, his armor dinted and muddy and his moustache caked in blood from what looked like a broken nose. Or maybe it was just as big and red as it usually was? Rymus was too drunk to tell. Or care.

"Mind passing me a cup?" asked Keldo, "All this killing makes me thirsty and I need something to take the taste of blood from my mouth."

Rymus made a grand gesture to the cask. "Haveasmuchasyouwant."

"Many thanks, Captain." He paused. "You shouldn't let your soldiers see you this way."

Rymus pointed an accusatory finger at his second in command and narrowed his eyes. "I don't need their respect, only their loyalty."

Keldo shrugged. "Respect leads to loyalty."

Rymus closed his eyes hard and leaned back. "Keldo, I am far too drunk to listen to your council right now. Sit down and have a cup of whatever it is I am drinking. That is an order!"

"As you command, Captain." Keldo poured a glass, took a sniff, and reeled. "Mighty strong stuff you have here."

"Could be fermented piss for all I know." Rymus took a long swig as Keldo plopped his fat ass beside him and drank. The sound of prisoners screaming filled the air.

As the sun rose, Rymus lay under the early morning sky nursing a hangover headache; beside him Keldo snored loudly. The empty keg had rolled off somewhere and he didn't have the least bit of interest in searching for it. Out of the corner of his eye he saw Elkus walk past.

"What did we learn from our prisoners, o' great interrogator?"

Elkus stopped and gave him a tired look. "Nothing we didn't already know. The Carinas are allied with the Aries and have started setting up bases by the northern rift. If we want any more information, we'll have to head up that way."

Rymus' head pounded like rocks down the side of a mountain. He gave his temples a rub, then gave Keldo a slight kick in the gut. The tubby man snorted awake and groaned.

"Who'sere?" he asked, liquor staining his lips.

"Me. We ride north today."

He sat up and rubbed his eyes. "There's nothing but mountains north o' here."

Rymus smirked. "Then take three guesses as to where we're going."

By the time Rymus was beginning to feel awake, Lydus was already on horseback, ready to head off scouting. He gave his brother a half-assed wave as his horse galloped off into the distance. A kind of rocky field dominated the landscape, with boulders dotting the horizon, chunks of mountain that had broken free. Small bushes and brambles littered the ground haphazardly and rustled in the wind. Rymus donned his chest plate and spit-shined his helm. The camp around them had come to life once more with the bustle of soldiers. The plan was simple: Move closer to the Aries central castle and take

RYMUS

down any camp in their way. Maybe if enough camps were destroyed, the peace banner would be coming over the ridge and they could avoid a siege altogether. Rymus wasn't afraid of a siege, but they were long and boring. He'd much rather a quick, exciting fight. A beetle walked by his foot and he crushed it under his boot, smiling. *We are the masters of this land.* Off in the distance the clouds were moving over the mountains. The sun's rays danced off them, sending radiant lines across his armor. *If only everything were so small.*

CHAPTER 11

JAIR 11

*T*he *King's quarters?* The words echoed in his head. "You're crazy," said Jair.

"No, just bold." Vikron gave him a toothy grin, and then looked to the axe in his burly hands. Flipping it around, he used its butt-end to give Jair another shove, harder this time.

"This square will be crawling with more guards any minute. How many of 'em you think will recognize you without your mask?" He leaned in close. "They'll think you're just another one of us, and they won't take kindly to you."

Jair knew there were many in the guard who would know and vouch for him. *More than likely they'll execute me for failing my king,* he thought. That left him in the same situation he started in. Begrudgingly, he turned towards the palace and began to move.

"Faster!"

Jair broke into a jog. Vikron and his insurgents followed. From the corner of his eye, Jair could see more guards pouring into the square from the surrounding city. With the crowd gone, there was no confusion as to who to go after. A bolt flew high over the group's heads and landed in the grass, sticking up like a twig. Another hit the cobblestone on the square and ricocheted like a stone skipping over water. Vikron urged him on until finally they came to the castle. As they stood before the marble walls, they heard a loud THUNK as the portcullis hit the dirt.

"Bugger!" yelled Vikron. "There better be another way in."

"There is, but I'll die before I tell you where it is."

"How about I take a few of those fingers, and then we talk."

Jair wished he wasn't such a coward. He motioned for the group to follow him around the side of the castle. Running his hand along the hedges surrounding the lower wall, he felt for a bump. When he found it, Jair shoved the bushes aside to reveal a small wooden door, only about two feet tall and the same wide. He tried to open it, but it was locked shut. Vikron growled and shoved him hard to one side.

"Jeremiah, get over here."

A muscular man moved forward, in his grip a two-handed sledge. Before Jair could protest, he smashed the door to bits, sending splinters flying.

Jair grimaced. "If those guards didn't know where we were going before, they certainly do now. They'll have the castle surrounded."

"That's what I'm banking on," sneered Vikron, before throwing Jair into the opening.

The room they found themselves in was only lit by the light from outside, but Jair knew he was in the lower storerooms. Past potatoes and parsnips, he led the insurgents up to the main level and into the castle wing that housed the domiciles.

"Where are all the guards, and all the bloody nobles?" asked one of the men."

Jair shrugged. "The guards are looking for us on the outside of the castle. The nobles have all locked themselves away in whatever room they feel is safest."

Jair thought of the royal treasurer, and the imported jeweled blade he had loved to rub in other's faces. The braggart wore the weapon on his hip all hours of the day. *Where are you and that sword now that the danger is at your doorstep?* Passing from hall to hall, the group came into no trouble until finally they arrived at a large ornately carved door with a pillar on either side.

"This it?" asked Vikron.

"Look for yourself," Jair motioned towards the door and stepped back.

Vikron used his big hairy foot to kick open the door with an audible *CRACK* as the mahogany snapped to pieces. Inside was a room five times the size of normal living quarters, along with an attached solar, loft, and shrubberies. Ornately woven tapestries hung round the room bearing the likeness of former

Kings of Ara. The space was so impressive that it could only have been made for a King. Vikron grinned.

"Looks like you get to live another day, 'cutioner."

Lucky me, thought Jair. One by one, the insurgents entered the room. Jair began to count how many he'd led into the heart of his King's castle. Twenty-one in all, until two final men came through a good three minutes after everyone else. Jair saw the large box the two of them were heaving in. One caught him staring.

"This doesn't concern you," he told Jair with a sneer.

When everyone was in, one person shut the door and stood guard. Vikron walked casually over to the fireplace, bent down, and started scraping armfuls of soot and half burned logs out onto a rug worth more gold than Jair made in a year. Once the fireplace was completely empty, Vikron pushed on its back wall and a panel was knocked loose. Jair could only stare in disbelief.

"How did you know that was there?"

Vikron looked back at him. "I'm sure Nathanyel would have loved to tell you. You can go ask him if you'd like. He's lying out in the city square."

Then he disappeared into the castle walls like an oversized rat, and the rest of the insurgents quickly followed suit. Even the big box was slid though, despite it almost being too big to fit. Whatever was inside thumped back and forth noisily. When everyone else had gone through, Jair stood alone, staring blankly, hardly comprehending what had just transpired.

JAIR

Then, without really thinking about it, he did something that surprised even himself: he followed.

Getting down on his hands and knees, Jair crawled head-first into the secret passage. He found himself in a pitch-black tunnel, too low to stand or even stretch. He wondered for a moment if this was what the Scorpios of the famous Scorpio Tunnels lived like. As far as he knew, none had been seen since some long-ago war. He grimaced and thanked the Gods that he wasn't born in that part of the Starscape. The tunnel began to dip more and more steeply, to the point where he almost slipped. Not long after, the tunnel widened into a dark room. By now Jair's eyes had adjusted to the lack of light and he noticed the walls were no longer the stone of the castle, but of dirt and clay. Suddenly a shadow came out of nowhere and clapped him on the shoulder.

"Decided to come with us, did you 'cutioner?"

"Yes," was all Jair muttered. Even in the dark, he managed to see Vikron's face twist into a smile.

"Good, I was hoping you would."

Together they continued walking until they exited through a small hole punched out of the ground. He covered his eyes as he birthed himself from the ground. The sun was still rising and it pierced his eyes. Jair saw one of the insurgents wiping off a hammer clearly used to break out to the surface. He surveyed his surroundings. To his shock, he found that they were well over a hundred yards from the castle walls and deep within the nearby King's Forest. He covered his eyes from the

 JAIR

bright light and looked at the top spires of the castle, poking themselves out from the top of the canopy. Around him, the insurgents were dusting off. Most looked giddy. Jair had seen killers, by all accounts he was a killer himself, but never had he seen a group of killers look so happy after a killing. Vikron grunted to get Jair's attention. When he turned, Vikron shoved his pole-axe back into his hands.

"Don't use this to kill us, OK?"

Jair frowned down at his weapon. "I could have just as easily led you all into a trap."

Vikron smiled. "But you didn't."

A young man with deep set eyes and curly hair gave Jair a look-over. He looked none too friendly.

"Don't mind him," chuckled Vikron. "It isn't often we get new members."

Distant shouting rose through the trees. *They've scattered the guard.* At one time, Jair had been a part of those scatters. Now, he found himself as the one being hunted. Vikron looked less than worried. With almost a skip in his step, he began forward again. Jair and the rest followed. The group made its way through the underbrush, not stopping to eat or rest until they came upon a river what seemed like miles away from the palace. Jair was exhausted, but at the same time filled with energy. It had been a long time since he had felt this exhilarated. Four small rowboats were tied to posts on the shore, bobbing lightly in the ebb and flow of the water. Vikron pulled a burlap sack out of the closest one and unbound it to reveal a bear pelt cloak, as well as tanned hide pants, a wool tunic, boots, and a leather jerkin. Before Jair knew it, Vikron had stripped himself down out of his prisoner's tatters and splashed himself with lake water. The captain turned towards the group, naked as a babe, with water matting the hair that covered him from lip to crotch. Jair reddened and looked away.

Vikron laughed. "Alright, if you've all finished ogling my pecker, we can get a move on!"

Jair looked back to see a new Vikron, a man fully dressed and more imposing than he could have ever imagined. He adjusted the horned helm resting on his head and smiled a wicked smile. The now uniformed Taurus Captain made quite a sight to behold. The others made their way onto the rowboats, cramming themselves in shoulder to shoulder. Jair took a seat in the middlemost rowboat, placing himself next to Vikron. He rested his pole-axe upright beside him. The large box got jerked and jarred until it got wedged in one of the other rowboats, causing it to nearly upend. From there, the trek across the river was made in silence, and the man sitting behind Jair seemed to have even fallen asleep. Once far enough out into the water they were safe. Even if they were to be spotted, their pursuers could do nothing. Arrows only reached so far, and there were no other boats within sight on shore. The water turned from blue, to fire red, to golden yellow, and finally a deep purple as the sun set and they reached their destination miles downstream on the other side of the lake.

 JAIR

☆ ☆ ☆

That night they camped out under the stars. Jair tried to pinpoint which one Vikron and the Tauri were from, but he'd never paid much attention to such lessons as a child. Beside him, a young boy sat cross-legged using a small knife to pry the gemstones from Jair's armor. His axe lay on the ground before him, already stripped naked of its adorning gold and jewels. He reached down and picked it up. It weighed only about half of what it did earlier that day. From it, Vikron had collected a small bag of gold plating which he meant to sell on the morrow. But for the time being, they simply sat and prepared. For what they were preparing, Jair did not know. He couldn't take his eyes off the crate that Vikron's men had taken with them. The big box was still tightly shut, though Jair thought he could now smell a foul odor emanating from it. He thought for a moment about inquiring, but he didn't think it a wise idea in his current situation.

Vikron may have accepted him into his ranks, but not everyone had. One man in particular sat by the fire and bragged to having personally killed three palace guards in the riot. He raised his sword above the light of the fire so everyone could see the dried blood, before pointing to Jair and threatening to make it four. The man had only gotten more boisterous when Jair had informed him that he wasn't a palace guard, but the royal executioner. Yet one word from Vikron and the man quieted like loyal dog.

But the real honour of the group had gone to a thirty some-odd man with short hair and a short scar on his chin named Arlum, who had been the one to fire both the bolt that gravely injured the scribe, as well as the one that had killed the King, or come close enough for it not to matter. Vikron had taken to calling him: "The man who broke the altar with an arrow," but soon after shortened it to simply "Altarbreaker." Jair had noticed that Vikron seemed to like giving his underlings nicknames. The small woman who had killed Sir Harkin with a sewing needle was known as "The Seamstress," another of the company was named "Frog," though Jair had yet to find out why, and of course Vikron had taken to calling Jair "The 'cutioner."

Around them, large pine trees swayed gently in the cool breeze. It was a beautiful night, though somewhat soured by the day's events. Jair found it hard to imagine what it was like back in the city. The townsfolk would be grieving over their ailing leader. King Jamarium was the only King that Jair had ever known, and he struggled to think what it would be like in Ara now that he was soon to be gone. Preparations were no doubt already being made. When the King passed, Prince Callum, the King's eldest son, would be crowned the new King of Ara, and the news would spread all across the Starscape. Jair had known Prince Callum briefly during his time as the royal executioner. "Vain" was the best word to describe him. Callum had the kind of bright blue eyes and long blond hair that made a young man a heartbreaker with women; couple that with his status as heir to a castle and a High House of the Starscape, and a night wouldn't go by without the prince sharing his bed with a new female companion. *He'll make a poor King*, Jair thought. *They won't take kindly to him.* He caught himself. *They.* Jair was amazed at just how quickly he had distanced himself from the others of his city. He'd been born there, grown up there, served there, and up until this morning was a highly respected and feared official there. Yet when the chance arose, he'd had no trouble leaving it all behind. He wasn't sure whether to be proud of that fact or disgusted, so he settled on a bit of both.

☆ ☆ ☆

The next morning Jair was awoken by the sound of far off trumpets blaring, marking what could only have been the ascension of a new King.

"All hail King Callum of Ara," he whispered sarcastically to himself.

Vikron was already awake, staring out over a hill at the running river below. His bearskin cloak flapped noisily in the morning breeze. Jair stretched and walked over to him. Vikron grunted a greeting without looking up.

"How did you know?" Jair asked him, following his gaze to the water.

Vikron gave Jair a sidelong glance. "'Bout what?"

"Trusting the royal executioner to turn traitor and help the enemy that just killed his King? That's a big risk. How did you know it would work?"

"Didn't," he said, bluntly. "But there was a look in your eyes that told me you weren't going to put up a fight."

Am I that easy to read? Jair thought, frowning. He watched a rotten apple float down the river, bobbing in the current.

"Captain!" called a voice from behind them. Frog was hurrying over. "Deleon spotted a dozen guards moving in from the south. He looked slightly panicked. "Do you want us to engage?"

Vikron spit down into the water and turned. "Only if need be. I don't want to risk anyone we don't have to. We lost five men back at the square. That was five men more than I could afford to have lost."

Jair was surprised to hear that Vikron cared about his men at all. Back when he was about to be executed, he'd bragged about murdering fifty civilians in cold blood. That kind of person didn't usually give two shits what happened to anyone but themselves, and sometimes they didn't even care about that much. Frog still looked anxious, but nodded and hurried back to camp. Jair and the captain followed in tow.

"Do you know how long it took me to get Eran on the inside?" asked Vikron.

Jair was confused. "Who?"

Vikron ignored him. "Seven bloody months, it took seven bloody months to get him on the inside, and it took you seven bloody seconds to kill him."

Jair's mind flashed back to the stage, and the mystery guard who'd attacked him.

 JAIR

Vikron shook his head. "Damn waste of a good soldier, but he served me well in the end."

Vikron seemed to know the surrounding forest better than even Jair did, and when they finally came to its edge there was no trace of a guard in sight. Two of the party climbed high into the tall sentinel pines and gave the rest of the group an all-clear sign. Jair breathed the fresh air into his lungs. He was amazed how light he felt without the gems on his armour weighing him down. The Seamstress had fashioned him a sash with leather buckles on the back to hold his pole-axe. It was much more comfortable than resting the thing on his shoulder all day. He shook the clasps to check them, and was pleasantly surprised with how sturdy they felt. It then dawned on him that the leather was probably cut from Sir Harkin's armour. The thought made him wince.

They saw that just past the treeline lay a small village. *Rotheston*, he thought. The town was mainly a lumber outpost, cutting the trees of the King's Forest and shipping them over the river by ferry. Jair had made his rounds as a guard here years back, even kissed a local girl. Parchment hung loosely nailed to a few of the trees nearer the village and blew in the breeze. Frog leapt over and pulled a poster down from a near-by tree, reading silently as he returned to the group. His lips twisted into a grin as his eyes scanned the paper. Jair caught a glimpse and snatched it from him. In big red letters across the top, it read "WANTED FOR KIDNAPPING THE KING." Below was an incredibly rough artist's sketch of Vikron. *That's not possible. The King was dying, he'd surely be dead by now. He was never... kidnapped.* Jair turned to look at Vikron, but stopped when his eyes fell on the large box. His gaze froze in place. *It can't be.* Vikron smiled at him, knowing exactly what was going through his mind.

"It is."

"Open the box." Jair commanded.

A man named Garrett was resting against the box with his arms crossed and only gave him half a look. "Not a chance."

Vikron smiled over at his man. "Open it," he said.

Garrett shrugged and lifted himself off the box. "You're the boss."

Drawing his dirk, Garrett wedged it between the crate's top and side. One twist and the lid popped off. He moved around and gave it an unceremonious kick. The crate tipped and out tumbled a body. King Jamarium fell to the ground and lay slumped in a blood-soaked pile in front of Jair.

"He... he's dead."

Vikron slapped him on the back. "'Course he's dead! You can't survive three days in a crate!" Vikron gave a loud belly laugh as Jair stared, more confused than ever.

"How... why?"

Vikron couldn't contain himself. "I left that prince o' yours a little note."

CHAPTER 12

ALGEN II

"Speak, child," King Caraq demanded again.

But Algen couldn't. He tried to make a sound, any sound, but all that came out was a low, feeble squeak. Caraq made a motion with his human arm and two guards walked over to Algen. Together, they lifted him from the ground and brought him closer to Caraq, who leaned in and came face to face with him. Algen could smell the fish on his King's breath.

"Can you speak?" Caraq asked him accusingly.

Algen was forced to shake his head no. Caraq slumped back into his throne.

"Pathetic," he said. "Take him from my sight."

The two guards hoisted Algen up again and pushed him toward the door.

"You disappoint me with your brood, Alperen." Algen heard the King say accusingly. "Maybe you should head home to that wife of yours and make a new one."

He found himself almost floating forward. The next thing he knew, he was on the ground, where he had been thrown. He watched as his father stormed past him, without even a second glace. Algen wanted to call after him, but the sound that came out couldn't even rival a seahorse. The King had been so disgusted that he hadn't bothered to choose a job for him. Algen considered for a moment about going back in and asking what he should do. *Oh right,* he thought.

The next few hours were a blur to him. The first thing he had thought to do was to go home, where maybe his mother would be more supportive than his father had been. After all, his mother wasn't exactly an incredible morph either. Once he arrived though, he found that his mother only showed him sadness and pity, neither of which he wanted. His father was nowhere to be found. At some point he found himself abed atop his seaweed bunk, crying softly to himself. The tears came flowing, but the sounds he made came out as hushed air.

Sometime later, after the dome had gone dark and the lightfish were swimming, Algen found himself wandering aimlessly from building to building, trying desperately to come to terms with his lot in life. He came across a rotten sea melon and imagined ripping into its rind with claws like his fathers, or teeth like the boy Gnash's. He held it up and scratched at it with his nails, which barely made a mark. He then bit into it

ALGEN

in rage, imagining his teeth were sharper. His soft teeth broke the skin and rotten juice welled into his mouth. He threw the melon against a wall and watched it explode, then bent over and retched. When he looked up, he saw Naylis standing above him.

"I heard you're mute now. Probably for the best, I could never get you to shut up before." He smiled a sympathetic smile and looked over to the stone wall where a large dark stain showed wet and sticky, with pulp dripping down onto the ground. "What did that sea melon ever do to you?"

Algen didn't answer. Even if he could speak, he wouldn't have known what to say. Instead, he elected to give a sad shrug. Naylis came close to him and gently held his chin, tilting Algen's head to the side so he could get a better look at the barnacle growths on his neck.

"Did it hurt to get those?" His eyes scanned, studying the growths."

Algen nodded, then grabbed Naylis' arm and starting rubbing on his skin.

"Ya, it gets pretty hot in there, I know." He pointed to the manta ray wings on his arms and face." These hurt like buggers."

Algen motioned to his throat.

"Your throat burned? That's not normally what happens."

Not normal. The words rang in his head. *It wasn't my gills growing, it was my larynx disintegrating.* He felt the tears begin to well up again.

"Hey, none of that," said Naylis. "You'll be a warrior, yet."

Algen looked at him, confused. Naylis rolled his eyes.

"Have you forgotten? I'm a soldier in King Caraq's Royal Army. One day I may become a knight, and a knight can choose any man to be his squire."

Algen's eyes widened. *Yes,* he thought. *Yes, that's right. He's right!* He wanted to thank Naylis, even hug him, but he couldn't bring himself to move. He'd always imagined he'd be his father's squire, to fight alongside him in battle. Before, he had wanted to prove himself to his father to honour him, but now he wanted to prove himself to his father to spite him. Naylis gave him a pat on the shoulder.

"My troop is moving out in the morning. The King has a mission for us. I think your father will be coming too."

Good, thought Algen, although a part of him still wished he were going as well. Naylis smiled and moved past him, patting Algen on his back as he went. Algen watched as he disappeared into the night, then, with nowhere else to go, he walked off in the opposite direction, passing by dark homes and closed markets, past quiet feeding tanks and sleepy guard posts. He kept moving until he reached the very edge of the dome. Placing a webbed hand on the glass, he looked off into the distant ocean. The water was dark and murky, with sand from the ocean floor moving haphazardly in the current. Without the lightfish peppering the waters, he wouldn't have been able to see past a few feet, but they were out in droves tonight and the water was lit up like what he'd heard of the stars of the night sky looking like on a clear day.

Around the glass dome, Algen watched colourful fish swim in massive schools, followed closely by great predators of the deep. Algen noticed a barnacle growing on the side of the dome and instinctively touched his neck. Again, he felt a stab of anger crossing his mind and attempted to peel the growth from his skin. When it would not come off, he slumped down and rested his back against the edge of the world. Algen's mind wandered as he thought about what to what he would do next. On the morrow, he supposed he may as well venture out into the water for the first time, now that he had his gills... if he even had his gills; about one in a thousand were morphed without them. *With my luck, that's probably me.*

But before all of that, he needed to find himself a job. Everyone over sixteen years living under the dome had one. If you didn't have a job, you didn't live under the dome; that was the rule, plain and simple. Algen had known a few morphs in the past who had chosen to leave the dome on their own accord, preferring to find their own way in the vast ocean rather than working for their King. Algen didn't feel that lifestyle would suit him very well. He had no claws to catch fish, no teeth to defend himself, and his new colouring made him stick out like a sore thumb for any would-be predator. Most new morphs were given positions by the King himself within minutes of exiting the chamber. But not Algen. The King had been so disgusted that he had forgotten to give him one. That or he didn't care enough to. Algen was left to find his own.

He found that he couldn't sleep that night, and by the time he was finally starting to nod off, the lightfish were being snuffed out by the morning sunrays cutting like orange knives into the water. The dark ocean around him slowly turned to a brilliant golden colour and the glass began to glow. Algen sighed and stood, knowing there was no point in continuing to try and rest. Out of the corner of his eye he saw a jet of bubbles cut the water and turned to watch as troops of the King's warriors rocketed out into the surrounding ocean. They were far away, but he thought he spied Naylis, though it was unlikely. Nine more jettisons followed as band after band was deployed. Algen thought for a moment about sneaking into their ranks, but the idea died instantly when he remembered what Gnash had done to the guard in the throne room. *How do you think they'll treat an intruder?* Instead, Algen began walking up and down the streets looking for an open shop willing to give him a job.

It soon became apparent to Algen that your morph mattered much more than he initially thought. He found out through rejection after rejection that the kinds of morphs you hired was a measure of status for your business, which left a barnacled reject like him well out of the running. Being a mute didn't help either. A lot of the time the shop owner couldn't even understand that Algen was asking for a job. Market after market, he was turned away by every vendor, until finally he came upon the royal kitchens. With nothing to lose, he ascended the cobblestone stairs and grabbed the big bronze knocker, hitting it loudly against the wooden door.

When no one answered, he chanced another knock. And then another. Finally, the big door swung open and the head chef met his gaze, introducing herself as Korra. When Algen did not introduce himself in return, she nearly left him right there and then, if not for Algen grabbing her arm and stopping her. She looked back to him, annoyed. Algen tried motioning to his mouth and his throat, desperately attempting to explain his situation in the only way he could. Korra stared back at him intently, until a light sparked in her eyes and Algen knew she understood. She was red skinned from head to toe; slender, with long sharp nails and webbing between her bony fingers. Her head was void of hair, but instead had a fin sprouting from her scalp. She sighed.

"I don't like hiring new meat here." She grimaced, showing the sharp white teeth that filled her mouth. "But lucky for you I don't have much choice. The King's decided to host all his Lords here within a fortnight and I'll need all the help I can get."

Algen gave her a smile and an appreciative nod. The head chef only rolled her eyes and shuffled him in. Within, the inner kitchens were hot and stale, smelling of old fish guts and bad seaweed. Korra pointed to a large pot in the far corner of the room.

"You want a job? You clean the pots and pans. Be fast, do a good job, and maybe I'll even pay you."

Algen hurried off without a second glance, picking up a scrubbing sponge and scouring the iron dishes. The metal was caked with burned bits of meat that took forever to chip off, but he wasn't about to quit. *If I fail here, then I will truly be out of options.* Sweat beaded on his brow as the minutes turned into hours. Chefs and serving boys entered and exited, bringing the King's Court their supper, returning again with empty plates, and all the while Korra surveyed the room from her spot nestled in the corner, making sure to test every morsel of food before it reached the people in the hall.

A young man who looked wholly inexperienced presented her with a plate of cooked shark fins. She picked one up and took a bite. Algen watched her expression turn sour as she spit the meat into the man's face, and knocked the platter from his hands as he attempted to wipe his cheeks. She pointed one of her talons at his nose.

"RAW!" she screamed at him. "This is your King we are serving, not some lowlife beggar with no taste buds!"

Algen watched as she shoved him back into the kitchen. He was beginning to feel the heat getting to him. The kitchens were directly positioned around the base of the natural steam geysers that heated the King's Dome. The kitchen used the vents to cook food, yet with no way of turning them off, the exhaust ended up cooking the chefs as well. Algen found himself wiping his brow just as often as he wiped the dishes that he was cleaning. There were no windows in the kitchens, so he had no idea what time it was until Korra came over and tapped him on the shoulder. He looked up and wiped the moisture from his eyes.

"Good work today, boy." She flipped him a small coin, which he caught and held to his chest. "Go home and rest, be back here tomorrow at sunrise."

Algen nodded and walked out into the streets, immediately overwhelmed by the cool air that greeted him. He smiled and sighed. Algen was surprised to find that the light from the sun above the surface had faded, and the water had turned dark again. He began on his way back home, but paused and instead turned back towards the kitchens. He waited for a moment to see if anyone was watching before sneaking back in and hiding behind one of the geysers. The hot, watery air that billowed out over him made him sleepy, and soon he was off dreaming. In his mind, he was still in the transformation chamber, and this time when he stepped out, he was a great beast, with rows of sharp teeth and fins tipped with great talons. And most of all, he dreamed of his father seeing him. In the dream, his father smiled.

CHAPTER 13

JOSHYA III

Joshya stood solemnly in the centre of the throne room, trying to look as princely as he could for his father seated before him. To Joshya's left stood the burly brickmaker, who's name Joshya had learned to be Lanoss, holding a mole fur to his head. The bandage was stained dark from dried blood. King Artemis sat before them on his throne, a seat ornately shaped from a rich red clay and surrounded by long stalagmite spires decorated by expert craftsmen with intricately inlaid patterns and etchings. His father looked grimmer than Joshya had ever seen him, stroking at the scruff of his beard. Then the king sighed and leaned forwards.

"Tell me exactly what happened," he began.

Lanoss cleared his throat, and shifted nervously from one foot to the other.

"Your Grace, I was working on th'bricks for the new chamber you'd asked for... when I heard this noise coming from out in the hall, you see, then –"

"What kind of noise was it?" the king interrupted.

Lanoss was set aback. "I..." he stammered. "It was a shuffling noise, like someone was... searching for something." He paused, seeing if the King would chime in again. When he did not, Lanoss continued. "I left my workshop and found a man rubbing his hands along the wall. I walked over and tapped him on the shoulder, but he turned around and knocked me on my arse. Made me drop my mallet too. When I tried to get up, he picked it up and gave me a good whack." He pointed with his free hand at the bandage.

The King gave a nod and Lanoss continued.

"Then, the bastard pulled a dirk on me and tried to hack my chest open. I was barely able to reach my mallet in time to defend myself." He looked over to Joshya. "And that's when your boy came in. If it weren't for him, Your Grace, I'd be a goner."

King Artemis shifted his attention to his son. "Speak Joshya. What happened once you arrived?"

Joshya recounted the events as he remembered them. The King's expression never wavered, his attention never faltered. Although, at the end, Joshya thought he may have seen a hint of relief.

"Did either of you see the face of the assailant?" The King asked.

Joshya and Lanoss answered in unison, but when Lanoss said "no" while Joshya said "yes", all eyes fell to him.

"Well... part of it," he clarified. "He had straight black hair that covered his face, and a large pointed nose." Joshya then pulled the mysterious object from his pocket. "I found this on the ground close to where the attack happened."

His father motioned and Joshya brought it up to him. King Artemis studied the object for a good while, and without looking up he said: "Lanoss, you may go."

The big man looked relieved. "Thank you, Your Grace." Lanoss gave a slight bow but it was obvious his balance was still somewhat off from the head wound. He disappeared out into the tunnel.

King Artemis motioned for his guards to leave as well, leaving just father and son together in the huge room. When they were alone, his father gave Joshya a half smile.

"You did well, Joshya." Joshya blushed and his father stood from his seat and patted him on the shoulder. "You saved the life of my best mason." He held up the mysterious object and fanned it out, running a dusty finger down its spine.

"Do you know what this is?" When Joshya shook his head no, he continued. "I'm not surprised." The King placed the object beside him on the armrest of his throne. "I want you to understand how serious a matter this is. Go home to your mother and sister. Tell them it will be some time before I'm home. I need to consult with my council."

Joshya nodded and started out the room, but his father stopped him.

"Once you have told them, come back here. I'd like you here for this."

Joshya's heart fluttered, and he rushed off with eagerness.

☆ ☆ ☆

When Joshya returned to the throne room, his father had adorned himself in his armour; thick gilded iron, gold inlaid, with black opal wrought in the shape of a splayed scorpion on the chest. He sat upon his throne with a sword across his lap, running the ball of his thumb along its edge. Joshya walked the length of the room and stood beside his father. Torchlight illuminated the smoothed floor of the large room, but the ceiling was so high that the light couldn't reach the apex. Joshya oft stared up into the darkness and wondered how far up it went. Sometimes, he wondered what he would find beyond. Though today he did not have much time to daydream, for he had a role to play.

His father had sent royal pages into the tunnels with a summons for any citizen with Corvusi blood. There were eighteen total citizens of the Scorpio Tunnels that could trace their lineage back to the Corvusi loyalists of old. This was the first time Joshya's father had asked he be included in a royal summons. His stomach fluttered with anticipation. One by one, the summoned began to arrive. The first to show was Galbard, known in the tunnels as the "Baby Crow," although at eighty-one years many had taken to calling him "Old Baby Crow." Galbard was the first child to be born of a Corvusi father after the retreat into the tunnels. His own daughter, Selsi, arrived along with him, interlocking her arm with her father's to help him into the throne room. Galbard made a rough attempt to kneel before his king and Joshya could hear the cracking in his knees from all the way across the room. The old man got only halfway to the ground before aborting the motion and standing up again with the help of his daughter.

Soon afterwards, they were greeted by Tult, a squire of eight years who seemed elated to be summoned to the King's presence. Rather than kneeling, the young boy elected to give the king a hug. Joshya was worried that his father would push the boy away, but was happy to see his father smile at the gesture. Not long after that, a total of thirteen more citizens that Joshya had either never seen or never bothered to learn the names of entered. Joshya watched as they murmured amongst themselves, obviously confused as to why they were being summoned.

Finally, the last two arrived: one young and one old. The younger was Himrel, Joshya's friend. The older was Himrel's grandfather, Sir Orrel, also known as the Half-Crow. Like the Baby Crow, Orrel's father fought in the war of the Crow King, a fact he wouldn't soon let anyone forget. When he received his knighthood near forty years ago, back when the Scorpios still bothered to knight their warriors, Orrel chose to crest himself with both the Crow of Corvus and the Scorpion of Scorpio, earning him the nickname of "Half-Crow." His pride for his father's faction had more than a little rubbed off on both his son and grandson. Himrel's father, however, had perished two years ago in a tunnel collapse. Orrel had been so furious that he'd stormed in on court to confront the King. He demanded infamously that those with Corvusi blood should be allowed to return to the surface because "Crows are meant to fly, not to be trapped in a cage deep underground." King Artemis refused the notion, saying any trip to the surface could jeopardize their position, as no one knew if the Corvusi army were still based atop their world. The Half-Crow had been hostile to the royal family ever since.

Joshya guessed that his father's suspicions lay primarily with Sir Orrel, and he'd only called upon the other eighteen as to not raise suspicions. If anyone was bold enough to attempt to murder a Scorpio, the likelihood lay entirely with the Half-Crow.

"My friends!" the King started, arms outstretched. "I trust you've all been well?"

Those before him nodded begrudgingly; none seemed too enthusiastic to be there, except of course for Tult. The King then turned his attention to Joshya's friend.

"Himrel!" he called warmly. "How are you, my boy?"

Himrel maintained his usual stoic demeanour. "I've been well, Your Grace."

Joshya gave Himrel a friendly smile, but his friend didn't move his gaze from the King.

"Why have you called us here?" asked one of the men Joshya didn't know.

The King wasted no time getting to the point. "There has been an attack within our tunnels," he began. "I apologize for the inquisition; however, I must know what has transpired. I need to know where all of you were last night, in the Hour of the Rabbit."

"And why do you suspect one of us?" asked another man Joshya did not know.

"I have my reasons," answered the King, noticeably colder in his response.

Joshya suddenly wondered if bringing them all in together had been a smart idea on his father's part. If even half of these men were hostile, they'd have no issue overpowering the King's two guards. Suddenly, Joshya wished he had thought to bring a weapon. *No changing that now.*

His father started by questioning Old Baby Crow. Galbard looked as though he'd been slighted.

"I'm an old man, my King. I couldn't even walk myself here without the help of my dear daughter. Do you think I could stage any manner of an attack?"

King Artemis shook his head, and moved to the Old Crow's Daughter. Selsi also denied her involvement. The King dismissed them both from his court. For each person his father questioned, he seemed to get no closer to an answer, until only Himrel and the Half-Crow remained with them in the great hall. Joshya understood the wisdom in his father's actions.

He'd gotten the two most likely suspects in a room alone without raising either of their suspicions. Before the King could even begin to ask them any questions, Himrel began to speak.

"I had nothing to do with this either, Your Grace. I was with my girl until you summoned me - honest."

"Shut up, Himrel," cautioned his grandfather. "Your Grace, I am almost two decades older than you so do not take me for a fool. I was knighted by your father while you were still crawling. I know you kept us for last because you suspect we were somehow connected. Tell me why, or I leave right now." He crossed his muscled arms and scowled.

The way that Sir Orrel spoke to the King was utterly disrespectful. The pettier of the other kings across the Starscape would have imprisoned someone for such impudence, but King Artemis only sat and listened, letting the slights wash over him. Without saying a word, he produced the strange black object from his lap and held it up for the Half-Crow and Himrel to see.

"Do you know what this is?"

"It's a feather, what of it?" the Half-Crow spat the words.

King Artemis opened his grip and let the feather flutter to the floor. "A black feather, more specifically. The kind of black feather you'd find adorning the majority of Corvusi armour, and you, my good Sir, are the only one in the tunnels to own such a set."

The Half-Crow reddened like a beetroot. "Are you suggesting that I donned my father's armour and attacked one of our people?" Joshya could hear the restraint in his voice. Likely if anyone else had accused Sir Orrel in such a blatant way they would already be on the floor with a broken jaw.

"The thing about living in tunnels," the King continued, "is that only a finite number of people can commit a crime and no one has anywhere to run. The King stood and clapped his hands. Just seconds later, a dozen guards came rushing into the hall and surrounded Himrel and the Half-Crow. The King's demeanor suddenly darkened and the fire entered his eyes.

"One of you did this, and until I find out which of you it was, I am placing you both in the containment chamber. "I do not wish to harm you so please do not resist." He waved a hand and two guards flanked each of them.

"What!" cried Half-Crow, as a guard forced his arms behind his back. The veins of his neck bulged. "This is an outrage!"

THUMP

The King looked around. "What was that?"

Joshya felt dirt fall on his shoulder. Puzzled, he brushed it off and looked up into the darkness. And then he saw the ceiling for the first time, as it came crashing down on top of him.

CHAPTER 14

GRELHYM II

Grelhym reached down to his belt and fumbled at the buckle clasping the hilt of his squire's dagger. His fingers trembled, but somehow, they were able to wrench it free. As he raised his hand in a feeble attempt to strike, the beady-eyed man grabbed his wrist and twisted, until Grelhym had no choice but to let go. The knife fell to the ground and clattered on the wood of the stable floor. With fear in his eyes, Grelhym looked at the beady blue-eyed man standing in front of him. His breath was sour and it filled Grelhym's nose with a stench of an intensity he had never before known. He looked around, but everyone else was gone from the area surrounding the stable. His heart sank as he realized suddenly that he was truly without help. The beady-eyed man reached down, still holding Grelhym's arm, and picked up his blade. Smiling, the man held the tip to Grelhym's chest and poked.

"Move," he said, his voice as rough as his skin.

I guess I don't have a choice. Grelhym started forward. As he turned, the point of the knife moved to press firmly against the small of his back. Grelhym was led across the yard to a cellar door on the side of the Roundhall. Forcing Grelhym to his knees with a shove, the man made him open the hatch. Grelhym did as he was bid. And when he was told to leap into the darkness below, he did that to.

When his eyes finally adjusted, he was surprised to find that the cellar stretched much further down than it seemed from the surface. He heard the sound of feet hitting soil behind him and felt the knife return to his back. Slowly, Grelhym began to move down the long, dark tunnel before him. The path wound and twisted, until finally he found himself entering a large chamber beneath what could only have been the center of the Roundhall. As he walked towards the centre of the stone chamber, Grelhym had to catch himself before almost falling into a massive gaping sinkhole. Stumbling backwards, he fell hard onto his ass and attempted to crawl backwards, but the beady-eyed man kicked him before he could.

"That ragged old fool Rygar won't miss you, I'm sure."

Grelhym's heart pounded, his hands buzzing with adrenaline and anxiety. Without thinking, he grabbed hold of the man's leg and yanked him to the ground. The man gave a soft yelp as his knee hit the rocky floor and gave a soft pop. All at once the dagger was spinning across the stony floor. The man cried out in rage and pain, clasping desperately at his knee-

GRELHYM

cap. Grelhym panicked and began to crawl after the weapon, scrambling on his hands and knees, scraping them against the hard ground as he went. Just as his fingers clasped the hilt, he felt a pressure on his back. His attacker was already on top of him, breathing down his neck. Grelhym felt his fingers stretch around the knife and he squeezed. It took all his strength, but he was able to roll himself onto his side despite having the weight of a full-grown man atop him. Closing his eyes, Grelhym began to flail his hand wildly. The first few swings hit nothing but air, but the fourth snagged some cloth, and the fifth punched deep into flesh. The man screamed, moving himself off of Grelhym in a jerking motion. Grelhym opened his eyes. In front of him, the man was again on his knees, looking down at his forearm where blood was spurting out from a deep puncture wound.

"Bas..." the man said, but his voice was too weak to say anything more. And as the man's beady blue eyes began to flutter, his words trailed off. The man's face had grown pale as ice and his sleeve was darkened red from elbow to finger.

Grelhym was taken over by fear, confusion, anger, and ten other emotions at once. He lunged forward, stabbing over and over and over until his shirt was wet and slick. Before him lay his assailant; or his victim, it depended on how you looked at it. The corpse lay still, thick red water welling like a fountain from the stone where it lay. Breathing deeply, Grelhym found his feet. Worried that someone would find the body, he dragged it to the lip of the hole, smearing blood across the stone as he went, and gave it a shove in. He never heard the body hit the

GRELHYM

bottom, only watched as it drowned in the darkness of the pit. Then came the vomit. That never reached the bottom either.

Grelhym wiped his mouth and stood. For the first time he noticed the bats hanging from the ceiling. Their chittering voices seemed to be mocking him. Grelhym tuned them out as best he could, his focus solely on the chasm before him. Only after his wits began to come back to him did he notice the wetness dripping from his tunic. He looked down to find himself soaked in hot blood. Panicked, he ripped the fabric off over his head and threw it down before him, watching it flutter as it fell. Then came his pants, shoes, and his socks. He spat on his hands and attempted to rub any blood caked on his skin, but instead it only smeared. At that point he even noticed the taste of blood in his mouth.

Finally, after his skin was rubbed raw, Grelhym felt confident enough to return to the surface. His mind was already filling with possible scenarios, excuses really, for his appearance. *I'll tell them I fell,* he thought. *That I cut myself bad on the way down. That I fell on my knife.* But he had no wounds, no proof that had happened. He knew he would have to think of something else.

He must have gotten turned around at some point. Grelhym found himself resurfacing through a similar hatch much further from the Roundhall than where he had entered. The rocks beneath his feet were black as the night and hot to the touch. Grelhym's heart skipped a beat when he realized he had was out in the badlands. He froze. The other squires had

GRELHYM

exchanged stories of wild men that lived out here, ones that were cold-blooded and hairless, that only ate their own droppings due to the lack of food, but were always on the hunt for fresh meat. The air swirled around him and he smelled the foul smog. His eyes watering, Grelhym turned back into the cave below, coughing. This time he found the right way out.

It was still night as he ran across the yard. He threw open a side door to the hall and slipped inside. Grelhym entered the bathhouse through the servant's door, walking as much in the shadows as he could. He breathed a sigh of relief when he saw the four empty steaming tubs. Grelhym slipped out of his undergarments and slid into the water, wasting no time before scooping the water up and over his chest and down his arms. Sighing, he dunked his head under the water and scoured his fingers through the tangles in his chestnut hair. He stayed under for a whole minute before splashing back to the surface and shaking off the water. He opened his eyes and wiped water from his brow, but stopped when he saw the torch flicker in a sharp gust of wind from outside. He sunk down into the water, dipping his chin below the lip of the massive tub. He listened as heavy footsteps descended the small stone staircase into the room. Whoever entered yawned loudly and sniffed, then cracked his knuckles. Grelhym risked a small peek over the edge with one eye.

The man who had entered stood with his back to Grelhym. He was almost six and a half feet tall with skin the colour of cocoa and rippling muscles down the length of his back. The

GRELHYM

man lay a broadsword against the stone wall under the torch and hung his chainmail jerkin on a wooden peg. He turned, only a little, but it was enough to cause Grelhym to reflexively duck back down. He winced as his movement caused the water to splash and he worried the noise would carry, though luckily the man did not move. Grelhym heard the heavy splash as the large man entered the pool furthest from him. He risked another look. The large man was holding a razor, and was running it carefully over the top of his head, shaving the thin layer of fuzz from his scalp.

Another man entered and the torchlight flickered. This man was smaller, with the light beige skin of someone from the Leo faction. The two men shared a glance and seemed to recognize one another. The bigger man placed his razor on the lip of the tub, pointing to his jerkin on the peg. The Leo reached into the pocket and pulled out a small vial. Nodding, the bigger man returned to his business, as the smaller man left.

It was near twenty minutes before Grelhym was finally alone once again. His heart raced with the anxiety of being seen, and he almost retched again when he could finally relax. Raising from the tub like a boiled crab, Grelhym decided not to redon his soiled undergarments. Instead he took a woolen robe from a side room and slipped it over his dripping body. The robe was fleece and white as snow. He knew that being seen in it would surely mean a beating from any of the great Lords in attendance, but being seen nude would have meant a worse beating. There was no chance of slipping back into the Squires'

GRELHYM

Quarters at this hour without being noticed, so he instead began searching the hall for a quiet corner to go unnoticed until morning. Twice he was almost spotted by roaming guards, but avoided detection. Grelhym eventually decided on one of the watchtowers spanning the outer rim of the hall. This particular one was broken on one side, and was no longer garrisoned. It was the perfect place to curl up without fear of being found. Listening to the gentle breeze, he was soon asleep.

As the sun crested the horizon, Grelhym's eyes broke their seal and opened. He rubbed at his face and noticed that his robe had opened, and his manhood was flopping before him. *Good thing no one can see me.*

"Never imagined I'd see you like this, Grels!"

The voice jolted him awake, the robe flapping at his hips as Grelhym leapt to his feet. The boy standing before him had a grin that could span a mountain range.

"Burmott!" Grelhym exclaimed.

Burmott was one of Lord Rygar's attendants. Like Grelhym, he had been brought along as a retainer, though Burmott's duties revolved more around maintenance of the Lord's supplies where Grelhym attended the Lord himself. Often Grelhym had been jealous of Burmott's duties, as the other boy rarely had to converse with Lord Rygar himself.

"What are you doing here?" Grelhym thought he must be dreaming.

Burmott laughed. "I think that's more a question I should be asking you! Don't you think?" He was holding a hammer and pointed it to Grelhym's crotch.

Grelhym blushed and covered himself.

"And a thank you may be in order," Burmott continued. "Twice I shooed away the other boys who were sent up here to help me, lest they see you here."

Grelhym was still groggy from sleep. "Help you with what?"

Burmott sighed. "In case you hadn't noticed, this tower's seen better days. A few of the squires were sent to help fix it. Imagine my surprise when I came up here to find none other than Grels lying tackle-out in my tower!"

Grelhym looked out over the ledge to the surrounding landscape. Out in the distance, he watched the smog roll across the badlands. A sinking feeling filled his stomach as the events of the previous night returned to him.

Burmott pulled the cork from a small potion flask and poured a viscous brown liquid over a cracked wooden beam. The syrup seeped into the breaks and filled them, leaving the beam looking next to new.

"Shouldn't you be at the delegation?" Burmott asked, not looking up from his work.

Yes. He thought. *But not until I'm presentable.*

Burmott must have known what he was thinking. Pausing, he pulled his tunic from over his head and a surcoat from his sack, and tossed the clothing to Grelhym.

"You owe me."

 GRELHYM

Grelhym allowed himself a smile. "I know."

The delegation was well underway when Grelhym entered the hall. Luckily, no one seemed to notice him as he snuck into the stands. Two of the delegates were locked in a heated argument and the others seemed to be trying to calm them down.

"Swine!" yelled a man in a burnished bronze helm crested with a centaur. "How dare you compare a loss of a few water fowl to the loss of an entire island?"

Another man was pounding his fist on the table. The long-braided hairs of his upper lip and chin jiggled with each strike. "Those water fowl are what sustains half my people, everyone from my rivers to my lakes." He paused for a moment and stared at the man. "And you will regret calling me swine, *Sir*." He spat out the last word like he didn't want the sound to touch his lips.

"ENOUGH!" Meikal yelled as loud as he could, but his old voice cracked and sent him into a fit of coughing. One of his pages brought him a pail and Grelhym saw him spit up a glob of phlegm then look at it in disgust. No one seemed to be paying the respected mediator any mind. The two kept up their banter while the rest grumbled their agreements. Meikal whispered something to the page who'd come and the boy disappeared. Two of Meikal's men at arms appeared in his place, each moving swiftly to one of the problem delegates.

"Get your hands off me!" the centaur knight yelled as the guard grabbed hold of him. But that only seemed to make him grip tighter. The centaur knight continued to struggle until the guardsman twisted his arm behind his back. The knight screamed and Grelhym winced, thinking the arm was broken. It seemed that it wasn't, as the knight quieted and allowed himself to be led from the hall. The second man went much more quietly.

That was when Grelhym noticed him. Sitting in the stands behind a delegate with a dog on his banner, sat the large dark-skinned man. Grelhym almost didn't recognize him. In the bathhouse, he'd been able to see the man's rippling muscles. Here however, he was dressed in a gown. From neck to ankle, he was covered and looked no stronger than a merchant.

King Terreon stood. "I would like to reiterate. This is a civil parley. Put your personal vendettas aside. Anyone else who engages in any more such outbursts and they forfeit their claim on the artifact *immediately*."

A murmur of acknowledgement rose from the room as Terreon sat back down. A man at the far side of the table raised his voice.

"May I speak openly, King Terreon?"

Terreon looked more than a little annoyed.

"You may, Lord Amalon."

The man stood, his fingers dancing across the table. Grelhym saw that the man's eyes were frosted over in a milky film, as if they were made of ice. *Blind as a bat*, he thought.

 GRELHYM

Amalon turned his head in the general direction of Terreon, though he was a bit off.

"We are all servants of different kings here; some of you are even kings yourselves. But we were all chosen to represent the best interests of our own factions." He tapped a knuckle against the banner displayed behind him. "See that? I may not be able to, but I know that that's a dolphin. What it means is that I represent every man, woman, and child who wears that symbol." He lowered his hand. "Now I would presume, Your Grace, that behind you is a banner depicting a brown archer on red, am I correct?"

King Terreon raised an eyebrow. "You are."

"So why, I ask, are you legislating to me as to how I can and cannot represent my people. If I must make a fuss, I will, even if it means I must duel one of you." He shook a finger at Terreon, though again he was a few chairs off.

"If you can face the right way, that is!" yelled a fat man under a whale banner.

Laughter broke from the table and stands alike. Even Terreon cracked a smile. All but Lord Amalon. Terreon calmly waited until the laughter stopped before responding.

"Lord Amalon, I will answer your question as plainly as I possibly can. You may be old and blind, but your spirit hasn't yet left you. I presume you have sons to inherit the lands of Swallowtail Rush once you pass."

"Three, Your Grace."

"And without this artifact, there may not be any land left for them, am I correct?" Lord Amalon stayed quiet and Terreon continued. "We are on an unclaimed planet in unclaimed territory where no one faction holds dominion. The war for this one small artifact could tear the Starscape apart. I stopped that from happening by calling this parley, or do you not remember the armies building out there in the badlands less than a moon ago?"

Lord Amalon continued to hold his tongue, but Grelhym knew he remembered. Truth be told, so did Grelhym. When he'd arrived with Lord Rygar and the rest of the Fornax preceding, he'd witnessed huge armies stationed across the black stony landscape. Banners flew all round, with war tents and temporary barricades littering the ground. The smog had masked the further armies from sight, but Grelhym knew that the camps must have stretched far into the distance. The Fornax armies had not yet been there, but it was only a matter of time. Grelhym wondered: If no parley had been called, would he be out there on the rocks, sword in hand, fighting for some ancient junk in the ground? *Or dying?* The thought unnerved him.

The huge doors swung open again and the centaur knight was back, this time with sword in hand. His armor was covered in blood. A few people gasped. Meikal stared at him with eyes like daggers.

"Sir Ambrose! Weapons are prohibited at this parley!"

"Exactly." He smiled and strode forward.

 GRELHYM

"Guards!" cried Meikal, and a few of the men at arms ran from the stands, but they were much further than the disgruntled knight. Ambrose reached the man who sat in the closest seat to the door, one with a peacock on his banner. The man leapt from his seat and attempted to grab Sir Ambrose's wrists.

The knight pushed him back. "I want Terreon, not you!"

When the peacock lord thrust himself forward again, Ambrose stuck him in the gut with the tip of his sword. The man fell back in his chair clutching his side as the guards surrounded them. King Terreon was among them.

"Stand down. He wants me." Terreon swiped a sword from the closest guard's hands.

Despite only wearing a leather surcoat today, he looked twice as intimidating as the enraged knight. Sir Ambrose simply stared. Terreon grimaced and outstretched his arms.

"You wanted me? Come take me then!"

Sir Ambrose raced forward and their swords met, then pulled apart and clashed together again and again. The sound of metal on metal filled the hall. None of the other delegates moved, except for the man under the peacock banner, who thrashed wildly on the ground. His medic was next to him, trying to pour a greenish yellow liquid onto the wound.

Sir Ambrose cried out and thrust his sword overhand, as Terreon easily stepped out of range. The King then swung above his head, cutting the centaur crest from the knight's helm. Ambrose felt at the top of his helm, and furiously ripped it off. His cheeks were cherry red and a vein had popped in his neck. Screaming, he charged at the King, but Terreon met his swing, knocking the sword from his hand. Then, in one swift motion, Terreon brought up a hidden dagger in his other hand and drove it sideways into Ambrose's temple. The point cut clean though to the other side of his head. The knight's eyes rolled back into his head as his knees gave out from under him. The room fell silent, apart from the cries of the injured lord below the peacock banner.

Meikal stood and peered down from his seat. "Terreon."

"Enough, Meikal. I told you I would not tolerate such behavior."

"That knife." He pointed to the blood-soaked instrument hanging from the King's fingers.

No weapons at the table, Grelhym realized. *What was he doing with a knife?*

Terreon closed his eyes and grit his teeth. "SEAL THE DOOR!"

CHAPTER 15

DERRON III

That night, the temperature dropped lower than it ever had before on their journey thus far. Waking, Derron found drool frosted in his beard. He stretched, and beat the hairs on his chin until the ice was gone. Then, he grabbed his jacket and laced it up around his chest. Melwick had done a lackluster job of stitching it back to its former quality. They had no duck down to refill what he'd lost, but at least the wind could no longer seep in. As long as he avoided doing anything too strenuous the patch would hold. *Out here? Everything I do will be strenuous,* Derron thought, frowning.

Outside the lean-to, the sun was yet again hidden behind a thick cloud cover. Light powdery snow drifted from the heavens and blanketed the world in a soft, white coating. Sitting with a wool quilt over his shoulders beyond the edge of camp was Mollens, staring intently at a tree. Derron walked over to him, and saw the caterpillar Mollens was watching, slowly ascending the bark, seemingly unaffected by the cold.

"Do you ever think about how strange it is that life can prevail over whatever nature throws at it?" said Mollens, without looking up.

Derron wasn't sure if Mollens was talking to him or just out loud. He picked the caterpillar from the bark and placed it on the ground, then pointed to a nearby tree where a puffy bird sat eyeing the bug.

"Sometimes everyone needs a little help. What's on your mind, Mollens?"

The boy rose to his feet and dusted the flakes from his trousers. His fingers were pale with the cold and dirt was crusted under his nails.

"I don't think we're ever getting home."

Derron frowned. "Not if we're in that mindset, no." He placed a hand on his friend's shoulder and moved him closer to the fire that Anthon had blazing at the centre of camp. He sat Mollens down on a stump and handed him a strip of dried meat. The slab was hard and almost black, but still relatively edible.

"Eat," he said. "You're hungry and it's affecting you more than you know."

Mollens took a strained bite and ripped the meat with his teeth with a considerable amount of effort. Anthon walked over and passed them each a steaming bowl.

"If you're hungry, you don't want that thing. Here, you'll love my leek soup." He grinned.

Derron looked at the steaming water in his hands. "Leek soup" was a stretch to be sure. In reality, it was more aptly called "boiling water with hunks of green". He hoped that the hunks were at very least truly leek.

Mollens only frowned. "I'm not hungry."

That worried Derron. Losing faith out here could mean a death sentence.

"We are close to the end of our travels. By moon's turn... one of them at least... we'll be on our way home, but if we quit now, in ten years' time there may not be a home to go back to."

Mollens looked up at him like a whipped puppy. "I trust you, Captain. I know you'll lead us home." He raised the bowl of boiling water to his lips and drank fully, only stopping once for air, before emptying the bowl completely.

Alymer and Melwick had already packed their tents. They were to take half of the men with them to the West. The others Derron would lead North, to where Melwick had noted something at the top of a steep ridge on the northern shore of the lake.

Derron stood and gave Mollens a squeeze on the shoulder. "Pack your things, son."

Within the hour, Derron found himself saying farewell to half the men he had spent the last six months with. And just like that, they were off, two parties where there had been one. Derron felt naked without Melwick's council, Alymer's wisdom, and Skoma's skill. Often in the earliest days of their journey, before they had known for certain that the region was unin-habited, Skoma had stood as Derron's protector. Now instead, he found himself flanked by a loping coyote, one that smelled of wet dog and bore a snarled tooth poking through its gums.

Will attempted for a while to walk of his own accord, using a dead branch as a crutch, but that did not last. Before mid-day Roman was back to carrying him. It was shortly after that that Derron called a halt to the procession. Atop a sloping hill, Derron could see for a mile around, but as the snowfall mount-ed, the visibility dwindled. Anthon knelt to kindle a fire, but Derron motioned for him to stop. It would not be a long break, just enough to gain their composure and orient themselves in the right direction. Derron took sanctuary under a massive pine with a bowed trunk. The canopy gave him enough respite from the drifting snow to concentrate a moment. His new pet sauntered up to the trunk and urinated. Derron unrolled the map and judged that they would have another half day before reaching their destination; on the morrow they were to recon-vene with the rest of their group by the lakeshore.

Across from Derron, a lone flower poked out above the mounting snow. Smiling, he reached down and picked it. He knew it from his homeworld: A small purple plant called the winter thistle that grew year-round, even in freezing tempera-tures. Derron rolled it in his hand. The flower reminded him of home. As a boy, his father had made sure to take time off from his royal duties to go on long hikes with his children. Derron

DERRON

and his three younger brothers had spent many long days scaling the foothills under the watchful eye of their father, though after the others had become tired, the king would take his eldest son just a little higher - just the two of them. Garron the Grey, he was known as to all in the Kingdom, but Derron had never seen anything but youth in his father, a light in his eye that could never be shaken.

On the final trip they had taken out, his brothers had turned back after three hours, but the two of them had spent another few to reach the summit of the highest hill. The air was cold with the first signs of autumn and the colourful meadow flowers had all lost their petals. All except the winter thistle, whose purple and white centre still quivered in the breeze. His father knelt and picked one, handing it to Derron. "You will rule these hills and beyond one day." He spoke calmly and slowly, handing the thistle to Derron.

Derron smiled at the memory and placed the thistle into his pocket. Behind him, Roman was attempting to free himself from a mud pit.

He wondered how his second son, Croft, was handling the situation in Leo territory. His father was able to end their slaving practices for a brief time, but after King Garron's death they had returned to the practice with more fervor than ever before. He had sent Croft as an envoy two years ago to halt the practice. The last letter he received, Croft was in Leo Minor space, having just destroyed a slaving outpost. He had mentioned at the end of the letter that he was off to the pits to bring the notorious slaver known as "Shackles" to justice. That was a week before Derron left on his own journey. He grasped his bear paw and said a small prayer.

By sundown the weather had turned from snowfall to snowstorm. As the glow of the sun faded from behind the clouds the temperature dropped to an unseemly low. And as the snow mounted, the hills and valleys of the forest slowly began to melt into one white horizon. The trees pushed past the surface, but most of the lower shrubs had been hidden away in snowdrift. Their fire had melted the ice around them, giving them the only ten-foot circle of sodden ground for miles around. Anthon and Gar were on the outskirts, breaking branches for firewood. The rest of them were huddled as close as they could get to the warmth. Derron looked over to the coyote lying at his feet. Pity overcame him and he tossed the rest of his meat down to the ground. The coyote raised its head and its tail began to wag. Within a few seconds the meat was gone, and the coyote was licking the grease from the dirt. Anthon walked up behind them.

"Are you sure you should be feeding that thing?"

Derron shrugged. "It can't hurt."

Anthon raised an eyebrow and nodded towards the bandage covering Derron's forearm.

"Well, it *was* starving. Maybe if I don't feed it, it will go for me again."

Anthon tapped the dagger on his belt. "If it does, it isn't getting very far."

 DERRON

The coyote looked up, ears back, its gnarled tooth hanging from between its gums. Anthon looked at it quizzically.

"No wonder that bite wound of yours was so bad, that snaggletooth of his is like a damned fang."

Derron smiled. "Well, then let's just hope Snaggletooth here doesn't get angry."

The group started out early the next day. Roman led the party, using a thick branch to push snow from the trail, while behind him Anthon wielded a hatchet to shear bramble from overhanging trees. Derron himself held the rear, keeping an eye on everyone and everything. The snow was falling so thick now that he could barely see the men ten feet before him. Gar's hand was firmly on his hilt, walking as though he was marching off to war. He had in the past, as Derron knew. So had half the men he had with him. Derron prided himself on leading his people through a prosperous and peaceful time during his reign. In the twenty-three years he had ruled, Derron had never waged an offensive war against anyone. However, that didn't mean his time had been without conflict.

Near ten years ago, a local lord named Boromund claimed to be the rightful heir of the Ursa Majors. As a show of strength, he'd kidnapped Derron's two youngest children during a royal procession and displayed them captive atop his holdfast for a fortnight before Derron mustered his army to lay a siege. But Boromund had amassed a larger following than Derron had anticipated, and the resulting conflict lasted near six months before Boromund was captured and the King's children returned. Afterwards, Boromund's holdfast was taken apart stone by stone until nothing remained but a barren stretch on sodden soil. Neither of Derron's children were harmed, but his second son, Croft, had taken an arrow in the shoulder during the final push that left him abed for a moon's turn. Gar himself had told Derron the story half a hundred times of how he had bravely protected the injured Prince on the field while attackers swarmed around them. Derron didn't give the story any credence, but every time Gar told it, he smiled and nodded. Mollens' father had also been present during that conflict, but Derron preferred not to recall his fate. The usurper, Boromund, himself was spared the sword, but not the dungeons. He died of a persistent chest cold three years into his imprisonment. Few mourned him, but that's not to say that none did.

Derron's foot caught in a hidden root beneath the snow and his mind immediately snapped back to the present day. He let out a grunt as he hit the snowbank, sinking a few inches in and sending a spray of powder outwards. Snaggletooth yipped as he leapt away to avoid the cold shower coming towards him. Gar took the hand from his hilt and offered it to his king, who took it and pulled himself back onto his feet, grimacing as his hurt forearm burned with the effort. Brushing the white off his jacket he muttered obscenities under his breath. A few of the men had stopped to turn towards him, but most paid his fall no mind. It was not the first time one of their number had

DERRON

fallen in the snow, and it would assuredly not be the last. He began to wonder if they should turn back, if waiting for spring would yield them an easier route. But they did not have the supplies to overwinter in the brush. Their only option was to push forward, until they found what he was looking for. Then, only then, would he allow them to rest. *If we make it...* With the weather turning the way it was, the odds were against them. But if Derron had one thing, it was hope. And hope was all he needed to have the confidence to press forward.

The procession was paused up ahead. Derron frowned, turning to Gar, who shrugged. With Snaggletooth loping by his feet, Derron made his way to the front, where he saw Anthon and Roman attempting to break through a large snowbank higher than their heads. Derron surmised that the snow had tumbled in a small avalanche from some hill close by. He could only guess though; the snow was so thick in the sky he couldn't see far enough to know if such a hill existed. Anthon was on his knees scraping loose snow from the ground as Roman cleaved large slabs of ice from the block before him. His grunts released a waft of hot stream of breath with every strike. He was so intent in his work, he nearly struck Derron in the temple on a backswing. The king ducked and tapped Roman on the back with his stick. The burly man flinched and spun, almost dazed. He panted.

"No going further 'til this blockade is broke," he said, his voice raspy.

"I think we're close!" called Anthon from where he knelt, snow piling on his dark hair. He had begun to dig around the trunk of a large tree whose canopy lay somewhere amongst the white fog above them. "Hand me that hatchet."

Roman tossed it to Anthon's feet, where the younger man picked it up and began striking at the wood.

"Can we go around?" Derron asked him."

Roman shook his head. "The brush is too thick, it would take us ten times as long, and in this snow there's no telling if we'd get back on track." He motioned and Derron handed him the map. "This map o' yours says that we're heading along this game trail." He pointed to a winding line near the top of the paper and traced it with a thick finger. "If we break from this path who's to say we don't get lost?"

Derron nodded. "That makes –"

He was cut off by the sound of wood cracking. Anthon suddenly jerked back, as the trunk began to crack through the snow and ice surrounding it. All at once, a shadow descended from the whiteness above. Derron leapt away, and felt a wash of snow cover him. Then the ground below him gave way, and his world became a tumbling stew of white snow and black mud. It was thirty seconds before he came to a rest, snow surrounding him on all sides. He cried out, but snow filled his mouth before any sound came out. Something grabbed his collar and Derron was being birthed from the ground. As his head broke the snow-drift, he saw Anthon standing over him, his face scratched and red from ice and splinters. Derron looked to his surroundings.

 DERRON

They had descended at least thirty feet down the hill by his estimate. He could no longer see where they last were, though he could hear his men yelling down towards them. Rubbing the snow from his eyes and coughing, he rose to his feet. The snow only came up to his knees, but felt like a mile. *Roman,* he thought. Derron called out to him. A muffled sound came from a few feet away where Roman was drawing himself up from where he'd fallen. Angry and red, the bald burly bear growled and snorted, but was no worse for wear it seemed.

"Bugger me!" He stood and beat his hands against his pants. He looked to Anthon. "Where'd that axe land?"

Anthon shrugged. "I lost my grip when I fell."

Roman grumbled something and began kicking at the snow, trying to uncover his lost tool. Derron and Anthon began to do the same, until they saw Roman bend down to pick something up. When his hand returned from the snow, however, it wasn't an axe he was holding.

"What in all the Starscape is this?' he muttered.

Derron walked over to him. He saw that Roman was holding a bone. No, it was too thin. It was carved.

"A knife?" Derron suggested. "Made from animal bone?"

Sudden realization washed over Roman's face as the two exchanged a glance.

"Thank goodness you're safe, Captain!"

Mollens was behind them, his peach face caked in frost. Smiling, the boy walked towards Derron, offering up his wool scarf. Frowning, he paused, and flared his nostrils.

"Does anyone else smell a wood fire?"

CHAPTER 16

ALMOND II

When Almond returned home, she found near half the village gathered around her farmhouse. Anxiously, she jogged up to the front gate, throwing her sword belt into a nearby bush as she ran. Coming up the front steps, she shoved past a dozen people to find her grandmother resting in the solar with her eyes shut and her breathing laboured. An old man was beside her, leaned over with his ear to her grandmother's mouth. After a few moments, he raised his head and nodded, squeezing her hand. But as Almond drew near, he vanished into the crowd, his white hair trailing behind him. She cautiously approached, and could feel her hands shaking.

"Grandma?"

Her grandmother opened her eyes, just a crack, long enough to lock eyes with her granddaughter before shutting them again.

"Oh, sweet Lefra," she said, using Almond's true name. "Lefra, Lefra, the gem of my life."

Her grandmother's face quivered as she formed a small smile, before exhaling deeply.

"May she rest." A man pulled his straw hat from his head and held it against his chest. Others did the same.

Almond felt the tears welling in her eyes. When Hagon the Fisherman put a condoling hand on her shoulder, she shook him off and ran out into the night. Someone shouted after her, but she didn't know who it was and she didn't care. Within a few minutes she was beyond earshot and away from the painful place, but her eyes continued to flow until well past dawn. She walked along the dirt trading road connecting Rimby to its neighboring hamlets as the stars overhead shone down like eyes watching her go. They reminded her of her grandmother, which only made her walk faster. Almond didn't care where she ended up, as long as it was far away from here.

Yet even in her sadness, thirst eventually crossed her mind. She moved from the road and down to the edge of the adjoining creek. Kneeling, she cupped her hands in the water and drew the liquid to her lips. Her tears dripped into her hands and Almond could taste the salt. *My father is gone. My grandmother is gone. I think that I'm gone too.* Her eyes welled up again and she let the water flow through her fingers and dribble at her feet. A light whinny cut into her brooding. She hardly looked up at the sound; nothing around her seemed to matter. She watched the shadow of moving of feet and heard the signature thump of a walking cane on dirt. Looking up, she saw a man with a large beard and broad shoulders silhouetted against the sky. She wiped her tears, and wished silently that he'd go away. Instead, the man reached a hand down and offered it to her. She took it, and he heaved her back onto her feet. Almond's dress was soiled with dirt and tears and she avoided his gaze, too embarrassed by her appearance. The man brushed the tangled hair from her brow and gazed at her face.

"You're Perro's daughter, aren't you child?" The man's voice had a gentle tone to it, but also had the kind of authority behind it that only came with age.

She nodded and the man smiled.

"Do not cry, child. I will bring your father back to you."

It was only then that Almond recognized him. He was the man from yesterday, the one attempting to rally the villagers into going after the Dogs. She then noticed that behind him was a carriage parked on the trading road, drawn by two horses: one snow white and the other ebony black. In it were an array of weapons, supplies, and chests. She wiped the tears from her eyes and attempted to meet his gaze.

"You're going after them, aren't you?"

"Yes, child, I am."

She straightened her back and stood as tall as she could muster, "Then take me with you."

The man was taken aback. "Where I'm going is no place for a child. I do not expect to return unharmed. And you have other family here who will miss you. What of your grandmother?"

 ALMOND

She felt the tears well up in her eyes again and sobbed. "She can't miss me anymore."

It took him a moment, but the man's face revealed that he understood what she was saying and he nodded. That was good; Almond didn't think she had the heart to explain herself any further without collapsing back into tears. The man bent down to one knee, gently, as it was obvious by the way he knelt that it was painful for him, and looked her in the eyes.

"If anything, *anything*, happens: You hide in the back of the carriage, understand?"

She nodded, and he led her back to the cart. She sat in the front, while the man picked up the reins and gave a tug. The carriage lurched forward.

"Hoss," he said, introducing himself.

"Almond."

The carriage rocked back and forth along the dirt road and somehow it soothed her.

"If worst comes to worst, you'll need to have a way of defending yourself. There should be a few daggers in the back there, pick one and don't let it out of your reach."

"I don't need a dagger, I have a sword," she said.

That made Hoss chuckle. "Do you now?"

She nodded. "It's outside my farmhouse... I'd like to get it back."

Hoss looked as though he were about to protest, but stopped when he saw the determination in Almond's eyes. With one tug on the reins, the horses turned and they started back for her father's farmhouse.

Almond hadn't walked near as far from the homestead as she had initially thought, and it took them less than an hour to return. Still, most of the mourners had left by the time they arrived. Quickly, Almond hopped from her seat and searched the bush for the sword belt. It cost her a few thorn-pricks to the arm, but she was able to retrieve it and bring it back to the carriage.

"That's a mighty big sword for such a little girl," Hoss remarked as the horses began moving again."

Almond fumbled with the buckle. "It doesn't fit me."

"Then maybe it isn't your sword," he laughed. Then he looked at her warmly. "I'll do some leatherwork on it in the evening."

They sat in silence for the first few hours of riding. Almond listened to the steady patter of the horses' trotting feet against the dirt. Rimby was far behind them, and even the adjoining creek had split from them miles ago. Hoss began humming a ballad beside her. His voice was deep and gravelly, but oddly calming. She knew the ballad he was humming. In other circumstances she may have even begun to sing along, but today was not a day for it. Even the sky seemed to mourn. The overcast had come rolling in over the hills during the day, and the clouds seemed to glow a foreboding orange. They stopped under a massive apple tree when Hoss had decided it was too dark to continue. He undid the bridles of the pull horses and tethered them loosely to the trunk of the tree.

"What are their names?" Almond asked, brushing the mane of the pale white mare. The black horse loosened itself from the tree, trotted off into the field, and began to chew the grass. Hoss paid the animal no mind.

"Day," said Hoss, patting the white horse, "and Night."

"May I ride Day?" she asked, surprising even herself.

"Maybe one day," he said, smiling. "But for now, we should get some rest."

Sometime later, Hoss was fast asleep and snoring in the cart beside her. Almond sat up, tired, but awake. She was too troubled to fall asleep. The horses were close by, breathing deeply. Her eyes scanned the hills around them, expecting at any time to see Jackan and his Hunting Dogs descend upon them. She tested the grip on her sword belt. Hoss had done a good job at reworking the leather. To the untrained eye, it hardly looked like it had been altered at all. She was also very happy that he had shifted the scabbard to the appropriate side. Whoever's belt it had been before was left-handed, but Almond used her right. The sword was still too big for her, but at least she would be able to draw it if it came to a fight.

Searching through the items in the carriage, Almond had found that Hoss also had another sword belt he had made as well. The work was immaculate, but the steel sword within was rusty and cracked. No doubt Hoss hadn't been a swordsmith at any time in his past. She had also found a wooden buckler, chipped and rusty on the metal boss. She wondered if Hoss had been some sort of warrior. Almond puzzled for a moment as she watched Hoss' sleeping face and wondered how old he was. His wrinkled skin and beard being closer to white than grey made her think him in his sixties, but the firm muscles in his arms and legs suggested he was younger. His other possessions were limited. She found a cowl for when it was rainy or overly sunny, a walking cane, two barrels of apples for the horses, and a chest filled with clay pots, iron pans, and rations. Almond wondered if this was all he had. Perhaps he was a drifter of some sort, or maybe he had some huge farm far away. He certainly wasn't from her own village. Perhaps she'd ask him in the morning, but for now she wanted only to lie down. She was finally getting tired.

When she got tired of watching the stars, Almond turned her attention to Hoss' steadily rising and falling chest. She saw the standard of a rabbit adorning his breast and thought of her father's attire, which in turn made her think of her father. She frowned, but was too exhausted to cry. The steady motion was hypnotic. Up, down. Up, down. Up, down. And before she knew it, Hoss was waking her as the sun rose up into the sky.

"Wakey, wakey," He said, smiling, as a grandfather would. "We have a long day ahead of us."

She covered her eyes from the bright light and felt a jog as the cart started up. Hoss must have already attached the horses. She stretched, and crawled out to the front of the cart, sitting beside the old man, who was whistling softly to himself.

ALMOND

"You're in a good mood this morning."

He smiled. "Because we're getting close."

She wasn't sure how to feel. "How can you tell?"

He pointed to the ground beside them where Almond could see the faint outline of horse tracks in the grass."

"That there is fresh," he said. "We'll be on those buggers within the day."

"How are we even catching up to them? They're riding war horses, and we're in a carriage."

Hoss gave her a smile. "One war horse, sure, but fifty? Fifty takes time, child, and remember, they stole food carts from us. Those carts go slow, and a procession is only as fast as its slowest horse."

Almond felt the first hint of fear since she started out. "What... what are we going to do when we do catch up to them? There's no way we can take on them all."

That amused Hoss and he laughed. "Sweet Almond, I am an old man. I'd be remiss to say I'd be able to take one of them, let alone all of them, and as for you," he patted her head, "I'm not going to be putting you that close to harm's way."

She frowned. "So, what are we going to do?"

"Well, first we wait for them to camp, then we free our people, and then we burn the buggers' camp down. Fifty men are no match for one big burning flame."

"Wouldn't they just run away?"

"Oh, without a doubt, but that just gives us more time to escape with our people. Revenge is satisfying, but the priority is to our own."

Almond thought of having her father back, and returning to a simple life at the farm. Hoss was right, as much as she wanted to destroy every last one of them, there was no way that was going to happen, and besides, having her father back would be sweet enough.

Hoss rose to his feet, and ever so quietly ruffled through the back of his cart for a hunk of flint.

They decided that they'd stop in the next village over for supplies and to water the horses. Hoss knew the mayor from his adventuring past, but Almond had never been anywhere near that end of the meadow. She knew its name, Sunspire, but that was it. The town was named for the towering stone spire at its centre. When the sunlight struck it, it cast a lengthy shadow across the ground that the townsfolk used to tell time. Her father had promised to take her there one day. *My father*, she thought, a tear forming in her eye.

When they arrived, she was shocked to find the tower no longer stood, nor did the rest of the village. As they drew near, the smell of charred wood filled Almond's nose and the sight of grass burnt black was all around her. From the crops to the west, to the creek at the south, the ground was covered in black soot. The village was now nothing more than a pile of debris. At its center, where the spire once stood, a pile of blackened stones took their place. Atop it sat a minstrel, his vibrant red

ALMOND

cloak muted with soot. He played a tragic ballad to the old men below, digging graves in the blackened soil.

"Bugger all," mumbled Hoss under his breath.

He urged the horses until their hooves began to tread over bits of crumbled wood. No one paid them any mind.

"You there! Minstrel!" Hoss shouted up to the lute player.

The musician turned and finished his line before giving them a sad smile and plucking a string on his lute. He said nothing.

"What happened here? Where's the mayor?"

The minstrel hopped from his perch and plucked another few strings.

"That be me I suppose, if anyone."

Hoss gave him an unamused look. "The mayor is a dear friend of mine. I know you not from a twig. Where is Ichabod?

"Ah, the former Mayor Ichabod. Yes, I believe he'd be in one of those holes."

Almond looked over to Hoss, his teeth gritted together. He looked ready to punch the minstrel in his pretty little mouth. Before he could, a priest walked between them, his robes soiled. He dropped to his knees before the graves, weeping softly.

The Minstrel played another chord and sang. "They took his son and killed his brother. Poor old, poor old priest."

"They?" mused Hoss. "The Dogs did this?"

"Who else? Old Ichabod couldn't pay."

"He could have," piped in one of the diggers. "He didn't want to reach into his coffers and so the whole town had to pay."

Almond looked to Hoss. His face suggested he believed the man, but was angered nonetheless.

"How long ago."

"Last night. We had to evacuate the town after Jackan torched the bloody square."

It occurred to Almond that the sky she had seen last light, the bright orange clouds, it had been fire and smoke.

"Wasn't all bad, though." The minstrel plucked another string. "Jackan is not as sharp as that claw that he likes so much. He torched a few of his own carts in the inferno."

"Our carts," Hoss corrected him sharply.

"Your carts," the minstrel agreed.

And as quick as Hoss' plan had been formed, it had disappeared. *Without carts, the dogs were no longer slowed.* Almond looked to Hoss, who by the look of his face, was thinking the exact same thing.

"Well, I'm afraid we can't offer you much hospitality here, friend."

"That's alright," said Hoss through gritted teeth. "We won't be staying long."

CHAPTER 17

RYMUS II

The three brothers stood side-by-side atop the wooden ramparts of their newly acquired stronghold, overlooking their masses gearing up for another early morning march.

"Two thousand strong," muttered Elkus, to no one in particular.

"The largest mobile army in all the Starscape," added Lydus.

Rymus said nothing, silently surveying the field below. He watched as the bodies of the previous garrison were piled into tall mounds and burned. In a few places around the camp, higher ranking lieutenants were drilling their underlings, but most of the soldiers were lazing around and enjoying the unusually warm weather.

"Rymus," said Lydus, turning to his brother. "I have decided that we are to split our army three ways."

Rymus furrowed his brow, not meeting his brother's gaze. "Why would we do that?" He motioned to the mass of people below them. "We have an army that can decimate anything those goats can throw at us."

"In close combat," Lydus admitted. He then pointed behind them to the tall sheer cliffs and canyons parting the ground from the sky.

"Remember your studies, little brother. The men who live here are masters of the longbow, and these mountains are peppered with their tower forts. If we send even a hundred men in together, it will be seen." He flicked the long blonde hair from his face as the wind caught it. "Then the volley of arrows will pop you and all these men like pox on an arse."

Elkus grunted agreement. "There are three main forts that guard the passages into these mountains. Lydus has decided on taking the largest one, I'm going to the second largest," he smiled, "and you, Rymus, you get the smallest, the one right at the very top." He picked a scab from his chin, flicking the dead skin to the ground, smirking at his brother with a row of dirty yellow teeth that could make a lemon jealous.

Rymus found Keldo attempting to buff a deep dent out of his armour to no avail, tapping a small mallet against the metal and frowning beneath his huge moustache. Dead to everything around him, Keldo did not hear Rymus approach until the boy knocked the visor of his helmet down over his eyes. The small man leapt to his feet, and instinctively reached for the hilt of his sword, which it happened he wasn't currently wearing. His burly hand gripped at the air beside his hip until realization set in. Embarrassed, he slowly raised his visor and blushed at his captain. Rymus only laughed, picked up Keldo's sword belt from where it lay on a stump, and tossed it to him. Keldo caught it and buckled it tightly around his gut.

"How'd the strategy planning go with the brothers?" he asked, fidgeting with the buckle.

"They talked, I listened. The usual." Rymus paused and looked to the cliffs. "How high do you think that tallest mountain is?"

Keldo squinted and stared for a good few seconds before answering. "Be near three miles high I reckon, and steep. I feel sorry for the dumb bugger stupid enough to try and summit that thing." He looked at Rymus, who raised his eyebrows.

Keldo sighed. "One day I'm going to kill that brother o' yours in his sleep, you know that?" He rubbed at his temples. "When do we ship out?"

Rymus scratched his nose. "Tonight; the vantage from that highest fort makes it impossible to go unseen in the daylight. Only under the cover of darkness can we be sure to make it to the base of the mountains without being seen. From there we take whatever path keeps us out of their line of sight until we're close enough for it not to matter."

"Any upside?"

"Lydus says there are enough goats - *real* goats - that live in those mountains to cover it like a sweater. We'll be eating well... If we can catch any, that is."

Keldo scoffed and crossed his arms. "Big if."

Rymus watched as Keldo left to do his usual prep. The nice thing about having Keldo as a second in command was it meant Rymus himself could be left with very little true responsibilities, and he liked that. Keldo was such a proud lieutenant he insisted on doing all the annoying prep work needed for gathering the force. Making his way to the armory cart, Rymus unlocked a special box which contained his custom-made spears. He had five left, all pristine, never having seen the wear of a battle. Reaching in, he grabbed one and weighed it in his hand, placing his finger beneath the centre and balancing it. Satisfied, he re-locked the box and went to his horse. The large beast stood grazing, tethered to a post beside his tent. When Rymus got near, the horse turned its head and gave him a soft whinny. Rymus smiled and patted him on the cheek.

"Hey, boy."

Rymus hadn't named the horse, fearing he would get too attached. In all likelihood the horse wouldn't survive long enough to make it home again. Of course, he'd never reveal his sentiment to his brothers. They would only laugh, to be sure. Reaching over, he unbuckled a special strap on the horse's saddle and latched on his spear. The horse didn't struggle, instead returning to his grassy feast.

"That's a good boy." Rymus smiled, patting him again.

Talking to some of the men under his command, Rymus discovered that his brothers only intended to send him off with two hundred of their soldiers; less than half of what he expect-

 RYMUS

ed. Gritting his teeth, he thought about protesting, but in the end, he decided that Lydus must have had a good strategic reason for it, and held his tongue. Instead, Rymus made his way to the baggage train and took the last crate of lamb jerky as a means of compensation.

When it was at last time to ride, Rymus sent Keldo to rouse the men. Keldo eagerly strode off to the line of tents. Rymus crossed his arms and smirked. He enjoyed having someone to do all the command-work for him. Instead, Rymus used the extra time in carefully armouring himself, slipping his helm over his head, buckling his jerkin, and lacing his riding boots in such a way his feet wouldn't be too sore after the ride. As a finishing touch, he pinned his blue enamelled Pisces insignia on his surcoat and gave it a shine with some spit and his thumb.

His horse was still tethered up next to his tent. Rymus patted the animal on the head and undid the rope. Mounting, he galloped to the edge of camp where almost thirty riders and two hundred foot-soldiers awaited him. Instead of stopping, he kicked his heels into his mount and sped past them all. From behind, Rymus could hear the others begin to follow as they galloped towards the mountain range. There was no need to ride in formation; it was entirely a matter of getting somewhere fast. Rymus kicked at his horse's flanks again and spurred him on even faster, letting the wind blow against his face. Out here, he felt at home. His horse swerved suddenly to avoid a pale granite boulder jutting from the ground. Without thinking, he pulled the reins and slowed, but soon his horse calmed and picked back up speed. The mountains loomed over him like giants scraping against the stars. As he rode closer, Rymus had to crane his neck back further and further to see the summit, until he was so close that he could no longer see the top. At that point, he stopped and dismounted, stretching his legs, and letting the blood flow back into his numb arse. He cracked his knuckles and watched as the rest of his men began catching up to him. Over the next fifteen minutes, two hundred soldiers including the thirty cavalry horses made it beneath the rock. Keldo was one of the last to arrive, limping and looking annoyed.

"Tripped over a damn rock," he grumbled.

"Perhaps you should have ridden a horse like I offered."

Keldo panted and coughed a wad of phlegm onto the grass. "You know I can't stand sitting on those damn beasts. I don't trust 'em."

Rymus shrugged. "Do you think anyone saw us?"

"I can't see twenty feet in front of me. I don't think they'll be seeing us all the way down here."

Rymus looked up the mountain, concerned. "I hope you're right."

It took them close to an hour of skirting about the foot of the mountain before finding a small passageway through the much steeper slopes. The way was only about three men wide, but it was the only path with a slope gradual enough to allow them to pass while still being horseback. Rymus placed his hand along the wall and felt the stone. He wondered if the pathway was natural or manmade. Natural meant there was no guarantee the path would continue to the top, but manmade meant the road may be monitored. He had sent a few of his best scouts up ahead to warn them if any guards blocked their way. So far nothing had come back, but that could either mean the scouts hadn't found anything, or they were dead and their position was compromised. He had no way of knowing until they got higher, so he decided to stay as alert as he could.

Rymus led the company, with mounted archers on either side of him. Keldo led the rear guard, with a platoon of swordsmen. If anything went wrong, he had faith Keldo would see it. Looking behind him, he could no longer see the beginning of the path. The camp was just a dot in a sea of green, looking like an anthill with tiny ants scurrying around it. His brothers had not yet left by the look of it. He breathed in. The air was cooler up in the mountains. He enjoyed it. On the Pisces homeworld, the King's castle was built on a small peninsula sitting on a beach between the world's two great oceans. The cool ocean breeze was never lacking. While up in the mountains, the air was distinctly drier, it still reminded him of home.

The sun was already beginning to rise by the time they reached a clearing large enough to make camp. Rymus reared his horse around and gave the command for a full stop. He then sent his archers further up the mountain in groups of four to keep guard. His scouts had still not returned, and that was concerning. The path had no forks so they could not have gotten lost. He dismounted and puzzled over it. Right now, an Aries army could be marching to their position and they'd never know it. A raindrop hit him on the back of his hand. It was... cold. Then another landed on his nose. He looked up and saw the sky had turned overcast. White rain fell and numbed him as it landed. He puzzled at it before it dawned on him. *This is what they must call "snow".* Lydus had mentioned to him they might come across it. Rymus had simply shrugged it off like most of the things his brother told him.

A cold wind swept over him and Rymus felt his muscles tense.

"You!" he yelled at the closest soldier.

"Yes, Captain?"

Rymus threw his rucksack to the ground. "Set up my tent. It's freezing out here."

The soldier tried to not look disappointed. "Yes, Captain."

As the tents began to sprout around him, Rymus dismounted and tethered his nameless horse to a stunted pine jutting from the rock.

From up the path he watched as a rider galloping almost too fast for his horse stumbled towards them. Rymus placed one hand on his sword hilt and the other on his spear, but as the rider drew near it became clear he was one of his own men.

"Rymus!" he called, halting his horse not two feet in front of his captain.

"What is it?"

RYMUS

"The road ahead..." he panted. "Trapped..."

"Who's trapped?"

The rider shook his head as sweat dripped from his temples and ran down his dust covered cheeks.

"Not some*one*, some*thing*. The road is trapped."

Rymus noticed then that the rider's face was pale. He reached up and peeled back the leather of the man's surcoat. Beneath, the chainmail he wore was split and the flesh beneath had bruised into a queer hue of black and green. Rymus lowered the leather and turned back towards his men.

"Get me a medic!"

No one answered from his ranks. It dawned on Rymus then. *My brothers have sent me with no means no care for my wounded.* A thud brought his attention back around. The rider had fallen from his horse and lay motionless in the dirt.

☆ ☆ ☆

That night, they sent the rider's body tumbling from the side of the cliff. A burial would have been too time consuming, and the ground was too rocky to break regardless. Rymus' mind raced. He knew the road ahead was set with traps. Yet he had no information on where or of what kind. The wound he'd found on his scout had been due to blunt force. When Keldo had checked the body for himself, he'd noted to Rymus that there was no gash, no puncture, not even a graze. Whatever had killed the man hadn't pierced his skin. Rymus decided that if they were to continue, he'd need to go on as a smaller force and attempt to circumnavigate the main paths. *And so, we break into smaller and smaller groups.* Any traps in the road could mean devastation for his army, and failure was not an option. It was best to avoid at all costs. Looking ahead, he noticed a side path that could possibly lead them to the top, yet there was no way to get any of his supplies or horses up with him. He would have to go on foot with just a few men. *But who to bring?*

"Keldo, get over here."

CHAPTER 18

ORLO II

Orlo awoke to find himself chained back in his cell. *I wonder if that mouse will come back to greet me,* he thought. But as his eyes adjusted, he realized it wasn't his cell. Far from it. The room was at least ten times larger than his original chamber; it even had a window, however small. The smell of warm food filled his nostrils, accompanied by the sounds of chewing, and suddenly it occurred to Orlo that he was not alone. Across the room was a long table raised just off the dirt floor. Six people sat around it, stuffing their faces and paying him no mind. Orlo rubbed his temple and noticed the bandages covering his arms and legs. His shirt was off and he wore only a pair of tattered shorts. He noticed his stomach, and how sunken it had gotten since being captured; and he was starving. Crawling, Orlo dragged his chains with him as he crossed the mud. They were attached to the far wall behind him and as he reached the table, they became taut. Straining the chain to the last link, Orlo had to force his way between two of the other feasters to reach any food, and they were none too happy to share.

On his left was a burly, dark-skinned man with hair that reached from his shaggy beard all the way to the top of his shorts. Presumably it went even farther. His forearms and torso were splattered with the sealed scars of half a hundred pit matches. On his shoulder, a new one seemed to have been added to the collection. Blood still dried down his muscled arm.

On Orlo's right was a woman, though without looking carefully you'd never be able to tell. Her auburn brown hair was knotted and tangled in the front, falling over her eyes. In the back, a crudely braided ponytail was held in place with a bit of bent bronze. Unlike the others, she wore a piece of fabric wrapped crudely around her chest, so small and threadbare that her midriff and the top half of her breasts were exposed. Tattooed on the skin over her heart was the crude image of a fox head with stars for eyes. Neither of them said a word to Orlo, only grunting and continuing to eat.

Orlo turned his attention to the food. Most of it was gone, but there were still the scraps of some shredded meat in a clay bowl. He wolfed it down and looked around for more. A few stalks of sugarcane, lay broken in front of him. He bit one in half and chewed. It was fibrous and not very sweet, but he enjoyed it nonetheless. Within minutes the food was all gone and the others seemed to settle. Orlo was still very much hungry, but wasn't going to complain. It was much more then he'd ever expected. A man with nine fingers wrestled another with half an ear for a bone with some meat still on it. The woman wiped her mouth and stared at them.

"Give it a rest, you two. Any more of that and neither of you eat for a week."

The two men paid her no mind. She shrugged and moved back to her section of the wall. The burly man soon followed, as well as the other, more timid man. This left only Orlo and the two bickering men at the table. Orlo picked up a grease-laden bowl and began to lick. He felt like a child, but he wanted it.

"You'll want to move back to the wall, freshmeat," advised the girl.

Orlo looked to her, but before he could ask why, the clasp around his neck grew tighter. Before he knew it, the chain on the wall was being winched in, causing Orlo to be dragged flailing along the ground until his back was flush with the wall. The two fighting men were also winched back. No longer in reach of each other, the bone lay somewhere between the two of them. A guard burst forth from the door, looking considerably angry. Storming over to the two men, he stepped on the bone with his bare foot, cracking it in half. Taking the two pieces, he whipped them through the air one at a time. He missed the nine-fingered man by an inch, but struck the half-eared man on the forehead. Without an ounce of dignity, the two men each picked up the bones and licked them clean, to the amusement of the guard.

Once the guard had left, Orlo could feel his chains loosen, and he once again had some range of movement. He cracked his neck and jaw, loosening his muscles. The woman beside him was smirking.

"You're in the advanced class now, freshmeat. The crowd loved you."

He looked at her, puzzled. "I only won a single matchup."

"Yes, but only half of all the people in the pit win a single matchup. Or did you forget that no one living in the pit has *lost* a matchup?"

He nodded, conceding the point. "And how many have you won?"

She held up four fingers and smiled, showing the crack in her bottom lip. "Next to Big Borrus here, I've won the most matches in this room."

"And how did you manage that?"

She proudly pointed to the foxhead on her breast. "It's hard to catch a fox."

"You're a Vulpeculan then? That faction is pretty far from here."

She nodded. "Not many of us around here. I'm Allysson."

"So, if you're so fast, Allysson, then how did they manage to get you in here in the first place?"

She frowned. "My bitch of a mother sold me out to the commander of the guard. I had a choice: be offered as a tribute to the Leo's, or lose my hand. Pretty clear choice if you ask me." She picked at her teeth and flicked a bit of meat across the floor to the nine fingered man. "Go ahead and eat that. I know you want to." She turned her attention back to Orlo. "What about you, freshmeat? What's the story behind the man to kill Mephis?"

Orlo shrugged. "I'm a butcher –"

"I'll say!" she cut him off, laughing.

He ignored her and continued. "I'm a butcher from a small town in the Mensa Faction; a group of mercenaries raided us, took everything they could. Of course, that included the people. Only thing was, they forgot that people need food, and by the time we arrived everyone but me was dead."

Allysson nodded. "I've heard that story a few times since I got here."

Orlo looked once again to his bandages. His arms didn't hurt, but he was afraid to take them off. Big Borrus held up his left hand, revealing a large black spot on his palm.

"Takes time to heal," he said with a thick accent. "Leave bandages on."

The other man across the room spoke up. He looked the least damaged of any of them. "For all these bastards do to us, at least they're good at patching us up. I saw one guy lose an arm to a flaming sword once, the next day he was back fighting in the pit."

"Did he win?"

"Oh no, of course not; the arm he lost was his sword arm."

☆ ☆ ☆

Night came and went. In the morning they were again pulled tight up to the wall. Moments later, two guards entered and unhooked the half-eared man from his bonds. He was then hoisted up and out of the room. Allysson attempted to see the fight from the small window in their cell, but gave up after five or so minutes. The half-eared man never returned.

About an hour later, a cleaner looking man came in to re-dress Orlo's bandages. As they came off, Orlo looked down to see small black burn marks coving his arms from wrist to elbow.

"Does this mean I'll be back in the pit soon?"

The man nodded, poking one mark with a stick and making Orlo flinch. "Tomorrow, and if you live, again in the melee."

After he left, Allysson whistled. "They must like *you*, butcher."

Orlo rubbed his temples, a headache beginning to start. "Why's that?"

Allysson smiled. "Melees, those are the big ones. That's when the Leo King comes down from his cavern of a castle and watches for the best of the best."

Orlo was confused. "For what?"

Allysson shrugged "No idea, but whoever wins gets a one-way ticket out of this hellhole."

That caught Orlo's attention. "To where?"

Allysson shrugged again. "How should I know?" She smirked. 'You best get into that melee, butcher, our plan depends on it."

ORLO

Orlo was back to be being confused. "Whose plan?"

Allysson only smiled.

☆ ☆ ☆

The next day, Orlo was standing barefoot in the mud of the pit. Cheers once again rose around him. His helm was stuck to his forehead with sweat as he stared down the nine-fingered man. His grip tightened on the leather hilt of the blue-steel sword that he held once again. It glinted in the light of the massive, low-hanging sun in the sky and sent rainbows of light dancing across the ground.

The nine-fingered man bore a quarter staff in his full hand, its end tipped with sharpened yellow quartz that shone brilliantly. On his right hand he wore a specially made glove where a small blade had been sown in place of his missing pinky finger.

Orlo sighed and raised the blue blade to the sky, hearing cheers from all around. He had liked the nine-fingered man, despite never learning his true name. In the week he had been in the meat locker, he'd had few enough companions, even if half of them did not speak to him. Yet it wasn't long before they were trading blows. For every swing of the nine-fingered man's mace, Orlo landed two blows with his sword, yet his opponent was very good at using his staff to defend himself. But his luck did not last forever. Orlo made a sweeping overhand blow that made his opponent flinch backwards. Orlo jerked his hand to the side, and instead of cutting over, he went under.

The blue blade cut through bone skin and muscle and suddenly, the nine-fingered man was the five-fingered man. Hot blood poured across the sand from a forearm that ended only halfway down, the bladed glove still adorning the severed hand. Miraculously, he was able to maintain to grip on his staff with his remaining hand, and used it in a feeble last swing at Orlo as he teetered from blood loss and shock. Orlo gave him a sad frown as the crystal tip bumped harmlessly against his chest. The one-handed man fell to his knees, his eyes darting randomly from sky to the ground, to his stump, to the crowd, to Orlo.

"Finish him!" cried a voice from the crowd.

Orlo saw no point - the man was dying anyway. But he also knew this was all just for the entertainment. So, with a heavy heart, he placed a foot on the man's shoulder, and slashed down, splitting his head clean in two. A cheer erupted from the crowd.

One of the Leo pit guards came out to bring Orlo back to his cell. For a moment he thought to cut down again, take out the guard and flee. But he knew that wouldn't be of any help.

Allysson was waiting for him in the cell when he was led back. There were a few bottles of rum on the sandy floor when he returned, but it was soon apparent that his companions had drunk them all. Big Borrus was passed out asleep in the corner.

"And then there were three!" Allysson called to him. One hand was fixed to her side where an arrow wound had been stitched shut. The other raised an empty bottle in a mock toast.

Orlo waited until he had been chained back to the wall and the guard had left before speaking.

"How much longer until the melee?"

Allysson shrugged. "No idea. How should I know?" She threw her bottle at Borrus' back. The glass shattered against wall behind him, but the big man didn't rouse.

Orlo slumped his back against the wall. "So, how do you expect to formulate an escape plan?"

"With this."

Allysson spit a key into her hand. It was roughly made, and coarse, but looked proper. She began jamming it into the grip around her neck as Orlo stared dumbfounded.

"Where did you get that?"

She didn't answer, instead grunting as the key slid into the lock. With a twist and a clack, the metal fell from her neck. Allysson rubbed at her throat where long red marks gouged under her chin. Standing, she made her way to the door and opened it a crack to peer out. When she was satisfied no one was there, she returned to the room, first looking to Borrus. It was obvious he wasn't going to be moving anytime soon, so her attention turned to Orlo.

"I need your help."

Before Orlo could respond, she was already at his collar, unlocking the chains.

"For what? I thought your plan was to escape during the melee."

She stared at him incredulously. "Yes, and how will we do that with no weapons? You think we'll have time during the chaos of an escape? No, I want to be prepared."

Orlo felt the latch open, and dropped the clamp to the floor. "Alright," he said.

The trip to the armory wasn't easy. Thrice they were almost spotted. Once inside, Orlo expected Allysson to pick the first weapon she saw and leave. Instead, she stood and browsed for a moment too long.

"Hide," hissed Orlo.

But it was too late, the Leo pit guard at the door had seen them. Reaching up, the huge man grabbed a war mace from the wall and took a swing at Orlo. He ducked the massive weapon, only to be knocked back by a fist, near as big as the mace, to his gut. Doubled over, he rolled to the side instinctively, as the mace hit the ground and sent a spray of sand from where his head had been just a moment ago. *Allysson left me. She left me.*

Orlo awaited the next blow with closed eyes. *Better to not see it coming.* But when it didn't come, he opened his eyes, and saw the knife protruding from the pit guard's chest. A silver flash, and then suddenly a second knife appeared in the flesh of his clavicle. A woman's hand gripped Orlo on the shoulder and yanked him back, just seconds before the big Leo man's body hit the ground with a thump.

Still dazed, Orlo allowed himself to be led from the armoury. Before he knew entirely what was happening, he was back in the cell.

ORLO

"Sit." Allysson commanded him.

Orlo snapped back to reality. He remembered the chains he was supposed to be wearing and began to put them back. After Allysson locked them around his throat, she did her own, just as a second guard came storming into the room. He took one look at them and grumbled. Allysson must have smirked, because the guard's expression soured and he stormed over to the girl. She suddenly tensed and prepared for the inevitable oncoming swing. That she had saved him was still fresh in his mind, and whatever came over him he did not know, but Orlo stuck out his foot and kicked the shin of the guard as he got just inches from Allysson. Pausing, the guard's complete attention turned to Orlo. *Dear Gods, what have I done?*

BAM!

The pain struck him like a lightning bolt, and fire seemed to spread down his skin. The world went dark for a second and Orlo's cheek scraped along the ground. He heard the door slam, but couldn't see it. All the vision in his left eye was gone, and it was beginning to swell shut.

"Thanks."

Orlo, woozy, sat up and looked with his one good eye to Allysson, who was staring at his other eye. He could taste blood from where it dripped down his cheek.

Allysson grimaced. "I think he broke your socket."

I think you're right, Orlo thought.

He put a hand over the left half of his face and felt the heat coming off of it. "That seemed pointless, we didn't gain anything, and they'll find that guard."

Allysson gave him a grin. "That's what you think."

CHAPTER 19

ALGEN III

Algen stood with his hands at his sides next to the King's throne. He was dressed up in the serving garb of a cup-bearer, a white codskin doublet and woven seaweed pants, waiting for His Grace to wave him over to fill his glass. He had been standing there for hours, and the heavy glass pitcher he held had started to make his shoulder ache. The King had yet to ask him to fill his cup, and the container was still as full and heavy as it had been when Korra had given it to him. Instead, the King sat staring blankly and boredly out over the empty tiles of his hall, his pincer rhythmically opening and closing as it always did. The skylight sent the King's shadow arcing over the length of the room, and his pincer cast the shape of the head of a sea dragon, its mouth opening and closing, bearing rows of small sharp teeth

Other than the two of them, the hall was all but empty. A pair of garrisoned guards were the only others in attendance, one flanking each side of the arched entryway. On the left was a guard he recognized from his transformation day. The other was new, a replacement for the previous guard torn apart by Gnash. Both stared unblinking at the King, still as statues, holding long spears crossed across the entryway. Algen had made a game of trying to determine which would flinch first - a dull game, but the only one he had to pass the time. At present, the new guard had flinched thirteen times while the old had done it just nine. Algen felt his arm grow numb and he shifted the pitcher to his other hand. *When will this be over?* he thought, miserably. But deep down he knew that this may very well be his life now. The job he did until the end of his days. *Or until Naylis takes me as a squire.* That thought made him smile. As far-fetched as the notion was, it was still a possibility, and that was all Algen needed to hold onto for now. Although Naylis had gone to the surface for some mission on the king's behalf. Perhaps he would never return. And in that case... *No,* he thought. *I mustn't think that way.*

Footsteps echoed from the far end of the hall and the guards parted their weapons. As they did, a third guard led five unmorphed children into the room. Even in less than a week of being a morphed man himself, Algen felt queerly alien to them, *better* in a way. Still, he realized that the odds were all five children would leave this hall as far more stunning morphs than him. As if to prove his point, one of the boys looked to

Algen with concern. Algen frowned. *He's thinking of how he hopes not to end up like me.*

The King finally sat up in his chair, excited at the prospect of new recruits for his army. His claw twitched again, and as it did, his eyes shone bright. Without looking, he raised his cup to Algen, who was so taken aback that he nearly forgot his duties. Pouring, he watched the green liquid fill up to the goblet's lip and spill out over the sides. He winced, thinking he would be scolded. Instead, the King took no notice and brought the cup to his lips, downing the contents in one long swallow and wiping his mouth with the back of his claw.

"Welcome!" he boomed. The King looked them over one by one, making eye contact with each as he had with Algen on his day. His eyes settled and he and pointed to a quivering boy in front.

Here we go again, thought Algen.

An hour later, five new morphs were exiting the hall. The quivering boy had become a seal morph, with soft white hair coving his body. After that was a boy who became a barnacle like Algen, only he was orange-yellow instead of Algen's bluish-purple. Then came two fish morphs: a boy and a girl. The last had been the worst. The girl came out so mutated that what remained needed to be scooped in a bucket from the chamber. One of the guards had poked his spear curiously at the lump lying on the ground, to Algen's horror.

The King had gone back to his brooding, frowning and gritting his teeth. It was an obviously disappointing bunch.

He rose from his throne and waved Algen off. Algen bowed his head and scurried from the hall. It wasn't the typical way for Cancer's to show respect, but without speaking it was all Algen could hope to do. He spent the next few hours scrubbing the exhaust vents for Korra, until finally she allowed him to leave for the night.

He left the kitchens sweaty and sore. He tried stretching his arms to relieve the tension in his muscles, but stopped when he realized he could stretch them all the way around his back. His rubbery skin was like elastic bending with his bone. The feeling made him uncomfortable and made Algen feel less like himself than he ever had.

The King's Dome had gone dark, only lit from the light-fish swimming outside, and the luminescent rods that lined the stone streets. As Algen walked, he produced half a steamed monkfish from the pocket of his tunic - he'd swiped it off the King's plate as it had come back to the kitchen for cleaning. He knew that if Korra found out he'd taken it, he'd be whipped or expelled from the King's service for sure. But the gruel they fed the serving boys was gritty and tasteless, and not even close to anything resembling filling. Algen was alone, except for a small group near the edge of the dome. As he finished his food, Algen decided to go look.

It turned out to be a party of twenty morphs preparing to depart for the Deep Dome. As the name suggested, the Deep Dome was the deepest of the fourteen domes under Cancer control, and housed many of the most freakishly deformed

 ALGEN

morphs, resembling what could only be described as horrible underwater monstrosities.

The hatch to the outside was being opened, and a few of the morphs had already started piling in for ejection. For a heartbeat it dawned on Algen that he could join them, leave and begin a new life in a new dome. But that idea was crushed just as quickly as it had begun. Two steps forward and a flat-headed man with huge watery eyes placed a hand on his chest.

"Name?" he asked.

Algen didn't answer, *couldn't* answer, only frowning.

"That's what I thought."

The man shoved, hard, and sent Algen sprawling back into a group of people. Algen's foot caught on someone's leg and they tumbled to the ground.

"I'm sorry," said a voice, hushed and sweet.

I'm sorry too, Algen wanted to say, but made no attempt to even try.

He got to his knees and offered a hand down to the morph he'd knocked over. As they locked eyes, Algen was shocked to see the pretty girl who'd been with him on his morph day. *What had her name been? Alanna. Yes, it was Alanna.* Alanna seemed to recognize him too. As she knelt herself, the fin on the back of her neck unfolded and gave her a brilliant crest. She took Algen's hand to stand the rest of the way up.

"Are you also being sent to the Deep Dome?"

Algen shook his head no.

"Oh." She looked sad. "The King's sending me to the store-rooms there. Where they keep all the gems mined from the seafloor? Apparently, there are hundreds of rooms filled to bursting with rubies and copper shards and pearls and black opals. And they have almost no one maintaining them all." She smiled at him. "So, where did the King put you?"

Nowhere, thought Algen. *I had to find my own place.*

He shrugged.

Alanna gave him a sad smile and slicked a hand over the back of her head, folding the fin back down again. Algen thought she looked as though she would say something else, but she never did. He watched as she entered the ejection chamber, and as the glass doors closed behind her Alanna saw him staring and waved. But before Algen could wave back, the outer wall of the dome opened and Alanna was gone, sucked out into the ocean, on her way to a dome he'd likely never see.

CHAPTER 20

JAIR III

The smell was still the worst part of it. As the small party made their way across the sweeping hills leading to the Rumblefall mountain range, Jair couldn't help but be hyper-aware of the rotting stench emanating from the crate being carried behind him.

"You couldn't tighten that lid, could you?" he called back to Garrett.

Garrett snorted, "It was tight before you made me take it off."

That was true enough. Jair supposed it was better than having to carry the thing himself, but even still he quickened his pace to put a few more yards between him and the odor.

"Bloody hell, I wish I had a horse!" Vikron was yelling to no one in particular while waving his arms in the air, making his fur cloak flap behind him. The tough leather boots Vikron wore upon his feet had each split their seams since they had left the river two days past.

Jair matched the captain's pace. "I thought you Tauri were supposed to ride bulls, not horses?"

That made Vikron burst into laughter, spittle erupting from his lips. "Ya, and the Lepus shit cotton. How gullible are ya, 'cutioner?"

Jair blushed. Never being off world had made him a bit of a shut in when it came to the other factions. Every now and again a travelling market would visit the castle, but otherwise he was sorely lacking in his experiences.

"So, where does the myth come from?" he asked.

Vikron shrugged. "Well, one of our Gods supposedly rode a giant bull across the stars into battle, but I don't believe it for a second. The only other man to do it was a knightly feller fifty years back. The beast kicked him off and trampled him. Serves him right, I say."

"Are you a knight?"

Vikron laughed again. "Heavens, no! You won't see me strutting around like a gussied-up cock!" He slapped Jair on the back. "How about you, 'cutioner? Should I really be calling you *Sir 'Cutioner*?"

Jair shook his head. "My father was, but I never came around to it."

 JAIR

"Was?"

"He died when I was young, fighting in one of the King's thousand nameless wars."

Vikron got surprisingly solemn for a moment. "Seems like everyone I talk to has a story like that."

They made the rest of their trip in silence, the only sound coming from their feet crackling against the underbrush and the air running through the trees. Despite being midday, the sky had gone dark with an overcast of plump grey clouds prepped to burst. They only paused once they reached the base of the Rumblefall.

"Why do they call it the Rumblefall?" asked Frog.

Jair turned to him. "Because if you hear rumbling you better be ready for something to fall."

As if on cue, a crack of thunder ripped through the air and rain began pouring down from the sky. Frog cursed and Garrett pulled his cowl up over his head. The drops made a hollow clanging sound against Vikron's helm.

"It looks like there's a cave up ahead," he called.

They climbed, careful not to slip on the smooth wet stone.

The cave turned out to be no more than a rocky overhang in the cliffside. *At least it's dry*, Jair thought, as Frog and Deleon piled tinder for a fire.

"Is that such a great idea?" he asked. "From where we are, that fire will make us stick out like a beacon for anyone attempting to hunt us down."

"Relax," said Frog. "One little cookfire for a few strips of bacon won't hurt."

It could, Jair thought. The castle guard may have fallen in strength over the past years but that didn't make them stupid. *They'll be watching.* Jair grit his teeth, but didn't argue.

They sat around the fire as the meat sizzled. Vikron had made himself a nest from his cloak and sat whittling the ends of his horned helm back into spikes. A few of the others were already asleep. Deleon bit into an overripe apple.

"Where you from, Jair?" Juice squirted from the corners of his mouth as he spoke.

"Ya, 'cutioner," piped in Vikron. "If you're going to be with us a while we may as well get to know each other a bit better."

Jair cracked his knuckles against the ground and shrugged. "Not much to tell. I was born here in the city. A few towns over is the furthest I've ever been."

Vikron looked up. "Never been through a rift then, eh?"

He shook his head. "I've never even seen one. I don't know where any of them are."

"You're in luck then. The closest one is just on the other side of these here mountains."

Jair stood and folded his arms. "What makes you think I'll be leaving with you?"

Vikron stared in silence for a moment, before standing himself, letting the helmet fall noisily to the stone. He walked over to Jair, getting right up face to face, though the Tauri was a solid foot and a half taller. His breath smelled sour and Jair felt the warm air from the bigger man's nose wash over his forehead as Vikron flared his nostrils.

"Because you got nowhere else to go, 'cutioner." He moved in even closer. "And I need a man that fights like you." He smiled. "At least, I assume you can fight, but how can I be sure?"

Jair bent down and picked the pole axe from the ground, but Vikron stomped it back down before it reached a foot off the ground. He tsk tsked.

"You won't always have a weapon. How well can you do without?"

Garrett moved up beside his captain, smirking and flexing his arms. Jair moved forward, fists up by his cheeks. Garrett scoffed and batted the hands down. Jair put them right back up, then took a jab. Garrett grabbed his forearm and twisted, until Jair lost his balance and fell to his knees. He followed up by kicking Jair in the side, sending him sprawling to the ground. Jair grimaced, but grabbed hold of Garrett's ankle where he stood, attempting to pull him off balance. Instead, Garrett used his other foot to stomp down onto his wrist. Jair cried out in pain, and immediately felt himself blush from embarrassment.

Vikron shook his head. "Get up and fight."

Jair raised himself to one knee, and lunged forward, catching Garrett off guard and sending them both tumbling. The two squabbled on the rock, trading blows. Jair felt an elbow smack him in the nose, but at the same time felt his own fist hit something soft. When they separated, Jair's nose was running with blood and Garrett's eye was beginning to bruise. Garrett looked dazed where he lay on the ground. Jair stood and wiped the blood from his face. His honour told him to stop, but this was no honourable fight. Jair stepped forward and kicked Garrett under the chin. He watched his opponent's body smack against the rock and moved in closer for a final blow. He heard a whistle from behind him and turned to find Arlum pointing a loaded crossbow at his face. Vikron stood next to Arlum, smirking.

"Rule one of this little group: no one fights fair."

Jair heard a rustle from behind him and before he could react a fist knocked him in the temple. Then everything went black.

☆ ☆ ☆

He awoke with no sense of how long he'd been out, but it was still dark outside. The fire had been stomped out and the company was asleep. He grimaced as he tried to raise himself. His head pounded and the world seemed to spin around him. His lips were stuck closed, and he tasted blood. Jair opened his mouth and felt the dried blood release from his upper lip. He sniffed and spat. What came out was entirely red.

"Awake I see." The voice came from across the rock. "You gave Garrett a good wallop there on that eye of his. He won't forgive you for that one, though he's also not like to call it a win for you."

 JAIR

Deleon was peering out over the forest below, legs swinging from the edge of the overhang, sword resting on his lap. Jair had never realized just how young the man was, if he was even a man yet at all. Dark hair spilled in tangles across his face. There wasn't a hint of hair anywhere on Deleon's cheeks, but even still, Jair got the sense of him being experienced beyond his years.

"Are you on watch?" Jair slowly raised himself to his feet. The cool air seemed to help his head.

"For another hour or so. You should sleep."

"I'm not tired." He walked up to the ledge and peered out. The castle was too far away to see from this distance. The only light came from the stars above and the firebugs in the sky. He watched as the insects swirled around in the breeze, lighting the air on fire.

"Good." Deleon looked up at him. "I could use the company."

He sat. "Don't you have a watch partner?" When Jair was in the castle guard, they had always taken shifts in pairs.

"Sometimes, but Vikron doesn't see us being in much danger at the moment."

That took Jair aback. "Not in much... *how*? You just committed regicide."

Deleon looked annoyed. "*Arlum* committed regicide. I thought it would be more beneficial for us to take the King hostage. Better yet, take that idiot Prince Callum hostage. That slime would pay half a castle easy to save his sorry skin."

Jair laughed "That he would." The clouds had passed and the trees seemed to have relished the rainfall, swaying in the now gentle breeze.

"What are you trying to accomplish?

Deleon shrugged. "Revolution? Is that the word for it?"

"I don't know, you tell me."

Deleon only laughed. "The winds are changing, Jair. The Starscape won't be the same for too much longer."

He reached into his pocket and produced a small pipe, which he pressed between his lips.

"Aren't you a bit young for that?" Jair asked him.

Deleon shrugged, took the pipe from his mouth and threw it down into the darkness.

"It wasn't mine anyways."

"How did you come to be in a group like this?"

Again, Deleon laughed. "I think Vikron is my third cousin... no, my uncle's third cousin... or is it...?" He shrugged. "I don't remember. Family."

"Distant family," quipped Jair.

Deleon looked out over the cliffside. "Family still."

JAIR

CHAPTER 21

JOSHYA IV

The sun beat down like a fire from the heavens, engulfing him in a warmth he had never felt before. Joshya tried opening his eyes, but as soon as he did, they forced themselves shut again. He cried out for help but no one answered. Dust filled his mouth and nose and he could not keep himself from coughing. The phlegm escaped his lungs only to be replaced by more dust. Joshya heard the faint sounds of shouting in the distance and he strained to call out again. He could barely move, and his lower body felt as though a giant hammer had mistaken him for a nail. He wiggled his fingers, then his toes. *Not broken, thank the Gods.* Still blinded, he struggled to shove the debris from his chest, but it was too heavy. Defeated, he lay back on the ground and prayed he would not die. The voices grew louder around him and he felt someone shoving the dirt from his chest. A hand then grabbed his shoulder and hoisted him up until he was on his knees. Joshya looked up, but his eyes couldn't make out who it was.

"My prince!" the voice said.

It was a male voice, that was for certain, and whoever it was had muscles. The man picked Joshya up and carried him like a babe in his arms. As his eyes slowly began to adjust to the light, he realized just what he was seeing for the first time. *The sky... I can see it! It's the SKY*! It was beautiful, but just as quickly it was gone, disappearing behind dirt and clay as the man took him into the open mouth of a tunnel. He watched as the natural light faded into torchlight as he was brought deeper into the dirt.

Finally, in the dim light he could see who bore him, but seeing the man made no difference; Joshya had no idea who he was. He placed the prince gently down onto a clay table in the infirmary chamber. Clay flasks lined the walls, and a scrawny man with a tuft of grey hair sprouting from his chin was fumbling through them. Faraday was the palace medic, being the only man with any remote amount of medical knowledge. Joshya felt him frantically poking and prodding at his body.

"He's alright," Faraday told the mystery man. "I wish the same could be said for the King."

Joshya tensed. "Where is my father?" he croaked. His throat was as dry as the soil surrounding him.

Faraday looked nervous. "King Artemis is alive, my prince, but he is badly injured and I'm afraid he's not yet awake."

 JOSHYA

Suddenly, Joshya remembered that they weren't the only two in the hall. "And what of Himrel and Orrel?

"In the dungeons, my prince."

Joshya could have sworn he misheard. "What did you say?"

'They're in the dungeons, my prince."

"For what crime?"

"My prince... are you unaware of what happened?"

Joshya shook his head. "The ceiling crumbled. Then I blacked out."

Faraday frowned. "My prince, we were attacked, by a Corvusi trebuchet battalion. Our soldiers are currently holding them off from on the surface."

From on the... It was too much for Joshya to take in at once. The questions poured out. "When did we have soldiers? How did they get on the surface? How did the Corvusi find us?" He sat up and looked directly at the mystery man. "Take me to my father."

"He is not fit to see you, my prince," Faraday interjected.

"Then take me to the dungeons. I want to see Himrel."

Faraday bit his lip as he and the mystery man exchanged a glance, but Joshya's wish was granted.

The dungeons were devoid of all light, so Joshya had to bring a torch in from the entrance. His legs were still sore, but he could stand on his own two feet. As he walked the corridors, the prisoners scampered to the bars, arms outstretched. The stench made Joshya wince. His mind was still fixated on the sight of the sky. He wanted to go back out, but Faraday had

told him it was too dangerous. The mystery man, who'd intro-
duced himself eventually as Dustin, led Joshya to a cell close
by to the mouth of the dungeons. Inside sat a dusty and bloody
Himrel. It seemed as though no one had bothered to clean him
off. Scrapes covered his arms and legs and dried blood was
evident on the floor. They had even stripped him down to his
undergarments. By his eyes, Joshya could tell that Himrel was
much more angry than he was injured. He glared out the bars
and gritted his teeth as they approached. Joshya looked back
in pity.

"Are you alright?"

Himrel spat. His saliva was laced with mucus and blood. "I
don't deserve to be in here."

Joshya moved closer. "That's not what I asked."

"Do I look alright to you?" Himrel snapped.

Joshya didn't answer; instead he asked: "What about your
grandfather, the half-crow?"

"Alive, but being treated like a full crow."

"Him -" Joshya started, but before he could finish, Himrel
threw a wad of wet clay in his direction. The muck splattered
on the wall inches from Joshya's cheek. A few bits plastered
onto his skin and dripped. Faraday placed a hand on Joshya's
shoulder.

"I think it would be best for us to leave, my prince."

Hurt, Joshya demanded again to be allowed to see his father. Not knowing what to expect, he was led back to the infirmary, where Faraday brought him to a small, dimly-lit cham-

 JOSHYA

ber. Joshya moved sheepishly into the room where his father lay. He could see his father's right leg was badly injured, but the worst was by far his head. His one eye was dilated and half of his head looked swelled to twice the size of the other. Awake now, The King smiled at his son and beckoned him closer. Faraday was nervously wiping one hand on his shirt and fidgeting with a small tool.

"Father," was all Joshya could muster.

Unspeaking, his father nodded, as if to say he understood. The light behind the King's eyes was still very much there, but the look on his face was a mixture of confusion, pain, and sadness.

"He'll live," said Faraday to the ground, as if not wanting to look. "He'll be indisposed for a while, but he'll pull through."

Joshya felt a tear stream down his face. He'd never realized just how much he cared for and loved his father, and how close to losing him he'd just come. A knock came from outside and in walked Aldar. Joshya attempted to wipe the tear from his face, but the flow had already begun.

"Joshya." Aldar looked solemn. "Please, come with me."

Aldar led Joshya to a part of the palace he had never been to before. A large table centered the chamber. As Joshya came closer, it shocked him to find that it was made of solid wood instead of clay. Aldar motioned to the chair obviously meant for the King.

"Please, sit."

Joshya was taken aback. "My father's seat."

JOSHYA

"This is a time of great crisis, and with your father incapacitated, we need you here." He motioned again.

Sitting in his father's chair made Joshya feel more important than he'd ever felt before. Aldar stepped out of the room, leaving Joshya to himself. He rubbed his hands along the rough armrests, also made of shaped wood. The chair was old, most likely made long before the tunnels were sealed. He thought for a moment about how much time and effort must have gone into crafting such a simple object. *It must have been quite the job.* Suddenly the feeling of responsibility hit him and wiped the smile from his face, just in time, as Aldar returned with others in tow. Joshya recognized Vylarr and his father's chief architect, Myka. The other man he did not know. Vylarr sat to Joshya's right and Aldar to his left. Myka, sat past Aldar and the last chair was filled with the weaselly man that Joshya had never seen before. Vylarr spoke.

"Prince Joshya, allow me to introduce you to Errgoth, your father's head of surveillance."

Joshya looked at the man, confused. "What exactly do you survey?"

"The surface, Your Grace."

"The...," he stopped and collected himself. Joshya tried to speak again, but he had so many questions that the words caught in his throat.

Aldar saw his look of bewilderment and gave him a sympathetic glance. "Your Grace, there is much you need to know."

 JOSHYA

Vylarr continued for him. "The war with the Corvusi never ended, only stagnated. We have had soldiers up on the surface ever since the tunnels were shut. Whenever the Corvusi army gets too close to our tunnels, our troops lead them away." He paused. "Evidently, they finally were able to pinpoint us and hurled a boulder through our front door."

"How many men do we have up top?

"Not enough," answered Vylarr. "For every soldier we have, the crows have five to match them."

Joshya's head was swimming. "So why keep this a secret?"

It was Aldar's turn to speak. "Our people think we're trapped down here. If they knew the truth there would be a revolt. Your father would be killed by the mob, then you, you mother, your sister, and anyone else they guessed was in on the secret. After that, they would head straight to the surface, be quickly spotted, and then they would all die. The entire population of the Scorpio Tunnels would go extinct in a matter of days."

Joshya thought he understood but wasn't certain. "So, what do we do now?"

Aldar spoke again. "Well, Joshya, that is entirely up to you. As the acting King you make the call. We are here as your council, but the ultimate decision rests solely with you."

Solely with me. He thought of his father, how he must have had to make similar tough decisions. Joshya had no idea what to do, but he needed to look strong. These were his people now, at least until his father was fit to rule again. Sitting up in his chair, Joshya tried to look as kingly as he could.

"Aldar, Myka, get the common people as low in the tunnels as you can; Vylarr, gather anyone able to fight and bring them to this room." He looked to the spy in front of him. "Errgoth, take me to the surface - I want to see what I'm dealing with."

The tunnel to the surface was hidden away better than Joshya could have imagined. As Errgoth led him from chamber to chamber he understood how its existence was kept a secret for so long. Left. Right. Up. Down. Past this pit and under that causeway. When they at last reached the final tunnel leading to the surface, Errgoth stopped and looked back towards him.

"Are you sure you are ready for this, Your Grace?"

No, he thought. "Yes," he said.

The two entered. As they walked up the winding tunnel, torchlight began to give way to sunlight, until it was so bright that Joshya could no longer see. He paused, covering his eyes with the back his hand. His skin burned, his eyes watered, and the air felt thin. A hand was placed on his shoulder, and he was led, blinded, across an expanse. The air was warm, but uncomfortable against his skin. Suddenly, he felt cool again and Joshya allowed himself to open his eyes. Errgoth had placed him in the shade of a large wooden pole, layered with smaller poles that ended in a thick green moss that protected him the harshness of the sun. Errgoth saw him staring and grinned.

"A tree, Your Grace. You'll find a lot of them up here."

Joshya surveyed the world around him in amazement as the words to describe it caught in his throat. He felt outside his own body, like someone had torn his senses from the confines of his mind. Everything around him was new. It looked new, it sounded new, the air even smelled new. He wanted to run and frolic, but his thoughts of wonder were cut off by the distant sounds of steel on steel. Errgoth tapped him on the shoulder and passed him a small knife.

"In case something happens."

The spymaster allowed Joshya a few minutes before pulling him from under the brush. For the first time. Joshya noticed that the ground was soft. *Grass*, he thought. *This is grass.* It sprawled over the landscape like an infection. Everywhere he looked it was green. Errgoth led Joshya across the field for close to an hour, until they reached the summit of a small hill, and the spymaster forced him down onto the ground and lay next to him. Joshya squinted as he watched a troop of men marching in a loose formation across the field. In tow was a huge wooden machine pulled by two huge beasts with horns. Oxen, Joshya guessed, from his recollection of Aldar's books. The machine they pulled was adorned with a large arm and net.

"Is that what brought down the throne room?"

Errgoth frowned "Too small. A trebuchet, yes; *this trebuchet*, not likely."

JOSHYA

They have more than one? Joshya thought, his nerves rising.

Errgoth nudged him and motioned with his head towards the ridge to their east. "Look."

An arrow trailing fire suddenly appeared from over the ridge and struck the machine near its top. Orange flames flickered and spread along the beams. The Corvusi column stopped. Standing strong, they drew their own bows and began forming a defensive line. A few of the soldiers attempted feebly to climb the trebuchet and beat out the flames, but to no avail. That's when more arrows came. This time in a volley, and this time directed at the men. A few Corvusi went down, but the majority of the arrows fell far short. After that, the arrows started flying in both directions. From his position on the knoll, Joshya couldn't actually see the assailants, but every now and again he heard the unmistakable shriek of death. He winced at the noise, clutching the knife Errgoth had given to him firmly to his palm.

A horn blew and a surge of armoured men charged over the top of the ridge, crying out and waving swords in the air. A few of the Corvusi dropped their own bows to draw black-handled dirks. The rest continued to loose arrows at the attackers. At the rear of the charge, a man with a heavy beard and iron half helm revealed himself as the horn blower, bringing it to his lips and blowing loud and long, waving a flag in his other hand. A Scorpius flag. With sudden realization Joshya gasped and looked to Errgoth.

"They are our men."

"Yes," said Errgoth. He was calm as still water.

"But... The surface, no one alive has ever seen it aside from you and my father and..." his head was swimming. "... not since the war."

"Joshya." Errgoth looked him in the eye. "The war never ended."

Joshya felt a tear roll down the side if his face, and he realized that he was scared.

CHAPTER 22

GRELHYM III

The doors shut suddenly behind them. All heads turned to the large wooden doors as the sound of large beams being jammed against the exit filled the room. Three men-at arms in well-placed locations around the room stood in their seats, and fired pre-loaded crossbows at the table. All at once, three of the delegates were face-down in their pudding. A gasp went up from the remaining men, including Meikal, who in a miraculous surge of strength stood and pressed his open palms against the long table, eyes darting from one man to another.

"This is outrageous! Which of you is responsible fo–?"

King Terreon had the point of his dagger nudged against the underside the old man's chin.

"Hush now, Meikal. You are a good man and I do not wish your death to be on my hands."

Meikal lowered himself back into his seat. "Terreon, please..."

The Sagittarius King frowned with his cold eyes and spoke slowly. "Not another word."

The three men-at arms had reloaded their crossbows, and were moving their aim around the table, looking for an excuse to fire. Closer up, Grelhym could see the unmistakable archer standard sown onto each of their breasts. None of the delegates made an attempt to move, but a few cursed beneath their breaths. A personal medic to one of the shot delegates was standing over him, trying pointlessly to staunch his already deceased master's wound. One or two of the squires beside him had taken out their daggers, but not Grelhym. He was frozen in place, unsure of what the best move was. Terreon stood to address the room.

"My fellow delegates, lords, ladies, kings, queens, knights, and other important persons, I regret that I must inform you of something." He addressed them with the respect and calmness that you'd expect from a gentleman, instead of the feckless backstabber he was. "The Sagittarius homeworld has been on a steep decline in the past five years. Now, over thirty of my cities are starving due to the lack of greenery. There is no produce to farm, no game to hunt, no fruit to pick. I'm afraid the situation is too dire to wait any longer in civility. As such, I will be taking the artifact."

"The hell you are!" The delegate for Eridanus spat the words as three crossbows simultaneously fixed upon his forehead. He was a knight with a bald head and braided beard adorned with gold rings. He stood and pointed a finger accusingly at Terreon, who seemed unamused by the interruption. "We all need that artifact just as much as you."

He reached down and unclasped a dirk from his side. But before he could raise it, a bolt pierced him in the temple, sending a sickening wet thump through the quiet room as he hit the table face first. Grelhym wanted to throw up. Terreon continued as though nothing had happened.

"I have a deal for those of you who wish to accept. Once I have successfully brought my world to its former glory, I will gladly forsake the artifact to any faction that does not stand in my way. In fact, I have already proposed this deal to some of you, who have graciously accepted."

The fat man with the whale standard stood from his chair. "I, Prince Dayvon of Cetus, accept this deal. You have my support."

Another man with a brown fur coat far too big for his body stood. "I, Lord Daxon of Canis Major, accept this deal. You have my support."

Grelhym was shocked as the next to rise was Lord Rygar, who cleared his throat before saying: "I, Lord Rygar of Fornax, accept this deal. You have my support."

Grelhym felt guilty by association. He hated his Lord, but never imagined Rygar could stoop so low. *Not to this level of cowardice.*

One of the men on the very far side of the table spoke up with a calm yet firm voice. "And if we refuse?"

The three men at arms trained their weapons at his forehead. Terreon gave them the signal to stand down. "If you refuse, Sir Halfort, then I will kill you here and now, without hesitation."

Another bolt flew through the air, but this time it landed square in the chest of one of the crossbow-wielding men-at-arms. With a grunt, he fell to his knees, crossbow dropping, still loaded. Sir Halfort smiled a wicked smile.

"Terreon, you fool. I have been charged with protecting my King and his interests for twenty years; did you think you'd be the only one to slip in a few armed guards of their own?"

The two remaining men-at-arms searched the crowd, waving their crossbows wildly from person to person as their comrade grasped feebly at the shaft protruding from his lung. The sound of steel sliding from scabbard filled the room. Sir Halfort drew his own blade, a red enameled great sword that matched the deep red of his three-pronged beard. Grelhym shrunk back into his seat. *So much for "no weapons at the parley".* Sir Halfort leapt onto the table and gave a great war cry.

The delegation room had suddenly turned into a battlefield, with secret soldiers coming out from every section of the gallery. Grelhym panicked and dived under his seat, in the space between the bench and the floor, curling into as small a ball as he could manage. It turned out that many, a good very many, of the delegates had snuck in their own guards to the gallery.

GRELHYM

Men at arms revealed compartments in the wood where large weapons were concealed, ladies in waiting removed daggers from under their skirts, and even some squires turned out to be highly trained. The sounds of battle cries and steel on steel filled the room for what felt like hours until finally, the noise died down and the battle of the round hall had come to a standstill. Only after a few more minutes did Grelhym allow himself to peek up over the divider and assess the results. One look and he was back down under his bench and vomiting. *Maybe today is the day I finally lose my mind.*

CHAPTER 23

RYMUS III

The fire atop the beacon house blazed against the night sky. Beside it, the shadows of two armed guards wearing helms adorned with curled iron horns paced back and forth. Their shadows cast dancing shapes along the mountainside, fifty feet high and black as pitch. Rymus had hidden his army down the mountain pass, awaiting the all-clear signal. Rymus himself was underneath the fort, poised amongst the iron support beams that attached the wooden fortress to the cliffside. The space was tight, and even tighter still since five of his men shared the crawl space with him. The mission was simple: his brothers had told him that whenever these forts noticed danger, they would turn the flame of their beacons blue. That would alert the lower forts of the oncoming danger. Rymus' job was to steal the powder that they used to change the flame to blue, leaving them no method of warning when Lydus and his men stormed the major castles below. It was a good plan, Rymus admitted, but if he failed everything would fall apart.

The air was cold and wind blew noisily between the beams. He could hear Keldo grumbling under his breath. Rymus clouted him on the ear and the pudgy man quickly quieted himself. For a moment he regretting hitting Keldo, but he wasn't taking any chances at being heard. Keldo was the man he trusted the most - the four others with him he knew far less well. One-Eye Watton was a sour greybeard with a breath like to kill a man. The battleaxe he had slung to his back was chipped from half a hundred battles. One of those battles had cost Watton his left eye, but ask him about it and he couldn't remember which. Beside him were the twin archers Pete and Pate, no older than sixteen. They huddled back to back, bows at the ready with quivers full. The only way Rymus could tell the difference was that Pate had a small scar above his left eyebrow... or was that Pete? Rymus could never remember. Lastly, he had taken a man known only to him as The Slippery Fish. The man was known for having an uncanny ability to get into any place he desired to go. *And by the weight of my coin bag, I'd wager he's gotten in there too*, Rymus thought.

Dust fell on them as a guard walked over the pine boards they were crouched beneath. They held their breaths and waited until the soft thumping of feet dissipated. One-Eye Watton unslung his axe and bared his teeth, or at least, the ones he had left.

 RYMUS

"Let's do it, now and quick like. I want to lick the blood of these goatfuckers off the end of my blade." His one remaining eye twirled madly in its socket.

Why did I bring this one? he thought.

Another guard passed over them and Rymus placed a hand on Watton's shoulder. The old man grimaced, but stayed put. Again, they waited for the sound to clear.

Rymus pointed to the outline of a trap door in the wood. The Slippery Fish had showed them this route. "Every fortress has a secret way to get out," he'd told the group, smiling. "Find that, and you find your way in."

Rymus began feeling the boards, as did the twins. It was Pate who smiled.

"I think I feel a latch!" The boy fumbled his fingers around for a while but couldn't seem to jar it open. He grunted softly as a sliver bit into his hand. Frowning, he looked back to Rymus. "It's locked from the inside."

Rymus frowned back at him. *Of course* it was locked from the inside; the trapdoor was for people to get *out*, not *in*. He thought on that for a moment, but before he could do anything, Rymus felt someone brush past him. Beside him, the Slippery Fish moved like a shadow, lightly moving Pate to the side. Without saying a word, he reached up and placed a thin knife between the wooden panels. He jiggled it lightly back and forth and within seconds the group could hear a light click. The Fish slipped the dagger back into his belt and motioned for Rymus.

Stunned at what he'd just witnessed, it took him a moment before moving forward.

Rymus placed his ear against the door, but heard nothing. *It could mean no one's inside, or someone's being very quiet.* Ever so carefully, he lifted the door, but only by a sliver, just enough to peek inside. The room was very dark, but Rymus' eyes were already adjusted. All he could see were two bedposts before him. *We're under a bed*, he suddenly realized. Rymus opened the trapdoor a little further, careful not to bump the bedframe above. He slid himself up and through onto the floor and motioned for the others to stay where they were.

Like a fish on land, he wriggled out from under the bed, and lay on his back. From there, he could hear the soft breath of a sleeping man. Rising to his feet, he could see the captain's helm on a nightstand beside the bed, and his sword propped and sheathed against the wall. The captain of the fort was sleeping peacefully, one hand dangling off the side of the bed and a line of saliva darkening the pillow beneath his head. Rymus drew a dagger from his belt. He took a deep breath before driving the blade though the man's heart. The captain would have made a gasping sound, that was, if Rymus hadn't placed a hand over his mouth. Before long, the captain grew still. Blood was soaking through the mattress and turning the entire bed a shade of dark red.

Rymus watched as Keldo attempted to pry his gut from under the lip of the bedframe. He looked like a piglet attempting to squeeze out of a trough and Rymus had to hold back the sud-

RYMUS

den urge to laugh. Without his waxed blue armor, Keldo looked more like an alley drunk than a lieutenant, although perhaps he was a little of both. Finally, he popped free and from behind him came the twins, then One-Eye, and lastly the Fish. The six stood together in the room. Watton couldn't keep his one eye off the body.

"Did he put up a good fight, Captain."

Rymus wiped the knife on his pant leg. "Just stay focussed on the mission."

The Fish slipped into the next room over, and gave them the all clear. The beacon was just across the fort from where they were. A guard with a loaded crossbow stood next to the great flame. Two more stood below. All three looked to be on high alert.

"How do we get across?" asked Keldo.

"We fight our way across," Watton piped in, tightening his grip on his axe.

Rymus looked sidelong at him. "No, only one of us needs to get across." He turned his attention to the Slippery Fish. "Think you can handle it?"

He nodded. Rymus watched from the window as his man crossed the dark fort's yard until he reached the back of the beacon tower. One of the guards was making his rounds and the Fish had to slip back into the cover of night to avoid being seen. Sure enough, the guard walked right by.

Suddenly, a door opened from behind them and a young Aries footman stood slack jawed in the doorway. Rymus' heart skipped a beat and he froze. One-eye lifted his axe and the twins drew their bows. Watton took a step forward, but the twins were quicker. Pete fired first. The arrow sailed over the footman's shoulder. Pate's arrow came less than a second later and sank deep into the boy's forearm. He looked to his wound, as the blood gushed from the skin, and then ran outside.

"Bugger," winced Rymus as he ran after him.

The rest followed. The twins even passed him. Pate was first to be out the door. Rymus called for him to wait, but the boy entered the yard anyway, where two loaded crossbows were directed at him. An instant later, Pate was stumbling back into the room, one shaft protruding from his collar, the other from his side. Pete held his brother as he collapsed, alive, but badly hurt. The blood spurted from the bowman's wounds and stained his brother's black jerkin. Pete was softly muttering to himself and began shaking uncontrollably. Rymus heard the distinct click of a crossbow being reloaded and slammed the wooden door shut - just before a bolt smacked loudly into the wood. One-Eye Watton latched the door and pressed his weight against it.

"We need to go." Keldo stood with his sword drawn, noticeably worried. "It's too late, they'll have blued the beacon."

Rymus chanced a quick peek out the open window.

"Not yet they haven't." He hoped the Fish was quick enough to have already secured the top of the tower. Pate was grunting on the floor, thumping his fist against the wood. His brother had removed the bolt from his collar and was pressing a strip

RYMUS

of cloth against the wound. The door was being pounded at from outside. Suddenly, the Fish was behind them. In his arms he held a sack of powder.

"I hope this was all they had."

Rymus nodded at him. "We have to go. Now."

Pate was still writhing on the floor and Pete was oblivious to anything Rymus might say. One-Eye shook his head as the wooden door began to crack behind him.

"That latch won't hold. They'll be on us before we're out." The window smashed and an Aries soldier holding a short sword climbed through. "Go!" Watton shouted.

Keldo needed no more coaxing than that. He took off back towards the captain's quarters as the wooden door split. Rymus nodded to One-Eye and followed his second. From the corner of his eye he saw Watton bury his axe in the neck of the soldier at the window as the door burst open. Then he was out of sight.

Keldo was first back in the captain's quarters. He grabbed the frame of the bed and tossed it on its side. The captain's body flopped to the floor with a wet smack.

"We have to keep moving. It won't take them long to find the trapdoor."

Rymus heard a scream from down the hall, but he had no idea if it came from one of his men or theirs.

Keldo opened the latch and leapt down through the trapdoor, followed by the Fish. Rymus was about to follow when he heard running footsteps coming from the hall. Drawing his sword, he had just seconds to parry as the enemy was on him.

Swords bit against one another and Rymus was thrown to the ground. A second blow came right behind the first, nearly taking off Rymus' sword arm as he rolled out of the way. Rymus was able to deflect the third blow, but it sent his blade spiraling through the air, disappearing through the trapdoor. *Just my luck.* Lunging forward, he head-butted his assailant in the chest, barreling him down onto the ground as a struggle ensued.

One punch hit Rymus on the jaw so hard he tasted blood. Another nearly broke his nose. Rymus then remembered the captain's sword lying against the wall. Leaning back, he gripped the handle and raised the sword from its sheath and above his head. Before he brought it down though, a different sword cleaved the man's head from his shoulders. Turning, Rymus saw Keldo removing his now bloody sword from where it stuck in the wooden floor. He grabbed Rymus by the shoulder and yanked him through the trapdoor. Once all three were down, the Fish shut the door behind them.

As quickly as they could, the three shimmied back down to the path. In the light of the beacon tower, Rymus watched as at least fifty bowmen, crossbowmen, and spearmen rushed down the mountain, leaping from boulder to boulder with footing as sure as silk.

Fifty is enough to be the death of us all. He thought, panicked. Still gripping the dead captain's sword, Rymus ran headlong down the mountainside, nearly tripping a dozen times before he reached the encampment of his men. There was no time

RYMUS

to mount up on horseback, they needed to be gone from the mountainside. Reaching his horse, he yanked his spear from its holster and held it in the air. A few of the men were startled to see him back so fast.

"Gather up!" he called. "We're setting off now!"

The men took no time waiting for more instruction. Within ten minutes the entire battalion was moving down the mountain. Rymus' heart beat faster than it ever had before. Sweat dripped from his brow and down into his eyes, but he made no attempt to wipe it. A call came from over the mountain and suddenly a wash of arrows cascaded over his men. Rymus held his hands above his head and crouched, as if that would do anything. Opening one eye, he saw that he was unscathed, though the same could not be said for all his men. The Aries men left them no time to gain their composure.

"Nock!" Rymus heard. "Draw!"

"Run!" he called.

CHAPTER 24

ALMOND III

They camped just within the treeline, at the point where the creek forked in two. It was a day's ride south to reach the next town over, but only half that distance to reach the rift. Hoss had decided they should rest under the cover of the canopy, though Almond wasn't sure it would matter. The thin brush surrounding the fork in the creek was too small to even be called a forest. From one side she could see right through to the other. The ground sloped down to its lowest point where the creek met the soil and gurgled noisily. A tree had recently fallen across, damming part of the water. Hoss sat on its remaining stump, poking at their mediocre fire with a dead branch. Almond could see the frustration displayed on his weathered face as he prodded the embers, trying feebly to reignite what was left. He grumbled to himself and spat into the leaves.

Hoss had surmised that Jackan and his pack would surely be heading south to the nearby town situated there, too tempted by the notion of picking up a few more captives before returning to the rift. Hoss had hoped to catch them before they reached the small brushed area around the fork, but they had been too slow. By the look of the hoof prints in the mud, the hunting dogs had been here near a day past. Almond herself had never been this far south of Rimby, but Hoss had, and he had told her that it was the only place between her town and the Rift with enough cover for a surprise attack.

Hoss angrily threw his branch into the water and stood. One last wisp of embers rose from the fire pit before going out. Almond frowned. She wanted to say something encouraging to him, anything, but nothing appropriate came to mind. She realized that there was nothing she could say that could help. Instead, she made her way closer to the shore of the creek, where she rolled her pant cuffs up to her knees and waded into the water. Hagon the Fisherman had taught her how to catch trout with nothing more than a sharpened stick. Earlier in the day, Almond had retrieved the straightest branch she could find, and had whittled the end to a point with one of Hoss' daggers. She stood in the stance Hagon had taught her and waited until she saw movement between her legs. But when she drove it into the water, the stick only struck the rocks beneath and snapped down its centre. She threw the broken half aside and crouched, hoping to get another chance. She did, but again she missed, and nearly teetered into the water.

ALMOND

If Hagon were here, we'd be feasting tonight, she thought. Almond missed the people of her village. She missed Grett and Falmir, the stable boys; Sweet Rosa and her powdered cakes. She even missed the ugly armourer's apprentice boy with the fat, pox covered cheeks who teased her. Yet somehow Rimby itself no longer felt like home to her. Without her father or her grandmother, it seemed more like a memory.

As the water rippled beneath Almond's feet, she caught a glimpse of her reflection. The nut-brown eyes that gave Almond her name were puffy, their edges circled in red. Her tears had long since dried, but the signs of her pain still remained. Something swam between her toes and she jerked forward, lost her balance, and fell hard against the stones below, sending water splashing over onto the grass. The fall sent her head beneath the surface and she scrambled back gasping for her breath. She brushed the soaking hair from her face and spat creek water from her mouth. Almond's eyes were doused in water and stung. Grimacing, she wiped them with her palms. When she could open them again, she was face to face with the butt of a cane. Hoss stood on the shore, arm outstretched with walking cane in hand. She grabbed the end of it as Hoss pulled her to her feet. Together they walked back to the fire pit where Hoss seemed to have gotten it alight again while she was in the stream. As Almond sat, the old man continued to the carriage where he pulled a bow from the baggage and slung it over his shoulder, then took half a dozen arrows and slipped them beneath his arm.

 ALMOND

"There's bound to be rabbit or something along this stretch," he told her.

Almond thought about asking to come, but decided not to. Her body ached with the cold water and she had no intention of straying too far from the fire. As Hoss strode off down the length of the creek, Almond pulled her shirt from over her shoulders and held it over the fire. Drops fell and sizzled in the coals. Even as much as she liked Hoss, she couldn't strip in front of him without feeling uncomfortable. After all, he was at least forty-five years her elder. Something in her told her that he knew that. They had food enough in the cart; Hoss had no true reason to go hunting. More like, he meant to leave her with some privacy for a while as she dried.

While she whittled a new fishing spear, her clothes hung from a truss above the fire, nearly dry. Day trotted up beside her and whinnied lightly. Almond brushed her on the cheek and smiled. The mare was the gentlest horse she'd ever met. Rising to her feet, she donned her clothes again, tucking the tattered bits of her shirt into her trousers and moved towards the carriage. Inside she pulled out a crate of red and green apples and picked the deepest of the reds, then paused and pulled out a second when she thought of the other horse. She wasn't as fond of Night, but the dusky gelding deserved the treat after the long day he'd spent pulling the carriage.

She whistled and both animals came loping towards her. She fed the first apple to Day, who lapped it up in no more than three bites as her tail whipped behind her. After another brush of the mane Almond turned to Night. The black horse was larger, and much sterner in its gait. Almond cautiously held out the other apple. Night took a sniff and snorted. Almond could hear laughing from down the way.

"Night don't like them apples. He only likes them sour green ones!"

When Almond turned, she saw Hoss coming towards her, smiling like a fool. In one hand he held his bow and in the other a fat duck with an arrow through its eye. He sat himself before the fire and began plucking the down from his catch. Almond joined him, but before she did she returned to the cart and tossed a hard green apple down Night's way. The big horse whinnied happily and munched at it.

"Do we have a plan for when they come?" asked Almond, studying the way Hoss plucked at the bird.

"The beginning of one," he answered, "but it all relies on Jackan returning to this fork in the road."

That puzzled her. "How can we be sure he'll come back?"

"We can't." He paused as he peeled the skin from the duck like a sock from a foot. "But if we ride south for Dunwell, then the dogs will be well gone by the time we arrive. And if we ride east for the rift, then we'll be meeting them out in an open field. One way we miss them, the other they can't miss us." He continued. "The way I see it, they need to take a bridge across the creek or risk their horses breaking an ankle, and one hundred yards from here is the closest bridge. Luckily the rift is on our side of the creek."

ALMOND

Almond helped him as Hoss skewered the duck onto a spit. "Do you think the people of Dunwell will be alright?" she asked him.

Hoss thought for a moment before answering. "Back when I was a little older than you are now, I knew a man, a great man. His name was Sir Jorge of Dunwell. He vowed that he'd never allow his precious town to fall. I believe he'll try to uphold that oath."

Almond walked back towards the carriage and pulled some spices from a chest "Do you think he can?"

Hoss did not answer.

"*That* old man?"

Almond's head shot around faster than she thought possible. Just behind the treeline stood a man with sharpened teeth, wearing black leather, and staring down at Hoss. *No,* she thought. *No, no it can't be!* Hoss was already on his feet. Almond's heart raced and she dove into the chest, sealing the lid behind her. It was cramped, but she could fit. *Had they seen me?* She wanted more than anything to jump out and help Hoss, but she remembered his words: "If anything, *anything*, happens: You hide in the back of the carriage, understand?"

And so she lay there, hoping that no one would find her, and cursing at her cowardice.

CHAPTER 25

DERRON IV

Derron lay under the cover of a large dying bush. The dirt beneath his fingers was cold as ice and snow was beginning to pile atop his back. He wanted to brush it off, but he couldn't risk the noise. Less than ten feet in front of him were at least fifteen men. They wore layered dry bark as armour over their chests and forearms and held thick clubs and bows made of yew. A few had their hair tied back with knots of grass and others were bald with painted heads. One thing was uniform, however: it seemed that every one of them had the standard of a Lynx carved deep into the palms of their left hands. It was hard to see, but every now and again one of them would walk close enough and the symbol would be clear as day in reddened scar tissue. These were no doubt men of Lyncis, a nomadic faction close-by Ursa Major in the Starscape. Where most of the factions over the years had prospered and grown into fully formed cities and towns, the Lyncis had regressed to little more than tribal clansmen. Derron knew the implications of what he was seeing. There were no Lyncis on his homeworld, which could only mean that they had come through a separate rift from their own world. In turn, that meant any number of factions could eventually be led here, and that thought scared Derron to his core.

One of the Lyncis stepped within touching distance of him. Derron breathed shallow breaths as to not be heard. He needed to stay as long as possible until he could find out why they were here, and if possible, where the rift was that they had come from. His eyes wandered, scanning the area. He knew Anthon and Gar were somewhere close-by, in case things turned sour. Knowing Anthon, he was probably crouched in some close-by tree, getting a bird's eye view. Gar was probably closer to the ground, like Derron, though he hoped that his man had found some place a bit more comfortable.

Derron heard the sound of geese migrating overhead and watched as a thin shafted arrow pierced one through the breast, accompanied by cheers from the camp. The bird fell somewhere over the treeline, and four men left to retrieve it. For a moment Derron pondered attempting to capture one of the men staying behind, but he had doubts it would be feasible and elected to stay put. The bandage on his arm had begun to soak in the moisture of the snow and mud, causing his forearm to go numb with the cold. Still, he didn't move. By his own es-timate, it must have been close to three hours before he overheard anything remotely helpful - a passing comment from one man to another about how they were to move north towards a large lake on the morrow. That caused a feeling of panic to strike Derron. They know something, but how? Most of the rest of the conversations consisted of talk about food, women, and war.

When the camp had fallen asleep and the watcher had gone off to piss, Derron rose to his feet. The hours of lying still in the cold had caused his muscles to seize and it took everything in his power to not grunt in pain. He moved silently in the snow directly away from the Lyncis camp back towards his own. As he moved, he heard a *THUMP* as Anthon leapt down from a nearby branch. Together, they found Gar fast asleep beside a large rock a good twenty feet from camp. Anthon gave him a light kick and he shot up to his feet. When he realized who it was, he blushed and had the decency to look ashamed. Derron didn't have time to be annoyed, though. He needed to rendez-vous back to the others before the Lyncis found them.

"They're coming here?" asked Alymer when Derron informed them of the situation.

Melwick was stroking his chin and looking contemplative, no doubt running through the same thought process Derron himself had. Roman picked up a long branch.

"Best begin to make something to defend ourselves. Only half of us still have any sort of real weapon on us."

DERRON

He pulled out a knife and began to whittle a spear. Skoma had the faintest hint of a smile on his face, feeling the edge of his ever-sharpened sword. Mollens looked paler than a ghost.

"So, what do we do?" the boy asked.

Derron looked at him somberly. "If they're here, it can only mean that they know something about what is here, and we cannot let them find it."

Mollens nodded. Roman handed him another large branch.

"Best get carving, kid."

Derron motioned to Melwick and the two of them walked away from the others.

"The Lyncis are tribesmen. There's no way they would be interested in coming here," said Melwick, when they were far enough away.

"But the simple truth is that they are, and they knew to come this way."

Melwick shook his head "There must be some other explanation."

"There may be, but until we know for sure, I need all of us prepped. Even you."

"You know that I'm a scholar, not a fighter."

"I also know that you have a longbow you've been carrying around."

Melwick looked at him quizzically. "You know that's for hunting game."

"Derron smiled. "Ever considered hunting a lynx?"

While the group prepped armour and weapons for themselves, Derron sent Melwick to watch the ridge for any sign of movement. The camp they had scouted was less than a day's walk from where they were and any number of Lyncis men could appear at any time now. Derron had no idea what was coming, so he was preparing for the worst, but nothing could have prepared him when Melwick came back, telling him that there were one hundred men positioned down the ridge. And their leader was asking for him.

"Asking for me," Derron repeated

Melwick nodded. "Specifically, for you. He stood atop a stump and called out for Derron."

Derron frowned. "Not *The King* or *King Derron?*"

Mewick shook his head. "No, only Derron." He paused. "And there's something else."

☆ ☆ ☆

Derron stood with his walking stick in hand, looking over the small army before him. To his left, Snaggletooth stood licking his lips and pawing at the ground. To his right, Melwick had an arrow notched on his bowstring. Behind him, the rest of his men gathered with swords, wooden spears, knives, and wood-axes. It made a less than intimidating sight, but he hoped that the man standing across from him would think it was a fraction of his force, instead of his entire strength. Even Will stood with them, in the very back leaning on a six-foot spear crudely carved with a fire-hardened tip. His leg was still bandaged but

 DERRON

hidden beneath his pants. Derron smiled and thumped his stick firmly into the snow-covered ground.

"Welcome, friend. Who do I have the pleasure of speaking with?"

The man across from him smiled back. A few of his teeth were missing from his mouth and the bark armour he wore was chipped and cracking. It'd obviously been in more than a few fights. In his right hand he gently swung a wooden club back and forth. Sharp pieces of flint were stuck all along the barrel of the weapon, jutting menacingly from the splintered wood. The man held up his left hand and showed his scarred palm.

"I am Chief Skel Bittertooth of the Red Lynx, slayer of Bannibal the Mighty." Skel lowered his palm and raised his club. "And are you the one known as Derron?"

Derron smiled. "Yes, but I'm afraid I do not have such glorious titles as you, Sir Bittertooth."

No need to tell him any more than he needs to know, he thought.

Skel turned his attention to the rest of the group. "And are you the leader of this tribe?" Derron nodded. "Good, then I propose to you a trade."

Two men were thrust forward from the Lyncis ranks and onto their knees. Each was covered in an array of cuts and bruises. Derron looked sadly upon his men. Fortho looked back at him, one eye swollen closed. Mallard couldn't even manage that.

DERRON

They followed my directions all the way to here, Derron thought, remembering the note he'd left for Fortho and Mallard.

Skel stepped a leather boot on Fortho's back. "Your friend here told me, *eventually,* that there is something important hidden here in this land. Yet no matter how hard I pressed him, he swears he doesn't know what it is." Skel looked dead into Derron's eyes. "Regardless, I want it, and I assume that you have it."

"And in exchange, you give me back my men?"

Skel laughed. "No, in exchange you get one of your men. You get the other when you give me all your food, weapons, and winter clothes."

Derron was fuming inside, but managed to keep his calm disposition. "That sounds more like extortion than a trade to me."

"This is how Skel Bittertooth does trades."

He pressed down harder on Fortho's back. Derron felt his men stirring behind him. He cleared his throat.

"I can have you drawn a map to the location of what you wish for."

Skel frowned. "I cannot read maps. Maps are for the weak." He spat. "Chief Derron will lead me personally."

It was Derron's turn to frown. A map he could fake, but you could only lead a person in circles for so many hours before they got suspicious. *But then again, what choice do I have?*

"Chief Derron will lead you personally only if you return his men to him now, with no further harm done to them." He felt like an imbecile talking about himself in the third person, but he hoped it would appeal to the tribesman.

Skel considered the offer for a moment, then pointed to Mallard. "You get that one now and the other one when it is found." He spat again, but this time onto Mallard's back. "That one is no fun, he has no fight in him."

Derron wanted nothing more than to charge the chief and beat him bloody here and now, but he held himself back.

"Deal."

Skel grinned, moving over to Mallard and hoisting him to his feet, then gave him a shove towards Derron. "You're free. Go."

Mallard hobbled over to the rest of the group. It was clear to Derron that something was wrong with his leg. He motioned to Melwick and the small man put an arm around Mallard and began to check his wounds. Derron gave Skel a nod.

"We need to take our man back to our camp to heal before we set out."

"You should let him die. He is weak. But I will allow you this." Skel gave a command and thirty of his men broke off and walked over to Derron's side. "These real warriors will go with you. Skel is not so stupid as to have you run off on him, Chief Derron."

Derron, in truth, hoped Skel *would* be so stupid as to do that, but thirty was better than one hundred.

"Return here at dawn, or I kill your other man." With that, he turned, and disappeared back into his ranks. Moments later, two tribesmen hauled in Fortho. Derron caught a glimpse of his face as he went. It showed pain, but also resilience. *If Fortho manages to make it out of this alive, there may be a knighthood in his future.*

One of the tribesmen with a scar stretching from his chin to a severed earlobe got right up in Derron's face. He was at least a foot and a half taller than him.

"Move. Do not keep the Chief waiting."

Derron watched as Melwick poked and prodded at Mallard. He went through half a jar of salve just to cover each of the cuts that covered him from his head down to his feet. Melwick gave him a sleep aid and updated Derron.

"Most of the cuts are deep, but will heal. His ankle is cracked by what looks like a deliberate hit, and his right eye is completely bloodshot. *Something must have hit him pretty hard.*"

"Will he be alright?"

"Physically, yes. Over time I think he'll make a full re-covery." Melwick paused. "Mentally, though, he seems pretty shaken. I don't think he's slept since he was captured."

Derron looked over at the broken man. Mallard was the childhood nickname given to Teagan, a farm boy from just out-side the castle next to Three Duck Lake. As a boy, Mallard had loved to go splashing with the waterfowl which had earned him his nickname. But now, at almost thirty, he looked more like a duck after being carved for a roast.

"I have to go collect some sticks for a splint." Melwick's voice broke his train of thought.

"Of course, but don't wander too far. I don't want anyone thinking we're trying to pull something."

From across the camp, he heard yelling as one of the tribesmen attempted to take a part of Roman's rations. Four men stood opposite Roman and Skoma. Each tribesman had a club ready, Roman pointed his spear and Skoma had his sword drawn. Derron ran over and placed himself between them.

"Enough!"

Roman lowered his weapon, but the tribesmen and Skoma did not. Derron glared into his man's eyes until the sword point lowered. One of the tribesmen spat on the ground.

"Your food is ours, grey-man. You are our prisoners."

Derron got up closer to them. "You are our escorts, nothing more, and if you steal from us again, there will be consequences."

The big man didn't seem to understand half the words Derron had said. Instead, he raised his club. A growl from behind him made him stop and turn, seeing Snaggletooth snarling, posed to lunge. Unnerved, the two men backed away. Roman walked up beside his king.

"I don't know what it is that's at the end of that map, but I know I don't want them to have it."

"Nor do I. As soon as there is an opportunity to get Fortho out of harm's way, we abandon them."

"And then what? These are forest-people. No doubt they'll be able to follow us."

Derron's head hurt. "I don't know yet."

As night fell, Derron sat on the edge of the lake, overlooking the moonlight shimmering off the freshly iced-over water. The cold had caused a layer to form, barely thick enough to walk on, where one wrong step would send you plummeting down. Most of the tribesmen lay asleep, but even they weren't stupid enough not to leave a few guards on duty. Derron himself had put two of his own men also on duty, and currently the four men sat in the middle of camp staring each other down. Derron had managed to slip past and find a comfortable spot to sit and think. The night was surprisingly warm, and the snow had stopped. He needed a plan.

Derron doubted his men could take on thirty armed tribesmen without casualty. Even if they could, once dawn hit, Fortho would be killed in retaliation, and Derron doubted he'd be the only one. He was trapped. The only option was to play along until an opportunity arose. If Melwick was correct, they had finally found what they were looking for, and that meant the Starscape itself could fall if Skel was brought there. Perhaps one life is worth sacrificing for everyone else. But he couldn't bring himself to do it. He would think of something. He had to. He gripped the wooden bear claw on his neck and rubbed his forehead. Rising to his feet, he snuck back into camp and lay

 DERRON

on his jacket. Hours passed and he couldn't sleep. When the dark grey sky turned light, he wasn't any closer than he had been at the start of the night. He heard the pounding of club against tree trunk accompanied by the shouts of "Get up!" and "On your feet!" Grabbing his walking stick, he rose and moved around camp, watching his men prepping, and where he could, hinting to keep their weapons at the ready.

As the group returned from the camp, they found Skel standing atop the ridge. Beside him, Fortho knelt, a fresh cut on his brow. Derron frowned and pointed the tip of his walking stick.

"You'll find none of your men are harmed, Chief. I wish you could have said the same for mine."

Skel grinned. "He tried to escape. What was I supposed to do?"

Derron took a deep breath, turned, and swung his stick into the nose of the tribesman beside him. The man fell to his knees, clutching his broken nose as blood dripped through his fingers.

"We are even now."

Skel began laughing. "I like you, Derron." He reached down and picked up Fortho, who rose to his feet. "Come, lead the way."

CHAPTER 26

ALGEN IV

A small drop of blood slid down Algen's fingertip, landing squarely on the pile of oysters he had been prying open for the past half hour. Algen winced and licked at his wound. His blood tasted different now than it had before his transformation, almost saltier. Dropping his oyster knife, he grabbed a leaf of seaweed and attempted to cover the slit before anyone noticed. Yet he knew that it had been too late when he felt the hard hand of Korra smacking him upside the back of his head. He turned to the head chef, and tried looking as sorry as he could muster. She took the bowl teeming with shelled oysters and dumped the contents into the nearest heat geyser. Then, she shoved the empty bowl into Algen's webbed hands and stared him in the eye.

"Do you understand who we are serving today?" she asked him, her sharp teeth grinding in an open scowl. "The Lords of every dome in the sea will be here within the hour to sup with our King. And if one dish doesn't meet their standards, then it will be my head in the next stew." She moved her finger in a motion across her neck. "But don't think that means I won't take yours first."

Algen nodded his acknowledgement.

She grabbed his cut hand and held it up before his face, squeezing just enough for another drop to well up and drip to the floor.

"And do you think they want this in their food?"

Yes, he thought. Pretty much every shark, eel, or ray morph under the dome enjoyed a little blood in their food; at least, his father certainly had. But he knew that wasn't what Korra wanted to hear, so instead he shook his head no.

"Right, so be careful."

She watched as he wiped his finger clean - the blood had stopped seeping by now. Then he picked up his knife and began the process of shelling all over again. When Korra was satisfied with his work, she left him to go harangue some other worker. It was good he couldn't speak, elsewise he may have been tempted to antagonize her even more than he already had. Algen looked again to his finger, where the skin had been sliced open. There were dried fish guts in a small room to the back. The Cancers used the guts as a kind of bandage. When Algen pressed the material to his finger, the innards adhered to the skin and made a seal that would help quell the bleeding.

He wrapped his finger tightly, bent it to test the strength, and moved back to his station.

It took him a solid hour to get back on schedule. Piles of oyster shells stacked near as tall as Algen was. The King's Dome never lacked for food, that was sure. The waters surrounding them teamed with fish, eels, corals, seaweeds, and most of all: oysters. Each morning, a team of morphs had to go out and scrape near two hundred from the outside of the dome. No one knew where they came from and fewer cared. It was an easy source of food and tasted good enough besides. The feast today would require a deal more than usual, however, as there would be close to one hundred and fifty people guesting in the King's Hall that evening. Lords, Ladies, knights, retainers, and they all needed more than a few steamed cod to satisfy them. Algen had heard it said around the kitchens that Lord Harren of the Frost Dome alone could eat the equivalent of ten men. Algen was curious to see if that were true.

By the time he had shelled the last oyster, Algen had enough shells to drown himself in. With the help of two other cook boys, they heaved the massive bowl of meat to sit over the mouth of the closest heat geyser. Instantly, the steam began to turn the metal bowl hot to the touch, and within minutes the meat within began to steam. Algen took a large handful of sea salt from a bag and threw it into the bowl. He winced, as the salt found its way into his wound. Wiping his hand on his leg, he tried to ignore the pain.

The cook boy next to him was chopping sea snakes into hunks for a stew. In one pile, nearly six dozen severed snake heads stared at Algen with dead eyes. The boy's hands were crusted with yellow and green scales which impeded the motion of his fingers and he struggled to hold the knife straight. As the blade wavered in his hand, it slipped, and clattered to the floor. He bent down, but his chubby fingers could not get between the blade and the floor. Algen took pity on the boy, and walked over to pick it up for him. Then, he took a second knife from his work station and began helping chop. The boy smiled, the corners of his mouth similarly crusted like his fingers.

"Thank you," he said with a slurred lisp.

Algen only nodded in acknowledgement. Together they finished the work well before they had anticipated and decided to rest for a short while upon the table as they waited for the water for a stew to boil. However, it was only a few seconds before Korra came bursting into the kitchens again. Algen scrambled to his feet, hoping she hadn't noticed their slacking. But instead of anger, her face showed worry and urgency. She called for the attention of the room.

"The Lords have arrived and my servers are nowhere to be found! I need two of you out there right now!" She searched around, until her eyes locked on the two of them. She pointed.

"Hanlin, Mute Boy, get out there!"

The two boys looked at each other, and hustled over. Korra threw them some fancy scale uniforms and shoved them down towards the serving hall.

"Stand up straight, retrieve for them whatever they ask for, and don't speak to anyone unless spoken to." She gave Algen a sidelong glance. "Shouldn't be too hard for you."

The door slammed behind them, and Algen was left standing in the middle of a hallway, not entirely sure what he was supposed to do, and without a way to ask. The other boy, Hanlin, shrugged and walked to the other end of the hall. Algen followed. The previously empty hall had been filled from end to end with wooden tables and chairs inlaid with whalebone and gemstones. The King sat atop his throne, with a high table before him made to rise all the way up to his waist. A goblet of thick green liquid sat in front of him. Other huge tables lined the walls, each with around twenty high men and women seated behind them, but with the central chairs noticeably empty. The Lords are about to make their entrance, he thought.

As if on cue, the guards at the door parted and three men entered together. The center one marched ahead of the other two and raised a brass horn to his lips, blowing in three short bursts. The two flanking men raised flagpoles that bore the standard of the Cancers: A red crab with shimmering stars for eyes on a field of navy blue. The centre man played a few more notes, before bowing and moving to the side. The two others stood on either side of the door, waving the standards high.

King Caraq took a long swill of his drink, and outstretched his claw arm motioning to the room.

"My people, stand, and welcome our great Lords."

ALGEN

His voice boomed, carrying throughout the huge room. Algen stood off to one side, ready to begin serving. Looking around, he counted fourteen high tables, to match the fourteen other Domes beneath the Sea of Cancer. Seven tables sat to either side of the King's, who wore red scale armor with a light fabric tunic underneath. The fabric was no doubt traded in from some other faction, most likely from the Cetus, who commonly visited the Cancer homeworld. The fabric fit tightly all the way down his right arm, but stopped at his shoulder on his left, no doubt to highlight his great pincer. The room fell silent and Caraq sat up in his chair as the first of the lords entered. The horn blower cleared his throat and announced in a loud voice:

"Lord Harren, of the Frost Dome"

Algen's eyes widened. The man was as fat as three average men and had huge tusks protruding from his mouth, so much so that his lips couldn't close and his cheeks stretched out to the sides to compensate. One tusk was broken about halfway down, but had since been reshaped and completed out of bronze. The break must have happened some time ago because the metal cap had long since rusted into a greenish hue and was riddled with small cracks. The Frost Dome was much further away from the King's Dome than any of the others, Algen knew, in an area where icebergs peppered the surrounding waters. He had heard rumours that the dome itself was freezing cold all year round, and frost often crusted the glass. He shivered at the thought. Lord Harren took his place at the seat closest to Caraq's left. The chair beneath him creaked, and for a moment Algen thought it would break. But it held, and he breathed a sigh of relief. He knew as the lowest rank-ing person in the hall, he was the most likely to be beaten if anything were to go wrong. The horn blower played a few more notes and called out again as the next lord entered.

"Lord Tenasil, of the Broken Dome!"

The man that stepped through the door wore no clothes other than a small cloth over his privates, and the reason was obvious: long tendrils of snaking yellow coral protruded down his back and up his arms and legs. A few pieces seemed to have been filed down behind his knees and in the crease of the elbow. Others, on his hands and head, had been noticeably sharpened to dangerous points.

"Lord Ormic, of the Iron Dome!"

The lord had an expression as though someone had poked a scalding rod up his arse, grimacing despite being the center of the hall's attention. With every breath, his entire chest in-flated like a balloon, causing the iron chains displayed around his neck to jingle against one another. He wore a fancy wool-en robe across his shoulders and a ring of metal links around his head. Algen grimaced. He knew each of the Lords thought themselves kings under their own dome, but he never imagined any of them bold enough to show such a display in front of their true King. He stole a glance over to the throne, where Caraq sat with a face of stone. His claw twitched open and closed, but the King said nothing.

 ALGEN

"Lord Bybel, of the Deep Dome."

Bybel entered wearing scaled armour very similar to the King's. However, where the King's shone bright red, his shimmered in eerie indigo. Four holes were crafted into the ribs of the chest piece, two on either side that allowed for four spindly legs that prodded in the air and sent a chill down Algen's spine. The Lord's true arms seemed deformed as well, with the three last fingers on each hand crudely fused together, and with the thumb and forefinger weak and bony.

"Lord Rav, of the Golden Dome"

This lord looked relatively human-like to Algen, compared to the other lords, that was. Still, he was covered in large starfish-like growths. One protruded from his left cheek and covered all the way from his temple to the bridge of his pointed nose. His eyes blazed with passion, but passion for what Algen didn't know. Algen began to wonder if some big announcement was coming. It appeared as though every dome was represented here today. For a moment he had a strike of sadness in his heart. I will never be chosen as the lord of a dome.

"Lord Lyagrim, of the Dragon Dome!"

As the man entered, Algen puzzled over the Lord. His skin was blue as the sea, but at the same time blacker than night. The hair on his head parted at the back of the neck to make way for spines that sprouted down his backbone. Crusted rough skin covered his cheeks and over one eyelid. His left eye had a green iris, but the rest of the eye was black. The right one looked natural, and bright blue. He wore no shirt, and his muscular body was covered in deep scars. Peculiarly, his right arm was bandaged completely from finger to shoulder in black cloth. His other was scaly and coarse, fingernails long and sharp as talons. The look of him disturbed Algen and he tried not to stare directly into Lord Lyagrim's black eye, but Algen found it impossible to turn away.

One by one, the other lords entered upon introduction to take their seats until all fourteen had entered. The crier finished with the Lady Mala of the Foggy Dome. Her hair fell down her shoulders like seaweed and her pink skin was translucent like a jellyfish's. She wore no shirt and Algen watched the outline of her heart beating inside her chest, mesmerized. Once the Lords had settled, the flagbearers stood to attention and walked out in unison, followed by the crier, who blew his horn twice as the guards moved in behind him. He felt Hanlin tap him on the shoulder and suddenly a platter of steaming tuna slices was being shoved into his hands.

"Korra says to pass these out," Hanlin whispered. He himself had a platter of mashed shrimp, and wheat crackers.

Algen paid no mind to the order of the lords, and simply moved first to the table closest to him, smiling and holding the platter to the sitting congregates. The lord before him was a large man of an eerie green colour, with skin rough and bumpy. He scowled and grabbed three slices off the plate. A few of his retainers did the same. Not sure what do next, Algen lifted the platter over his head and hurried to the next table over, where the starfish-mottled Lord Rav sat discussing something with a slimy fishlike man next to him. Rav waved him along without looking up. At the next table, where Lord Bybel sat, he watched as the people at the table wiped the platter clean leaving none for anyone else. Algen noticed a serving boy, no older than thirteen and not yet transformed, sitting close beside the Lord. Because of his malformed hands, the boy placed the food into Bybel's mouth and wiped the spit from his chin when necessary. Looking over, he saw Hanlin being surrounded by the retainers of the Frost Dome, all wanting a taste of wheat cracker, a rare delicacy traded from the surface. Being so far to the north, the Frost Dome had little trade, so for them it was quite the treat indeed.

As of yet, the King himself had eaten nothing; instead simply watching over his Lords. Each one had been appointed by him at various times in the past, though it must have been half a decade since he'd seen some of them. Having them all together was truly a momentous occasion.

"Save some for us, Lord Large!" came a cry from the table hosting the congregate from the Garden Dome.

Lord Harren stood, looming over the table and searched for the source of the sound. Caraq banged his claw on the table, sending a long echo through the hall. The sound quelled any trouble that may have started. *Perhaps the Domes aren't as amicable as I had thought.* Algen moved back towards the kitchen door, where another of the cooks handed him a plate of puffer roasted in algae. The food smelled delicious, but he dared not taste it. He passed a little to each table, making sure to be quick enough not to let any one lord take it all. He had learned his lesson fast.

By this time the feast was well underway and the smells of food mingled with the sounds of fervent discussion. The King had stood again, and this time he held a war mace in his left hand. He raised the weapon above his head. The room fell to a hush.

"My Lords!" His voice carried through the hall like a sledge. "For too long have the Aquarii peoples of the surface held us down here in our Domes. They are weak! And yet they rule over us like the sky rules over the land." He pointed the mace forward, pointing at each of the Lords in turn. "I have chosen each of you in the past to rule over one of my fourteen outer domes. Today I ask of you a deal more." He pointed the mace up to the hall's roof where the night sky was visible through the glass. "Today I ask you to take on the role of commanders, in the war I shall wage on the scum that walk the sand!" He beat his claw against his armoured chest. "In a moon's turn, I will be leading an assault upon Water's Edge, the port town closest to this very dome. Who will join me?"

The green skinned Lord stood immediately and growled, pulling a steel sword from its scabbard and raising it high.

"I will, my King!"

Lady Mala stood almost immediately after, and a squire passed her a trident forged with snakes as the tines and she held it over her head.

"I will, my King!"

The King nodded approvingly.

"I will, my King!" blubbered Lord Harren through his tusks as he raised a massive hammer.

"I will, my King!" spoke Lord Bybel.

One by one, every Lord pledged to go to war, leaving King Caraq grinning. Algen didn't really expect any other outcome; the Lords only received their positions through the King, and they could be taken away just as easily for disloyalty. None of the Lords had much of a choice in the matter.

King Caraq raised his arms outstretched.

"Then feast, my Lord Commanders, as tonight is a night for celebration!"

He brought down the mace to the table, splitting the wood in half in a single blow to the sound of cheers erupting from the hall. Algen shook his head in disbelief. *So, it begins.*

CHAPTER 27

ORLO III

O rlo stood and took a deep breath. The hot sun was making sweat bead off his forehead already. For a moment, he could see his reflection in the metal of his half-helm as he held it out before him. Then, closing his eyes, Orlo donned the shiny helm atop his head. There were fourteen of them in the pit for the melee. Orlo's gaze went to each one, attempting to spot any weak points in their armour and sizing them up for who to take on first. *Just live long enough for Allysson to make her move*, he told himself. She had told him not to worry, but of course, Orlo still did. Any moment now, Allysson would be making her escape, and she had assured him that Orlo would have his chance to escape as well. *Live until then*, he told himself again. *Have faith.*

He just wanted to go home more than anything. To see his small town below the mountains, to hold his wife in his arms and sleep beneath his own roof again. He wanted to drink peach ale under the shade of a hazelnut tree and play with his children by the river.

Sweat stung his eyes and he wiped his brow. He hoped that the heat would at least let up. He was having enough trouble as it was without worrying about the weather. Just as Allysson had said, the King of the entire Leo Faction was in attendance. He sat perched atop a great podium next to the Lord of the Pit, with the best view of the action below. Orlo noticed one of the other contestants held a bow and for a moment he wondered if the man would attempt to fire upon the King, but sadly, he did not.

One by one they took a bow before the King. Nine of them were obviously slaves by the way they carried themselves, reluctant to move at all. They, like him, wanted nothing more than to come out of this with their lives. Another two were young travellers looking to find glory in the pit. Their armour was bright and shining, made of expensive castle-forged metal. Orlo suspected they had bought it for the looks over the practicality. The metal looked so thin a pin could cut through it. The King seemed amused by the men, probably figuring they'd fall in spectacular fashion.

The Lord of the Pit's own brother, a gargantuan man named Zonday, was competing as well, also for glory. He wore no armour, just a simple loincloth. His chest muscles rippled in the sun and his black hair fell over his shoulders. Zonday circled the wall of the pit, hammering the blunt end of his flat, wide sword against the outer panels of wood, pumping himself up and hollering like a wild animal.

The final two contestants were some of the Lord's personal career fighters. Allysson had pointed them out to him earlier in the day. The first was a man known as Haza. He displayed a tattered red cloak over his shoulders with a matching hood over his face. Underneath, he wore nothing more than simple clothes. In his right hand he held a whip, and in front of the entire crowd, he took a torch and lit the oiled hemp. The blaze carried up to the hilt, where the flames stopped. Haza spun the flaming lash twice around his head before flicking it. The end CRACKED against the sky, sending embers flying into the air as the crowd erupted into cheers.

The other career fighter was named Bofur, a huge man who, like Zonday, wore no shirt or pants. Instead, he wore the skull of a bear over his head and two iron gauntlets. On the finger of each gauntlet was nailed a bear claw. Orlo could see that the claws were old, half were cracked and the others chipped. They were yellowed with age and stained pink in places from blood. Suddenly, Bofur pawed at the ground like a bear, and a deafening growl erupted from his throat. The crowd again roared their approval.

Before coming, Allysson had explained to Orlo how the grand matches worked. The rules were simple: if you lived longer than everyone else, you had the honour to become one of the Lord's personal pit fighters.

ORLO

"Do you get the option to just leave?" he had asked her, hopefully. "I thought you said winners got their freedom?" But she had just laughed at him.

Pampered and enslaved is at least better than mistreated and enslaved... or dead, he thought, shifting his sword from one hand to the other. He hoped that *neither* would happen, but in case something went wrong with Allysson's escape plan, he at least wanted to know where he stood.

The Lord of the Pit outstretched his arms, and a cheer went up around the stands. In his hand he held a mallet, which at the peak of the cheers, he smashed against a large suspended bronze disk. The sound it made rang across the dirt and signaled the game was on. Orlo made a silent prayer and tightened his helm. Then, cautiously, he moved towards the centre of the arena. His eye throbbed with every step, but at least they had rubbed a numbing salve on the area before kicking him into the ring.

The rest of the contestants were also stirring. One of the glory-seekers immediately charged towards Bofur, lance pointed at the career fighter's bare chest. As if snapping a twig from a tree, Bofur wrapped one of his mailed hands around the shaft and twisted. The force made the attacker lose his grip. The bear man then snapped the wood over his knee, before watching the once gung-ho young man scurry away to the sound of laughter from the crowd.

Across the oval, the bowman was loosing arrows around the edge of the arena. For the first time, Orlo noticed that the man wore two rabbit ears nailed to his helm. Suddenly, Orlo saw the bowman meet his gaze and loose an arrow towards him. Gasping, he ducked, before realizing the arrow hadn't gotten anywhere close to him. Glancing back up, Orlo saw that the bowman seemed to be favouring his right side, obviously injured. Whatever wound he had sustained was obviously affecting his aim. *He won't last long like that.*

A scream went up and Orlo watched as one of the pit slaves sunk the tip of a sword down into the chest of a second slave. Then, not two seconds later, that slave had his head separated from his shoulders when Zonday rushed up behind him and cleaved his weapon into the man's neck. Orlo frowned. *Coward. Killing a man when his back is turned.* Orlo's thoughts were broken when a third slave charged him from the side. Orlo's instincts kicked in and he brought his blue sword up to parry, but he was a second too slow and the opponent's sword cut into his ribs. The cold steel slid along the outside of the bone and left Orlo with a large gash. A scream of anguish escaped his lips, and without thinking, he slashed back. The other man tried to scream, but all that came out was a gurgle as blood filled his throat. Holding his side, Orlo took a few deep breaths. The wound was bad, but not lethal. He just needed to hang back. *Allysson, whatever you are doing, do it fast!*

Haza, whip still burning, was caught in between the other, still armed, glory seeker and a slave. The two had him flanked and were closing in with swords brandished. It seemed like Haza was doomed, but the other two hadn't considered that

ORLO

the whip had a great range to it. As soon as the glory seeker stepped within fifteen feet of the caped pit fighter, the whip snapped, and flicked across his cheek. The flame burned and sent the man reeling back. Pivoting, Haza made another flick and the whip wrapped around the slave's leg, bringing him to the ground. The man fumbled, trying to untie the rope without burning his hands. As the flames spread up his clothes, the slave panicked, but was too slow in escaping. Bofur took him in the back of the neck with a great claw.

Within only a few minutes of the start of the melee, just seven of the fourteen remained: Orlo, Zonday, Haza, Bofur, the bowman, and two of the other pit slaves. The other half lay strewn about the field. The Leo King whispered something to the Pit Master, who relayed the message by yelling it to Bofur, and pointing to Orlo. *That one is injured.* Still clasping at his side with one hand, Orlo raised his sword as the bear-man charged at him. A great claw came swinging towards him and barely missed as the gauntlet was deflected off of Orlo's sword. Growling, Bofur took a second swing. Orlo met him again with sword. This time, the blue steel cut clean through two of the claws and the bone fell to the floor. A cheer went up from the audience, amongst some boos. Bofur was clearly angry. Growling once more, he swept in for a killing blow. Orlo capitalized on his brashness and buried his sword in his bear skull mask.

Leaping backwards, Bofur cried out, the sword still stuck where it hit the mask. A stream of blood welled from under the skull, and beaded off his chest. All around Orlo the crowd

ORLO

was cheering now, apart from the King and Pit Master themselves. Momentarily forgetting the fight going on around him, Orlo reveled in the glory. And that's when he saw her: Allysson was up in the higher stands. A man stood next to her. Both had loaded crossbows in hand, one pointed at the King, the other at the Pit Master. Everyone else was too focused on the arena to notice it seemed. Orlo and Allysson's eyes met and she smiled cunningly down at him, finger ready to pull the trigger.

THUNK

The crowd's cheers died down to a hush. Orlo frowned, expecting to see the King fall from his seat. His eyes went back to Allysson, but her crossbow had not been fired. She looked... sad.

Oh. That was all that went through Orlo's mind as he looked down to see the arrowhead protruding out from his breast. He made a motion to grasp it, but his hands didn't seem to want to work. Suddenly, his knees hit the dirt and he had to use his other hand to prop himself from falling further, but it didn't help. Orlo fell to his side, then rolled to his back.

What a beautiful day, Orlo thought as his eyes fluttered closed, and his lifeblood welled around him. *A beautiful day to die.*

CHAPTER 28

RYMUS IV

Behind him, Rymus saw guards closing in along the mountain pass. He looked ahead to discover that more soldiers were circling around every ledge and jut out on the cliffside above. One of his men panicked, and loosed an arrow at a nearby Aries soldier, missing him by near ten yards. This turned out to be a fatal mistake, as the reply came in the form of five bronze-tipped arrows crashing down around the Pisces man. One took him in the calf, another in the chest. He was dead before his body hit the ground. No one else dared make a move after that. Rymus' men stood still, in a hush that covered the pass like a fog. Above them were the enemy poised like hawks. Any wrong move and they would strike. Rymus was desperately scanning the area for any chance at an escape when Keldo slowly moved up beside him, being careful to not make any sudden motions lest his belly become a pincushion.

"My prince," he whispered. "There appears to be an opening due south of us."

Rymus looked to the right, straining his eyes as far as he could without actually tilting his head. It was just enough to see that Keldo was right. Between two half-dead evergreens there looked to be a small cave opening, and Rymus could see the faintest bit of light crowning from the other side. The opening was a good hundred yards away, but doable. He didn't have another option. If Rymus was captured, it meant game over. Most likely he'd be tortured into giving away the positions of his brothers, then he would be killed. Then his brothers would be killed. Then his father. At that point the throne would pass to his quivering Uncle Gyrus, who would be more than happy to submit to any demands the Aries were wont to give him. Rymus glanced back at his men. Around one hundred and eighty were still with him. He estimated that less than half would make it if they had to sprint. He closed his eyes. *A necessary evil,* he thought to himself.

"Get ready," he whispered to Keldo. The stout man nodded, bushy moustache bouncing. Rymus took a deep breath.

"WITH ME!" he called out, raising his spear high in the air.

Before looking to see if anyone was following, Rymus took off running down the rocky cliffside, leaping swiftly over small boulders and rocky outcrops. He heard the unmistakable swish of arrows flying, and the impact of arrowhead on flesh. Out of the corner of his eye, he saw one of his soldiers running close beside him, but the man was unaware of a small break in

RYMUS

the ground below them. Rymus jumped, but the soldier's toes caught and the momentum sent him careening headfirst into the ground, yelping and gripping his ankle. But Rymus kept on running. He didn't have time to stop and help, even for the men who looked up to him. For a moment he wondered why they looked up to him at all. Just twenty yards away from the tunnel opening, Rymus could see his destination more clearly now. The tunnel looked man-made, about eighty feet long and carved by pickaxe. The most important thing was, however, that there were no Aries soldiers on the other side.

Only once Rymus was beneath the safety of the tunnel's stone ceiling, did he stop to catch his breath. He noticed that Keldo was also there. He silently marveled at just how fast the stout man could run with such short legs and big belly. He then forced himself to look around at his men. Around seventy of them were also in the tunnel, and as more and more reached the safety of the opening, Rymus himself was forced further and further into the tunnel. The opening could fit about eight men side-by side, and as more of his men made it in, the more uncomfortably packed the tunnel became. When Rymus had sufficiently caught his breath, he yelled out again.

"Forward!"

And slowly, the party moved towards the far end of the tunnel. He knew they couldn't wait for long. The Aries archers may be out of range now, but they inevitably knew these cliffs like the backs of their hands, and would soon reposition to an easy vantage point. Keldo waddled up beside him, breathing heavily.

"My Prince," he panted, "I feel –" He was cut-off by the sound of rock crumbling.

Without warning, a massive black boulder fell squarely in front of the tunnel entrance they had just come through. It hit the ground with a smacking *Thud* against the dry ground and sent dust spewing through the tunnel. Rymus looked worried. Keldo looked confused.

"Why would they block off the side we just ran from?" he asked.

"That's why," Rymus answered him, pointing with his spear to their only remaining exit.

Where it had once been clear, at least a century of Aries soldiers armed and armoured to the teeth now stood. Their weapons drawn, they began moving into the tunnel. The eight frontmost of them held great tower shields that when put side-by-side made one long barrier from wall-to-wall. Each had a small notch at the top where the next row of eight soldiers rested eight-foot-long lances.

"Bugger me," mumbled Keldo as he drew his notched and bloodstained sword. Rymus was the closest man to the barricade. He could have fit seven more men beside him as well to match his enemy, but Rymus' men had swords, so being shoulder to shoulder meant none could swing with any sort of power or precision.

"Four men, up front!" he called.

RYMUS

Two of his soldiers took their places on either side of him, swords drawn. He was half surprised to see Keldo as one of them, standing directly to his right. Keldo must have seen his shock.

"It is my place as your second, Captain."

Rymus nodded curtly and turned to the soldier on his left. "What is your name?" he asked. The man looked to be around twenty-five.

"It's Fen, Captain."

Rymus pointed the tip of his spear at the man's forehead. "Don't die on me, Fen."

Rymus was about to give the command to charge when from the other end of the tunnel came a shout, and the shield wall started to move forward. Suddenly it became clear to Rymus. *They aren't trying to barricade us. They mean to crush us.* He lowered his spear.

"Hold your ground!" he called.

Either they would fight them here, or fight them there. Rymus thought it best not to tire his men in a charge before the two sides clashed. The shield wall kept moving. *Twenty-five feet... Twenty feet... Fifteen...* Rymus adjusted his grip on his spear.

"AND HALT!"

The call came from behind the shield wall. The tips of the spears were so close that Rymus could have reached out and touched them. The two shield bearers in the middle parted and let through a large man in white enameled armor and a helmet shaped with golden ram's horns curling from the top.

"Prince Rymus!" he called, being surprisingly courteous.

Rymus knew immediately who he was staring down.

"The White Ram of Aries."

"Please, My Lord, call me Sir Artell." The Ram took a slight bow.

Rymus had half a mind to wedge his spear into the knight's gullet right here and now, but he knew that would only result in the death of every last man around him including his own. *Besides*, he thought, *there must be some reason he trapped us instead of outright slaughtering us.* At least, he hoped there was a reason. Sir Artell of Aries, also known as The White Ram, had a reputation around the Starscape. He was well known for being so unconventionally honour-bound that at times it bordered on being theatrical. Rymus had never met the man before, but he'd always wanted to. He never imagined, however, that the name "White Ram" would be so... literal.

"You're a long way from home," The Ram began. "May I ask what brings you to our fine Aries homeland?"

Rymus gave him the most genuine smile he could muster. "Curiosity," he said.

Sir Artell made an exaggerated look behind Rymus and the hundred odd men standing with weapons drawn. He made a large motion with his hand indicating them.

"I suppose these fine men are just here to join you in your... curiosity?"

 RYMUS

"Most of them, yes."

"And the others?"

"The others carry my things."

Sir Artell smiled. "I could kill you right here and now, you know."

"I do."

"But alas, what honour would there be in that?"

Rymus raised his spear. "Not sure. Never really cared about honour."

Despite his cocky veneer, Rymus was incredibly nervous about the situation at hand. His mind fluttered from one idea to the next, trying to think of something, anything that could help him. But there was nowhere to run, no room to fight, and nothing he could say... except:

"You caught me." He dropped his spear to the ground. "Capture me, but don't hurt my men."

"You have my word," said Sir Artell. "After all, there is no honour in killing a caged animal."

Artell gave a command and the shield wall moved up and around Rymus. His hands were bound and he was stripped of all weapons. Sir Artell then marched him out from the cave and onto a pack donkey. His feet were then hooked and locked to the donkey's saddle.

"Is this all really necessary?"

Sir Artell laughed as he himself mounted a large muscular horse with a shaggy mane. He smiled down at Rymus.

"For one of the Princes of Pisces? Yes, I believe so."

It was Rymus' turn to chuckle. "The least of the three."

"Too true." Sir Artell gave his palfrey a kick and began down the trail. "Time to reunite you with your brothers."

CHAPTER 29

JAIR IV

The windswept grassland stretched for miles, contained on three sides by the High Mountains. Jair stood perched on a boulder, surveying the land. He'd never been out this far from the castle. In fact, he'd never even known just how high these mountains went. Stretching up from the grassland and hills, the peaks of the High Mountains broke through the clouds like an oar through water. Snow capped the summits, hugging to the rock face. Out in the distance, a small town sat dead-centre in the middle of the field, far enough away as to see the entire town at a glance, but close enough to smell the waft of roasting meats and hear the sound of laughter. Jair's stomach growled. Out in the forest, he had the luxury of eating nothing but pine nuts, bush berries, and the occasional rabbit. He'd never realized how well he had been fed at the palace until he turned traitor.

Licking his lips, his tongue touched the scruff of his beard. He raised a hand to his face and prodded the hairs. At the execution, he had been clean shaven, but now his cheeks, chin, lips, and neck were all covered in a sandy brown fur. Jair debated for a moment using his pole-axe to shave himself, but quickly dropped the idea. Frog was lying on the ground beside him, deep in sleep. Jair used the butt of his axe to nudge him awake. Frog awoke with a jolt, but quickly turned to annoyance.

"I was having a dream, you know. A good one, 'bout a girl I knew."

Jair grinned. "Why not find a girl in that town down there?" He motioned with the head of his axe.

Frog shook his head. "No, I'm saving myself for this one girl. Dalia, her name is. We grew up together."

Jair felt a stab of awkwardness. He'd never been with a girl either. In all honesty, he'd never spent much time in the company of others at all, now that he thought about it. Vikron, Frog, and the others may be the closest thing to friends he'd ever had. And he wasn't sure they were even that to him. Jair spotted Vikron suiting up in his leather armor and loosening the clasps on his hand axes. Hopping off the boulder, he strolled over and caught Vikron's attention.

"Are we expecting a fight down there?"

"Expecting? No, but I'd rather be prepared, wouldn't you, 'cutioner?"

Jair wasn't nervous either way. No one in a small town like that could possibly take on a palace trained soldier like himself. Garrett moved behind a boulder to take a piss, and the Seamstress was finishing the final touches on a tightly knit scarf. Deleon stood out in the field, practicing his swordplay, and by the way he was doing it, Jair hoped for his sake that they wouldn't run into trouble. As a final touch, Vikron donned his bull's helm and shrugged on his bearskin cape.

"Move out, boys."

The town was smaller than even Jair had expected. Eight loosely scattered houses, an inn with an attached tavern, a blacksmith's shop and a tanner's hut, all on two crossed gravel roads. A few dairy cows roamed the surrounding fields and a small dog slept in the shade of what seemed to be the only tree around. The tanner was the first to greet them as they entered the town.

"Hello friends," he started. "Welcome to Harlstown. My name is Tanner. What can I do you for?" Tanner cracked a smile that revealed three missing teeth and a fourth looking to join them.

Vikron snorted. "A tanner named Tanner? You picked the right profession."

Tanner smiled again. "My father was the last tanner of this town, his name was also Tanner, as was his father and his father's father and his father's father's father. Seems ta' me it's the only thing I could've done was become a tanner Tanner. It's a legacy thing."

"Sounds more like a curse thing to me," muttered Frog.

Tanner led them to the door of the inn, as if they couldn't find it on their own, and left them to get back to his work. *The Roc's Talon*, the sign read. As a young boy, Jair's mother had told him stories about massive birds that soared above the clouds and would descend to take naughty little boys far away from home; funny how he only ever heard that story after he had done something wrong. Entering, they found the inn and its adjoining tavern were surprisingly packed. A few patrons had the looks of locals but over half the patrons looked as though they had come from every which way but here.

Three men in red feathered armour mingled with two men with skin as brown as mud. A pair of twin brothers drank with two women in exquisite dresses: one green and gold, the other purple and cyan. One man sat alone in the corner with an eye-patch over his right eye, which hardly covered the deep scar that stretched from his widow's peak to the corner of his lips. When the man opened his mouth to drink, Jair could see that all the teeth on the right side of his mouth were gone. There were many others in the tavern, but all fell to obscurity once Jair's stomach took over. His nose perked up again as a cute redheaded serving girl walked by him with a steaming plate of seared cod and roasted carrots. Jair's eyes followed the girl until she placed the plate in front of an ugly man who looked just as like to eat the serving girl as he would the fish. Vikron nudged Jair in the side.

"That's the man."

JAIR

Vikron took Jair as well as Arlum to the ugly man's table. The rest of his company scattered amongst the crowd. Jair hoped that he'd get a chance to share in the fish, but as the three of them walked up, the ugly man grabbed the entire cod and took a monstrous chomp out of it. Juice sprayed in all directions and chunks of flesh hung from the man's oversized mouth. Jair's heart sank as he sat down into his chair. At this distance, Jair could see that the man's skin had a slight green tint to it. His eyes were red and his teeth were sharp as a dog's. Wrinkled skin hung off his jowls and wobbled as he ate. His cheeks shone with grease as much as his bald head did.

"Well?" asked Vikron, "aren't you going to say hello to your old friend?"

The ugly man stopped gorging for a moment to look up. "All my friends can go bugger themselves."

"*Friend*," Vikron corrected. "Far as I know, I'm the only one you got."

The ugly man only grunted. Arlum attempted to pick a roasted carrot from the plate, but was met with snapping jaws and a growl. *Is this man even human?* Jair thought. He knew of Cancers that would transform themselves into hideous beasts, but as far as he knew they only mutated with marine life. The man sitting in front of him looked like a cross between a dog and an under-ripe tomato.

"Welcome then... *friend*." The ugly man spat out the words.

Vikron rolled his eyes. "My friends, allow me to introduce Gutless Gror, the most handsome and bravest man this quarter of the Starscape."

Gror sniffed in a load of mucus and coughed, making his jowls bounce. Jair wondered why Vikron would ever associate with such a man, but got his answer right away.

"I may be ugly, but I could bury you alive in all my gold back at The Grorsfort."

"Aye, you could," Vikron agreed, "but there is something that even money can't buy that you want. And I have it."

"Where?"

"If I told you that, you wouldn't need to give me anything."

"So, what is it you want?"

Vikron smiled and leaned back in his seat, unclipping his cloak and hanging it on the corner of the chair. "Jair," he started. That was the first time he'd ever referred to Jair by his name. "This may take a while; will you bring us some ales?"

"Make mine so dark it's black," piped in Arlum.

Jair stood. Either Vikron was trying to show his might by treating his underlings as servers, or much more likely he just didn't have any money. The man behind the counter gave Jair a look over.

"What'll it be?"

"Four dark ales."

The man nodded and disappeared into the back. Jair leaned himself against the wall. He looked over at Deleon who was nursing a mug of cider and not so subtly ogling the girl in the green dress. He glanced up as the tavern door swung open and his heart skipped a beat. Five heavily armed palace guards strolled in, eyes darting from person to person. Jair lowered his gaze to the ground and turned his back on them. *How did they find us all the way out here*? One of the guards moved up beside him at the bar.

"Barkeep!" he called, slamming a freshly forged sword down on the table.

The barkeep returned with four large mugs, passing all four to Jair, who in return placed four silver coins in the barkeeps hand. On his way back to Vikron, he gave Deleon a slight kick, making him spill his cider. The boy was about to protest, but held his tongue when Jair nodded towards the guard just a few feet away. When he returned to the table, Gutless and the Captain were deep in discussion. As soon as he placed down the mugs, Jair's hand swept up and swiped the distinctive bull horn helmet off Vikron's head.

Vikron stopped mid-sentence "Oy boy, what are you doing?"

"We have company."

Vikron's eyes showed that he immediately understood what Jair was talking about. He turned back to Gror.

"Alright, Gutless, lets' get this done now. I give you the location where I'm hiding the King, and you give me what I need."

Gror took another bide of his cod. "No."

Vikron unclasped one of his axes and placed it lightly on the table. "Wasn't asking."

Jair and Arlum exchanged a wary look. The Altarbreaker unslung his crossbow from his back and pulled a bolt from his tunic. Jair put a hand on the dirk sheathed on his belt.

"Hey, I recognize you!" The voice came from far behind them, partnered with the distinctive sound of sword sliding on leather.

Jair turned to see a guard staring down Frog, sword unsheathed. Frog was staring back, wide eyed and pitifully under-armored. The guard reached out a hand and grabbed Frog by the arm.

"Where is Vikron?" His voice boomed with authority.

"He's right here!" Jair spun around to see Gror, smiling, and pointing with a greasy finger at Vikron.

And that's when all hell broke loose.

Two of the guards rushed over with swords drawn. The guard holding Frog shoved him to the ground and joined the others. The last two stood firm at the door. Vikron unsheathed his other hand-axe from his belt.

"Bastard set us up!" he growled.

Gror was erupting with deep belly laughs, until Vikron's axe slammed down into the table with a thud, and two of Gror's pudgy green fingers rolled to the floor. Arlum was prepared, bow loaded, and turned to fire. His finger pulled back on the trigger without hesitation and the bolt flicked through the air. It glanced harmlessly off the closest guard's chest piece, and ricocheting into a nearby wooden column.

 JAIR

Tavern patrons scattered, knocking over tables, chairs, mugs, and plates. One of the twin brothers drew a longsword as the other hid under a table. The two dark-skinned men pulled strange looking gauntlets covered in spikes from their bags and slid them on. The feathered men cowered behind them. Deleon had drawn his own sword, as had Garrett, and both were pushing through the crowd to reach their captain. Vikron, however, didn't seem to need their help. In one motion, he dislodged his weapon from the table, stood, and kicked his chair back. The chair caught in the legs of the first guard, sending him falling face first towards them. Vikron buried his one axe in the back of his exposed neck and raised the other to deflect a blow from the second guard's broadsword. Jair fumbled with the clasps for his pole-axe. In the close quarters of the inn, it was hard to grab. Gror was slumped back in his chair, crying out and gripping the remains of his right hand with his left. Blood gushed from between his clasped fingers. Jair finally unhooked his weapon and brought it up just in time to stave off a swing from a third guard. For a brief second, the guard's eyes widened as he recognized Jair, before Garrett's sword exploded from the centre of his chest, punching a hole right through the armor. Vikron was already finished with the two guards that had attacked him, and was marching to the front door to face the last two. They stood side by side, making a hard wall of steel. A bolt slipped past Vikron's ear and into the neck of the guard on the left. Blood spattered the other guard and made him flinch.

Before he had time to recover, Vikron's axe was hanging from what remained of his face.

"Stop right there!" Everyone turned to see that the barkeep had produced his own loaded crossbow from under the table, and was pointing it square at Vikron's nose. "Drop it!"

Vikron raised his hands and dropped his remaining axe to the ground. Jair looked over at Arlum, but his quiver was empty.

"Kingnappers!" the barkeep continued, trigger finger trembling. "You're the people who took our king!"

A hush fell over the entire room. Even Gror's screaming had stopped: the fat man had passed out and was slumped on the floor. Suddenly, a tightly knit scarf appeared over the barkeep's neck and drew him down as the crossbow fired harmlessly into the ceiling. Gurgling noising and struggling could be heard from behind the counter, then stopped. No one else made a move.

Vikron picked up his weapons and loudly clanged them together.

"Leave." Vikron muttered.

No one moved.

"NOW!"

The patrons, serving girls, and even chefs rushed out through the front door and into the field outside. When the last person had left, Vikron used one of his axes to bar the door and moved towards the counter. Stepping not-so-respectfully on the dead barkeep's body, he selected a cask and chopped at it with his other axe. Three hits in and ale began gushing out the gash. Vikron placed his lips up against the wood and drank fully, letting the rest cover the floor. Wiping his mouth, he moved back to the table, and looked down at the unconscious Gror.

"Axe." He held out a hand to Jair, who passed him the executioner's axe.

Vikron took the spiked head and drove it down through Gror's sternum. Jair grimaced as he heard a lung pop. Vikron wasted no time looting the corpse. When nothing was found, he stood up, took a deep breath, and then began kicking at the body in a rage.

"I take it you didn't find what you were looking for."

Vikron shook his head. "The bastard set us up. He never meant to have an honest trade. He wanted the bounty on my head, and if he got the location of the King then that would have just been a bonus."

"Do you think he even had it to begin with?"

Vikron ran his fingers through his hair. "Oh, I know that he did."

"So where is it?"

Vikron sighed. "You heard him, 'cutioner. It's at the Grorsfort." But that's all the way in Musca space."

Jair shrugged. "Is that far?"

Vikron laughed. "No, but the only way there is through a rift in the heart of the Grus High Family's castle." He paused. "If you think the bounty on my head *here* is big, you ain't seen nothing yet, 'cutioner."

The Roc's Talon was in a state of disarray. Vikron strode over to one of the last upright tables and used the flat of his blade to smack a half-empty mug across the room and against the wall. The mug shattered into a spray of glass and its contents dripped lazily down the bricks. Frog walked over, rubbing his neck.

"So how do we get to The Grus High Castle from here, Captain?"

Vikron looked over at him, annoyed. "The closest rift is across the next damn river, and the only bridge for fifty miles is owned by the royals. We'll be caught the second we step into view."

"Looks like we're in for a hike," said Garrett.

Jair piped in. "Not necessarily."

Vikron looked up. "Speak."

"There's a small dock half a mile downriver from the bridge. The crown has been trying to get it shut down for years, but the dockmaster pays off any guard that comes to destroy it."

Vikron frowned "How do you know all this?"

Jair grinned. "Not important. What matters is that we can use one of his boats to cross without being bothered by any guards."

"Sounds simple enough," said Garrett.

Vikron scratched at his cheek. "They could be watching both docks. Word travels fast."

"We would have to know their rounds if we mean to sneak by them," piped in Deleon.

JAIR

Vikron rubbed at his chin, then looked to his men and pointed at one of them, beckoning him closer. "Brighteyes, come here."

The man walked over to them, concerned. His hair fell in curls around his shoulders and his skin was fairer than Jair had ever seen. To top it off, his eyes seemed to shine with a bright blue fire. *He probably does well for himself.* Jair mused, half jealous. Vikron slapped the boy on the back.

"I got a mission for you, 'eyes."

The boy looked surprised. "What is it captain?"

"I need you to join the 'cutioner here in going down to the docks."

"Me, Captain?" The boy was genuinely puzzled.

Vikron leaned down and whispered in his ear. "One of those guards is bound to have a lady friend who knows something."

☆ ☆ ☆

From afar Jair could see that the bridge had changed since his last time here. It had only taken him and Falmir, or as Vikron called him, Brighteyes, half the time he had expected to get from Harlstown to the bridge. *The world is so much smaller than I thought it was.* He'd had that thought a few times since joining up with Vikron and his ilk. The last time he'd been here, the bridge had stood alone. Now, he saw that a small village had sprouted on either side of the river. Guards were posted on both ends of the bridge, and more skulked throughout the village. Vikron had been right: the small dock was be-ing patrolled by at least five guards, and although he couldn't see that far, Jair knew that more men waited in the village on the other side of the river too. *This will be difficult.* He bit his lip and pondered their chances.

Next to him, nervously biting at a fingernail, stood Falmir. The boy looked more than a little uncomfortable. And under-standably so, if he was to follow through on Vikron's plan. Jair would have rather they simply took their chances at the bridge, but Vikron had told them no, in no uncertain terms.

The captain and the others had split off and were going to tie up some loose ends, or so Vikron had said. On the morrow, they would be back. By then, Jair and Falmir were to have se-cured safe passage to the other side. Falmir pointed.

"What about him?"

Jair followed the direction of his finger. The guard was travelling towards the brothel house, yelling bawdy comments at the women above.

Jair shook his head. "He's just pissing. Watch."

Sure enough, the guard stopped for a minute by the bush-es, then moved right back to his post. From where they were positioned, Jair had a good vantage point for the brothel and a few of the guard posts. Eventually one of the men would enter, and then they would make their move. Jair looked to where the sun was setting over the horizon. *And it better be soon.*

Half the night passed before they finally saw something. Jair was lying on his back, only half paying attention when Falmir nudged him.

"Hey! Look over there."

Jair gave a sidelong glance in the direction he was referring too. He caught the tail end of a guard kissing a woman in a pink dress, before they parted and she disappeared inside. Jair sat up.

"Yep, that's our way in." Reaching, he loosened the buckles on his poleaxe.

Falmir began fussing with his hair. "Does it look okay?"

Jair chuckled. "You look fine, princess."

"What if this doesn't work?"

"Then we go about this another way."

"What's the other way?"

Jair tossed Falmir his short sword. "That's the other way."

Falmir sheathed the sword between his belt and jerkin. Together they walked to the door of the brothel, making sure to keep their heads low. Jair figured no one would recognize him this far out of the capital, but you never knew. One of his old brothers-in-arms may just have been posted out here.

They made sure no one was around, and Jair took a seat on a step a few feet away while Falmir went up and knocked on the door. The same woman came to the door, wiping her hands on her dress. Jair watched as Falmir began to smooth-talk the woman. Her face went from annoyance, to interest, to desire as Falmir stood and talked. *He has a talent*, Jair thought. Before long, she moved aside and ushered Falmir in with her. Less than ten minutes later, he returned with his hair disheveled and his face red.

"Well?" Jair asked. "Did she say she'd do it?"

"Yes."

The woman appeared again, and the two followed from the shadows as she trotted off to the post and greeted her prior companion. Laughing, she gripped him round the shoulders and whispered something into his ear. The guard smiled and nodded. Together, the two of them walked out into the night. Jair and Falmir followed subtly behind, just far enough away as to not alert him. Every time he seemed to get suspicious, the woman planted a kiss on his cheek or nibbled at his ear.

"You must have really gotten that girl to like you," Jair quipped quietly. Falmir only blushed.

Their pursuit ended when the guard stopped at the water's edge, before a small raised building with an iron lock on the door. He pulled a key off his belt and placed it gently into the lock. As soon as the door was open, Jair sprung to action, removing his dirk from its sheath and lodging it deep into the guard's neck before he knew what was happening. The woman stood in stunned horror, not moving.

"Hurry," said Jair.

The two of them quickly grabbed suits of armour before locking the door and grabbing the body. Falmir gave the girl a kiss as they left. Heaving the body over the railing, they watched as it tumbled down into the water with a slight splash.

 JAIR

Quickly, they donned their plate and chainmail and left, just moments before a small group of common folk came to investigate the commotion.

Down at the dock, they relieved two of the other guards of their duty and began releasing the ropes tying a large ferry to the shore.

"What in the bloody hells are you two doing?" asked one of the other guards.

Jair expected that. "Captain's orders."

"*I'm* the Captain of this guard." The man drew his sword.

Damn. Jair winced, and reached for his axe, but Falmir was quicker with his words.

"OK, you caught us. We were off to try and bring the bastards who are holding our King hostage to justice. Long live the King of Ara."

"Long live the King of Ara," the captain echoed. "But I have not given you my leave to go, soldier."

It was Jair's turn to speak. "Our apologies Captain, we will ask first next time."

The Captain grumbled, clearly annoyed. Gritting his teeth, he sheathed his sword and nodded his head towards a building. "Bring me a mug of ale from the tavern up there, and might be I forgive this transgression." Jair nodded, and motioned for Falmir to stay while he went back to the village.

The tavern was near empty, and the barkeep seemed all too happy to take Jair's money. As he waited for the mug to fill, Jair could hear the sound of someone sharpening their sword. Looking around, he was surprised to see that it was

Taking his mug, Jair walked to where the large man sat and coughed to get his attention. Vikron looked up, and in seeing Jair he grinned. Jair frowned in return.

"The plan was that you weren't supposed to be here until morning."

Vikron shrugged. "It matters not, now. It was a stupid plan anyway, so I changed it." Before Jair could ask him what he meant by that, Vikron was already donning his helm and leaving.

Together they walked to the dock, Jair lagging only slightly behind Vikron. As they reached the shoreline, he was surprised to see the rest of the company awaiting them on the ferry. The bodies of the garrison were lying strewn below, and Jair had to step over the corpse of the captain he had bought the drink for. One at a time, Jair and Vikron were heaved onto the deck as the bow of the ship drifted into the water. Garrett sat at the helm, wiping the blood from his sword, while beside him Arlum checked the fletching of his bolts. Jair looked at the full mug still in his hand and made to toss it over the side, but Vikron grabbed it out of his hand before he could. In two great gulps, the liquid was gone. Raising his hands, he smashed the glass against the wooden deck and cheered.

"Always good to be a little drunk before a battle."

They reached the east side of the river without so much as a peep from the guards on the bridge. Jair found it odd that the dock was completely empty when they arrived, and was near dumbfounded when he saw that the surrounding village was quiet.

 JAIR

Vikron leapt from the boat and undid the clasps on his hand axes. Arlum was doing the same with his crossbow. Even the Seamstress had a sewing needle tucked in her sleeve. Jair unclasped his pole axe and held it up before him.

"This is where you told Prince Callum to meet you, isn't it?"

Vikron smirked. "You're a smart one, 'cutioner."

Falmir and Jair still wore the stolen outfits, and Falmir's chainmail was jingling as he looked around frantically. "Where's Deleon?"

Arlum raised an eyebrow, "I thought he was with Frog?"

The treeline broke before them and a man stepped forward.

"I see him," said Jair.

CHAPTER 30

GRELHYM IV

Grelhym sat, his attention darting back and forth between the living and the dead. The living sat round the circular table, in a momentary truce. Weapons adorned everyone's hand. Those delegates unfortunate enough to not survive the squabble lay unceremoniously strewn about on the ground. By Grelhym's count, only around half the delegates were still delegating. Even fewer of the men at arms and other called-on guards remained. Their dead lay amongst the bodies of the highborn delegates. In death, they were all equal. Grelhym looked to his left and right. The benches had been full when the day started. Now, they looked emptier than the world outside. Down below, Meikal was saying something similar to the delegates.

"You are a fool, Terreon!" he cried out, wiping blood from the brow of one of his pages. "When word of this incident reaches the homes of these men and women, they will blame you for their loss. You have assured war on your people."

"Spare me the lecture," Terreon snapped back, his face hardened in frustration. "It will matter not when the artifact is mine."

Sir Halfort had his helmet on the table, and was rubbing his temple. "Bloody hell, you still believe that after this anyone will let you walk away with it? I will die before seeing the artifact in your hands!"

Prince Damien was wiping the blood from his battle-axe. "Sir Halfort is correct, King Terreon. You'll be lucky to leave this planet with your head, let alone anything else. When my father hears of this, you can believe it will not be taken lightly."

"If your father ever returns, that is," quipped Prince Dayvon, chins wiggling. "Your daddy is dead, cub. The entire Starscape knows it!"

Grelhym watched King Emerton's snow-white ermine scurry across the floor like a rat. Its fur looked more crimson than ivory. King Emerton himself lay dead with half an arm sheared off at the elbow. Grelhym looked down with hatred at his Lord Rygar, who sat unscathed in his seat, fumbling with his mustache. *Of all men, why must he survive?* In fact, all three of Terreon's loyal delegates had survived, though Lord Daxon had a large gash cut across his chest, and his face was pale as an egg. On the stand closest to him, Grelhym noticed a crossbow and a small quiver of bolts. Thinking of the uselessness of his own squire's dagger, he reached down and placed the weapon under his seat, just in case.

"I need a stiff drink," said Rygar, interrupting some other delegate at the table. He began rising from his seat when the delegate closest to him held a sword up and pointed it at his throat.

"No one is leaving this room."

Rygar frowned and turned to the stands. When his eyes found Grelhym they stopped.

"Squire! C'mere boy!" Grelhym gingerly rose from his seat. "Now!"

Rygar pointed to the ground before him. Grelhym hurried himself down, careful not to slip on the still drying blood coving the wooden floor. He stood at attention before his Lord, who stared back at him.

"Go get me a glass of red... no, a bottle of red. This has been quite the day."

Grelhym shifted uncomfortably from one foot to the other.

"My Lord, King Terreon sealed the door."

"Not for long."

The sound of the doors opening made Grelhym jump in his seat. The man standing before them in the open doorway was smirking as though he had just done some great deed, his arms outstretched as the great wooden doors struck the walls. Though he looked familiar, Grelhym didn't recognize him. Even Meikal seemed to be surprised, and he supposedly knew everyone at the parley.

GRELHYM

"Greetings, brother!" The man shouted across the hall, hand raised like some prophet as he took a bow. "I have arrived!"

As he strode into the hall, the cape around his shoulders flapped and Grelhym caught a glimpse of his sigil: an archer.

"You're late, Carrell." Terreon sounded more than a little irritated. "The first carrier pigeons have already flown."

His brother shrugged and sat upon the great roundtable. Unfastening a flask from his belt, he took a long swig. "These badlands are so dry. I had to turn around to get more wine." He sniffed and turned the flask upside down. A few drops came out but it was empty. "Bugger," he whispered.

Terreon stood and moved around to where his brother sat. The younger man looked near identical when the two stood side-by-side, although where Terreon had a regal composure about him, Lord Carrell had a drunken grin.

"I'm parched brother. Do you happen to have a wine cellar around here somewhere?" He paused and looked down at his feet, running his shoe over a swatch of dried blood. "Am I sitting in a dead man's spot, Terry?"

King Terreon struck him backhanded across the face. "Never call me that! Do you understand me, Carrell?"

The younger brother rubbed his cheek, where fuzz was only starting to show the first signs of facial hair. He looked down to his feet. "I understand, Your Grace."

Sir Halfort saw an opportunity and rushed Terreon from behind. One of Terreon's hidden soldiers stepped forward and easily parried the tired knight's swing. Another two soldiers grabbed Halfort – one on each arm, and dragged him back to where the other survivors nursed their wounds.

Terreon paid the situation no mind. He pointed to the floor. "We were set to have a powerful hostage from every faction in the Starscape. But because of your little... *detour*, we're going to have to run damage control. We have less than thirty hostages now and over forty noble deaths to cover for. Does that sound like a situation worth a bit of booze to you?!"

Carrell sniffed again. "No, Your Grace."

Grelhym watched as the two brothers quarreled. They wore the same coloured armour, though Carrell's bore no elaborate insignia on the breastplate, only the rough sewn one on his cape. From the great wooden doors, two columns of soldiers marched into the hall, each led by a flagbearer holding the standard of Sagittarius. The rest were armed with loaded crossbows and short swords. King Terreon held up a hand and motioned for them to stop.

"It's done," he sighed. "Round them up!"

Although a few resisted, it wasn't long before all the survivors were being shackled. Within minutes, Grelhym watched as a procession of delegates in fetters were being led from the Roundhall. Carrell watched as well as they passed. "Who do we have?"

Terreon sighed and took stock. "Prince Damien of Ursa Major, Lord Hustace of Pavo, The Knight of the Sandstorm, Sir Kennett of Columba...," he listed them as they passed.

 GRELHYM

Soon, only King Terreon, Lord Rygar, Prince Dayvon, and their loyalists remained. Lord Daxon had slumped where he sat, and Grelhym wasn't sure if he were living or dead. Not even Meikal was spared; the old man was led chained from the room. *As if he had the strength to resist.* Lord Carrell had left to see them off back to a prison on the Sagittarius homeworld, a prospect King Terreon seemed none too convinced his brother would be able to do properly.

"I'm still waiting for that wine, boy," Rygar grumbled.

Grelhym gingerly took a step towards the exit, having to work his way around bodies and bloodstains. One man looked up at him with dead eyes, his innards hanging outwards from his gut. On his breast was the sigil of a phoenix.

"Halt." Terreon's voice cut through the silence. Grelhym stopped, and nervously turned. "I have need of him."

GRELHYM

CHAPTER 31

JOSHYA V

Joshya stood side-by-side with the rest of the javelin battalion. Despite being part of the high family, he was treated no differently than any of the other boys around him. He watched as Captain Vylarr made his way down the line, correcting the recruits' stances and readying them with a few words of encouragement. All the true Scorpio warriors were down the hill, closer to the oncoming army. They were all men who were within the King's inner circle. They all knew of the surface world's existence and had been here before. Men not even Joshya recognized. On the contrary, the green boys Joshya was to fight alongside had never known anything but the tunnels.

They were an auxiliary force, only to be used as a last-ditch effort if the situation turned sour. Joshya knew that as the highest-ranking member of his father's small army, Vylarr's place was with the vanguard, not commanding the children.

He figured that the only reason the captain was there was because of him. *He's here to protect me and only me,* he thought to himself. Joshya wanted to say something, but he was too afraid; afraid that without Vylarr he would not survive long enough to complain, so he kept his mouth shut.

Next to him, Esho was scanning the sky, mesmerized by the clouds and the birds. His eyes glazed over, looking into the blue that seemed to go on forever. Joshya nudged him.

"Stay focused. Having your head in the clouds just makes it that much easier to cut off."

Esho turned, still in a daze. "All my life I thought the surface was just a myth, some story my mother used to tell me. Now that I can see it, I... I never want to go back under."

Joshya frowned. Truthfully, he felt the same way, but if there was one thing his father and councillors had trained him to do, it was not to get distracted. Right now, the twenty or so boys on the hill had a job to do. They could worry about enjoying the fresh air later.

Joshya rotated his arms, testing the range of movement that his new armour allowed him. Vylarr had given him the same clothes as the other boys: a steel breastplate painted with a black scorpion and bronze bracers adorned with the same insignia. Vylarr bent down to meet him face to face. Joshya noticed for the first time the ceremonial scorpion broach that clasped Vylarr's white cape.

"I hope you learned at least something from those sessions." Vylarr's face was as sour as ever. He put a gloved hand on Joshya's elbow and twisted him like a doll until Joshya stood in a throwing position.

"Remember to stand like this. Eyes forward. Keep your breathing calm and throw at anything that comes near."

From the distance Joshya could hear a horn sounding. Vylarr's ears perked and he stood, drawing his sword from his belt. The blade glinted in the sunlight in a way Joshya had never seen before. The metal looked identical to the ones they used in training, but this one had a sharpened edge. Lethal. Joshya also had his own sword of sorts - a dirk, slipped unceremoniously inside his belt. Vylarr had given it to him in the off case he found himself with no other protection. All the swords, short swords, maces, and axes had been given to the soldiers on the front line. The rest of the boys had only been given small daggers, except Joshya, who had been given Vylarr's own dirk. Joshya had learned recently that each soldier was supposed to carry both a sword and a dirk onto the field of battle, but Vylarr had forgone his to give Joshya the extra protection.

"I will not be far," the veteran had told him. "But if I fall in battle, you will need to protect yourself."

When he looked over the treeline, Joshya could see the sinkhole in the ground where the throne room had caved in. He thought of his father, still abed in the infirmary chamber. Of his mother and sister and grandfather. Of Himrel and the Half-Crow. He looked to Esho beside him. The boy was staring out over the field now, his javelin in hand.

"If this goes sour, promise me you'll say I died bravely?" Esho had a genuine look of fear in his eyes.

Joshya nodded and tried to think of something clever to say back, but nothing came to mind. He watched as Vylarr descended the ridge and began yelling orders at a group of archers. Together they nocked and drew, but just as they were about to fire, a huge boulder came cascading over the hill, eclipsing the sun. The archers scattered, Vylarr with them. The boulder hit the ground with a deafening *THUMP* and rolled, digging up the ground as it went. One unlucky archer found himself in its path, and before he could react, the rock had crushed him, leaving a red smear where a man once stood.

Joshya grimaced and he heard a few of the other boys gasp. But the moment was short lived, as legions of black clad soldiers swarmed over the hill. The council had been right. For every one of the Scorpio's soldiers, at least five Corvusi descended to match. The two sides clashed, and Joshya watched as man after man fell to the onslaught. Below, Vylarr had reassembled the archers and was running back towards Joshya. From their vantage point atop the hill, Joshya could see the entire battle. Arrows flew, swords clashed, men screamed. He watched as a Corvusi soldier attempted to cut down Vylarr as he passed. The captain parried easily, and stuck the assailant in the gut before continuing up the hill.

"Throw!" he called out as he ran towards them. "For the love of the Gods, *THROW*!"

Joshya had nearly forgotten what they were supposed to be doing. He stared stunned for a second before releasing his javelin into the air, without even taking the time to aim. It struck the ground thirty yards from a soul below. Embarrassed, he grabbed another from the stockpile. The boys beside him were throwing as many as they could, but none seemed to make their mark. Then Joshya watched one boy's javelin strike a Corvusi archer in the heart. The weapon went clear through his chest and pinned the man's body, dying, to the dirt.

A cheer went up from the rest of the boys, but it was short lived. An arrow came in retaliation and took the same boy in the side. He cried out, and fell from the crest of the hill, tumbling down the steep cliff below into the fray. Joshya felt tears welling in his eyes and he grabbed at his hair, unsure how to process what he'd just seen. Vylarr came from behind to grip him by the shoulders and throw him to the ground, just as a volley of arrows swept over them. Four more of the boys fell dead from the cliff, and another two were injured, scuttling back from the lip. Joshya saw Esho lying beside him. His heart skipped a beat and he crawled to his friend. Esho blinked.

"I'm... I'm OK." He rolled to his back and felt at his body as if to check for any arrows sticking out.

Another of the boys on the ground was wailing in pain, an arrow sticking out from his calf. Vylarr ignored him.

"Get up!" he called. "I count thirteen of you still good enough to fight!" He pointed with his sword to the remaining javelins. "Now grab one of those and follow me." Joshya made a move to follow, but Vylarr placed a hand firmly on his chest. "Not you."

As the others descended the hill, Joshya wondered if he'd see them again. There were no javelins left for him to throw and he felt utterly useless. Of the two injured boys, one had died from his wound. The other had quieted, slightly, but was still whimpering and grasping at his leg. Suddenly, conviction overcame Joshya. *I will not stand back just because I am the prince.* Rising to his feet, he drew the dirk from his belt. That's when he saw it.

A boulder, big as an ox, was hurtling towards the crest of the hill directly at them. Joshya froze in place, unsure of where to run. He saw Vylarr screaming at him from below, but it was too late. The rock impaled the hill, sending hunks of soil and grass in all directions. Joshya felt his feet leave the ground... *Or did the ground leave my feet?* For a moment Joshya was suspended in the air. And then everything went black.

CHAPTER 32

ALMOND IV

Hoss had slowly moved himself to the carriage, and had removed his sword and buckler from where they lay in the back, placing a rusted half-helm on his head. Almond wanted to leap out of her hiding place and help, but she knew that she couldn't do that. The cart was surrounded and she still wasn't sure if Jackan or his Dogs had seen her. All she could do was peek out from the lip of the lid.

"What do we have here?" Jackan japed, pointing towards Hoss. "Old-man farmhand is playing hero?"

He picked up Hoss' walking cane, where it lay by the fire. The sunset light glinted off Jackan's fangs and made them look even more sinister than they already had seemed. In one swift motion, he brought the cane up and snapped it against his knee, throwing the pieces at Hoss' feet. The old man had hatred in his eyes. With his sword raised, he pointed the tip at Jackan.

"I am Hoss of the Royal Lepus Army. I served my people for thirty-five years, and I challenge you to a duel, cretin!"

Jackan laughed. "Cretin? I hope you have more to offer than mean words. And as for that sword of yours? It seems to have seen better days, no? And that shield...?" he tssk tssked. "Well, I doubt it could stop a wasp sting."

Hoss paid him no mind and tightened the grip on his hilt. "Answer me, scum, do you accept my challenge?"

Jackan pretended to think about it for a moment, making a not-so-subtle motion to show that he had Hoss completely surrounded. "I don't think so, no."

Two of the hunting dogs moved in and attempted to grab at Hoss' arms. The old man slashed at the nearest one to his sword-hand, but the black-clad dog jumped lazily out of the way. The other one rushed in and grabbed his shield, twisting it until Hoss' arm looked ready to snap. A third dog leapt onto his back. Before Hoss could swing his sword, the first dog had moved in and was gripping his wrist, snarling and twisting until Hoss released his grip on his sword. The rusted metal dropped to the dirt with a feeble plop. The buckler was ripped from his arm and thrown to the ground as well, where one of the dogs split it in half with a hatchet. The old man struggled, but couldn't break free. Almond wanted to do something, anything, but she knew she couldn't. Jackan walked over and knocked the half-helm from Hoss' wrinkled forehead.

"You have a lot of fight in you. The Pit Master would love to have a man like you. What do you say?"

Hoss' eyes blazed with fire and he spat on Jackan's boot. "To the depths of hell with you."

Jackan shrugged. "Don't say I didn't give you the option." He raised his clawed fist, and in one swift motion, slashed it clean across Hoss' throat.

Almond shut her eyes as soon as the metal touched skin, not bearing to watch. That didn't help with the sound though. She sunk down into the darkness of the chest as the lid shut above her and the latch fell into place. When she heard someone walk by, she froze where she lay. The latch jiggled and for a moment Almond thought she would be caught, but the lid never opened. Then she heard Jackan's voice, muffled through the closed wood.

"Take the carriage. We need a new one after you idiots let the others burn."

Almond could feel the cart getting loaded, with every new crate or barrel jerking the back of the carriage. As the last of the cargo was loaded, she thought the weight would have snapped the rickety old cart and she felt a lurch forward accompanied by the sounds of horses trotting. The motion was oddly soothing, and despite her fear, Almond soon fell asleep.

"Hand them over, dog, before I throw you in with them."

She awoke to the sound of two men arguing. It must have been night, because the entire world was dark. *No*, Almond thought as she remembered where she was.

She could hear the muffled sound of Jackan grumbling, and then the cart lurched forward again. As the carriage slowly rocked along, Almond felt herself growing increasingly anxious. The air had grown stale within the crate, and Almond was beginning to have difficulty breathing. She unsheathed her sword from the scabbard beside her, and used the tip to pick at the wood of her crate, in a feeble attempt to carve an air hole. She was cramped and hungry and had to relieve herself. The uneven wheels on Hoss' carriage made the ride a nightmare for her back muscles, and there was no telling how long it would be until she'd have a chance to attempt an escape. She managed to cut a splinter from the wood but not much else. Through the opening she could see nothing more than other crates and boxes. She pressed her lips to the wood and sucked in. It was all the air she would get.

It took hours before the cart came anything close to another stop. Almond was playing with her orange gem, the one hanging around her neck, when she felt the cart slow to a canter. A queer tingle went through her fingers and she panicked for a moment. Then, all of a sudden, she was warm. Very warm. She looked again through her hole, but could still see nothing. Although... there was no green outside where there once was grass. Only what looked like... *sand*? she thought. Before she could process anything, the cart lurched forward again and she was off.

When the cart finally did stop - *fully* stop, her head pounded so hard that she could barely think. The stop was jarring. Almond could hear cursing from outside and held her breathe.

"Leave it," someone called out. It might have been Jackan, but the voice was too distant to tell.

Don't move, Almond told herself. *They still could be out there. Don't move.*

Almond waited in silence for over an hour. Well after the last sounds of hoofs had cantered off. Her stomach betrayed her, though. Outside her box, she could smell the start of a cookfire. The thought of food made Almond's stomach growl and she winced at the smells. Unable to last a second longer within her confines, she raised herself to her knees and attempted to lift the lid of the crate. The latch stopped it from moving even an inch. Frustrated, she drew up her sword again. There was no way to swing it, but she could still jab. With all the strength that remained to her, Almond began chipping at the wood, until the tip pierced through and sent a wash of fresh air in on her. Her relief was short lived, however, as she heard a gasp from the cookfire, and the sound of feet rushing over. *I'm dead*, she thought.

The latch jiggled and the lid opened. Almond was ready. She lunged forward, eyes closed and screamed as loud as she could. Sword in hand, she thrust forward and heard a woman yelp in pain. Almond came to a hard landing as her shoulder

ALMOND

hit the hot sand. *It is sand.* Confused, she opened her eyes. All around her was a sea of red sand. The air even seemed to have a red tint to it. Turning, Almond lay on her back, breathing in the fresh air and staring at the night sky. But it was different; the stars were all wrong.

"Who?"

The voice was timid. Almond propped herself up on her elbows and stared. None of Jackan's dogs were in sight: only a lone girl, clutching a skinny hand to her right palm, where blood dripped from a long gash.

"I," she started again, but her voiced choked and tears welled in her eyes.

Almond looked around. The girl was alone. Almond was standing in the middle of what looked like a desert. To the east was a large wooden fort - so big that it could have been easily mistaken as a castle. Hoss' carriage was lodged in the sand, one wheel had come off the stone path and cracked in half.

"I thought it was abandoned!" she stammered again. "I'm sorry!" She looked down at her hand as the blood dripped at her feet. "Please help me."

Almond sat on a leather-bound hardwood chair, wrapping gauze around her new friend's wound. *A wound that I am to blame for.* Almond had never hurt anyone before, and she didn't like the feeling that had come with it. The girl's name was Halley, as Almond has learned, and she was a serving girl for Queen Eidaya of the Phoenix Faction. *A rift.* Almond was astounded. *Jackan took me through a rift into another Star Faction.* The thought terrified her, but excited her just as much. She looked to Halley, the first person she had ever talked to from off-world. Together, they sat beneath a wooden archway, off the west flank of the Queen's Palace. The wooden fort was much nicer on the inside. But all around them was sand, without so much as a pond of water in sight – only the remains of the carriage. Jackan had decided to ditch the cargo once the carriage had broken. To Almond, it seemed like such a waste. *You killed Hoss for that carriage, and yet you throw if away so easily.* She had come to realize that Jackan valued nothing in this world - not property, nor life. *He values that gauntlet of his, though*, she thought, bitterly.

Almond counted herself lucky on finding Halley, elsewise she would have been lost on this world without a hope of getting back home. And although she had trouble admitting it, Almond knew that talking to Halley was helping distract her from thinking about Hoss. *Stupid old man. You were supposed to help me save my father, now I have to mourn both of you.*

Halley had told Almond the general direction to go to find the Rift back to her own world, but in exchange Almond was to take Halley's place as a serving girl until her hand healed. If Queen Eidaya saw the sword wound, she would know Halley had been outside of the Castle, and that was prohibited for servers.

 ALMOND

The palace itself was hardly conventional. Without an ounce of stone to be found, the entire structure was built like a massive wooden boat and half buried in the red sea of sand. Even the main tower looked half like a mast. Halley had told Almond that at one point the sand sea had been a wet sea, but that time had dried it until all that remained was salt and sand.

As the sun rose over the horizon, Almond was struggling to stuff herself into Halley's serving clothes. The girl was young, eleven or twelve by the look of her, Almond never asked. As she finally squeezed herself into the tunic, Halley reached up and placed a red feather in her hair and gave her a ponderous lookover.

"Queen Eidaya can never tell one of her servers from the next," she said. Talk as little as you can, and she'll never know the difference."

Almond hoped that the girl was right. As she left, she turned back to see Halley flexing her hand, the bandage creasing.

"Don't do that." Almond said, frowning. "You'll irritate it."

"It itches," said Halley. "I think I got sand in it."

Almond gave her a look. "You'll be fine." She hoped she was right about that too.

As Almond drew closer to the room where she was to go, the one with the feather carved above the door, she took a deep breath and tried to compose herself. *You'll be fine. You only have to do this for a few days, then you can return home and cry all you have to. For now, be strong.* The sounds of heated discussion emanated from within. Stepping through the door, she attempted to make as little noise as possible, as to not draw attention to herself. Inside, the Queen of the Phoenix Faction sat at her table, with five of her advisers sitting facing her at the other end. One was in a heated discussion with a knight in bronze armour that reflected the light in all colours of the rainbow. Halley had warned her of this man, a hotheaded knight named Sir Heleron. Stare at him too long and be prepared to be talked down to in front of everyone.

"I told you thrice already, Heleron," said the first man. When he spoke, his brown eyes twitched like a bug. "We haven't the material to fix the armoury. You'll have to wait until the shipment arrives from Hell's Fall."

"The shipment was due a fortnight ago!" Sir Heleron slammed his fist onto the table. "It is not going to arrive; those dogs have probably already sacked the caravan. I swear by the gods I'm going to tear off each and every one of their–" He paused and looked to Almond. "And pray, who are you?"

Oh no. All eyes were on her now. "I'm Almond", she almost said.

"I'm... I'm to care for the Queen's legs." She produced a bottle of ointment that Halley had given to her.

Heleron looked as though he was going to protest, but before he could, Queen Eidaya waved her hand dismissively.

"Of course, get to it."

Almond walked sheepishly to the older woman and rolled up her pantlegs. Then she began to apply the ointment to the

ALMOND

skin. *No wonder Halley needed me. With the cut on her hand there's no way she would be able to do this without the Queen questioning her.*

Sir Heleron began to fidget with his sword belt. "I simply must protest that –"

"Enough." The Queen's voice was soft, but stern. "Drop the issue, Sir Heleron, we have many more matters to attend to before we adjourn." A letter lay before her on the table and she slid it across to the other side.

"My cousin Elroy fears that the parley on Armonth is simply a front for King Terreon to take control."

"Your cousin is a fool," Sir Heleron scoffed.

"Yes," added the Queen. "But regardless, I'd like you to send a garrison of soldiers to make sure. A dozen should suffice."

Sir Heleron nodded. One of the other men spoke up and produced a parchment.

"We have also received a letter from the Aquarii town of Water's Edge, Your Grace."

The Queen frowned. "Really, what do they want?"

"They fear the Cancers are preparing their assault on the surface soon. They beg for any friendly factions to come and help protect them. There are signatures at the bottom of the Lords from Tidefall, Black Isle, Widow's Well, –"

The Queen cut him off. "I needn't hear the names of every measly Aquarii town. Why have they not sent to their own Queen?"

"Queen Delphini is busy collecting hired swords for war. They are already being harried on their western shores by the Grus Faction. The new Grus Queen seems bent on further expanding her realm by the day."

Queen Eidaya shook her head. "This Starscape... Too full of bloody wars." She looked down. "You may stop child."

Almond rose to her feet and wiped her hands on her tunic. "Will that be all, Your Grace?"

"It will, thank you."

As Almond left, she could hear the discussions continue, and knew they wouldn't be stopping anytime soon. Her father had often been a part of council meetings back in Rimby, but the matters of a small village were nothing in comparison to that of an entire Star Faction.

Halley was waiting for her back in the serving quarters. She had made soup, and handed a bowl to Almond as she entered.

"How did it go?"

"You were right - she didn't notice anything different." Almond took a sip of her soup and spat it back into the bowl. Embarrassed, she wiped her mouth. As she felt her cheeks turning red, she mumbled an apology to Halley, but the girl seemed to understand.

"Fresh water is hard to come by here, so it's reserved for the Queen and her people. Boiling it helps, but you can never really get rid of the taste."

Almond nodded, and took another sip. It wasn't nearly as bad as she had thought. "What's the meat you have in here?"

Halley smiled. "Rabbit."

The word made Almond think of her people, and suddenly, Almond felt sick all over again.

CHAPTER 33

DERRON V

The chief stood opposite Derron, his century of men dwarfing the two dozen with Derron. The old king shifted uncomfortably from foot to foot.

"Well, show me the way," Skel repeated. "The Bittertooth does not have all day."

A light freezing rain had begun to wash over the field. It was getting warmer, but that wasn't saying much. Derron pulled the collar of his coat up around his neck to stave off some of the chill, and yet somehow, the tribesmen standing across from him didn't seem phased by the cold despite being woefully underdressed. Unable to think of an alternative, Derron walked forward and beckoned the tribesmen to follow. He barely got two steps before Skel stopped him with a gesture and a smirk.

"Hand over your weapons," he commanded, left hand outstretched, with his right in a tight grip around his own club.

Derron paused and thought for a second. "There are beasts in these woods. Just a fortnight ago we came across a great ten-foot wolf," he lied. "We need our weapons to protect ourselves."

That only made Skel laugh. "You take me for a fool, don't you, grey-man?"

A few of the tribesmen murmured agreement to one another. Derron could feel the tension cutting through the air like a blade through silk. He allowed his grip on his walking stick to release, and the wood made a soft PUFF as it hit the snow.

Skel scoffed. "Pick up your stick, grey man. The red lynxes are not afraid of an old man's cane." He pointed. "It is the steel that we do not like."

Derron watched as the few members of his party that owned daggers, axes, and swords dropped them to the ground. Skoma was the last to do so. He almost looked as though he would cry as the steel disappeared beneath the snow. Derron felt a rip in his jacket as Skel pushed the butt of his club into Derron's back, the flint tearing at the wool.

"Guide us. Now."

Derron led the group up the eastern side of the lake, passing by the carved rock where he'd been bitten. As they got close to it, he felt his arm tingle. Snaggletooth whimpered beside him, no doubt remembering the hook that pierced his nose here. For a moment, Derron considered showing the rock to Skel, but in the end decided not to. *I will give them as little as I dare.* He had no idea how much Skel knew. Perhaps he knew more than Derron, perhaps less. Derron had to assume the latter, as Skel had questioned Fortho so sharply. Lucky for Derron, Fortho's own knowledge was limited as well. Although, you only question someone if you know there is information to be obtained. Skel must have known there was information to give. He was pondering that when Skel suddenly and violently went into a coughing fit.

Derron came back to reality, and turned towards the chief. "Are you alright?"

Skel smiled. "Never better." He grinned and pointed to a rotten brown canine tooth on his bottom jaw.

"Bittertooth," Derron mused.

"I once killed a man by biting him with this tooth." He boasted. "It's lucky"

"It's rotten is what it is."

Skel frowned, and for a moment looked as though he would hit Derron over the head with his club. "A sign of strength."

"It's infected." *Why am I advising this savage?* He continued anyway. "It needs to come out."

That did anger Skel. "If it does, Skel will no longer be the Bittertooth!"

Derron shrugged. "If you say so."

Derron counted himself lucky. There were no further issues between the two groups of men, even when the night grew close and the tribesmen grew rowdy. As the light dimmed, the path before them was also thinning. The weather had grown warm-

DERRON

er, and a few of the trees had snow melting off their canopies. *The weather here is as fickle as a child*, he thought. Not a day had passed since they were bracing for the coldest winter they had known, and now the snow was melting in droves. When he looked up, he could see the two moons coming through what remained of the cloud cover. If it kept up, the group may even get an entire day of sun tomorrow.

Skoma was walking beside Derron, with his hand adorning the hip of his belt where he typically holstered his sword. Snaggletooth wasn't far behind. The group kept waiting for Skel to call a halt, but the command never came. Even tired and hungry, they had made incredible progress for a single night, travelling well beyond the northern shore of the lake. Before them was a steep chasm, and when Derron consulted his map, he found that they were already at the northern ridge.

"Where next?" asked Skel.

Derron scratched at his beard. "We need to reach the bottom of this chasm."

"Then we climb."

Derron laughed. "Then we fall!"

Skel scoffed and spit over the ledge. "A lynx can climb anywhere."

"You are no more a lynx than I am a bear."

"Bears can also climb."

Derron decided to halt this folly of an argument. "You may climb down, but my men are remaining right here."

Skel frowned and pushed a finger into Derron's chest. "You are guide, for me."

"Then we take another path."

Skel paused, annoyed. Derron could see that the small amount of reasoning skills the wild man possessed were being put to use. A vein in the chief's forehead bulged. "Bear, there is no other way down."

Derron shook his head no. "There is, but we have to double back the way we came."

Skel nodded, bitterly, biting his lower lip in frustration. "Alright, grey-man. We go your way."

Skel moved fast to his men, barking commands to turn around. Derron stayed by the ledge gazing out into the snow filled chasm. It was a lazy excuse, but it had worked. In truth the ridge was more than traversable, but the detour would work to give him more time to think of a means to escape. Derron stared over the ledge, deep in thought, only looking up when he saw Alymer coming towards him. The old man glanced over his shoulder and took a deep breath before speaking.

"I have a plan," he said in a low voice, almost a whisper.

Derron looked over to him quizzically and nodded. "Then I'll hear it."

After a short pause Alymer spoke. "The ice of the lake is still thin: the cold spike could not have frozen it through, and in this weather, its assuredly starting to melt. Perhaps it's thick enough to walk on, but only until it cracks."

 DERRON

Derron stopped him. "Are you suggesting that we flee across the lake?"

Alymer grinned. It was a sad grin. "Quite the contrary, I'm suggesting we make them think we're fleeing across the lake." He pointed to the map Derron had in his hand. "The Lyncis are here, searching for us north around the site." He circled the red marking with his finger. "We are here, directly north-west of the lake. If we escape, then eventually, they will find us. However, if we make our position known, then we can choose when, where, and on what terms that happens. If that place is on the lake, these people will not hesitate to charge us down... and then the lake will shatter."

"Causing all of us to fall in with it," Derron finished.

Alymer looked up. "Or just one of us."

Derron stared at him wide-eyed. "Out of the question, I will not allow it."

"With all due respect, my King, I see no other way. And it is my job to protect you."

Derron ground his teeth together. "Alymer, we are in this mess because of me. I brought you all along and it is not my intent to lose you here."

Alymer smiled a sad smile. The skin at the edges of his mouth bunched up. "You're going to lose at least one of us whatever way this goes down. Let me keep that number down to just one."

Derron wasn't sure what to say, so he said nothing. Alymer spoke instead.

"When I was a boy, still living on my father's farm, my brother and I were always challenging each other. I never could beat him. When we decided to leave and join your father's castle guard, my brother told me that I would never do anything of note, that he would be the great warrior. I promised myself I'd prove him wrong. I was sixteen when I made that promise. Sixteen. I'm sixty-five now, Derron. I'm nearing the end of my life and I still haven't fulfilled that promise. Let me go out on my own terms, to give my life meaning."

"Your life *has* had meaning." Derron placed a hand on Alymer's shoulder. "You've served me faithfully for your whole life. You've guarded my home for as long as I've been alive. There is no guarantee this plan will work. Don't throw your life away."

But in his heart Derron knew no words could persuade him. Alymer's mind was made, and there were no better options on the table. He sighed and stroked his beard.

"We would have to escape first," said Derron, and that was when they thought of the chasm. "We do it tonight."

It took some convincing, but Skel eventually caved to allowing them to camp for the rest of the day. Derron had argued that the men needed sleep to face what was ahead, but Skel asserted that the Bittertooth didn't need sleep, though his tone changed slightly after he noticed half his men asleep in the brush.

"We post guards. Keep you in one spot and keep eyes on you."

 DERRON

It would be smarter to keep us apart, Derron thought.

It was lucky for them that the temperature had risen. Skel had refused to allow Derron's men to construct any kind of shelter for themselves. Instead, they huddled in a group for warmth. Ten sentries surrounded them at a distance, in place of a true barricade. While together, they had been circulating the plan around the group: they were to make a break for the chasm on Derron's signal. They had even checked on Will to make certain he would be OK on his leg, expecting the man to be fearful. Will had been quite the opposite.

"If they catch me, it just gives you all more time," he'd said, to which Derron stared at him, disapprovingly.

They would only have one good shot, Derron knew, as he stood before two of the sentries. He had asked one of them if he could speak to Skel, and now he waited for the chief to come. Derron's hands nervously gripped his walking stick. Each sentry had a hard-wooden club, and neither let up their eye contact with him. One had his hair tied back with a piece of dead grass, the other was bald, with blue paint running in curves around his cheeks and chin and up his bald head. Derron gave the bald man a light smile, but got nothing in return. Behind him, many of Derron's men pretended to sleep, imitating the long-drawn-out breaths of slumber. At least, he hoped that they were pretending. Skel had positioned guards in all directions, though at the moment only two stood between the chasm and the group. Derron needed it to stay that way for just a few minutes longer. Skel was stretching as he walked towards him.

DERRON

"Why does the grey man wake me?"

"I did not think I'd wake you. I thought the great Bittertooth never slept."

That made Skel laugh. "Make it quick."

"I'd like to discuss with you how we will divide the treasure when we come to the end of our journey together." Derron watched Skel's eyes flicker with a hint of interest.

"You know what treasure lies at the cross?"

The Cross. Derron frowned, thinking of the symbols he had discovered. *So, the man does know much of what we are after.*

"Gold" said Derron. "There will be gold."

"Skel has no need for gold."

"Perhaps a golden tooth?"

"Skel does not need a –"

CRACK!

Skel's head shot to the side as Derron's stick hit him in the jaw. The Chief went stumbling to the ground as blood gushed from his swollen lips. A small brown tooth lay in the snow a few feet away.

The Guard with his hair tied back made the first move, raising his wooden club and growling. That was when the newly carved bone shank punched into his chest. Skoma twisted and released and the man fell to his knees. The bald guard seemed too stunned to move, so Derron took him in the temple with his stick, knocking him out cold. Behind him, he heard the sounds of a struggle as his men overpowered the two tribesmen nearest the chasm. One lost a wrestling match with Roman and was flung from the lip, landing in the snow thirty feet below without a sound. The other had his club wrestled away from him, and one of Derron's men used it wallop him in the forehead. From where Derron stood, he wasn't sure if the man was unconscious or dead.

As the other tribesmen swarmed, the group began descending the wall of the chasm. The climb was rough, but not impossible. Derron himself reached the bottom in less than five minutes, and most of his men had done the same. A few of the tribesmen attempted to follow. Many hadn't. As Derron began walking from the cliff deeper into the underbrush of the chasm, he passed a pile of stained snow. At first, he thought it was a tribesman, but as he passed, he saw the bear sigil and knew it was the body of one of his own men. He said a silent prayer and clutched the carved bearpaw on his neck

As quickly as it started, the escape seemed to be over. They were out of sight of the Lyncis at least for now. Derron paused for a moment to account for his men. Three were not there. Somehow, Snaggletooth had been able to descend the rocks and so had Will, although he had badly reopened his wound on the way down. Roman was holding him like a baby, the blood seeping fresh from beneath his Will's pantleg and down the bigger man's thigh. Derron knew that they needed to move, and fast. He could already hear the sound of feet shuffling down the rockface behind them.

DERRON

CHAPTER 34

ALGEN V

Algen watched from his place at the side of the throne as King Caraq bent down to pick up his goblet from amongst the splintered remains of his high table. The King raised the goblet to his Lords and laughed.

"We feast!" he cried. "More food!"

Algen hurried back to the kitchens, where Korra was scrambling to produce something for the guests.

"The King requests more food!" she was yelling. "Get cooking!" She saw Algen come in and forced a platter of something warm and oozing into his arms. "Take this! Go!"

Algen nearly knocked Hanlin to the ground in his hurry to back to the hall. Bursting from the archway he stumbled past the throne to the nearest table, seating the envoy from the Frost Dome, where Lord Harren took one sniff of the food and nearly retched.

"You giving us rotten food, boy?"

Algen paled and moved on before the Lord could ask him why he did not answer.

The next table over housed the delegate from The Iron Dome. Lord Ormic was bolstering himself, laughing and drinking, and telling the men at the next table of all his great accomplishments. When he laughed, his belly jiggled and rang with the clinking of the chains around his neck.

Algen hurried to the front of the wooden table where an armed guard stopped him, looked down and snarled. Then, with a hand protruding with shell pieces, he reached down and pulled a large handful of food from the platter, and stuffed it in his face. Algen felt bits of spittle drip against his cheek as the man ate.

"Kali!" yelled Lord Ormic between gulps from his goblet. "Save some for your Lord!"

The man named Kali nodded, and swiped the platter from Algen's hands. Turning, he reached out to present it to his lord. Ormic reached out a yellow hand, but before he could touch the platter it suddenly slipped from Kali's grasp. The food splattered against the table, soon followed by Kali himself.

Ormic stared wide eyed at his man as the Iron Dome guard writhed upon the table, sending cups and plates clattering to the floor. Algen stepped back, and his eyes locked with Kali's, for just a moment, before the seizing guard's burst with blood. The entire hall had become hushed. No one dared speak.

"Poison!" Lord Ormic had swelled thrice his original size, bursting from his robes, his pasty yellow-white chest glinting in the light of the skylight. "Someone dare try and poison me?"

King Caraq stood, noticeably distraught. "Take him to the Steam Cells!" he bellowed.

It took Algen a moment before he realized that the King was talking about him. *No!* he wanted to scream. *No, it wasn't me!* Algen felt two large hands grip him on the shoulders, and before he could even put up his hands to protest, he was on the ground and being dragged from the hall. From behind him he could still hear the ravings of Lord Ormic, and the jingle of his chains.

As he was dragged to the lower levels under the dome, Algen couldn't help but try and escape. *I'm innocent!* he screamed in his head. But of course, there was no way to convey that to the man grasping him. The guard was holding his wrist in a tight grasp and didn't even bother looking down at him as Algen was dragged across the stone tile. His leg scraped over a jagged crack in the cobblestone that left a scratch running down his thigh, but when he reflexively yelled out, nothing happened, and the guard continued to pull. For most of the trip Algen was on his chest, but every now and again his body flipped and he got a good look up at his jailer. The man was big, incredibly so, with open holes covering his cheeks that oozed a watery slime. The man wore no shirt, and his exposed skin was greenish and crackled. The guard did not speak either, but Algen assumed that was by choice.

Suddenly, he was hoisted to his feet and thrown forward like a wet bag, tumbling until his back hit the stone wall of the back of the cell. The rock was burning hot to the touch and Algen had to scramble away to avoid being burned. He glanced up and watched as the barred door closed with a loud screech and the guard walked away grinning.

Algen felt the sweat beading off his brow already. The steam cells were just as they sounded: hot and muggy. The geysers that heated the King's Dome were directly below two places: the kitchens, for cooking food. And the cells, for cooking prisoners. Algen knew that his father had brought many men down here in the past, and he had told Algen all about this place. Although, Algen had never imagined in his wildest dreams he'd inhabit it. *The steam heats the cells to an unbearable temperature,* his father's voice spoke in his head. *It saps a prisoner of any energy to escape. A day inside and they're ready to do anything you want in return for release, three days and most have gone mad. A week, well, I've never seen a man live for that long. We usually find him cooked well through by morning, and have a little feast for breakfast.* Algen always wondered if that last part was true. He'd always assumed it was a joke, but now he wasn't so sure.

In his cell there was no bed, no chamber pot, no food, no water, and no light besides some luminescent algae hanging tentatively from the ceiling. Just sitting on the ground made his backside uncomfortably warm, and standing only shifted the pain to his feet. He finally decided to remove his clothes, piling them in the center of the room and sitting on top cross-legged. That alleviated some of the feeling, but it did nothing to help the air, which was hot and moist, making it feel like he was drinking every time he took a breath. It must have been hours, but eventually the slimy guard returned and threw two raw fish into his cell. Algen was more concerned about water, feeling more dehydrated than he ever had before. But when he motioned to his tongue and throat the guard only chuckled, leaving him to his fish. The food was mediocre at best, but at least not rotten like he expected it would be. With something in his stomach, Algen was able to compose himself, if only a tiny amount. However, the heat was beginning to make him dizzy and he felt close to passing out.

Algen thought about how he would escape, but his mind kept returning to thoughts about what his punishment would be if he failed to do so. The murder of a lord, even the attempted murder of a lord, was punishable by death. He knew deep down that the only reason his head still rested on his shoulders was because of his father. No doubt, King Caraq was contemplating the idea of losing the support of a major lord if he wasn't punished, and losing his best general if he was. Either way, it would be a blow to the war effort. Algen hoped that Caraq wouldn't figure out that he was as good as dead to his father the moment he stepped out from the transformation chamber.

He studied his bluish-purple hands and bent them around. He'd noticed more recently that his transformation had made him more flexible, almost bendy and jelly-like. He twisted his

ALGEN

arm and watched as his hand turned painlessly from being palm down, to palm up and then some. When he let go, the arm swung back into place and jiggled. He then experimentally bent his fingers back until the nails touched the back of his wrist. It felt no different than bending his fingers normally. Reaching down, he picked up the remains of his fish and hurled them at the bars of the door. They hit the bars, but still made it through the gap. And suddenly, Algen had a wild idea.

Getting up, he donned his clothes and walked over to the bars. His feet were numb to the heat at this point and he hardly felt anything on his soles. He peeked out. The guard was no-where to be seen. Gingerly, Algen slid his hand all the way to the elbow out of the bars. The gap between the iron bars was roughly the same width as his forearm, so normally that would have been as far as someone could reach. But as he pushed, Algen felt the skin and muscle on his arm squish as he made his way up to the shoulder. Then, the bones of his shoulder popped and shifted in his body, until that too was outside the cell door. He stared in disbelief at what he was doing. Next came a foot, which was easy. Then the knee, where his kneecap shifted to the side as it too went through, realigning itself on the other side.

Within two minutes, Algen had gotten all the way to his neck, where one half his body was free. His skull was the hard-est to push through, but even it, bending to fit the hole, made it through. Not long after that the rest of his body followed. It took a moment for his mind to comprehend what had just happened, but Algen realized he was free.

He felt disconnected from his own body, unsure how it happened, but knowing that it had. And then he ran. As fast as his feet could take him, he ran. Other prisoners yelled to him as he went, some cheering, some screaming. Algen was sure that a guard would hear them, but there was no place to hide anyway and so he kept going. The closer he came to the main level of the dome, the cooler it got, and the easier time he had breathing. When he reached the top of the stairs, he stopped, afraid that he'd been seen. Looking around, he saw a small window that looked out over the palace's courtyard. Not ten seconds after he had climbed through to outside, Algen froze, the sound of panicked thumping footsteps up the stairs filling his ears. Once he had his bearings, Algen made a mental map as to which was the King's Hall and promptly ran in the opposite direction.

Algen didn't stop until he knew he was well away from the towering walls of the palace, and even then, he kept going until he physically could not go any further. *I have to leave*, he thought, as he pressed a hand up against the glass. His thoughts turned to Alanna, and seeing her being shot out from the ejection chamber. Before fully considering what he was doing, Algen found the closest chamber and sealed himself inside. As the glass on the outside of the dome opened, Algen felt the seawater rush in, yanking him like a hand from where he stood. Instinctively, he held his breath, until he could do that no longer and sucked in. His gills took over from there.

Turning this way and that, the water's current threw Algen in a flurry of motions before dropping him in a reef. He lay amongst crimson sponges gasping for breath. Breathing through his gills was a foreign feeling. The water rushed in under his chin, and then out again. Somehow it gave him the oxygen to breathe. But water is much thicker than air, and each breath was a chore. A few times he accidentally breathed in through his nose, and ended up coughing water from his lungs, only to be replaced with more water. He composed himself, feeling the sandy floor with his webbed hands. His eyes were still adjusting to the motion of the water. It made him dizzy just trying to focus. Algen tried to calm himself, breathing as deeply as his gills would allow. Then, composed, he pushed from the seabed and jettisoned himself upwards towards the light.

CHAPTER 35

RYMUS V

The trip through the mountains was long and jarring. Rymus felt as though his tailbone had shattered and his ass had fallen asleep, though the ass he was riding on was still well awake despite carrying him for at least the last five hours. When they were at last in sight of the small fortress, Rymus tried his best to determine which it was, but soon determined that he'd never seen it before. Most likely, it would be Sir Artell's fortress, and everyone inside was likely under his command. *Well, everyone except my brothers, if The Ram is to be believed.* Rymus was anxious to find out.

When they arrived at the portcullis, a man released Rymus from his chains. As Rymus dismounted, he struggled to stand on his own with his numb legs, the ground beneath him seemed to churn as though he were still on horseback. Sir Artell wandered over to him and clasped his arm around Rymus' shoulder. With his other hand he pointed at Rymus' legs.

"Having some troubles, aren't you, Prince?"

Rymus nearly fell as he tried to take a step. "Bugger yourself, Goat."

Artell frowned and removed the hand from Rymus' shoulder, only to use it to shove him to the ground. Rymus' legs collapsed beneath him. Sir Artell stood above him, eclipsing the evening sun dipping behind the mountains.

"Where'd you get this sword?" He threw Rymus' scabbard to the ground, revealing the pommel carved in the shape of a ram's head.

"Flea market," he lied as he rose to his knees. "Bought it as scrap metal."

That didn't amuse The Ram in the slightest. Sir Artell picked the blade from the dirt and hooked it to his belt. "Don't get comfortable, Rymus." Sir Artell pointed an accusatory finger at him. "You're my prisoner right now, so don't go forgetting that."

The rest of the walk up through the fortress hallways was in silent tension. At the peak of the highest tower, Sir Artell opened an oaken door and Rymus' heart sank. Sitting at a table, with chains dangling from their wrists, were Lydus and Elkus. Lydus looked up with as much embarrassment as hatred as the pair entered the room. His long hair was drooped over one half of his face and Rymus could only see his one eye. Elkus had more of a look of boredom, though his expression was also mixed with pain. As Rymus was brought to his seat next to his brothers, he saw that the skin on Elkus' right hand was stitched all the way from between his middle fingers to the back of his wrist. *He must have gone down in much more of a fight than I did.* He didn't resist as The Ram clicked the chains around his wrists. He was scared to know that his brothers had been captured, but even more, he was happy to find them still alive. Sir Artell had gone to the brazier and lit a fire. Lydus' serrated sword hung above the mantle like a trophy. Sir Artell noticed him looking and smiled.

"You like that? A fine trophy, I think. The famed Prince Lydus' serrated sword!" He smirked. "Well, my sword now, in truth."

Rymus fidgeted in his seat. The table had been set with spoons, forks, plates, mugs, and even a lit candelabra, but no knives. *It would be easy enough to go for his eyes with a fork.* Rymus considered for a moment doing it, but his better sense took over. He wouldn't leave himself that vulnerable. Rymus sat. The table itself was big enough to seat at least thirty, and looked absurdly big when only four were seated.

"Are you hungry?" asked their host.

Lydus didn't answer. Elkus made only a grunt.

"A little," said Rymus.

His brothers turned to look at him. Sir Artell smiled and called his servers, who brought them trays of vegetables and meats. One serving boy placed a bowl of perfectly ripened fruit in front of Elkus. His brother reached for a peach, but as he did

RYMUS

the chains that bound his hand snagged and the stitch in his hand burst. Blood trickled out over the entire bowl, spotting the peaches red. Artell was unperturbed. Snapping his fingers, he waved a server over to remove the bowl. Elkus took his napkin and wrapped it tightly around the open wound.

"Let's begin," Artell said. "Why are you here?"

"Heard your mother was in town, ha!" said Elkus.

Artell ignored him.

Lydus spoke up. "Your king stole a very important heirloom from our father. We are here to retrieve it."

"And you thought the best way of going about that was to invade our land and kill our men?" The Ram took a bite out of an apple.

Lydus shrugged. "Would you have rather we politely knocked on the front door?"

"On the contrary, I would have rather you had come looking to fight me first." Artell took another bite from the apple. It made a wet sound as he broke the skin with his teeth. He continued, "Let's say that I know where this... heirloom, is. If you had it, would you leave this world?"

"Promptly," said Lydus.

Sir Artell clapped his hands together. "Well then, it's a shame that I cannot give it to you."

Elkus spat a peach pit to the floor. "And why in the hells not?"

The White Ram smiled a white smile. "His Grace the King of Aries has given it to me for safekeeping, I cannot betray my word to him that I would protect it.

Rymus frowned. *Honorable to the end.* He paused. *Although maybe...*

"How did you come to capturing my brothers, Sir?" Rymus was trying to sound as knightly as he could.

Sir Artell laughed. "Prince Elkus I caught with his trousers around his ankles, taking a shit, with the rest of his men half a mile away! Prince Lydus was a harder nut to crack. I waited until his camp slept before I descended the mountain. He never dreamed we could traverse a cliffside so steep as the one he was beneath, but that was where your brother was wrong!" Sir Artell seemed to delight in regaling the tales of his prowess.

Rymus smiled. "Sneaking and tricks? Not a very honourable way to go about capturing your enemy, Sir. Tell me, do my brothers frighten you?"

The Ram's expression immediately turned sour. "No."

"No?" repeated Rymus. "Then why not take them head on, in an open field. Or better yet, man to man?"

Sir Artell was gritting his teeth now. Pushing back from the table and standing, he threw his apple mere inches above Rymus' head and snorted. "Then fight me now, Pisces Prince, and I will prove to you my might."

Rymus looked to his brothers. "Oh, not me. Lydus is the heir. If he beats you in single combat, on your honour you must let us go."

 RYMUS

"And when I win?"

"If you win, you can hand deliver us to your king. We will not resist." Rymus looked to his brothers for support. He found none in Elkus, but Lydus was ever so slightly nodding. Somewhere in those eyes he thought he saw a flicker of a brother's pride.

The Ram drew his sword and brought it down on the chain clasping Rymus' hands to the table. The metal snapped and Rymus rubbed at his wrists. Sir Artell gave him a cold stare. "Done."

The garrison of the Ramsfort marched the three brothers, hands bound, to a small clearing a mile up the mountain. By the time they were allowed to sit, Rymus was exhausted. Elkus even looked as if he were going to throw up. But if Lydus was the least bit tired, he made no show of it. The clearing was a circle only about thirty feet across from side to side, with two of those sides falling off into steep cliffs down to the rocks below. Sir Artell put his hands on his hips and breathed deeply.

"Smell that? Mountain air be the freshest air you'll ever smell."

"I prefer the smell of the sea," Rymus said.

The Ram made no response, but Artell's face showed that he had heard. He motioned and a young soldier moved behind Lydus to cut his bindings. The other brothers got no such treatment. Lydus stood and stretched his arms, getting the blood to circulate freely again and loosening his muscles. Another of Sir Artell's men gingerly handed him his serrated sword, then quickly moved away, as if Lydus was going cut him down where he stood without hesitation. Lydus felt the edge of the blade to make sure Artell hadn't dulled it. Rymus knew that Artell wouldn't have. After the fiasco over honour back at the fort, he would be remiss to play such a trick. Judging by Lydus' reaction, Rymus knew that he was right.

The White Ram himself was donning his own armour. The white enameled plate shone against the light of the sun. His golden horns made Sir Artell look like a sort of goat god. Sir Artell's weapon of choice was a broadsword, long and sharp. He used two mailed hands to give it a practice swing.

"Clear the field," he boomed.

Rymus and Elkus were moved to the rocky edge of the cliff, along with the thirty or so soldiers Sir Artell had brought along. Rymus glanced behind him and paled as he stared down the jagged cliff and the rocks below. *Don't look that way, Rymus,* he told himself. Lydus had donned the simple iron chest piece Artell had supplied for him and buckled the clasps. The two combatants stared each other down from across the field and both looked ready to say something, but The White Ram spoke first.

"You don't know how long I've wanted this, Prince."

"I'm honoured." Although by the sound of his voice, Lydus was anything but.

"I do hope your father isn't too disappointed in the loss of his heir," Artell continued.

RYMUS

"If I die, my father will grieve for me, but the dominion of Aries will shudder at his wrath."

The two moved ever closer together, until they were practically touching.

"Then best not die!"

The White Ram made the first swing, a two-handed sweep that Lydus leaned away from. Lydus then made a swing of his own, which Artell deflected on the backswing. Artell jabbed with the point of his weapon and Lydus had to sidestep out of the way. The fight raged on with each exchanging blow after blow. At first, the White Ram was taking on the offensive, until a few minutes in when Lydus become more aggressive and pushed Artell all the way back to the edge of the field.

He smiled. "This is exactly what I wanted."

The combat went on for several more minutes before both started to tire. Lydus had a deep cut under his upper arm that had significantly hurt his swing. Artell had a light cut on his cheek. Any deeper and the teeth on Lydus' sword would have torn out the entire cheek no doubt. Rymus, for the first time, had a pang of worry that his brother may not survive this fight. He looked beside him and saw Elkus squirming in his bonds.

Artell raised his sword. "You're dead, Pisces."

The Ram ran forward and made a hard swing downward onto Lydus, who lazily brought up his sword in defense. The two weapons struck and serrated teeth from Lydus' sword broke free and flew in all directions. One piece struck Lydus under the left eye and stuck into the flesh. A small trickle of blood seeped from behind it and dripped onto his shoulder. The ring of metal on metal filled the air. Lydus looked to be tiring, the blood loss from his arm seemed to be affecting his ability to react. Sir Artell reeled back for a killing blow and Lydus, in a last-ditch effort, forced all his body weight into him, sending the knight stumbling backwards into the crowd of onlooking soldiers. *He's coming right at me,* Rymus noticed. As the White Ram stumbled ever closer to the edge of the cliff, Rymus subtly stuck out his foot, and Sir Artell clipped it. Rymus and Sir Artell's eyes caught each other for a split second before the White Ram went sprawling over the edge, falling down, down, down into the rocks below. No one saw him hit the ground, but a red stain on the side of the mountain told all.

Rymus couldn't believe what he'd done - it was a reflex, he did it without thinking. He looked around, but no one was looking back at him. All the Aries soldiers were staring off the cliff.

"He.... He's dead," said one of the men.

Elkus frowned. "'Course he's dead. You don't survive a fall like that. Now untie me!"

The stunned soldier behind Elkus blinked and nervously cut Elkus free. Another guard did the same for Rymus. *Did no one notice?* Rymus thought, stunned. He had imagined he would have been thrown off the cliff right afterwards. While everyone else was staring in disbelief off the cliffside, Rymus turned and looked over to see Lydus lying face-down on the grass. Wide eyed, he rushed over, flipping his brother to his

RYMUS

back, and feeling his pulse. *Alive,* he thought, b*ut losing blood fast.* Ripping off his own tunic, he tore a strip and tied it tight onto Lydus' arm. The blood was seeping and caking into the fabric.

"Wood!" he called. "Bring me wood!"

The Aries men were still too stunned to react, but Elkus wasn't. Running to one of the only trees in the clearing, he broke off a large branch and hurried back to Rymus.

"And flint! Get me flint!"

One of the soldiers fumbled in his pouch and produced a large chunk. Elkus snatched it, and then ripped the man's dagger from its holster. Striking it against the flint above the branch, he soon had a small fire started. Not a lot, but enough for heat. Rymus held Lydus' sword with both hands above the open flame. He didn't want to wait too long, but if he pulled out too quickly, he'd have to start again. With the metal as hot as it was like to get, he placed it on Lydus' wound: over cloth and all. Lydus jerked, but Elkus was holding him down. Rymus just held the metal there, unsure what to do, until finally, the metal was cold to the touch. Lydus' arm looked a wreck. The bleeding had stopped, but in its place was a patch of melted fabric and pus. The smell of burned flesh and wool filled his nose. Lydus remained conscious, but just barely. Rymus looked up to the thirty onlooking Aries men.

"My brother is the champion. He won the fight fairly, and now you have to escort us down to the Ramsfort."

Begrudgingly, they complied, but the trip was far from easy. Lydus had to use Rymus as a crutch to make it all the way down the mountain and one Aries man tried to start a revolt about halfway. He drew his sword and turned towards the brothers.

"Why are we doing what they want? They killed Sir Artell! There are thirty of us and just three of them, and one's almost dead already!"

Elkus moved in closer to him. "This is why."

In one swift motion, he stepped forward, pushed the sword out of the way, and buried his newly obtained knife deep into the man's throat. Blood shot up like a red geyser and the man fell to his knees.

☆ ☆ ☆

It was three days before Lydus was strong enough to continue on their journey. As each hour passed, tensions in the fort grew higher, and half a dozen times Rymus was sure there would be a revolt. But luckily, there never was. It was on the third day, as the brothers were preparing to set out and rejoin their lost armies, that they were greeted at the portcullis by a strange and dirty man riding on a pack mule.

"Who are you?" Rymus asked, as he unsheathed a sword he had taken from the fort's armoury.

The man didn't reply. Instead, he gripped a bag from behind him on the mule, and tossed it underhand from where he sat. The bag rolled and came to a stop at Rymus' feet. Puzzled, he stared at it for a second, before stepping forward and picking it up. Rymus undid the tie on the bag and pulled from it a leather quiver painted in the ocean blue of the Pisces. Inside were three feathered arrows. When he pulled one out, he saw that it was tipped with an arrowhead made of an eerie sky-blue steel. He rolled the shaft in his hand.

"That is what you came for, isn't it?" the man called down. "It's yours. Take it and be gone."

Rymus lightly touched the tip, and his skin immediately opened. He licked the blood from his finger and nodded, satisfied that it was the real thing.

"You do not look like the King of Aries, but how else could you have come by this?"

The man grimaced. "I am no King, Sir. I am a humble herder, who wishes you to leave this place."

"And how did a humble herder come into possession of such a unique item?" He slung the quiver around his back.

The man smiled. "A humble herder may also be a master thief."

As the strange man rode away, Rymus turned and smiled to his brothers.

"Let's go home."

CHAPTER 36

JOSHYA VI

The world stood still - quiet, apart from the rustling of feet on grass and the caws of birds. Out of the corners of his eyes he could see the faintest traces of movement, blurs under a dark sky. Joshya blinked, clearing his eyes of the crust that had formed. He looked down to the bracer on his right arm, where the ornately painted Scorpion had been at the beginning of the day. Black on beige, it was then, but now the design ran dark crimson on red, the colours of the leather mixed with his blood. The broken end of an arrow shaft jutted out from the scorpion's head. Only then did Joshya feel the pain. *When did that happen?*

He lay dazed, his head pounded, and he could not seem to remember why he was here. Slowly though, the events were coming back to him. *Vylarr,* he thought, *I have to find Vylarr.* Joshya tried to stand, put pain shot up from his knee to his hip and he cried out, not able to move. *My leg,* he thought. Joshya forced himself up on his elbows and looked. It wasn't a pretty sight. His leggings were ripped from cuff to knee and the leg beneath was contorted in a such a way that the calf was almost turned around. *Dislocated,* he realized, dismayed. He tried, unsuccessfully, to move it, but ended up doing nothing more than sending another shockwave of pain up his body. Joshya collapsed back onto the ground and cursed; cursed everyone and no one all at once. He cursed the Gods and the people, the Scorpios and the Corvusi, Vylarr and his father. But most of all, he cursed himself.

Stupid child, thinking you could play soldier like your father. He was mad, but deep down he was also relieved. His wounds would hurt, and they would take a while to heal, but they weren't life threatening. Propping himself up again, he took another look at his leg. The bone was out of the socket, that was certain, but there was no break. Slowly, Joshya grasped his calf and twisted, as Aldar had once taught him to do. The bone set with a large *POP* and Joshya reeled with pain, but immediately afterwards his leg felt much better. Once he had mustered enough strength, he tried rolling to his good leg. Looking around he spotted the broken shaft of a javelin. Joshya crawled towards it, picked it up, and used it to push himself to his feet. He wondered if he had been the one to have thrown it.

Surveying the landscape around him was a hard thing to do. Joshya saw the bodies of Scorpios and Corvusi alike, strewn about in hideously misshapen ways. The view was far too much

JOSHYA

to take in all at once and Joshya keeled over to vomit, almost losing his balance in the process. *Who won?* he thought. *There was no way the Scorpios could have won. There were too many of the enemy. But if the Corvusi won, then why am I still alive?* He pondered that as he started the slow journey back towards the tunnels.

Joshya had seen many things in his years within the tunnels: giant millipedes the size of your arm, cave fish with no eyes, and, worst of all, the result of his grandfather's illness. But never in his life had he seen a dead body before. Now, as he looked around, he saw hundreds. Some no longer even looked human, with features so grotesque from damage that an arm could begin to look almost like a leg, and a face could disappear entirely.

Halfway back to the keep, he came across a small onyx scorpion broach lying in the dirt that signified the rank of captain. Just a few feet away from it he found Vylarr, or what was left of him at least. Half of the man's face had been caved in by a heavy blow from a morningstar, his one remaining eye left open in a look of shock and sadness that was petrified to his face. His once prided red armor looked no more impressive than a rusted tin can down in the mud. Too sad to look any longer, Joshya made a mental note of where he lay, with intentions to come back later and give him the burial he deserved. In life, Joshya had hated Vylarr, but when it really came down to it, he knew that Vylarr's harshness was only to protect him. And in the end, protect him he did.

As Joshya drew closer to the tunnel entrance he saw other Scorpio survivors either guarding the mouth of the tunnel or licking their wounds. No one there seemed to recognize who Joshya was. He liked it better that way. Joshya found Aldar on a rock doing the best he could to cauterize a soldier's arm where a dirk had nicked a vein. Mathas was next to him, holding a candle as Aldar heated a metal rod. The scribe's other hand held a blood-soaked rag against the man's arm. But as Joshya drew closer, Aldar noticed him, and his attention shifted immediately. Jumping to his feet, wide eyed, the old man rushed over, scanning Joshya's wounds. Joshya in return gave him the most genuine smile he could muster, despite the pain that he was in.

In a hurry, Aldar brought him to a rock and made him sit. Taking out a vial, he poured a liquid over Joshya's leg, making him grit his teeth as to not cry out, though the sound came out nonetheless. Aldar then grabbed a steel bar from his nearby sack and wrapped it against his leg with fur and hide, sealing the end with a flame. He then cut off Joshya's bracer with a knife and poured more liquid into that wound. Without warning, he pulled the arrow from the muscle and immediately covered that wound with hide as well. Joshya grimaced, but this time managed to stay silent. Only then did Aldar slow down and return his attention back to the other man.

"You're damn lucky," he said, pointing to Joshya's arm. "If that had been two inches to the left, you'd have severed the artery and bled out in the field."

"Sorry, I didn't plan on being shot," he retorted, somewhat annoyed.

"No, but you were supposed to stay out of harm's way."

"I did." He remembered how Vylarr had made him stay atop the hill while the others went into the fray, and how he had been about to chase down after them. "My people were dying. I couldn't sit back and let that happen."

"Well, now you'll be sitting back for quite some time. That leg won't heal right if you don't keep your weight off it. Better have Vylarr teach you how to fight while on your ass."

The mention of his name made Joshya frown, only slightly, but Aldar caught it.

"Didn't make it then, eh?"

Joshya shook his head.

Aldar nodded, clearly perturbed. "Then I'll make damn sure I don't let any more of his men die today."

Joshya watched Aldar work, seeing him mend one wounded man after the next. He was anxious to check on his father, his sister, and his friends. After all, he still did not know what happened to Esho. *Did he make it?* His head pounded and his limbs ached. Joshya's mind was tired enough that he wanted to go back underground and sleep for a week. None of that could happen right now, though. Without his father around it was up to him to stay and see this through. By the looks of it they had won. *But who knows how soon it will be until the Corvusi come back?* He didn't have to wait long.

From across the field, a man dressed in all black, holding a long thin sword, approached, followed closely by two hundred men. They spread out, and created a semi-circular wall around the area where the wounded sat. A few of the Scorpio soldiers made a move to attack, but none clashed with the newcomers. The leader of the Corvusi approached, flanked by a man on either side. He spoke with a voice that was both authoritative and condescending.

"You have lost the battle, and what was yours is now ours. In the name of King Olathe the Second, King of the Corvusi, the Scorpio tunnels and all its riches now belong to the faction Corvusi. Long live King Olathe."

"Long live King Olathe," the rest of the men echoed.

He continued. "As such, all remaining Scorpio citizens will be removed from the tunnels immediately. All surviving Scorpio combatants will be brought before King Olathe for judgement. Any who resist these demands will be punished. Insubordination will not be tolerated."

The man raised his weapon in a show of might, as the others descended on the camp.

"Drop your weapons!" called out Aldar. "We are in no shape to resist."

Joshya could tell that was the opposite of what Aldar really wanted them to do, but it was the most intelligent option. He watched as the surviving men threw down their swords, spears, and axes, as the Corvusi bound their arms in rope. Joshya himself threw down the half a javelin he was using as a cane. As the Corvusi swept the camp, they began collecting the weapons from the ground. When they reached Joshya and Aldar they paused.

"You," said one of the Corvusi, pointing at Aldar. "You'll come with us into the tunnels to make sure no one resists." He then turned to Joshya. "Can you walk?" Joshya shook his head no.

The soldier sighed, and called over one of the other soldiers who was on horseback.

"Take this one. His leg is injured badly."

The mounted soldier looked unamused. "Why not just kill him? The King won't notice one less captive."

The first soldier shook his head, obviously annoyed. "Dorian, you know our orders. The prisoners are to be taken alive."

The soldier named Dorian shrugged. "Alright, you're the boss."

He dismounted and pulled Joshya from his seat, hoisting him not so gently onto the back of the horse.

"I hope you end up being worth it," he japed.

Joshya wanted to tell him right then and there who he was, but kept his mouth shut.

The group was brought into a large clearing already filled with tied up Scorpio soldiers. Joshya noted Myka, his beard and naked chest matted with sweat, and a few of the boys who had stood with him in the javelin battalion. Lanoss the

Brickmaker was on his knees, the wound on his head bleeding fresh. There was no sign of Esho, Errgoth, or Faraday.

The clearing was surrounded on three sides by a thick treeline. In the center, a large throne had been constructed from the surrounding wood. It stood fourteen feet tall and sitting in it was an old man smiling wickedly at the tied-up men below. His hair was white and wispy, so thin it was bald in more than one place on his head. His skin was wrinkled and pale. On his shoulders sat a thick capelet of black feathers that looked thick enough to be a blanket. He wore no crown, but instead a large ruby around his neck, bigger than Joshya's fist. The weight of it seemed to give the man a hunch. The King held a cane in his hands, and as he slowly descended the steps, Joshya could see that the handle was made of bronze and shaped like the head of a crow.

The Corvusi soldiers knelt as the King reached the bottom step.

"Rise!" he called out, "For today we have finished what our fathers and grandfathers started decades ago!" His smile made Joshya want to punch him and knock out whatever few teeth he may have left. Dorian pushed him from the saddle and Joshya fell to the ground like a sack of rocks. He cried out when his leg struck the ground and the King seemed to hear. Walking over, Olathe the Second hunched above Joshya. As he looked up from where he lay, Joshya saw that the old King's skin seemed to be as white as the moon.

"Pick yourself up and kneel," the King demanded.

Joshya did as he was bid as best as he could, but his braced knee wouldn't bend. He remembered the dagger that Errgoth had given him. The blade was tucked in his boot and without thinking he grabbed the handle.

Joshya lunged forward, dagger in hand. The old king before him stared in hushed silence as the blade ripped through his feathered capelet. Joshya fell to the ground and the brace separated from his knee. King Olathe grasped a paper-thin hand to his throat where the fabric was cut. The tunic he wore welled red, with a drop of blood trickling down his chest. The rage was evident in his eyes.

"Kill him!" he cried. "Kill him now!"

Joshya felt himself raised roughly from the ground. His arms were locked tightly behind his back with a rough yank and he felt a dagger at his throat. *What did I do that for?* He thought to himself.

"NO!" It was Lanoss who had called out, the old mason staring intently. The King turned to him.

"And just why not?" He spat the last word like it was poison.

"Because that's Prince Joshya of Scorpius, grandson to King Luthor of Scorpius."

That seemed to pique the Corvusi King's interest. "You?" He sounded almost amused. Moving forward, the King lifted Joshya's chin to study his features. Nodding, he let go. "Yes... I believe you are. Take him to my tent."

 JOSHYA

Joshya sat under the fabric canopy, alone, waiting for the King to see him. He wanted to escape more than anything, but knew that even as the prince, he could only expect so much patience from King Olathe. And so he sat, listening to the guards outside bicker over who had landed the killing blow to one of Joshya's soldiers. Suddenly, the tent flap opened and Olathe entered, the ruby still about his neck. There was a guard beside him with sword drawn.

"To make sure you don't try to kill me... again," Olathe smirked.

Sitting, he laced his fingers together in front of him and stared menacingly into Joshya's eyes.

Joshya felt like he should say something. "Are you going to live in our tunnels now?"

That made the King cackle. It was a wheezy kind of laugh that deeply unnerved Joshya. "No, of course we aren't. All we want is what's within."

"Our precious metals."

The King nodded. "But the rest of the Starscape won't take kindly to us wiping out an entire faction for a few rocks. King Terreon alone would bring the might of his wrath down upon the Corvusi." He shook his head. "No, I need a more... orderly approach." He pulled a parchment from beside the table and lay it before Joshya.

"What is this?" he asked, unrolling the paper. When Joshya's eyes read the first few words, his heart skipped a beat.

"A marriage pact," the King answered. "To my dear grand-daughter."

CHAPTER 37

ALGEN VI

His head surfaced and Algen was birthed from the sea. The sun beamed down on him and for the first time he truly felt its warmth. Algen sputtered as he tried once again to breathe the air. All at once, the water in his lungs burst from him and he gasped a long and deep breath, coughing. All around was water, except for a single mound of land far off on the horizon. *Nowhere else to go.* And so, he swam.

It took Algen until dusk to reach the beach, and when he finally did, he collapsed immediately and lay exhausted and dripping on the sand like a beached whale. He knew he couldn't stay there, but the sand was so soft, and dry, and oddly comforting. The night was cold, and Algen could feel a chill coming. He yearned for the warmth of the heat geysers. Slowly, Algen made his way up the beach to where tall trees grew. He huddled under one, gripping his arms and shivering, listening to the crash of the waves against the shore and the odd caw of birds. It was all new to him, and the sight of it all made his head swim. So much was he enveloped in the new world around him, that Algen never heard the man behind him.

"Get up," he heard, as the butt of a spear was thrust against his back.

Algen grimaced and turned. Looking down at him was a middle-aged man, with slicked back silver hair, and an equally silver goatee. His one eye was light blue and the other deep green. The man looked none too happy to see him.

"Cancer scum." He looked down on Algen as if he were an insect sitting on his food. "I told you, get up."

Another man appeared from the night air, this one younger and clean shaven.

"A scout?" he asked."

The first man spit into the sand. "By the looks of it. A young one."

Algen had never seen anyone older than sixteen who hadn't been morphed. He puzzled for a moment before it dawned on him. *These are Aquarii men.* A panic ran through him. Before he knew what took hold of him, Algen scrambled to his feet and took off running towards the shore. *They can't follow me once I'm underwater.* Algen's feet kicked up sand as he ran. He could hear yelling from behind him. He fled, the water rushing up to meet him with every tidefall. Suddenly, something swept beneath his ankles and his feet were taken from the ground. Algen flew for a moment, before crashing down face-first into the sand. The water rushed over his head but he couldn't move; someone was pinning him down.

"Antonatos," called the voice from on top of him." Help me tie him up."

Two hands grabbed Algen by the wrists and pulled his arms taut. A rope was bound around them and drawn tight. He attempted to wriggle free, but the bars on his cell allowed for much more room than these did, and he realized that he couldn't escape these binds.

As before, the butt end of a spear was thrust against the small of his back, twice as hard this time. Then a second time, before he was pulled to his feet and spun back towards the land. The younger man had him by the arms and the older man was looking him over.

"What's your name, creature."

Algen didn't even bother trying to convey that he couldn't tell them.

The younger Aquarii grunted. "He's not going to tell us anything."

"Neither will that other scout we caught, but eventually we'll get them to talk."

Algen was brought past sand dunes with intermittent patches of grass. He wished he could have stopped to explore this above-water land, but the men who had him didn't stop for rest. Finally, they came upon a small fort attached to a dock.

"Welcome to Water's Edge, creature."

Pushing him inside, the men led Algen through the fort and down some stairs. Scoffing, the older guard kicked open the door and threw Algen inside a small room, and he found himself back in the exact same situation he had been in not two hours ago: trapped in a cell.

"We'll be back in an hour for you, freak, so don't get comfy," said one of the men from outside the door.

Algen sighed, and made his way to the back corner of the cell to lay down. At least this time the room wasn't going to boil him alive. He tried to close his eyes, but something was bothering him. He wasn't alone.

"Well, I'll be damned."

Algen turned to see Naylis smirking, slumped against the wall with blood crusted down his hip from a puncture wound in his side. The skate morph attempted to stand, but grimaced and slumped back down where he sat. The coagulated blood on his side split and fresh blood wept from the wound.

"Bugger," he breathed under his breath

Algen rushed to his friend.

No, he thought, *no, he can't be here. He was with my father!*

"You're probably wondering what I'm doing here, hey?" Algen nodded and Naylis rested his head against the wall. "I'll give you some advice, Algen: don't go for Aquarii women - they don't like our kind."

 ALGEN

Idiot, Algen thought. *You incredible idiot.* Whatever mission Naylis and his father had been on had no doubt already been comprised because Naylis couldn't control his lust.

"They know we're coming, Algen. They all know. I didn't tell them, but I know that they know." Naylis sounded almost sad, not scared.

I know too, Algen wanted to say, *and someone already tried to poison one of our lords.* But instead he only nodded, and helped press against Naylis' wound to stop it bleeding.

Nearly two hours passed before Algen heard the door open again. Outside was the silver haired guard with the spear.

"Now," he started. "Which of you are coming first?" Algen was about to stand when Naylis called out.

"Me."

The Aquarii nodded. "On your feet."

But as Naylis rose, a call from without took the guard's attention.

"Raiders!" someone shouted. "They're here!"

The guard looked to Naylis, then to Algen, and grimacing, he ran from the room, spear brandished in his hands. To Algen's surprise, he did not close the door behind him.

Naylis laughed. "Probably doesn't think us enough of a threat." His laughs turned to coughs. "Go, Algen - that would be your father out there."

Algen frowned and tried to lift Naylis to his feet, but to no avail.

ALGEN

"Go," he said again. "I'll be fine." Naylis gave Algen one last smile before Algen left.

Outside, the bodies lay strewn from shore to fort. The garrison of Water's Edge had been reduced to just five men, including Algen's guard. The men stood in a small circle, back to back, brandishing silver-tipped tridents and spears at their assailants. Six armoured Cancer mutants slowly descended upon them. One had the head of a hammerhead, and wielded a hooked staff. Next to him was a man near eight feet tall and looking to weigh at least a tonne. His body and head had merged together to looking like that of a whale. Then was a man with his fists and head adorned with hard conch shells. The shells had been sharpened on the ends of his fists into long points. Next to him was a man with a long nose and albino white skin who wore no shirt; a large blue sail ran from the crest of his head down to his tailbone. Each of his forearms displayed protrusions ending in needle-like spikes that jutted at least a foot past his hands. The fifth was a bald, slimy man who skulked from behind a rampart. And at last, the final mutant came into view.

Father, Algen thought, tears welling in his eyes

One of the Aquarii made a thrust with his weapon at the albino. The mutant parried with his own arm spike, then thrust the other into the man's throat. The giant man laughed as his ally removed the body from his arm, letting it fall with a wet smack against the sand. Another of the Aquarii garrison seemed to anger at the jeering, and made a clumsy attempt at

ALGEN

the giant's face. The trident merely scratched the skin, unable to penetrate. In response, the giant gripped the man's head in his massive fist and Algen heard a pop. The remaining three men dared not move, and two threw down their weapons. That proved to be a fatal error, as the hammerhead man showed them no mercy, effortlessly using his hooked staff to end them where they stood.

The last Aquarii standing was Algen's guard. Standing solemnly in the wake of his countrymen's demise, he gave no indication of fear. From where Algen watched, he was close enough to hear the words coming from his mouth, but was too far away to understand them. The man was addressing his father, standing opposite him.

He watched as the hammerhead forced the guard to his knees, and removed the steel helm from his head. Then, the slimy bald man took a step forward, and placed a mucus covered hand upon his forehead. A *ZAP* cracked the air and the guard threw back his head, his muscles convulsing uncontrollably. As soon as he stopped moving, he was struck again,

They're torturing him, he thought, horrified. *My father is having that man tortured.*

It was too late when he noticed the monstrous shadow towering over him. Turning, Algen was suddenly gripped at the throat by a hand near as wide as his chest. It only took two of the massive fingers to cover the entirety of his neck. He flailed wildly, but the grip was too tight. The air was being squeezed from Algen's lungs. His face would turn blue most like, if it weren't already that colour. He gasped. The giant mutant was grinning with a smile made of massive square teeth.

"Boss!" he boomed.

His father turned, looking annoyed. Sudden realization swept over his face. He pointed a grey finger at the giant.

"Drop him, now."

Algen was suddenly greeted by the ground as it came up to meet him. He lay sprawled in the sand, dazed and sucking in breath, coughing, as sand reached his lungs. His father's muscled hand pulled him to his feet and he was face to face with his father for the first time since his transformation. And his father's face was as sour now as it was on that day.

"Why?" was all he asked.

Algen looked broken, and it was all he could do not to wet himself.

"They know," his father almost whispered, releasing his grip. "You followed me, you stupid child, and they know!"

As if on cue, a massive trumpet blared and the sound of a portcullis opening filled the air.

"No." It was the albino man who spoke.

The march of feet on ground filled the air as drums began to pound.

Algen's father looked at him.

"Do you know what you have done?" His hand struck Algen across the face, leaving three long gashes where claw tore flesh and split the barnacles. From where the grizzled Aquarii guard lay, he began to laugh uncontrollably. The slimy man gripped

 ALGEN

him by the throat and zapped him so hard that Algen could smell the flesh burning.

"They're coming!" he heard from above on the hill. Algen watched as the water of the ocean swirled and bubbled, as ten thousand Cancer mutants broke from the surface and charged up the beach, wailing and screaming, a thousand different kinds of marine life freaks swinging a hundred different kinds of weapons. Some had no need for steel or bronze, instead waving claws or baring teeth. Algen watched as one army ran up the beach, and the other ran down. Thousands of Aquarii solders gleaming in silvered armour met the mutants in their charge.

"Alperen, we have to go!" It was the hammerhead who spoke.

His father nodded, and left Algen where he lay on the ground. Unmoving and unspeaking, Algen lay face up, his cheek bleeding into the sand. Around him, a battle raged.

Help me, was all he could think.

CHAPTER 38

ALMOND V

It had taken a few days, but Almond had finally become comfortable in the Queen's presence. More recently, she had even made friends with the large red bird that the Queen kept in a cage beside her throne. At first, she had feared the bird and its incessant cawing, but over time Almond had come to marvel at the bird. Sir Heleron was another story entirely. Every time the two happened upon one another, Almond would hide her face and hurry off in the other direction. Most days, that was possible, but today the big man stood guard next to the Queen's throne as she sat brooding over a letter in her lap. The note was stained red with blood and Almond couldn't help but speculate on the one man she thought would have sent it. Almond was only halfway done sweeping the floor when she heard the Queen speak for the first time that day.

"Go."

Almond looked up, but the Queen did not meet her gaze. "Me, Your Grace?" she asked, timid as a rabbit.

"You," answered Sir Heleron.

Almond frowned at him, unsure whether to wait for the Queen to answer. She did not.

"Need I tell you again?" Heleron put a hand on his sword hilt and bared his teeth in a scowl.

Almond did not have to be told again; collecting her broom and pan, she scurried from the room without a second glance. Halley was shocked when she returned.

"Back so soon?" Halley's hand was nearly healed, the long scab now less red than it had been, and crusted over. It would leave a scar, that was to be sure, but at least now it wouldn't be such a shock to the Queen. Almond's time as her double was nearly at an end.

"The Queen received a letter," Almond told her. "She seemed to want to be alone."

"Alone with Sir Heleron, you mean," added Halley without hesitation.

Almond nodded. Halley continued. "It's those dogs coming again."

Almond nodded again. She had known it as well. "Do they take your people, too?"

It was Halley's turn to nod. "Yes, the Queen has been wanting to be rid of them for years. Perhaps today will be the day she finally puts things into motion. If their leader steps into that throne room, I don't think the Queen will let him leave alive."

Almond had a sudden urge come over her. "I want to be there. I want to see him die."

Halley began to pick at her scab nervously, seeing the determination and rage in Almond's eyes. "There is... one way you could be there."

She had shown Almond a secret crevice, a hole in the wall really, accessed through a small panel in the kitchens and leading to a small hole between beams above the throne. Halley said she had come here as a young child, to avoid doing chores before she had become a serving girl. There was a crack, large enough to see out of, but inconspicuous to anyone in the room. If Almond had any malice towards the Queen, this would have been a perfect place to nestle a crossbow.

There were already guards within the room, seemingly awaiting Jackan's arrival. And arrive he did. Almond sank back into her hiding place and watched as Jackan approached the red feathered throne in stride, five hunting dogs flanking him, brandishing polished steel blades. Jackan himself displayed his daggered gauntlet of black steel. The tips of the claws dripped with warm, fresh blood. The sight of it made Almond think of her father.

"We ran into some trouble on the way in," Jackan said, flicking red drops to the wooden floor. "Apparently your guards didn't feel it necessary to let us in."

ALMOND

He smiled his sinister smile, flashing his sharpened teeth. The other dogs gave similar smiles, and cackled to themselves. The Queen sat, unamused, stroking the underside of her bird's throat with the back of her meaty knuckle.

"*SQUAWK*! Let us in! Let us in!" The bird repeated, flapping its big red wings.

Sir Heleron, standing at the Queen's side, clenched a mailed fist, and stepped forward. He drew from his scabbard a broadsword made of the same rainbow-shimmering metal as his armor. The knight slashed the tip of his sword down into the floor with an intimidating *THUD*. The short red-brown whiskers on his chin and lip twisted into a scowl.

"Leave this place, dog, lest I remove that wretched gauntlet from your wrist with your hand still inside."

Jackan grinned once more. "Try, please. It would give me all the reason I need to haul you off to the pits. I'm sure the Pit Master would love a shiny new toy like you."

The knight flustered for a moment, his cheeks reddening, and then tensed his grip on the hilt of his weapon. "Should I assume the castle is surrounded?"

Jackan laughed. "Surrounded? No, we'd need five times our numbers for that. Besides, the sand is too hot. We'd much prefer occupying your halls and drinking your sweet wine."

He motioned to one of his men, who handed him a flask. He took a long swig and licked his lips. Purple-red liquid dripped from his lips and stained his teeth. Then he smashed the half empty container on the floor, sending an explosion of liquid splashing across the floor. The knight looked gobsmacked, but the Queen continued to keep her composure. Jackan chuckled.

"So, here's the deal: We take all the wine you have in this rubbish heap you call a castle, and in return we forget your little indiscretion."

The knight was about to speak, but Queen Eidaya held up a hand in a motion of silence. A few moments passed before she spoke, her voice cool and collected.

"You would have us die of thirst then, Jackan, is that it? Wipe your dirty paws clean of us without having to lift a finger yourself?" She pointed an accusatory pudgy finger. "You know as well as any of us that the water of this planet is no longer safe to drink. Without the wine there wouldn't be enough boiled water left to maintain a tenth of this castle."

Jackan moved a step closer. "Oh, Your Majesty, I revel in the dirty work." He raised his claw and licked at the blood. "So, am I to take this as a no?"

The Queen darkened. "You are to take it as a warning. Get out of my palace now, or I will have you and yours hanged by sundown."

Heleron swung his sword in a half circle so the point was facing upwards, and moved forward. A mailed hand outstretched with his weapon ready to strike. "You heard Her Majesty. Be gone."

Six heavily armoured Queen's men appeared at the doorway to the Throne Room. Jackan's eyes fixated for a moment on Heleron's steel blade, and then to the door. After a few tense moments, he turned and moved back to his men. "You know what I've always wondered, Eidaya?" He took another flask of wine from his man. This one had a cloth plugging into the top. Jackan struck a match against his pantleg and touched it to the rag. "Can the Phoenix Queen be reborn from the ashes?"

He lurched towards her and hurled the flask at the Queen's feet, where the glass burst and sent tongues of orange light snaking up her legs. The bird on her armrest leapt upwards and flapped to the ceiling, narrowly avoiding the flames. Queen Eidaya screamed and rolled back in her chair. The panels of the wooden floor below her were already burning. Almond sank back in her hiding place, heart racing. As the smoke rose and filled her nostrils, she watched as Jackan and his men ran from the throne room, while Sir Heleron and the six other men rushed in the other direction, struggled to suffocate the flames and help their Queen.

Almond crawled backwards until she could move no further. Then, she pounded on the soft wooden wall with her feet until it gave way. She could smell burning wood and the smoke had already caught up with her. She thought about the layout of the castle. *Wood. The entire castle is made of old, dry wood!* She panicked for a second, thinking of all the people in the castle that had no knowledge of what was going on. But a second was all she had, before her thoughts were cut off by the sound of yelling and pots being dropped.

A woman ran by her yelling: "Fire! Fire!" The woman was so preoccupied she hadn't even seen Almond crouched there.

Soon the entire castle seemed to be in a buzz, trying to find an exit; however each door seemed to have been barricaded shut. As the flames spread, so did the panic. A few were screaming for their Queen to save them; another bunch cursed her and began looting what little they could. Almond soon found herself drifting away from the group, looking for any small hole there may be. But every wall she found seemed to be kissed by the fire, and she couldn't risk staying for too long.

Support beams began falling around her, opening a pathway the next section of the palace. She leapt forward, over a burning beam and onto the other side of the curved castle wall. As she moved forward, her belt snagged on an exposed nail and caused her to fall. Feeling the warmth of the wood beneath her, she panicked and scrambled to her feet, scraping her hand in the process. The pain didn't even register. As she squeezed through the wood, she found herself close to the serving quarters.

"Halley!" she screamed. "Halley!"

A hand gripped her from behind. Almond turned to see Halley's pale face staring back at her. "What happened?"

"Jackan lit the Queen on fire!" The words sounded almost surreal coming from her mouth.

Halley gripped her by the arm and led her to the serving door. To their dismay, it wouldn't budge. Almond unsheathed her sword, and in one swing, she cracked the wood of the door. As smoke billowed in from behind them, the two girls splayed forward out onto the sand. Almond could hear the creaking of

the wooden castle behind them, ready to collapse. From afar, she saw a group of black horses riding off.

They found other survivors burnt and coughing along the sand, including the Queen herself, who looked nearly as grotesque as a corpse. Queen Eidaya lay writhing on the ground, clutching at the remains of her face. The hair on her head had been singed off in ragged patches and replaced with plum-coloured blisters. The muscles of her arms were exposed and her fingers twitched as they bent. She alternated between screaming and coughing out smoke.

Sir Heleron was frantically pacing, desperately trying to figure out what to do. His attention was fully fixed on his Queen, despite having multiple severe injuries himself. Blood dripped from his ear where a support beam had struck him and the skin on the back of his hand was hanging by a thread. Almond wondered if the wound went further up, but Heleron still wore his tightly fitting rainbow armour. However, soot had made the armour look cheap and covered its luster with a matte grey.

The six dozen or so other castle inhabitants that made it out varied from almost unscathed, to good as dead. A kitchen maid sat in the sand prodding at what looked like a broken toe. The girl sitting beside her had fainted. Almond wondered if she was dead. Looking down at herself, Almond counted herself lucky to have come out so unscathed. Her sword belt still clung to her hips, but the sword itself was nowhere to be seen. Suddenly, all her rage flowed back to her and tears welled in her eyes.

She fell to her knees and punched at the ground, sending sand up in a wash before her. *Jackan won't get away with this.* She clenched her fist and a stab of pain shot up her arm. For the first time, Almond noticed the large gash from one side of her palm to the other. She watched a drop of blood drip from her wrist and steam against the hot sand below. Next to the blood lay her gemstone, the one from her grandmother. The chain had frayed and must have slipped from her neck. Her grandmother's words rang in her head.

Lefra, Lefra, the gem of my life.

Longingly, she reached down and picked it up, not caring about the blood from her hand dripping on the stone. Her emotions took over and she imagined the gem as her grandmother's hand, warm and pulsing. In fact, the gem was warm and pulsing. Shaken, she dropped it. And then she saw it: her hand, the wound, it was... *sealed.* She turned her hand over and looked at it from all angles, making sure she wasn't imagining it. There was a line, there had been a wound there, but it looked as if it were years old and long since healed.

She knelt, wide eyed and open mouthed. Picking the gem up again, she walked over to the kitchen maid. Without saying a word, she pressed the stone's surface against her toe. The maid looked up at her, confused, until they heard a light snap as the bone reset itself. Almond then moved over to the next girl, who lay unbreathing on the ground with a severe burn down her arm and side. She pressed the stone against the damaged skin, but she felt nothing. She pressed it harder, but the stone stayed cold as ever.

"She's dead," said the maid sympathetically. "Whatever manner of magic it is you have there, it can't bring someone back from the dead. Nothing can."

The Queen's screams penetrated her consciousness once again.

"Help her," offered the maid.

Almond rose to her feet and hurried over. Heleron stopped her in her tracks, shoving Almond to the ground. She crawled forward, but Heleron placed a foot on the ground in front of her.

"Stay away from the Queen!" he demanded.

"I can help her."

"If I cannot help her, then you cannot help her. She is beyond saving."

Almond looked him directly in the eye. "Then let me try."

Sir Heleron paused for a moment, then sighed and let her pass. Up close, Almond could see that the Queen was far worse than she had thought. The blisters covered her entire body. Gold and silver bangles had melted right onto her blackened forearms and three of her toes were missing. Almond fumbled with the gem and pressed it first against the queen's cheek. She felt the warmth and buzz again. Before her eyes, the skin lightened, turning to a more normal tone. The blisters shrank and smoothed. Quieting, the Queen opened her eyes and peered at Almond, who moved the stone across her forehead, to her scalp, and back down to her neck. As her hand moved, the skin healed, and before long the Queen looked more like a person than a piece of burned flesh. When Almond moved to the toes, she expected to watch them grow back, but instead the stone sealed them off, as if cauterizing the wound. At that point, the Queen sat up.

"Thank... Thank you, child."

The Queen had foregone her tough persona and now sounded meek as a mouse.

She raised her forearm where a bangle had melted and picked the pieces of metal off her arm. Below, the skin was perfectly fine, except for a slight darkening. She sat in disbelief.

"Who are you?"

"I'm... Almond, Your Grace."

The Queen smiled. "You are my saving grace, Almond."

Queen Eidaya looked past her and looked over her injured people. Heleron looked as though he'd seen a ghost. Her eyes fixed on his flayed arm.

"Please, Almond, I beg of you: save my people."

And she did. By the time she was done, over fifty people destined for death stood unharmed and in awe. Three bodies lay where death had arrived first. The Queen hobbled over to her, testing out her maimed foot. Only the big toe and second toe remained to her right foot, and even the latter was missing the first joint. She smiled and braced herself on Almond's shoulder. Almond blushed and looked up at her. The Queen smiled back, then turning to the crowd she announced: "My

ALMOND

people, for I have failed you." She looked back at the burning ruin of the castle. "But all hope is not lost." She grabbed hold of Almond's arm and pumped it into the air.

"Bow down before Almond, the savior of the Phoenixes!"

Before Almond's eyes, six dozen men and women, knights and ladies, serving boys and girls in waiting, all took a knee before her. Even the Queen slipped down to her one good leg and lowered her head. The remaining curled locks atop her head fell over her face as she bowed in gratitude.

It had been a miracle she had performed, Almond knew, as a million questions raced through her head at once. Sighing, she allowed the praise to wash over her and stared up to the sky. She could not accept their love. Not from these people, not yet. All she wanted right now was one thing: *revenge.*

ALMOND

CHAPTER 39

JAIR V

The moon was set high in the sky, surrounded on all sides by puffy grey clouds. Around him, the grass of the open field surrounding the dock took on a purple tint in the moonlight and Jair felt a cool, wet breeze cross his face as he surveyed the men before him. At least thirty palace guards surrounded them in a tight semi-circle, keeping the group pinned with the river at their backs. The Prince's guard stood less than ten feet before them, half with bows notched and drawn, ready to fire at Prince Callum's command. Callum himself stood in their centre, wearing a smug, stupid expression. The intricately carved dagger he held pressed up against Deleon's throat shone pale, moonbeams glinting off the metal. Deleon pressed his head into Callum's chest, trying to move as far from the blade as he could, but Callum only pressed harder.

"My father," he demanded. "Bring him to me or this one dies."

Falmir was looking intently at the prince, his face clearly showing his fear. Garrett was more composed, and even looked ready to charge, but as there was an arrow pointed directly at his face, Jair thought it unlikely. A few of the palace guards had moved forward and both Frog and the Seamstress had been surrounded. The rest of the group stood warily, weapons drawn, but waiting for Vikron's command. Jair himself was nervously opening and closing his grasp on his poleaxe, looking from one guard to the next, and trying to ascertain if he recognized any of them. Vikron took a deep breath and spoke loudly and clearly.

"I have him chained in a secret location. Call off your guards and I will bring you there."

Callum snickered. "Just how stupid do you think I am?

He thinks you're very stupid, Jair thought. Though in the position they were in, he didn't know if it would matter. Jair noticed Deleon sneaking a hand to his belt for a knife. *Idiot.* Callum noticed it too, and pressed the blade deeper. A trickle of blood welled on the knife as Deleon's hand went back in the air with the other.

"Captain Vikron comes with me," said Callum. "The rest of you cretins will stay here."

Vikron shook his head. "I can't do that."

Callum frowned. His light blonde hair waved like silk in the breeze. "I will kill every last one of your rats until you come!"

JAIR

"If you kill them, I won't show you the location, then you'll never find you dear old dad."

That sent Callum into a rage. He removed the knife from his hostage's throat and pointed it menacingly at Vikron. "You'll pay, worm!" His voice cracked as he said it.

Deleon wasted no time. Using the little leverage that he had, the young man shoved his back into Callum's chest and knocked the prince off balance. But it wasn't enough to knock him over. As Deleon tried to run towards the group, Callum caught him by the arm, spun him around, and lodged the dagger deep into his neck. A stream of hot blood rose up as Deleon's eyes rolled back in his head. Jair froze. So did Vikron. Arlum let out a cry and fired his crossbow. The bolt pierced Callum in the shoulder and sent him screaming to the ground. Deleon dropped with him.

"Kill them! Kill them all!" Callum's voice squeaked.

Garrett ducked as the arrow pointed at him was fired. The shaft soared just an inch over his head and nearly grazed the scalp. Lunging forward, Garrett brought his sword up in an underhand swing into the archer's belly. As that man fell, two more advanced. The rest of Vikron's company had matched the other guards head-on, and the tranquility of the night broke into the sounds of steel clashing, blood spraying, and soldiers dying. Callum himself even tried to join in the fighting, but the bolt had hit the shoulder of his sword arm, and he grimaced with every movement. The Prince soon gave up before even engaging and left the job to his men. Jair cut down the guard be-

JAIR

tween him and Callum. As the body fell, the two of them locked eyes for the first time since before Vikron's arrival.

"Executioner?" Prince Callum exclaimed in shock. "We wondered where you had went!"

He doesn't even know my name.

A sword swing from his left broke Jair's thoughts. Leaning back, he watched a guard make a clumsy approach. Four seconds later the guard was on the ground, a gaping hole in his breastplate. Jair glanced around the open field. Bodies from both sides littered the grass like bumps on the skin. Jair knew that the battle would soon be over. He turned on the ball of his foot and used the butt of his poleaxe to knock the prince to the ground. Below him, Callum writhed in pain, clutching his shoulder and crying out for his guards to protect him. None came; they were all either fighting, dead, or dying. Jair placed his boot on Callum's wounded shoulder, causing him to scream out in even more pain.

Jair was ready to end it there and then but paused. Who knew what Vikron was planning with the Prince? Instead, he flipped the crying prince onto his back and held him to the ground. Arlum walked up beside him, sweat dripping from his brow. He looked over at Deleon's lifeless body, growing visibly angry. Before Jair could say anything, Arlum raised his loaded crossbow and fired a bolt into the bony part of Callum's ankle. Jair grimaced as he heard the sound of the tendon shredding. Callum cried out again and started weeping. Arlum knelt down and retrieved his bolt. Blood welled in the open hole it left.

The fight was over now. Every last palace guard was dead or dying, as was half of Vikron's group. Frog held his side where he'd taken a light slash wound. Vikron himself was covered in blood, though little of it was his own. He looked up and yelled like a beast at the moon. One of the bull's horns on his helm was sheared off at the base and his bear pelt cloak was nowhere to be found, but shreds of it clung to his muscled back. What was left of the group gathered in the center of the field as Vikron strode towards Callum. Together, Jair and Arlum hoisted the prince to his feet to meet their captain face to face. Vikron only stopped when his scraggy chin was inches from Callum's. Jair could smell his breath heaving. Reaching forward, Vikron moved his hand around the back of Callum's neck and grabbed a chain. Yanking, he snapped it off and held it up. At the end was a small ruby. Vikron smiled and placed it in his pocket, then gave Callum a light slap on the face.

Callum looked defeated. "Just tell me where my father is."

Vikron laughed. "I put him in the ground."

"You killed him?"

Vikron smiled. "Your Grace, your father was dead the moment the fighting started back at the city square."

Callum looked dumbstruck.

Vikron chuckled. "So, I suppose I should say: "All hail the new King of Ara!'"

Jair could see the dismay on the new King's face. All hope was lost in those eyes.

 JAIR

Garrett walked over and placed a large stump at Callum's feet.

"Kneel," commanded Vikron.

Garrett forced the King to his knees and his chin onto the stump. Callum hardly put up a fight. Vikron looked to Jair.

"Well, 'cutioner. Do the honours."

Jair paused for a moment, unsure what to do. Then, he felt clarity, raised his long-axe, and brought it down, cutting clean and true. The axe head stuck in the wood, as the new King's reign ended. And for the first time in a long time, Jair felt good.

CHAPTER 40

DERRON VI

Derron stood next to Alymer, Melwick, and Anthon. The rest of his men were above him somewhere, hiding in the trees. All around them, the Lyncis were searching, including a much angrier and bloodier Skel. Derron and his men had been luring them close to the lake for the past five hours, only making the faintest of sounds to lead them in the right direction. As they went, more and more scouting parties had joined in until almost all of the tribesmen were on the trail. At the moment, they were clubbing down bushes and kicking snowdrifts less than a hundred yards away in search of the group. Derron was giving it another minute before they made the next sound cue, the final sound cue, before Alymer would make his move.

"When you return, tell my brother what I did," said Alymer, calm as ever. "His name is Alyras. He lives back at my father's farm. I suppose it's probably his farm now."

Derron nodded. "Of course." He paused. "Are you ready?"

Alymer nodded, and tightened his grip on Derron's walking stick.

Derron gave a signal to Anthon and Melwick, who began throwing rocks at the dry leaves down on the ridge. The Lyncis were immediately aware of the sound. Slowly, the tribesmen made their way towards the lip, where Alymer stepped out and allowed himself to be seen. Cries went up and the men began to scramble headfirst up the ledge. Derron and the others had already fled the safety of the underbrush, silently placing themselves in pre-dug holes and covering themselves with dirt. Alymer moved to the lakefront, and stepped cautiously onto the ice, then moved further out. Derron watched as the tribesmen began summiting the cliff, stopping before the lake. Skel himself moved to the front.

"What's the holdup?" He looked down at the ice and then out to where Alymer was. He took a step, then another. "It's frozen solid you pansies! Lyncis are not afraid of water!"

The men looked at one another, then began crossing. Alymer was already well out into the lake by that point. Derron heard the faint *CRICK* of breaking ice from his position, but the layer did not give way. When Alymer got a good hundred yards out, he pretended to slip and fall, and by the time he rose back to his feet there were thirty men almost on him, including Skel, with another thirty close behind. A few had refused to cross the lake despite jeering from the rest, and around ten were still very close to the edge. Alymer stood and faced the oncoming men. Derron thought he saw Skel say something, but he was too far away to hear what it might have been. Then, all at once, Alymer lifted the butt of the stick, and smacked it down onto the ice. A cracking sound pierced the air and a fracture line cut from Alymer to the water's edge. The Lyncis had no time to react before the ice shifted and the surface crumbled beneath them.

Derron watched as men dropped from sight, suddenly swallowed by the water. Alymer had already vanished. Suddenly, the other half of the plan was in action, as the rest of Derron's men charged from the treeline and took the remaining Lyncis off-guard. With Skel nowhere to the seen, Derron's men found little resistance. A few of the Lynx swam towards the shore, but were quickly tangled in the stew of ice chunks and drowned before making it back. Those too far from Derron's end of the shore attempted to reach the other side of the lake. Yet the other side was out of sight and Derron knew it was a longshot for anyone to swim that far. And even *if* anyone made it, they would be in no shape to seek any kind of vengeance. He was not worried.

When the last of the Lyncis' heads dipped below the water and didn't resurface, Derron knew it was over. He knelt down and said a silent prayer for Alymer, then rose to his feet and looked to the sky. The sun was out again, if only for a brief moment. Derron took it as a sign that they could rest.

Mollens was scanning the faces of the bodies on the shore.

"Did anyone see Skel?"

 DERRON

Derron shook his head. "He's either frozen or will be soon. Either way, he won't be bothering us."

It was Mollens who made the suggestion to name the lake after Alymer, and the rest of the men had nodded their approval.

"He will be missed," said Skoma and a few of the men echoed the sentiment.

A silence fell upon the group as they made their way back to camp. On their way, the clouds parted and the sun shone down on them. Derron gripped the carved wooden bear paw around his neck and smiled despite himself.

Mollens cleared his throat and mumbled. "Where do we go now?"

Derron scratched his beard. "Well, now we could –" Something made him pause. He couldn't quite figure out what. *Something about the light? Yes.* He watched as it filled the chasm.

"Melwick, give me all your maps."

Startled, Melwick rustled through his sack and produced his maps. Derron crouched down and lay them on the ground before him, the snow making them wet. He overlapped them where the terrain was the same and... yes... it was.

Anthon looked over his shoulder. "Those ridges look kind of like that -"

"Cross symbol," Derron finished. "The ridges make a giant cross. And the centre is... We go west."

With new found vigour the group set out. It wasn't long before they had their hopes realized. In the space where the two crevices crossed lay a clearing. A huge tree with gnarled old branches centered the area, stretching fifty feet in the air and at least thirty-five in all directions around. Below, the roots split, revealing a rift nestled below.

"Mother above," Will said in a hushed tone.

Derron smiled, and walked through.

CHAPTER 41

RYMUS VI

Rymus stood on the prow of his ship and watched as the castle rose into view along the horizon. To his right sailed Swordfish, the ornate ship of his brother Lydus. Further right sailed Proudfin, Elkus' ship. And behind them, going much slower, was Whalebelly, the huge cog that carried the bulk of their forces. Although, it was noticeably less crowded compared to when they were here last. Rymus had never bothered to learn the name of its captain. Like as not, he had died on the Aries homeworld and a new man had taken his place. Rymus had named his own ship Trout's Tail. Keldo often bickered with him over the name, but his calls to change it only made him love the name more.

Out on the open sea, Rymus felt more at home. He felt safe aboard the wooden planks beneath him. He liked being able to see in all directions, unimpeded, and his little jaunt through the mountains had only served to strengthen that conviction.

Something else could be seen over the horizon. *Ships.* He frowned. *This isn't the harbour.* He moved back from the prow and looked down the hole to the lower deck. He called out to his oarmaster.

"Derry!"

An old man with a bald head and thick beard appeared a few moments later.

"Yes, Cap'n?"

"Full stop. I don't want us any closer."

The old man nodded. "Full stop!" he called down to the oarsmen.

The boat slowed and Rymus walked to the railing where he held up a signal to the man at the helm of Swordfish. The man saw, and Rymus could hear him yell something to Lydus. Within moments, both boats were slowing, and soon Proudfin and Whalebelly joined them. Once they had stopped, the gangplank was lowered, and Rymus moved over to his brother's ship. Lydus met him at the railing.

"Warships from the Carina faction," Lydus said, eyes blazing.

Rymus nodded. "All around the castle."

From across the ship, he heard another gangplank drop and saw Elkus running across.

"The buggers have the castle surrounded!" His jowls wiggled.

 RYMUS

Rymus looked out at the water. *Only by sea.*

"The Carinas are blocking our way from the front, not the back."

"We can't get our army to the back. There are no docks."

"But we have rowboats."

Lydus crossed his arms across his chest. His left was bandaged from shoulder to elbow. "To what end?"

Rymus gave him a half smile. "To pay our dear father a visit."

The small wooden vessel was lowered by winch into the water. Rymus and his brothers could fit, but only just. There was no room for anyone else. During the time he'd be away, Rymus was leaving Keldo in command of Trout's Tail with orders to keep out of sight. Keldo seemed all too happy to take command and Rymus hoped that he'd be able to get his ship back once he returned. As the oars dipped into the water and they moved north towards the shore, Rymus marveled at the home he hadn't seen in a month. The tallest tower must have stood one hundred feet high, with gulls circling its peak. Contrasted with the golden sand, the grey stone almost looked cheap. But Rymus knew that the thick walls could keep any invader at bay.

It took no time at all to reach the posterior gate, and luckily the brothers found that castle had not yet been taken. Once inside, they entered the study to find their father sitting morosely in his armchair, staring deeply into the koi pond that centred the room. A fire blazed in the corner hearth and its light glinted off the sapphire encrusted crown clinging to the last few wisps of hair on the king's head. Hallus of Pisces made for a sour sight. Most other royals from across the Starscape referred to him as "The Saltfish" due to his demeanor, but never to his face.

"Kneel," he boomed, not looking up from the floor.

The brothers moved in unison, taking a knee and bowing their heads. As he knelt, Lydus' long black hair fell and shrouded his face. Rymus could see from the tops of his eyes as his father stood, relying heavily on his arms to lift his weight. Beside his chair was a crutch, which the King used to prop himself. Decades ago, in some conflict long forgotten, King Hallus had had the mast of his ship topple from a scorpion bolt. The mast had crushed his left leg as it hit the deck, shattering the bone. The medics after the battle had said it was astonishing that he had survived such a thing, but he had. They had then advised amputation, but Hallus had refused, saying his body would decide whether or not the leg came off. Eventually, the leg had healed, if you could call it that; it was bent at an angle, thin and sinewy, and could support no weight, but under the King's fine blue robe, no one was like to notice. As he crossed the room, the king almost tripped, but maintained his balance until he reached his children.

"Rise," he commanded, and they did.

Hallus did not smile - at least, Rymus had never seen him do it. Nor had he ever seen him cry, not even when their mother had died. He showed no more emotion today, as Rymus slipped the quiver from his back and displayed it for his father.

 RYMUS

"We have succeeded in our mission, Father."

He looked to each of them. "Are you the only ones to return? I gave you half my army. Do not tell me they are all lost."

Lydus spoke. "The rest of your army waits on the ships, Father. We saw the Carina Navy at our doorstep and thought it best not to engage."

"Pity. Might have been that you were able to drive them away."

Elkus then spoke. "What are they doing here? Can't be to sing us our praises."

The King grimaced. "They threaten to besiege the castle, if their demands are not met."

Rymus frowned. "And what do they demand of us, Father?"

"Not of us, of me. The King of Carina lost a grandson on the Aries homeworld, no doubt to one of you three. He wants retribution. And as I have no grandsons, he says he will settle for a son."

Rymus smirked. "Surely he knows that you would never follow through with such a deal?"

His father looked him dead in the eyes. "What use do I have of *three* sons?"

Before he could process what he had just heard, they were on him. His brothers, or once they had been his brothers, leapt into action at their father's word without a moment's hesitation. Elkus acted first, tackling Rymus to the ground while Lydus unsheathed his serrated sword. Rymus beat his hands against his brother's chest until he was off, then stood. He reached to his belt and drew a dagger, but as he did, he heard the whoosh of steel through air and felt a terrible sting as Lydus' blade cut into his arm. It was only a graze, but the teeth ripped open the flesh. He dropped the dagger and gripped his arm as blood welled through his fingers.

Elkus was on him again, this time from behind. Rymus tried to shake him, but his brother's grip was too tight. Lydus made another swing of his sword and this time the blade grazed the leather of Rymus' jerkin and sheared it open. It was obvious to Rymus that his brother was only trying to wound him enough to the point he would submit, otherwise he knew he'd be dead already. Elkus' grip faltered for a moment and Rymus was able to break free, only to be gripped again. The two of them twisted and turned in a queer dance until Rymus' foot caught the lip of the koi pond and they went splashing down amongst the fish.

The water was shallow, but it was deep enough at least to cover Rymus' head. He panicked for a moment as he realized he could not surface; Elkus was atop him. His heart beat faster as he struggled to free himself. As Rymus' vision started to go grey, he was able to push his lips above the water and take a breath before he was shoved back under again. In a moment of desperation, Rymus rolled onto his back and used his knees to lift Elkus off him. Gasping, he turned and landed a punch on his brother's chin. His fist was wet and the strike only glanced off. Before long Lydus was also on him, this time without a blade. He felt his brother's hands wrap around his throat and tighten.

 RYMUS

Panic gripped him again and he reeled, catching a glimpse of his father's unwavering face. In a rush of adrenaline, Rymus remembered his brother's wound and his elbow connected with the bandage on Lydus' arm. Hs brother screamed and let go, stumbling away, clutching at his bicep.

Rymus saw the quiver still lying on the floor where he'd dropped it. He reached a sopping wet arm out and tried to grab it, but Elkus pulled him back. His fingers grazed the feather of one of the arrows and somehow, he held on. As Rymus was pulled back into the pool, so was the arrow. He could not see, but at this point he did not care. He flailed backwards and slashed the arrow around as it if were a knife, feeling it connect with flesh. He heard a scream and thought to see if his brother was alright. But before he could, a fist came from nowhere and hit Rymus in the jaw. The impact sent stars to his eyes and the world spun into darkness.

Rymus awoke to find himself lying face-down on a wooden floor with a splitting headache. He felt as if the world was shifting beneath him. Then, he smelled the sea air and realized the world *was* shifting under him. He tried to raise himself up but his hands were tied firmly behind his back. His legs were also tied together, the rope digging deeply into his skin. All he could do was roll onto his back, and even that was hard. He squinted as the sun shone directly into Rymus' face. Something bent over into the sun's path. Looking down at him was a grinning face he did not recognize centered on a clear blue sky. The man was smoking a pipe, holding it in his mouth and flashing a golden tooth. His beard was sporadic and curly and one eye was hidden behind a black leather eyepatch.

"Awake, I shee." His words were slurred with the pipe.

Rymus squinted. "Where am I?" he asked

The one-eyed man laughed, the pipe clicking in his teeth.

"Why, yur' on the deck o' the Old Samson, finest ship in the Carina fleet."

He blinked and let it sink in. *Carina*. He tried to raise himself to his feet, but a wooden leg struck him in the chest and he fell back to the ground.

"Don't be trying any of that, now!" The man laughed a deep belly laugh.

Rymus could only look up, watching three gulls circling above. *My brothers. They gave me away.* One lone gull flew a good hundred yard from the other two. "That's me."

"Eh?" The one-eyed man looked at him. "Who are you talkin' to?" He blew a ring of smoke. "They calls me Rumbeard, for this red beard of mine. That's me."

"I'm Rymus."

"I knows who you're!" Rumbeard looked annoyed. "That's why you're on my ship!" He blew another smoke ring, this time at Rymus. "And best you get comfortable - it's going to be a long trip."

 RYMUS

CHAPTER 42

GRELHYM V

Grelhym found himself once again in the tunnel below the Roundhall. King Terreon stood brooding at the ledge of the pit with Lord Rygar and Prince Dayvon. Grelhym leaned against the rocky wall, fiddling with his squire's knife, eyes fixed on the bloodstained ground next to the ledge.

Beside him stood four of Terreon's men. Foremost was Byron, captain of Terreon's person guard. He stood as still as a statue, his wrinkled face unwavering, except for the motion of his jaw as he chewed a wad of tobacco. Behind the captain, two men at arms talked noisily to one another. Because of their conversation, Grelhym had learned their names to be Len and Hadrian. Hadrian, the shorter of the two was showing off his bloody sword to Len. According to the soldier, he had cut down King Emerton during the chaos in the hall. Len fawned over the bloody steel, declaring that Hadrian should be given a knighthood or a captainship for killing a king. *The Starscape would be much better off giving him a swift execution*, Grelhym thought.

The last of Terreon's men stood off to one side, heaving on a winch Grelhym hadn't noticed the last time he was down here. *Having a knife in your back really steals all your attention.* Slowly, a wooden platform was heaved up to the lip of the pit, where the winch-man held it in place as King Terreon and his cronies stepped forward. Terreon motioned and his men at arms joined them.

"You too boy!" shouted Rygar.

Begrudgingly, Grelhym did as he was bid and stepped onto the platform. The winch-man moved and the entire platform jerked down a foot. Grelhym fell to his hands and knees, nearly off the side of the outermost wooden beam. He stared down into the abyss, where there was no bottom in sight. He froze in fear.

"Careful with that!" Terreon shouted to his man.

"My apologies, Your Grace. Won't happen again."

They descended again, slowly this time, and smoothly. Terreon lit an oil torch and handed it to Dayvon. The big man looked nervous holding the fire. The light was eerie in the blackness of the pit, and illuminated the stretch marks below Dayvon's third chin. He looked like an overstuffed pastry with a face.

Grelhym expected the pit to get cooler the further they went, but instead he had started to sweat. He lost count of

GRELHYM

how far down they had gone, but the ledge of the pit was no more than a pin prick of light above them. Suddenly, the platform struck bottom, and something beneath the wood made a squishing sound. Grelhym winced knowingly, and was left staring into the dark void of another tunnel. Beyond the reach of the torch he could see nothing.

"By the grace of the Gods it is hot down here." Prince Dayvon looked as though he were about to faint. "Squire, take this."

Perhaps it was the heat, or the fear, or both but for some reason Grelhym decided to refuse.

"I don't take orders from you."

The backhanded slap was inevitable, though this time it was from a mailed fist.

He landed on his ass and his eyes were forced shut.

"Boy, you do as the prince says."

When he opened his eyes again, he was face to face with the tip of Terreon's sword. His clean proper beard had become longer and scraggy over the past few days, and he had a deranged look in his eye.

"What is your name?"

Grelhym blinked. "I'm Grelhym... Squire Grelhym. Of Fornax."

"And who do you serve?"

"Lord Rygar, of Fornax."

Terreon frowned and ran the tip of his blade across Grelhym's cheek, just below his left eye. Grelhym could smell the blood running down, and tasted it on his lips.

"Wrong. Rygar serves me, which means all of you potion-sniffers serve me. Now, who do you serve?"

"Terreon," he squeaked. "King Terreon of Sagittarius."

Terron smiled, and sheathed his sword. "I'll have no doubt here on who here is leader," he said to the group. "Your loyalty must be absolute."

Without hesitation, Captain Byron knelt to one knee. Len and Hadrian followed almost as fast. Then Dayvon and Rygar joined. Grelhym never thought he'd see the day when one faction knelt to another. He was already on his arse, so he needed only to raise himself to a knee to join the others.

"Excellent. You all may rise and follow me."

He took the torch from the whale prince and led the small party down into the tunnel. Grelhym wanted to ask how all this was found, but he didn't want to risk another cut. His right cheek had started to swell.

The tunnel narrowed to the point where the others had to bend over to make it under the ceiling, and then they had to crawl. Eventually, only Grelhym was small enough to keep going. While the others waited, Terreon ordered Grelhym to continue.

"At the end of this tunnel, you will find a small metal cube. It will look like nothing you have seen before. Bring it to me."

 GRELHYM

Grelhym nodded, and continued alone into a deep and dark passage. Although he had torchlight, he struggled to keep the flames from licking at his arms in the tight space. Suddenly, the rock dropped and he gave a cry as he fell into an open chamber. Steel fragments littered the floor.

"What do you see?" he heard Lord Rygar yell. "Grab the artifact, and bring it to your King, boy."

"There's nothing here," he whispered.

"Boy!" Rygar yelled again. "I don't hear you moving!"

"Nothing is here!" he called.

All Grelhym heard was silence. Then, something was breathing next to him. And that's when his torch went out.

CHAPTER 43

EPILOGUE

These badlands aren't all that bad. As far as targets went, this had been easy. Dray took the strange metal cube from his pocket and tossed it up in the air behind his back. It arced over his shoulder and landed squarely on the back of his hand. Then, in one motion he flicked his hand up, bumped the cube off his elbow, and caught it back in his pocket. Smiling, he started dreaming about all the riches he could buy with all the gold he was about to make.

A chill came over the wasteland just as Dray found himself outside the entrance to a small stone hut. The structure was the only one for miles around, aside from the odd tent and, of course, the huge round building he had just been under. Grimacing, he remembered the body he had stepped on on his way down the shaft, and the gruesome state that it was in. Had he not had a torch to let him see, Dray would never have known what it was that had gicked to the bottom of his shoe. Even then, it took him a few seconds before realizing it was human. Shuddering at the thought, he knocked on the wooden door and waited. Absentmindedly, Dray pulled the cube from his pocket and began juggling it between his fingers, flipping it into the air. As the object reached the peak of its arc, a large black hand came from the darkness of the doorway and grabbed it from the air.

"Be careful with that."

The man stepped forward. His skin was the colour of chocolate, and his head was void of hair. Over his chest he wore steel chainmail with a black tunic beneath. With a big meaty finger, the man beckoned Dray enter. Shrugging, he did. Dray was almost twenty now, and had been on his own since thirteen. This stranger did not frighten him.

Inside, the room was small and dark. As the man before him lit a wall sconce, Dray noticed the broadsword leaning against the wall. Instinctively, Dray's hand moved to his hip, where a dagger was concealed beneath his belt. The man seemed to be amused.

"No need for that."

Dray released his grip warily. "Are you the man who wanted this? I was told I'd find a man here to make the sale. So, are you going to pay me, or what?"

"That would be me, yes." Pulling a sack from a shelf, he tossed it haphazardly at Dray's feet. The top split, and golden coins showered across the floor.

Bastard, Dray thought as he knelt to pick up his reward. Suddenly, Dray was aware of the extra pair of eyes on him. Looking up from where he knelt, he met the gaze of an elderly man seated before him. The dark-skinned man chuckled.

"I'm the one who's paying you, but it's him who wants this." He placed the metal cube in the old man's lap.

Dray wasn't sure what to say. So instead, he simply cleared his throat and rose to his feet. "Um... who are you?"

The old man smiled. His robes seemed to shimmer in the pattern of a galaxy.

"They call me the Starcharter."

To order more copies of this book, find books by other
Canadian authors, or make inquiries about publishing
your own book, contact PageMaster at:

PageMaster Publication Services Inc.
11340-120 Street, Edmonton, AB T5G 0W5
books@pagemaster.ca
780-425-9303

catalogue and e-commerce store
PageMasterPublishing.ca/Shop

ABOUT THE AUTHOR

Evan Chaika is an author and musician, born and raised in Edmonton, Alberta, Canada as the only child of parents Darin and Leanne. Evan began writing stories at the age of five, by telling his mother about the adventures of an anthropomorphic mouse as she wrote them down into little books. Starcharter is the first of many novels Evan intends to publish, ranging in genre from fantasy, to documentary, to perhaps a mixture of both. One of his main sources of inspiration is looking towards the night sky and wondering what could lay beyond what the naked eye can see; making Starcharter the natural introduction into a long career in writing.